Rock Chick Renegade

Discover other titles by Kristen Ashley:

www.kristenashley.net

ISBN: 0-6157-7423-7
ISBN-13: 9780615774237

Rock Chick Renegade

Kristen Ashley

Dedication

This book is dedicated to the memory of Rebecca Ann Mahan-Womack
or Auntie Bec
her birthstone was amethyst

and to William Womack
his birthstone is emerald

⇥⇤

and lastly to Cedric, the inspiration for Boo and the best cat ever

⇥⇤

Chapter 1

Law

Well, I guessed eventually it would come to this. It wasn't like I wasn't expecting it. I knew when I started this crusade that something like this could happen, probably would happen, and here I was, in a dead end alley, facing down Vance Crowe.

Shit, Lee Nightingale's tracker.

Of all the fucking bad luck.

Rumor on the street, Crowe was third in command at Nightingale Investigations, after Lee and Lee's right hand man, Luke Stark.

This was saying a lot, considering all the men employed by Nightingale Investigations were the crème de la crème of private investigations, security, surveillance and bond skip tracing, with a small dose of head-cracking thrown in for shits and giggles. In fact, Nightingale, Stark and Crowe had a guns-drawn facedown with some lowlife drug dealer at a society party just a month ago. Crowe had blown off the guy's hand.

Rumor had a lot of things about Vance Crowe. In fact, I knew two women who'd had a couple of things from Crowe; by their reports, very good things, though he didn't stick around to give them more than a couple very good things, much to their dismay.

"Put your gun down," Crowe said to me.

"Back off," I returned, keeping my gun aimed at him.

I wasn't going to shoot him, of course. I was anti-violence. That was one of the reasons why I was in this mess in the first place.

He kept walking toward me, unarmed and apparently unafraid.

I took aim at his Harley. It would kill me to harm the Harley, but I'd do it.

"Shoot my bike, there'll be consequences," Crowe warned in a voice that said he meant it.

Fuck.

I aimed at him again.

"Back off," I repeated as he kept advancing.

"You're Law," he told me.

Kristen Ashley

Damn, he knew who I was.

"Stop moving," I said, ignoring what he said.

He got about a foot away from the barrel of my gun, which was pointed at his chest, and he stopped.

"I work for Lee Nightingale."

"I know who you work for and I know who you are," I told him.

Then I stared at him.

Damn, but he was good-looking. Native American coloring, straight, black hair pulled into a ponytail at the back of his neck. He was about three inches taller than me, with a fantastic body, dark brown eyes, thick lashes, unbelievable bone structure, high cheekbones and a square jaw. It should be a crime to be that hot.

"Put the gun down, Law," he ordered, using my street name.

My street name was kind of a joke. The kids gave it to me. My real name was Juliet Lawler. Most everyone called me Jules, but the kids called me Law because at the Shelter, what I said was "law". It had taken on a life of its own these past four months, and now I wished they'd never given it to me.

"Step back, Crowe. I'll just get in the car and go. I have no argument with you."

And I didn't. I had a lot of arguments with a lot of people, but not with anyone at Nightingale Investigations. From what I heard (which was a lot) they weren't exactly lily white, but any fool would be crazy to go head-to-head with a Nightingale Man. I was a fool, but I was pretty sure I wasn't crazy.

"I'll say it one more time," Crowe informed me quietly. "Put the gun down."

"Step back," I returned.

He moved faster than I'd seen anyone move, and before I knew it, I no longer had the gun.

Not only that, but he had my arm twisted behind my back and he had slammed my front up against his hard body.

I struggled.

This was not a good choice. I'd had a free hand and some of my pride left. In seconds, he shoved my gun in the back waistband of his jeans, had my other arm twisted behind me and he moved me, shuffling me back until I hit the side of my car. Then he pressed into me full body.

I tilted my head back and shouted in his face, "Let go and step away!"

2

"Two cops were standing in Fortnum's when you had your showdown with Cordova. They saw the whole thing. You got a permit for that gun?" he asked.

"Yes." This was true. Zip got it for me. Zip was a benefactor. Zip supported my crusade. Zip taught me how to shoot and Zip was a good shot, therefore, so was I.

Though, it was a little worrying that two cops saw me face down Sal Cordova. However, I didn't figure Sal was going to run to the police and tell on me, considering he was a criminal, and a total jackass to boot.

"I'm takin' you into the offices. We're gonna have a talk," Vance said to me.

Oh crap.

I didn't know what he thought we had to talk about, but I was having no part of it. Lee Nightingale's brother and father were cops, and so was his best friend. No way was I going to any offices with Crowe.

I kept staring him straight in the eye. It was kind of hard, since he was so hot. I was beginning to feel weird about it, especially with him pressed up against me. I kept at it all the same.

"I haven't done anything to you. Just let me be on my way," I said.

He got closer. If you'd asked me the second before if he could, I would have said no. But his face came within an inch of mine and his body pressed deeper into me.

"This is a dangerous game you're playin', Law. Vigilante justice," he told me.

I knew that, though I didn't say.

When I didn't speak, he went on, "You've got the attention of Darius and Marcus. This is not a good thing. Do you know what I'm sayin' to you?"

I felt a little thrill go through me, and not the kind that was going through me with just his body pressed against mine.

Darius Tucker and Marcus Sloan were the two biggest crime heads in Denver, Colorado. I was happy they knew who I was. I didn't figure they were scared, but I intended them to be.

Well, maybe one day.

Crowe must have seen something on my face because his eyes flashed.

"I should take you to the offices, lock you in the safe room and keep you there until you've had some goddamned sense talked into you."

He said "should". This I decided to treat as a good thing. I didn't know what the safe room was, but I didn't want any part of that either.

I kept staring at him and kept my mouth shut, thinking maybe he'd let me go.

He stared right back.

We were both silent, staring, his body pressed against mine.

I kept my chin up and hoped I kept my face blank.

"Jesus, you think you're fuckin' Catwoman," he muttered.

"I do not. Catwoman wore a leotard and stupid ears and fake claws. That's just silly."

I had no idea why I shared my views on Catwoman. I should have kept my mouth shut.

I thought this primarily because what I said made Crowe's face change. He wasn't looking at me like he was the pissed-off, badass boy trying to warn off the helpless, hapless female who dared enter his turf. He was looking at me in an entirely different way. A way that made me even *more* aware of his body pressed against mine.

"Where'd you learn to shoot like that?" he asked, and even his voice had changed. It was deep and masculine, but now it was also smooth, sliding across my skin like silk.

I decided it was best to go silent again.

He tried a different question. "Why was Cordova chasing you?"

I kept my silence.

Then something else about him changed. It changed the way he looked. It even changed the atmosphere.

I'd been staring at him to keep a brave face and tough out a difficult situation. With the change, I was staring at him because I had to. It was like I was drawn to him. My body softened; even my arms (which he still held behind me) that had been rigid with tension, relaxed.

"I could make you talk," he threatened, his voice low and quiet, and I knew, in that instant, he could.

"Let me go," I whispered, beginning to lose my fight.

This was a first. If Nick knew, he would freak out. He told me I'd been a livewire since he met me at age six, always beating up kids on the playground who bullied other kids, sometimes losing, sometimes winning. Always phoning and writing senators or congressmen and telling them what I thought and how

4

they should vote. Always having some cause that I'd fight with a passion that was nearly an obsession.

Crowe kept staring me in the eyes, which kept me stuck to him by some magnetic, macho man forcefield.

"You need to stop what you're doin' or you're gonna get hurt," Crowe told me, his voice still silky low.

"I can't," I admitted. Don't ask me why, but I had to say it.

"Then somebody has to stop you."

Somewhere along the line, he'd let go of my hands and he was just holding me. Actually *holding* me, his arms around me, mine lose at my sides.

It took a lot, but I shook off whatever was keeping me entranced, lifted my hands and pressed against his chest, hard.

He didn't budge.

Fuck.

"Let me go!" I shouted.

His arms tightened with a jerk and my hands slid up his chest to rest on his shoulders. I immediately began pushing. This didn't work, but it sent a message so I kept doing it.

"I'll let you go and I'll talk to Hank and Eddie. But I hear you're on the street, I'll find you and shut you down."

He could find me, I knew it. He found people for a living, and if word could be believed, he was really good at it.

I knew who Hank and Eddie were, too. Both good cops, Hank Nightingale and Eddie Chavez; Lee Nightingale's brother and best friend. I was guessing this meant Crowe would get me off the hook for shooting out Cordova's tires in broad daylight in the middle of Broadway, one of the busiest streets in Denver. It had been showy and stupid and I knew better. Zip would be disappointed. Nick would be furious.

What I didn't know was how Crowe would shut me down.

"All right, Crowe. Let me go, I'll stop," I lied.

At my words, he grinned.

I stared (again).

He had the most arrogant shit-eating grin I'd ever seen in my twenty-six (nearly twenty-seven) years of life.

My belly fluttered.

A belly flutter? What was *that* all about?

"What?" I snapped and ignored my belly.

"You're lyin'."

"I am not lying," I lied again.

He shook his head. Then, to my surprise, he let me go and stepped back. I stood there, feeling weirdly bereft.

"That's it?" I asked.

"No," he said.

I waited, then waited more.

"Well, finish it," I demanded when he didn't say anything.

"I get the feelin' I'll see you again," he told me.

Oh crap.

I didn't figure that was good at all.

He pulled my gun out of his jeans, released the clip, and with a casual overarm throw, he tossed it well away. Then he leaned in and shoved the gun in the waistband of my cords, right in front, by my hipbone.

He turned and walked away, threw a muscled thigh over his Harley and roared off.

I stared until I couldn't see him anymore.

Then I pulled my gun out, lifted up my sweater and checked to see if there was a mark where his hand slid against me.

I did this because it still burned.

⋙⧏⋘

I parked Hazel (my vintage red Camaro) in the garage behind my house, scanning my mirrors while the door came down just to be certain I was safe. These days there was no telling.

I got out of Hazel and did the routine of walking the fifteen feet from the garage to the backdoor. Eyes open, gun at the ready (I had an extra clip in my glove compartment), listening and praying no one was out to get me.

I unlocked the door and walked through the shared back room of my duplex where Nick and I kept our washer and dryer, an extra freezer, tools, old paint cans, and the kitty litter, which Boo, my cat, could access through the cat flap in my backdoor.

I unlocked that door, unarmed the alarm and flipped the light switch to my retro kitchen. Pink metal cabinets, pink fridge, pink oven door, huge black and white diamond tiles patterning the floor. One wall was brick, the rest painted steel gray. It was cool as shit, but not on purpose. Only that it had been there so long, it had come back into fashion. I'd bought a high, fifties-style black Formica-topped table with gleaming stainless steel sides and kickass retro stools with black leather swivel seats because the kitchen demanded it.

Boo approached from the other door and began immediately to tell me about his day.

My cat was black with dense, soft fur and yellow eyes. He was too fat, unbelievably proud, and he was the only clumsy cat I'd ever known. Boo pretended he meant to fall over and miss his leaps from furniture to table or whatever, but he was just not coordinated. At all.

"Meow, meow, meow. Meow meow. *Meoow,*" Boo told me, obviously having a full day and feeling I needed to be kept apprised of every second of it.

I threw my gun and bag on the table and swiped him off the floor.

"*Meow!*" Boo protested.

"Shut up, Boo. Mommy's had a very bad day. She did something stupid then got cornered by a hot guy and now she's pretty much fucked."

"Meow," Boo replied, thinking his news was more important than mine.

To shut him up I gave him kitty treats, feeding him from fingers to fangs.

This made him happy until I stopped giving him treats and he complained, "Meow."

"That's it," I told him. "Only three or the vet is going to yell at me again."

"Meow." Boo didn't care what the vet thought.

"Whatever," I wasn't in the mood to argue with Boo.

I dropped my cat, walked into the hall and pulled off my boots.

Nick owned the whole of the duplex. He let me stay in my side for half the mortgage, kind of. Even though I was now twenty-six (nearly twenty-seven), he didn't like me paying for anything, even my rent. So I put it in a bank account each month and gave him a check on New Year's Day every year. He tore up the check so the money just sat there earning interest.

Sometimes you just didn't argue with Nick.

The duplexes were weird. They weren't in the greatest part of town, though I thought it was pretty, or at least part of it was. It was officially Baker Historical District, but the not-so-good part.

We were on Elati and had a park in front of our house, but there was a subsidized high-rise apartment building on one side of the park and a low rent apartment building across the park opposite it.

Our house was historically registered and Nick kept it in great condition regardless of the 'hood. He'd redone his side; knocked out walls, put in a bedroom and tore out his pink kitchen.

I had not redone my side.

So my side was a lot like a loft. Nick had put in a new bathroom for me and I'd carpeted the whole place in a thick, soft gray. The front room had huge arched windows, a brick wall, the other walls painted a soft lilac, and it was enormous. It fit all my fancy furniture, including the dove gray velvet chaise lounge that sat by the front window and my sweep-lined lilac couch, which flanked a gleaming, square pub set with midnight blue leather-studded pads on the benches and a blue-gray overstuffed chair and ottoman. My antique oval walnut dining table was at the inside wall. The half circle-backed chairs I'd had reupholstered in the same dove gray velvet as the lounge.

There was a closet that separated the living room from the bedroom, though you could only loosely call it a "bedroom". It was really a king-sized mattress set on a platform that sat four feet above the floor and was open to the hall. I had to climb up three narrow stairs to get to it. There was storage underneath it and big areas cut in around the side walls of the bed that were above the lowered ceiling of the hall and closet. This was where I kept books, candles and a television set. This was my refuge. A little, feminine cave with fancy cream sheets, a fluffy green and cream patterned comforter, and an overwhelming array of pillows from standard to European to bedrolls to toss.

Then there was the bathroom and the kitchen. The hall was lined with floor to ceiling bookshelves that housed my massive CD collection. Mostly rock 'n' roll.

I loved my duplex and it was all for me. I didn't have parties because I didn't have very many friends, and none of them I knew well enough to ask to a party. I didn't have a rollicking good time in my bedroom refuge because I'd never had a boyfriend.

In my life, it was just Nick and me.

Before that, it was Nick and Auntie Reba and me.

Before that, before I could really remember, there was Mom and Dad and Mikey and me.

8

But when I was six, Mom and Dad and Mikey died in a car crash. Well, Mom and Dad did, instantly. My brother Mikey died in surgery a couple hours later, though it was the same thing. I'd been with them and survived, even though I'd been in the hospital for three months.

Then I went home to Nick and Auntie Reba.

Auntie Reba was Mom's only sibling, much younger than Mom. My Dad had no siblings and all the grandparents were dead except my Mom's dad, and at the time he had Parkinson's and was in a home (now he was dead too).

Auntie Reba and Nick had only been together a few months when my family died. They got married a few months after I got out of the hospital.

When I was fifteen, Auntie Reba died. She'd had a routine surgery. All went well, and then a couple of days later, she just died.

A blood clot dislodged in her leg and lodged in her heart and then… gone.

Nick, who wasn't even my real family, didn't turn me out.

Something happened between us, losing Auntie Reba like that.

The only love I knew growing up (or remembered, really) was Auntie Reba and Nick's love for me.

And I knew Nick's love for Auntie Reba.

He loved her in a way that was indescribable. It wasn't like she walked on water or was the earth and moon and stars.

It was different.

It was breath.

It was necessity.

She was the last of my blood and she was life to him.

So we hung onto each other. It was the only thing we could do.

Nick put up with me, which was saying a lot. I was a difficult child, an even worse teen, always on a mission to save a broken-winged bird, a shy school-mate, a forest in Brazil I'd never even see. I didn't party or get out-of-control in any normal way, but I was out-of-control just the same.

I became a social worker, which had Nick worried. He didn't think I needed any more causes.

"Christ, you've saved the trees, you've made the wilting violet into the prom queen and you've marched to take back the night. You can't save the world, Jules," Nick said.

"Maybe not, but I can try," I retorted, full of youthful bravado.

"Then I hope the Lord saves us all from you *trying* to save us all," Nick finished.

After graduating from college, I had a few jobs and kept my boundaries. Nick was surprised. He was certain I'd run amok in my quest to save the world.

This unfortunately put Nick at his ease. He'd thought I'd settled down.

Then I got the job at King's Shelter for runaway kids.

This went well, for a while. The kids responded to me and I'd found my niche.

That was until about four months ago, when I walked into the Shelter and Roam and Sniff were looking funny.

⎯⎯⎯⎯⎯

I walked back into the kitchen opened a bottle of red wine and poured myself a glass in one of my big-bowled red wine glasses. I went back through the hall to the living room and threw myself on the chaise lounge.

Boo jumped up and settled in my lap.

"Meow," he said to me.

"Quiet, Mommy's thinking," I told him and then slid my finger under his jaw and rubbed.

He purred.

I looked out the window, and even though I didn't want to, I remembered.

⎯⎯⎯⎯⎯

Roam, Sniff and Park were my boys. We were close. It took months, but I worked hard and got them to trust me.

They'd been on the street for years, but none of them was over sixteen. I'd rounded them into the Shelter, going day in and day out to 16th Street Mall where they hung out, and talked to them. I got a lot of kids from the street into the Shelter, then into counseling, then to reunions with their parents (if it worked), then family counseling and then home (if it really worked).

Roam, Sniff and Park were never going to go home. They told me about their homes. Their homes were evil and there was no way I'd finagle that kind of reunion. So I just worked at keeping them clean, safe, fed and educated. That day, that, shitty, awful day when I arrived at King's, I noticed Park wasn't there and I knew that Roam and Sniff knew something.

I cornered Sniff, the weakest of the pack, and asked where Park was.

"Dunno," Sniff replied.

Park had a crush on me. I knew this and used it. It was not that I thought I was all that, even though Auntie Reba and Nick told me I was, in Nick's words, "extraordinarily beautiful". He said this because he loved me. I did have a mirror, though, and even though I didn't think I was the hottest of the hotties, I was nothing to sneeze at. I had Dad's black hair, but on me, because I wore it long, it had a bit of wave. I had Mom's violet blues eyes and pale skin and Mom's curves, too. I wasn't going to win any beauty pageants, but no one was going to hand me a bag to put over my head, either.

To be honest, I had a crush on Park too, but obviously not the same kind as he had on me.

He was funny, sweet and smart as hell. He made me laugh so hard my stomach ached and he looked at me in a way that made me know I was making a difference.

I was beginning to realize I wasn't going to save the world, but I sure as hell was going to save Park, even if it killed me. I knew I should have boundaries, but I loved that kid. I loved all three of them.

Park knew I'd be at King's that day. He wouldn't miss a chance to see me.

"Sniff, no pudding cup for you if you don't spill," I threatened.

Sniff liked his pudding cups.

"Dunno, Law. Just… not here."

The sacrifice of the pudding cup was a surprise and heralded bad tidings. Sniff knew something was going on, and Park could be problematic. He was too smart for his own good and needed challenges to keep his active mind moving, especially moving away from a life that was pretty much shit. He got in trouble a lot, searching for adventure and release and a way to get away from it all. I had my hands full with him. I had my hands full with all three of them.

I grabbed the material of Sniff's overlarge sweatshirt at his arm and dragged him to Roam.

"Let's go boys. We're finding Park."

They came with me mainly because it meant they could ride in Hazel.

We found Park. It took hours. We searched all his places, and there were a fair few, but we found him.

I'll never forget it.

The syringe was resting in the alley by his lifeless hand.

Bad dope.

He was stiff. Rigor mortis had set in. His eyes were open, his usually beautiful skin was pale.

I took one long look at him and then shouted, "Goddammit!"

Sniff puked.

Roam put both of his palms to the top of his head, his eyes never leaving the dead body of his friend.

I cursed a bit more (okay, maybe a lot more) then crouched low by Park and stared at him.

It didn't even look like him. I'd never met a person with more life than Park. Seeing him lifeless was like looking at another human being.

I dropped my head and cursed some more.

Then I pulled out my phone and called the police. When I was done, I stared at Park again.

After a while, when the vision of him was burned on my brain, I closed my eyes and found the vision of him was burned on the insides of my eyelids.

That was when I knew what I had to do.

It just came to me.

I got out of my crouch and looked at Roam. "Who sold him the stuff?"

Roam was black, tall, gangly, and when he filled out he would be a looker. Sniff was white, overly-thin, short and had acne. Park had been Mexican-American, medium height and already handsome. If he'd reached an age, he'd have been a knockout.

I knew from my work with him that Roam was sliding across the edge. I never knew if I was going to get through to him. Every day I went to King's I held my breath, hoping he'd be there as that was the only indication that what I was doing was working.

Roam's black eyes stared at me, but he didn't say a word.

I put my hand to his chest and shoved him against the wall of the building next to Park's body. Then I got in his face.

Roam was fifteen, but five inches taller than me, and if he tried, he could take me.

He didn't try.

"Who sold him the fucking dope?" I demanded.

"Don't know his name."

"Can you take me to him?"

Roam's eyes moved, quick as a flash, surprised but not wanting to show it.

"Law," he said. That was all he said, and I knew he could.

"Tonight. You take me to him," I ordered.

Roam's face went hard and I knew why. Roam and Park had been friends since they could remember. They knew the bad times at home and the better-but-still-shit times on the street. Sniff had come later. New on the street, Park had taken him under his wing. The three had been inseparable ever since.

Until now.

"Yeah," Roam agreed, and I knew why he did that, too, and that wasn't going to happen.

"You aren't getting involved. You show me who it is and then you're a shadow."

"Law," Roam repeated.

"No, Roam. This isn't a discussion."

"Ain't no place for white bitches. These people'll fuck you up," Roam told me.

"Don't worry about me. And don't call me a bitch, it's rude."

What could I say? I was still the adult in the situation.

That night, Roam showed me who it was.

I didn't go after him. I wasn't that stupid. Instead, I followed him and I planned.

I also went to Zip's Gun Emporium and bought a gun.

Zip was as old as time. White, short, wrinkled, skinny and mostly bald except for about a dozen long, white hairs that were attached randomly to his skull.

Zip watched me as I handled the guns in his shop, making my decision.

"You ever held a gun?" he asked.

"Nope," I answered.

"You buyin' it for protection? To put in your purse?"

"Nope," I repeated.

Zip watched me some more. "Goin' after your ex?" he asked.

"Nope," I said again.

Zip's eyes got wide for a fraction of a second then they narrowed. "Goin' after someone else?"

I looked at Zip.

Then, I didn't know why, maybe I needed to talk about it, maybe I needed someone to talk me out of my plan, but for whatever reason, I told Zip about Park.

Then I told him about my plan.

He stared at me for what seemed a long time.

Finally, he walked down the display case, opened one up, pulled out a black gun and said, "Glock 19, nine millimeter. It's light, it's dependable and it'll fit in your purse."

Hallelujah.

"Sold," I said.

"Got a shooting range out back. Every day, you're in here for at least an hour. Every day, I'll give you the hour free and I'll teach you. You don't go on the street until you can handle that gun. And I got some boys I want you to talk to. They'll show you how to handle yourself. Be here tomorrow at six."

I was a little shocked, but I wasn't going to look a gift horse in the mouth so I nodded.

"Let's fill out the paperwork," Zip finished.

Zip made me practice shooting until my arms ached. Sometimes one of his boys, Heavy or Frank, would come get me and take me out and they'd show me other things. They taught me about knives; mostly how to avoid them, but also how to handle them. They also taught me how to scrap; how to punch, how to duck. They taught me how to drive, how to use stun guns, Tasers and mace, how to be quiet, how to be invisible and how to disappear.

Most importantly, Heavy taught me, "You get in a tussle, go for the go-nads. Always."

It was good advice, but I didn't expect to get that close.

I expected to be a nuisance.

I was going to use guerrilla tactics.

And I did.

I followed Park's killer, and while he was off making a sale I used one of Zip's knives and slashed all his tires.

Sure, it might seem silly and immature, but you make a drug sale, you want to get away and make another sale, not call AAA.

Then during one of Park's killer's sales, while hidden, I threw a smoke bomb at them, interrupting the sale and freaking everyone way the hell out. I didn't expect he lost his customers. Drug addicts would get over a freak out when they needed a score. Still, it would aggravate the dealer, and that was what I was after.

I followed Park's killer some more and saw his supplier.

Then I followed his supplier and I slashed *his* tires.

I did this a lot, messing with their heads, doing stupid, annoying shit that got right up their noses. My favorite was the plastic wrap I attached back and forth on the doorway when the dealer was taking a break from destroying people's lives and banging his girlfriend. When he was done, he walked through the plastic wrap on the door and, for a second had no idea what he'd walked through. He'd started yelling and carrying on, throwing his arms everywhere, plastic wrap clinging to him.

I watched the whole thing and nearly peed my pants laughing.

During the day, I listened to the kids.

At night, I eavesdropped on the dealers, the suppliers and the junkies.

This was how I learned the street, or part of it, anyway.

I paid attention. I memorized faces, names and places and I spent a lot of time with Zip, Heavy and Frank.

And I widened my net.

Sal Cordova was my first mistake.

Cordova was a small time supplier and part-time dealer and I got up his nose too, just for the hell of it, mainly because he was a swaggering jerk who thought he was God's gift to women. Following him, hiding in the shadows in bars and watching him, I noticed he seriously thought he was God's gift to women, even when the women didn't agree. I worried that Sal Cordova was the kind of guy who would *make* a woman agree.

One could say Sal was good-looking. He was a couple inches taller than me, decent body (not Vance Crowe-esque but then again, who was?), light brown hair, blue eyes.

Problem was, Sal was a jerk, he was a letch and he was so stupid, I got cocky.

One day I got close, sliding into the opposite side of a booth in front of him at a greasy spoon.

He looked at me, surprised, then he smiled, thinking I was coming on to him.

"Hey darlin'," he said and winked.

Um... *pu-lease.*

"I'm Jules," I told him, trying not to vomit.

"Hey Jules." His smile widened.

Okay, so that was all I could take.

I didn't waste any time and told him why I was there.

"Sell dope to kids, any kids, including the runaways, you'll be out of business. Remember, I'm watching."

Then I got up and left.

As I said, cocky.

And cocky was not good.

That was when people—not the right kind of people—found out who I was.

Zip was not pleased.

"Girl, you got a screw loose," Zip said.

When I told Nick (I told Nick everything; I did this because he'd find out anyway, I learned that a *long* time ago), to say he was not pleased was an understatement.

"Are you out of your flippin' mind?" Nick yelled.

I didn't answer. I learned a long time ago, too, that silence was the best way to go with Nick.

It was Roam and Sniff who spread the name Law.

Roam knew me, he knew what I was like and he'd heard about my antics on the street. He figured out it was me right away and he made a mistake. He told Sniff.

Sniff could never keep his mouth shut about anything, and he loved Park. They both did, so Sniff and Roam thought what I was doing was the shit.

By the time I talked Sniff into keeping his mouth shut, it was too late. I was Law and that was it.

Sal took my approaching him in the greasy spoon as a challenge. Not that he wanted to "shut me down" as Crowe did, but that he wanted something else entirely from me. Something icky, when you thought about doing it with Sal (way *not* icky when you thought about doing it with Crowe, but I didn't go there).

So instead of coming after me to stop me from getting up his nose, if you could believe this, Sal Cordova was actually trying to get me to go out with him.

Yes, that's exactly how stupid he is.

All of this brought me to my current predicament.

Sal had caught up with me and made his intentions clear.

I'd told him to go fuck himself.

He got a little excited and there was a bit of a car chase.

We ended up in a guns drawn faceoff in the middle of a busy one-way, four-lane street, right in front of a used bookstore that was the known hangout for Lee Nightingale and his boys.

The rest was history.

$$\approx\mid\approx$$

"Meow?" Boo asked, staring at me and knowing with feline instincts that my life was fucked, and probably wondering if something happened to me who would feed him.

"Yeah Boo. You called it. Meow," I answered.

Chapter 2
Levitate

My phone rang and I got up. I mentally shook away my memories, dislodged Boo on an angry "Meow!" and walked across the room to pick it up.

"Hello?"

"You're fuckin' loco. Loco!" Zip shouted in my ear.

I guessed word of my faceoff with Cordova had made the rounds.

"Zip—" I started.

"You're off duty. You're lyin' low. Least a week, maybe a month, maybe forever," Zip interrupted me.

"I'm not lying low," I told him.

Zip talked over me in full rant.

"It isn't Cordova. You could handle Cordova. Hell, a five year old could handle Cordova. We're talkin' Lee Nightingale now. *Lee Nightingale*. Do you *know* who was in fuckin' Fortnum's Bookstore watchin' you be a hotshot, shootin' out Cordova's tires like you were in a goddamned Hollywood movie?"

"Um ... " I mumbled.

"No?" Zip didn't let me answer. "First off, Lee fuckin' Nightingale. Then Hank fuckin' Nightingale. Make matters worse, Eddie fuckin' Chavez. Two officers of the goddamned law."

"Zip—" I tried to butt in.

He ignored me.

"And if you already weren't screwed three ways 'til Sunday, Luke fuckin' Stark, Kai fuckin' Mason and Vance fuckin' Crowe."

"Well, I knew about Crowe," I said.

And I guessed the rest, or some of them.

It wasn't good that I had the attention of the Nightingale brothers and Chavez, but Crowe had said he'd talk to them. Having Stark and Mace witnessing me facedown Cordova was kind of embarrassing. If word was even remotely correct, Stark was one badass mother. Kai Mason, known as Mace, was also known for not being far behind Stark in the badass mother stakes, not to mention he had a reputation for having a seriously short fuse.

"Oh yeah? How's that?" Zip asked, interrupting my moment of mortified reflection.

"He kinda caught up with me," I told Zip.

Silence.

"Zip?"

"He there?" Zip asked.

Zip's question confused me. "Sorry?"

"Crowe, is he with you now?"

"No. Of course not. We had a talk. He let me go."

"He's not there?" Zip asked, surprise evident in his tone.

"Um… no." I drew out the "no" thinking maybe Zip had finally lost what marbles he had left.

"You sure he isn't there?"

That was when I got a chill up my spine and looked out the front window.

No Harleys in sight.

I let out a breath.

"He's not here Zip. What are you going on about?"

"Crowe's got a way with the ladies. You look like you do, which you do, you get in his sights, he'll nail you faster 'n snot."

I rolled my eyes to the ceiling.

Pu-lease.

"I hardly think so," I said.

"Girl, you're loco. Pure loco. What'd Crowe say during this talk?"

"Not much," I lied.

I was already freaked out, and Zip was pissed-off. I didn't want to get Zip more pissed-off, which would serve only to heighten my freak out.

"He get a good look at you?" Zip asked.

I would guess the answer to that was "yes", considering his face was an inch from mine and his body was pressed against me.

My belly fluttered just thinking about it.

I ignored the belly flutter (again).

"Yeah. Zip, don't worry about it."

"These boys got a way about 'em, Jules. They don't fuck around. They see somethin' they want, they get it. They're fuckin' famous for it. A woman don't stand a chance. He seem interested?"

I had no idea the answer to that and I didn't care (well, maybe a little, but I had bigger fish to fry).

"Listen, Zip, honestly, there's nothing to worry about. We went our separate ways. I'll be smarter, I'll be more quiet. I'll be—"

"Laid, good and simple. Crowe got a good look at you, you're his. You're gonna be fucked and I mean that literally."

"Zip!" I yelled, shocked.

He ignored me. "Though, this may not be a bad thing. Crowe won't want a woman of his gallivantin' around town, lettin' off smoke bombs, slashin' tires and puttin' herself out there. You've been noticed. You're gettin' a lot of attention. It makes me *un*-comfortable. You get me? You were supposed to be invisible, you ain't invisible. Everyone knows about 'The Law'. Heavy and Frank and me been talkin'…"

Oh crap. Not Zip, Heavy and Frank talking. That was not good.

Every once in a while they got worried about me, a lot more often lately. I found ways to calm them down, but I didn't figure this would last forever. I needed them. I had a lot to learn and they could teach me. I also liked them and I liked spending time with them.

They were the closest things to true, good friends that I had. It might be a little pathetic that a twenty-six year old social worker's friend posse included an old, bald gun shop owner, a guy whose nickname "Heavy" said it all, and then there was Frank, who looked like he could hole himself up in a cabin with fifty years of provisions and mastermind a violent world takeover on a computer.

But I didn't care if it was pathetic, they were my friends and that was all I cared about.

"Zip, stop and listen to me. Vance Crowe is not in the picture. I'm fine and I'm not stopping."

"Jules."

"Zip," I said quietly and then, with feeling, "No."

He was silent again. He knew what my quiet voice meant. My word wasn't law for nothing.

"Zip, I promise, I'll do better," I assured him.

He was silent for another beat then he gave in.

"Jules, you be safe, you hear? Keep your eyes and ears open and your head down. I want you in here tomorrow, got me?"

I smiled. Crisis averted.

"Got you."

"Fuckin' loco," he muttered and hung up without saying good-bye.

⇛⇚

I was getting ready to go out and wreak some havoc on bad guys when I heard a knock at my backdoor and Nick came in.

"Jules? You home?"

"Yeah," I called from the bathroom.

I finished wrapping the band around my ponytail and went into the kitchen.

Boo was telling Nick about my day, snitching on me in kitty language.

Luckily, Nick didn't speak kitty language.

I looked at Nick.

He was tall, with salt and pepper hair, blue eyes, glasses, kinda stocky. He was only sixteen years older than me and I figured most of the salt in his hair was put there by me. He was dispatch for a trucking company, and because he loved doing it, he worked as a DJ most Friday and Saturday nights. He was responsible for my love of music, but mostly my love of rock 'n' roll.

He took one look at my black turtleneck, black jeans and black Pumas and muttered under his breath.

"Nick—" I started.

"I don't wanna talk about it. Talkin' about it flips me out, so I don't wanna talk about it. You're old enough to make your own decisions. The fact that they aren't the *right* decisions is outta my hands. I've been practicin' my morgue face for when I have to go identify your body. Wanna see it?" Nick said then he arranged his face in this kind of mock, sad, shocked look and slowly shook his head like a world with vigilante social workers mystified him.

"Good?" he asked.

I couldn't help myself. I laughed.

"You aren't going to have to identify my body," I told him.

"I hope not. Your timing, it'll be during a Broncos game. That'd piss me off."

I smiled at him. "Okay, I'll try not to get killed during a Broncos game."

He gave me one of his looks, the kind he'd been giving me for four months. The kind that made my gut twist. It was fleeting and he hid it fast, but I saw it and I knew he was worried.

I decided not to go there.

"Do you want me to make you dinner?" I asked.

His eyes got huge. "What? Now you tryin' to kill *me?*"

It was safe to say I wasn't the best of cooks.

Auntie Reba could cook. She was the queen of time-economy cooking. It took her about fifteen minutes to prepare a delicious, three course feast for thirty people. She was a kitchen goddess.

Unfortunately, while she was doing this, Nick and I were listening to Stevie Wonder or Elton John or The Marshall Tucker Band, depending on our mood. Therefore, I never learned to cook.

"I was thinking quesadillas," I suggested.

Anyone could melt cheese between a couple of tortillas. How hard could that be?

"You eaten yet?" Nick asked.

"Nope," I told him.

"Goin' out tonight?" he went on.

"Yep."

"I'll make dinner," he decided.

We both knew that was probably best.

And most nights Nick made dinner anyway.

⌦⧓⌫

I sat at a table in the back of the bar, my back to the wall, watching Darius Tucker.

He was a tall, lean, black man with twists in his hair. He was very good-looking and had a way of holding himself that made you notice him and he was also a very bad guy.

I knew as much, and was surprised by the fact that he was reportedly close to both Lee Nightingale and Eddie Chavez. Nightingale worked for money, and from what I could tell had a foot planted on both sides of the fence. But Chavez was a cop.

This relationship intrigued me.

I'd been on the tail of one of Darius's boys, a dealer. The dealer led me to Darius and I was watching.

It was late. I was tired. I'd had a shit day, not to mention I'd mentally relived the whole Park nightmare. I wasn't sure I was in the mood for mayhem so I'd decided to give the night over to reconnaissance.

Know thy enemy.

I was keeping my eye out for Crowe or any of the Nightingale boys. I'd only ever seen Crowe. The rest of them were still shadows for me. Though I'd heard enough about them that I could probably pick them out in a crowd.

I was sitting on my phone and it vibrated against my ass.

Not taking my eyes from the room, I pulled it out, flipped it open and put it to my ear.

"Yeah?"

"Law?" Sniff said and he didn't sound right.

My back went straight. "Sniff?"

"Law... shit. Law, he'll kill me if he knows I told you but... Roam..."

I was already standing, my body tense, my mind wired.

"Tell me, Sniff," I demanded, hitching the strap of my black purse over my shoulder.

"He's been talkin' lately, got this idea to help you out," Sniff told me.

Fuck!

I was worried that something like this would happen.

"You with him?" I asked, moving through the bar, keeping people between Tucker, his dealer and me.

"Watchin' him. Law, shit... he's gonna kill me."

"Where are you?"

"He's followin' someone. I'm followin' him. Goin' down Speer Boulevard bike path, close to Logan."

"Which side are you on?"

"South side."

"What direction are you headed?"

"West. Shit, Law."

He sounded scared.

"I'll be there in ten minutes. You stick to him, Sniff, but do not get near. Do you hear me? Something happens, you don't call me. You call the police. Got me?"

"Law, can't call the cops."

"You think something's gonna go down, you get out of there and call 911. Promise me."

"Law, I call the cops, Roam'd never talk to me again."

"Promise me, Sniff."

I was at the Camaro and Sniff hesitated.

Then he said, "Fuck. I promise."

"I'll be there in ten," I told him. "And don't say fuck."

I swung myself behind Hazel's wheel, started her up and drove like a madwoman. I parked in the Fox TV station lot, pulled my mace out and shoved it in my front pocket. I shoved my gun in the back waistband of my jeans and held my stun gun in my hand. I got out, locked up and pocketed the keys.

I crossed Speer, which wasn't easy. It was a busy three-lane street, even late at night. Then I headed to the bike path, keeping my eyes open.

I moved swiftly and quietly.

It was nearing midnight. It was dark. The street was bright, but the bike path wasn't well lit.

I saw nothing and kept going, hoping they stayed on the path. I couldn't chance a call to Sniff. I didn't know if Roam and whoever Roam was following would hear it. So I just moved as fast as I could without making any noise.

What seemed like an eternity later, but was probably five minutes, I saw Sniff's gray sweatshirt. We were almost to Broadway when I got to him.

He was standing, trying to hide, but you could see his sweatshirt. I approached him from behind and touched his shoulder. He jumped and whirled, dropping his phone with a clatter.

"Shit, Law!" he hissed.

I bent down, got his phone and gave it to him. "Roam still here?" I whispered.

"Yeah, up ahead," Sniff whispered back.

I handed him my car keys. "Camaro's in the Fox station lot. Go to it, get in, lock up and wait for me."

"Law…" he hesitated.

I got close and clipped, *"Move!"*

He took off.

Told you my word was law.

25

I moved forward enough to see that there were people in front of me, standing, pretty as you please next to a streetlight. A dealer making a sale. Anyone else might have thought they were just talking, on the Speer bike path, at midnight.

I knew it was a sale because I'd witnessed a lot of them the past four months.

Roam was nowhere to be seen.

I got into the shadows, watched and waited.

The sale went down. The buyers took off West, the dealer came my way. Shit.

The dealer got close and I recognized him. Name was Shard. A low level player, just a piece of scum caught in the wheel of the big drug machine.

I made a decision, came out to the path and started toward him like I was taking a moonlight stroll. I figured I'd walk by him, find Roam and get the hell out of there.

Shard noticed me, hesitated, and then, for no apparent reason, his body jerked and he whirled.

I stared, not knowing what was happening and wondering if maybe he suffered from epilepsy or something.

He jerked again, then again, then caught sight of something and ran toward it, away from me. He jerked again while he was running and I finally noticed Roam, standing a bit away, throwing rocks at Shard.

Oh shit.

I ran after Shard. Roam saw us both and shot out of his hiding hole and took off.

We were all running, flat out, and I realized in a panic there was no way I'd catch Shard and Roam. Roam was quick. Shard was quicker.

I did catch up with them, though the only reason I was able to was that Shard caught up with Roam, did a flying tackle and brought him down. They struggled. He rolled Roam to his back and reared to punch him, but before he did I made it to them, grabbed Shard's wrist and twisted it, spinning him off of Roam.

Shard rolled into me, took me down and my stun gun went flying.

"Roam, run!" I shouted as Shard got on top of me. We were struggling, his hands at my wrists. He was stronger than me, way stronger. I looked for my opening to knee him in the 'nads when Roam body tackled him sideways.

We all went rolling, Shard taking me with his hands at my wrists.

We stopped rolling, still scuffling. Shard was working to free himself from Roam and me when all of a sudden he was lifted clean up into the air, like he was levitating, arms and legs reeling.

I stared in shock. Roam went still and then Shard was slammed face first on the ground next to me.

That's when I saw Crowe.

He was crouched low. He planted his knee in Shard's back, pulled Shard's hands behind him and secured his wrists in cuffs like Shard wasn't struggling like a mother (which he was).

Crowe straightened, jerking Shard up with him. Crowe cocked his knee to the back of one of Shard's, taking Shard down.

I was lying on my back, staring up, unable to move.

Roam was lying on his side next to me, up on an elbow.

We were both (I hate to admit it) in awe.

I didn't have to wonder why Crowe was there. He was following me in order to "shut me down".

Shit.

Crowe pulled a gun out of a holster on his belt and trained it on Shard.

"Don't move," he said to Shard. His deep voice was scary.

Then his head turned and even in the shadowed light I knew he was looking at me. I knew it because I felt his eyes burning into me.

"Get up," he ordered.

I did as I was told, frankly too scared to do otherwise. He *was* holding a gun, and he seemed a bit pissed-off, and he'd made a grown man levitate. Even *I* wasn't fool enough to spit in the eye of that kind of tiger. Then I turned and helped Roam get up.

Crowe pulled a phone out of his back pocket, flipped it opened one-handed and hit a button.

I breathed heavily, staring at him.

"You... are... the... *man*," Roam whispered. He was staring at Crowe, too, eyes wide with wonder.

"Jack? I got a pick up," Crowe said into the phone. "Speer bike path, south side, close to Broadway," he hesitated, listening, then went on briefly. "Yeah. Out."

He flipped the phone shut and looked at me again.

"You wanna tell me what the fuck's goin' on?" he asked me, his voice still pissed-off.

I didn't, really, so I didn't say anything.

"How'd you do that?" Roam asked, cutting into Crowe's short, one-sided conversation with me.

I looked at Roam. He was still staring at Crowe like he was a god among men. Then I remembered to be angry at him and turned to face him.

"What did you think you were doing?" I shouted.

Roam's eyes came to me. "Law——"

"Don't 'Law' me. I should knock some sense into you. You could have got hurt, pelting drug dealers with rocks. Are you nuts?" I yelled.

"You do it," Roam said, assuming a teenage boy's pissed-off-yet-pouty stance of jutting lip and slightly leaning body.

"I do not pelt drug dealers with rocks. That's a fool thing to do. Honestly, Roam, what am I gonna do with you?"

"You're Law?" Shard said, butting into my tirade and looking up at me.

I caught his look, and even shadowed, it made me shiver.

"Quiet," Crowe told Shard, but Shard kept staring at me like he was memorizing me. I knew this wasn't good and that shiver turned into a quiver.

"Eyes to the ground," Crowe ordered Shard, and when he hesitated, Crowe's hand snaked out, shoving the back of his head so he faced down.

I felt the disquiet of fear crawling along my skin, but I pushed it away and turned back to Roam.

"We're not done. Go find my stun gun, I dropped it. I'm taking you back to the Shelter tonight. Tomorrow, we'll talk."

"Seriously, Law, I was only tryin'——" Roam started, but I interrupted him.

"Stun gun. Now. Talk. Tomorrow. Go," I snapped.

He grumbled something about "fuckin' bossy white bitches" and stomped away.

I stared daggers at his back.

"What'd I say about calling me a bitch?" I yelled at his back.

"Law," Crowe cut in.

My head rounded to him, and I'm afraid to say I'd had about all I could take.

28

"Not now. I've had a bad day. I have to get these kids to bed and then I'm gonna go home and have a bubble bath. Then I'm gonna sleep like the dead. I have to be ready for tomorrow because tomorrow, I'm going to kick some black-teenage-kid ass."

Crowe didn't say anything. Then again, what could you say?

I looked down at Shard then back at Crowe.

"You have this covered?" I asked, like I'd been helpful in some way taking down Shard.

"I'm thinkin'... yeah," Crowe told me.

"Good. Great. Marvelous. Have a fabulous evening."

Then I stormed up to the bike path where Roam was waiting for me. He held out my stun gun and I snatched it out of his hand.

"Let's get to Hazel. Move. Sniff is probably scared shitless. I don't even *know* what to say. You get out your phone and call your friend. Tell him you're okay..."

And the whole way down the bike path, even while Roam was on the phone with Sniff, I reamed him.

And most of the way, even though I didn't know it, Vance heard me.

Chapter 3
The Interrogation

I took the boys to King's and got them to their beds.

King's had six bedrooms, each with three sets of bunk beds. Three rooms for boys, three rooms for girls. Not many of the kids spent the night there. Usually they came during the day to hang, play pool, eat, and if we were lucky, talk to the social workers or work with the tutors.

I talked Park, Roam and Sniff into staying most nights there. They'd had permanent beds for months. Roam on the top of the last bunk by the window, Sniff in the bunk under him.

Park had slept on the top bunk in the bed next to Roam. Even though it'd been months, no kid had slept there since Park, mainly because Roam frowned on this.

As they settled, I stood beside their beds and looked at Roam. He was on his back, hands behind his head, staring at the ceiling and ignoring me.

I knew he was angry. Not only had Sniff ratted him out and I cut into his action, but I'd embarrassed him in front of macho man Vance Crowe.

"Be mad at me, Roam," I said softly. "But don't be mad at Sniff. He did the right thing."

Roam didn't reply.

I didn't touch the boys, touching was not right. I might nudge them or shove their shoulder playfully, but I only did these things after months of getting to know them. The only other time I'd touched Roam was to slam him against the building when we found Park.

After hesitating, I laid my hand on Roam's chest.

"Something happened to you, I don't know what I'd do. We lost Park. I don't want to lose another one of you," I whispered.

I felt his breathing go heavy like he was fighting emotion. He still didn't say anything and I left him alone.

I bent to Sniff. He was also lying on his back, arms to his sides. I could see his eyes staring at the top bunk.

"You did the right thing, Sniff," I told him.

Sniff turned his back to me.

Oh well. So be it. For now.

I left them to their thoughts and went home.

I let myself in, set the alarm so the door and window sensors were activated, but the motion sensors were not. I took a long, hot bubble bath and let the tension seep out of my body. Then I got out, toweled off and slid open the door to the under bed storage.

I had two dressers under there. My clothes were mostly utilitarian, chosen for comfort with only a bit of attention to style.

My nightwear was anything but.

Outside of decorating my house, my only extravagance was sexy nightgowns. I had two drawers stuffed full of them.

I pulled out a nightie and put it on. It had smoky gray lace at the triangular bosoms and at the hem, which came to my upper thighs. The thin straps and body of the nightie were the palest pink satin.

I climbed into bed and Boo settled in beside me.

I shut down my mind, and just as I told Crowe, slept like the dead.

<hr>

I woke up, groggy from sleeping heavily, and felt strange. The covers were tucked close to my back, an odd intense warmth coming from there. And for some reason, even though he'd never done this, Boo was draped over my waist.

My eyes opened slowly and I saw Boo, lying beside me, watching me and waiting for me to get up and give him his morning portion of wet food, the favorite part of Boo's day.

I closed my eyes again. My morning alarm buzzer hadn't gone off so I figured I had time to sleep some more.

Then my eyes opened again and I stared at Boo.

If Boo was lying beside me, then what was draped over my waist?

My mind cleared.

Oh crap.

I moved quickly, dislodging what was on my waist and heading out.

At my sudden movement, Boo went flying on an angry, "Meow!"

I was snagged around the midriff and thrown back to the bed, my head hitting the pillows, and Vance Crowe rolled his body over mine.

I stilled and looked up into his dark, lushly-lashed eyes.

"Oh my God," I breathed.

"'Mornin'," he said to me, like we woke up next to each other every day.

"Oh my God," I breathed again.

His hair was not in a ponytail, but falling around his face and shoulders, and I kid you not, he looked like a Native American Warrior God.

"Do I have your attention?" he asked.

Yes, he had my attention. He seriously had my attention.

"How did you get in here? My alarm——" I started.

"I disabled it."

"Oh my God," I said again.

My alarm was a good one. Nick had it installed for me. It had settings for when I was home and when I was not. The motion sensors had been specifically placed so Boo wouldn't set them off, even if he used his kitty flap. When an intruder tripped it, an alarm sounded and it immediately called a security dispatch then the police. It was not a rinky-dink alarm. It cost a fortune, not only installation but monthly maintenance fees.

"How did you disable it?" I asked.

He didn't answer. Instead he gave me his shit-eating grin.

Then it came to me where I was, where *he* was and I bucked to throw him off.

This didn't work.

"Get off me!" I yelled.

"We're gonna talk," Crowe replied.

"No... we... are... not. *Off!*" I was using my Law-at-the-Shelter-telling-off-the-kids voice.

This had no effect on Crowe.

"Don't make me hurt you," I warned, mostly for show.

The shit-eating grin spread to an amused smile, and that pissed me off.

"Like to see you try." He said it like he would, indeed, like to see me try.

It was a challenge, and because I was all kinds of fool, I took him up on it.

Heavy and Frank had shown me a number of moves and they'd made me practice them until my body ached. Unfortunately, these moves were mostly done standing up, but I used them all the same.

We wrestled and I realized Crowe knew all my moves, knew also how to deflect them, and he had far more moves in his arsenal, not to mention he was a hell of a lot stronger than me.

Nevertheless, I pushed him off, got my opening and surged to my feet on the bed in order to run. This was not smart, considering the platform where my bed sat had a five foot ceiling.

I slammed the top of my head against it and then went down, hard, on my knees. I saw stars and my right palm went to my head, my left palm came out to steady my body and landed on Crowe's chest. I settled my ass on my calves.

"Jesus, Law, you okay?" Crowe asked, coming up from his back, taking my hand with him.

I blinked to take the stars away. This didn't work so I blinked again.

"Jules?" Crowe called, using my real name for the first time. One of his hands went to my hip, the other one was sliding up the arm that was lifted toward my head.

With effort, I focused on him. "Yeah, I'm okay."

I was sitting back on my calves, my hand still on his chest. He was sitting up, torso twisted to me, hands on me. His face had softened to concern, a look that did something to my heart rate.

I took him in.

He was wearing his clothes from last night, without the jacket, a black henley now untucked and jeans. His feet were bare.

For some reason, I stared at his feet.

Most feet weren't very attractive, but his were somehow sexy. How he could have sexy feet, I did not know, but I figured if anyone would have sexy feet, the unfair laws of the universe that made *everything* about Vance Crowe sexy would also give him sexy feet.

This reminded me I was pissed-off.

I made a move, hopeful that I'd take him off-guard, but, alas, I didn't.

His hand moved from my hip. His arm swept under my legs, pulling them out from under me, and I landed, head on the pillows again.

He got on top and we struggled. I looked for a chance to knee him in the 'nads, but he got up and sat astride me, making my legs useless even though I kicked out to dislodge him. He caught my wrists and held them down at the sides of my head and loomed over me. I pushed my wrists against his hands and bucked my hips. He didn't move.

"Get off!" I shouted.

"No. You lose, now you talk," he said.

"Get... off," I demanded.

"What were you doin' last night?" he asked, ignoring my demand.

I stared at him, stopped struggling and kept silent.

"Who was that kid?" he went on.

I kept my mouth shut.

"Is he from King's?" Crowe continued.

I felt my heart begin to race, but I kept my face blank, or at least I hoped I did.

"He one of your street kids?" Crowe kept at it and I kept silent.

"This have to do with Park?" he carried on, and I couldn't help it. My body stilled at his use of Park's name and my head turned slightly to the side in an attempt to hide my reaction.

How he knew about Park, King's and my "street kids" I didn't know, and I didn't want to know. But he told me.

"You're on record as finding Park's body. You made a statement to the police, told them you were workin' with him at King's. Park had a juvie file a mile long, last few years of his life. Your name is in it," he paused, "Jules, your name is in it a lot."

I looked back at him and frowned but kept silent.

He changed tactics. "Tell me about Cordova."

I clenched my teeth and just stared at him. When I didn't speak, he stared back at me.

Then he did the change. I saw it, felt it and was captivated by it.

I watched, enthralled, as his head came toward mine. My racing heart skipped into overdrive and I felt a belly flutter so strong it had to be off the charts.

When his face was an inch from mine, he said, his deep voice silky, "See I'm gonna have to make you talk."

"No," I finally spoke, but it was too late.

His mouth came down on mine and the belly flutter broke the Richter scale.

You should know about something I hadn't yet shared.

See, I was not exactly experienced in the boy department. I'd had a few dates here and there, some kissing, some groping, but other than that, nothing.

Yes, I was a twenty-six year old virgin.

Many women would be embarrassed by this. Not me. I had no interest in sex, relationships or romance and I had no time for it. I was out to save the world, or at least save a few kids. And anyway, people in my life had sad and awful ways of dying on me, Park being the latest. I had to guard my heart and I did, like a vicious, trained Rottweiler.

My body tensed and I tried hard not to react, but the kiss was nice. I liked his hands on me, even if they were holding me down, and I liked his heat.

Then his tongue touched my lips and I felt a strong, pleasant tingle strike between my legs. I opened my mouth to say something, get him off me but his tongue slid inside. He slanted his head and the kiss got serious.

I was not experienced, but I could tell he was good at it, mainly because I melted. My lips fitted themselves to his and I kissed him back.

His mouth disengaged from mine, but he kept kissing me, lightly, softly, then he said against my mouth, "I wanna know about Cordova."

I shook my head, not only in a "no" to his request, but also to clear it, and he kissed me again. The between-the-legs-tingle strengthened and emanated out through my body and my mind muddled again, focused only on what his mouth was doing to me. My wrists pressed against his, not to get away but so I could touch him.

I wanted to touch him, *needed* it.

His grip tightened, likely thinking I was trying to struggle even though I was kissing him back.

His mouth came away just a fraction and he spoke against my lips again. "Who taught you to shoot?"

I was breathing heavily and I just stared at him, trying to clear my head.

"Who's in on this with you?" he asked.

I kept silent.

"Who're you after?" he persisted.

"Please get off me," I said softly.

He shook his head, his lips turned up a bit and he kissed me again.

I lost any clarity that I had gained with his mouth not on mine and kissed him back, struggling against his hands at my wrists. His mouth moved away, down my cheek to my ear and he said, "I'll keep this up all day. You're gonna talk to me, Jules."

I twisted my head, and don't ask me why—I was just driven by something I couldn't control—I touched the tip of my tongue to his neck.

This caused an interesting response. His knees slid down so his body came to rest on top of mine and his hands let go of my wrists. My arms went around him immediately. He brought his lips to mine again and his kiss changed.

This wasn't a muddle-your-mind, get-you-talking kiss. This was something entirely different.

My body reacted instantly, softening, melding itself to him, and one of my hands went under his shirt, my fingers tracing the hard muscle and soft skin of his back above the waistband of his jeans then they slid up the indentation of his spine.

He made a noise, low in his throat, that shot straight through my body and pounded between my legs.

He rolled to his side, taking me with him, kissing me, hot, hungry, his hands gliding over the satin of my nightie. I could feel the calluses on his fingers snagging at the material, and for some reason, this thrilled me.

His leg moved. He pushed a hard thigh between mine and his hand slid down my back, over my bottom, up the back of my thigh, lifting my leg at my knee and hooking it around his hip. Then his thigh pressed up between my legs.

It was then the phone beside my bed rang.

Vance ignored it and so did I. We kept kissing, Vance using his talented tongue, then he'd give me soft, quick kisses, then he'd use his tongue again. My hands moved up his back, feeling him and pressing him to me at the same time.

I hadn't gone the way of voicemail. I still had an answering machine, mainly because I liked to see it blinking on the very odd occasion that someone phoned me.

My voice could be heard asking the caller to leave a message as Vance and I kissed and groped, totally oblivious to the sound.

"Jules? This is May. I know it's early, hon, sorry. Listen, do you know where Sniff and Roam are? Their beds have been slept in but they're gone…"

My body froze for a nanosecond then I pulled away from Vance. I rolled, came up on my knees, my ass again on my calves and I snagged the phone.

"May?" I said into the phone, slightly breathless.

May was a volunteer at the Shelter. She worked more than most of the paid staff. She was a sweetheart and a soft touch, but she hid it just enough so the kids wouldn't walk all over her.

"Hey hon," May said into my ear. "You sound like you were running."

"No, just… never mind," I said, not about to explain it. "What's up with Sniff and Roam?"

"They're not here. Thought you might know something. The kids are talking, but not straight out. We think something is happening, or has happened, and we're a little concerned."

I closed my eyes and dropped my head.

Then I took a deep breath to calm my heart and mind and said, "I'll be there as soon as I can."

"Okay, hon. See you when you get here."

She disconnected. I put the phone back and turned my eyes to Vance.

He was on his side, up on an elbow, watching me.

"Sorry. Gotta go," I said.

And before he could respond, I scooted to the end of the bed, and not using the steps, I jumped to the ground, landing lightly on my feet. I headed straight to the kitchen.

I went to the table, pulled my cell out of my purse, found Roam's number and called it. It rang to no answer and Vance walked into the kitchen. He stopped, leaned a hip against the counter and crossed his arms on his chest, watching me while I left a message.

"Roam, you get this message, you call me immediately. Got me?"

Then I hit the off button and scrolled to Sniff's number.

"You gonna share?" Vance asked.

I kept my eyes on him while I listened to the phone ring. What I didn't do was share.

Sniff didn't pick up either, so I left the same message.

I flipped the phone shut, threw it on my purse and headed to a cupboard. Boo was circling my feet. Oddly absent during the bed area frolicking, he was now ready for breakfast and told me so repeatedly. I got out his wet food, got out one of his bowls and made him breakfast.

Vance watched me, and I was acutely aware that I was only wearing my nightie.

Though considering he had his tongue in my mouth and his hands on my ass (and elsewhere), being prudish about the nightie seemed a bit silly.

"Jules," Vance called after I'd put the food down.

I headed out of the room, right past him.

"I'm going to King's," I informed him.

I walked down the hall and went to the closet in my living room. I pulled out a pair of jeans and yanked them on under my nightie.

I had them zipped and buttoned when a hand curled around my upper arm and I was shifted and pressed into the wall. Then Vance got into my space, seriously into my space, head bent close to mine.

"We were in the middle of something," he told me, like I didn't already know that and wasn't trying my utmost to forget it.

"Yeah. I know. Sorry about that," I said airily, like it was all the same to me (even though it was *not*) and his eyes flashed dangerously at my tone.

Um.

Yikes.

I decided to explain. "It's probably for the best. We don't want things to get complicated."

He came closer. "We don't want things to get complicated?" he repeated what I said.

"Um… yeah," I replied.

"You think things aren't *already* complicated?"

He had a point.

I remained silent.

He got even closer. His hands slid around my hips to the very top of my behind and he pressed my body into his. His head tilted so it was a hairbreadth from mine. I put my hands between us, but this didn't serve any purpose at all, because Vance didn't let it.

"I know about Cordova. I know he wants to get in your pants," he told me.

My eyes narrowed at him. "If you knew, why did you ask?"

He ignored my question and said something that threw me right off balance.

"Jules, listen to me. Since *I* intend to get in your pants, he's gonna have to back off," Vance announced, rocking my world. Then before I could process his words, he finished. "I'll take care of Cordova."

Oh crap.

"Vance," I whispered, not sure what I intended to say, but I intended to say something.

For some reason, this made him smile. It was a new smile to me. It made his eyes soft and sexy and I felt my breath catch so I didn't say another word.

Kristen Ashley

"I like that," he said quietly, his voice back to silk.

"What?" I whispered.

"You sayin' my name," he told me. "I'll like it better when you moan it, tonight, when I'm inside you."

My stomach plummeted. You would think this was a terrible sensation, but instead it was thrilling, like being on a roller coaster.

"Oh my God," I breathed.

"Tonight, at dinner, we're gonna talk about what you're doin'. After dinner, we're gonna finish what we started this morning."

"Vance," I said, at that moment, wanting to have dinner with him like I wanted oxygen to remain present on the earth. And wanting to finish what we started like I'd wanted nothing else before in my life.

However, I knew this wasn't smart and it was not going to happen.

He kept talking. "I'll pick you up here, six thirty. You're not here, I'll find you."

"Vance, listen to me," I said.

"You feel like talkin' now?" he asked, his head cocked, and his eyes flashed again.

At his scary, threatening look, I forgot what I was going to say.

His mouth came to mine. "Six thirty, Jules. Be here."

Then he kissed me, hard and deep.

After he kissed me, he let me go, walked away, grabbed his boots from the floor and walked down the hall.

I moved to look down the hall but he'd vanished.

I heard the backdoor open and shut and I knew he was gone.

Chapter 4

I Wanna Be You

I swung into King's and knew immediately something was up.

King's Shelter was a huge, ugly building off Evans, close to I-25. It consisted of a big rec room with a pool table, television and bunches of couches and chairs, an enormous kitchen and dining area, six large bedrooms, a conference room where we did our family reunions, an open plan office, and three smaller rooms where we did counseling and tutoring.

There was a manager who ran the place and raised the money to keep it going, two full-time social workers, myself included, and one half-time tutor. We had two half-time professionals volunteering, one a social worker, one a tutor. Last, we had five volunteers who came and went as they pleased, three men and two women. They cooked, cleaned, spent time with the kids and stayed the night to let kids in or out and to keep an eye on things.

The place was packed when I walked in and everyone's eyes swiveled to me and most everyone stared. Not good. King's usually had a number of kids hanging around, but this, in my experience, was an all-time record.

May saw me the minute I walked in and she approached me.

May was one of our daytime volunteers and did most of the cooking. She was well into her fifties. She was short, black, round, and straightened her hair then arranged it so she looked like a heavy-set, African-American Jackie Kennedy circa the White House years.

"Hey, hon," she said when she made it to me.

"Hey, May. Any sign of Sniff and Roam?" I asked.

"No, girl, but we gotta talk."

I didn't like the sound of that.

Before she could lead me away, Josefa, a thirteen year old Mexican-American girl who'd been on the streets for six months before I got her to King's, approached us. She'd been reunited with her family a couple of weeks ago and they were in counseling. She wasn't my kid. In other words, I wasn't working her case, but I knew her all the same. I knew all the kids.

"Is it true?" she asked.

A gaggle of her girlfriends were standing close and staring at me in awe, much like I stared at Crowe last night (and possibly this morning).

My heart stuttered, thinking she knew something about Sniff and Roam, and I asked her, "Is what true? And by the way, hello and how are you today?" I not-so-subtly reminded her of the pleasantries of conversation.

She ignored my reminder and said, "That you've partnered with Crowe. Is it true you and Crowe are patrollin' the street and takin' down the dealers of Denver? A vendetta for Park?"

Oh crap.

"Mm-hmm. This is what we gotta talk about," May told me.

I looked from May, to Josefa, to her posse. "No. It's not true," I replied, and it wasn't, *exactly*.

"But I heard you and him took down Shard last night," Josefa said, looking disappointed.

I closed my eyes. Sniff and his big mouth.

Then I opened my eyes. "Josefa, I have not partnered with anyone. Don't believe everything you hear."

It wasn't exactly a lie. I hadn't partnered with anyone, and it wasn't me who took down Shard, it was Vance. I wasn't going to share this with Josefa however.

"But I heard," Josefa went on.

"Josefa, girl, enough. Leave Law alone. Go on. Scoot," May cut in.

Josefa stared at me, so did her posse, then they shuffled away.

May caught my arm, dragged me to a quiet corner and turned to me.

"Well? Is it true?" she asked, her eyes lit with a fire I'd never seen before.

"May—"

"Don't think we don't know what you've been doin'. These kids talk. They been whisperin' about you for weeks. I've been keepin' myself to myself, not likin' you out there alone, but not disagreein' with you either. Park was a good kid. We all loved him. You partner with the likes of Crowe, well, I'm thinkin' that's a bit of all right."

"May, I haven't partnered with Crowe. Something happened yesterday and... erm... last night," and that morning but I didn't go into that, "I met him. We've talked. He helped me with a situation and that's it. We aren't partners."

"He as cute as they say?" May asked, eyes still dancing with excitement.

Crowe? Cute?

I couldn't help myself. I threw back my head and laughed.

"What's funny?" May talked over my laughter.

"Vance Crowe is *not* cute," I said when I got myself under control.

May's nose scrunched. "That's damned disappointing. I heard he was a little hottie."

"Oh, he's hot all right, but he isn't cute. You don't describe a man like that as *cute*," I told May.

May's eyes lit again. "How *do* you describe him then?"

I thought about this and couldn't come up with anything. He was simply indescribable. You had to see him, and if you were lucky (which, surprisingly, I was) *feel* him.

"Just… not cute," I answered.

May must have caught something on my face because she smiled wide. "Bet he wouldn't describe you as cute either," she told me.

Whatever.

Time to move on.

"You hear anything about Roam and Sniff?"

"Not word one. They're out on the street, of course, probably spreading this 'Crowe and Law Death to All Denver Dealers Crusade' story far and wide. I was you, I'd get those boys in here. Pronto."

I nodded because she was so right. Then I went into the office to get what I had to get done done so I could go and look for my boys.

I checked my email, my voicemail, did a few return calls and took the two morning appointments I'd made with a couple of my kids. I had a free afternoon, which I was going to use to do some paperwork, make some calls and sit out in the rec room and talk to the kids, but I grabbed my purse and headed out to Hazel.

Hazel and I cruised the streets of Denver checking out Sniff and Roam's places, then checking out places where all the kids hung out, the whole time keeping my eyes peeled for Crowe or Cordova.

I came up with zilch. No one had seen them. This meant no one was talking.

I got myself some chicken tenders, an M&M cookie and a Diet Coke from Safeway and sat in the car, eating and thinking of where Roam and Sniff would go.

Then it hit me.

Shit.

I put my head to the steering wheel and said to Hazel, "Please tell me no."

Last night, Roam had looked at Crowe like he'd stepped right up to the Messiah. There was the vague possibility that Roam would try to tail Crowe, especially if he was shit-hot to "help" me in my crusade and looking for a mentor. This meant Roam would look in three places.

One was the Nightingale Investigations office. I didn't know where this was, but I figured a phonebook or the Internet would tell me (and Roam).

However, I doubted Roam would approach the offices. Watch them, maybe. Approach them, no.

There were two other Nightingale Boys hang outs that I knew of.

One was Lincoln's Road House, a biker bar.

The other was Fortnum's Bookstore.

I threw my chicken tenders bag on the passenger side floor, sucked down some diet, ignored my cookie (for now) and headed to Fortnum's.

Fortnum's was in my 'hood.

I'd been there a few times to buy books. It was only four or so blocks from my house. It had been there forever and had that feel about it. In fact, I was pretty certain some of the books had been there since it opened.

It was huge, smelled musty and had three big rooms. The front room had an espresso counter against the side wall facing Bayaud, a book counter facing Broadway, and a door that opened from the corner. There was a couch, its back at the store length Broadway window, another couch facing it and a coffee table in between. There were bunches of tables and chairs and a few comfortable armchairs. Behind the book counter there were rows and rows of shelves, then another, smaller room full of more shelves, and a table topped with open milk cartons stuffed full of old, vinyl records, then a huge back room filled with more shelves and books.

It was popular, and getting more popular by the day. They had a coffee guy the last time I went there who made unbelievable lattes. Rumor had it he got into trouble, dragging the bookstore's owner, India Savage, with him. Luckily for Indy, her boyfriend was Lee Nightingale, thus explaining why the kickass

Nightingale Boys chose to hang out at a bookstore. So her problems were sorted pretty damn quick.

The coffee guy took off and I heard they had a new coffee guy, and he was supposed to be a maestro of espresso, the best of the best.

I parked the Camaro on Broadway and headed in. The bell over the door rang and everyone looked at me. When they saw me, most everyone stared for a second then most of them smiled.

Except one.

"Oh shit," a super-deep, gravelly voice said. The voice came from a man behind the book counter, and he was the one not smiling. He had long, gray hair pulled back in a braid, a red, rolled bandana wrapped around his forehead and a thick gray beard. He had on a black Harley Davidson long-sleeved t-shirt, over which he wore a black leather vest.

Standing beside him was a gorgeous redhead who I knew was Indy Savage, the owner of the store and Lee Nightingale's woman.

Sitting on the counter was a beautiful blonde woman wearing a killer outfit, and next to her was a woman who looked exactly like Dolly Parton, wearing a velour powder-blue tracksuit, the top unzipped and showing so much cleavage she'd be arrested in some places.

Behind the espresso counter was an enormous man with lots of wild blond hair and a russet beard, and beside him was a pretty blonde.

Looking at the women I decided there was another, more obvious reason the Nightingale Boys hung out at Fortnum's.

Even though it was well in the afternoon, way past coffee time, there were three customers waiting to give their order, two waiting for pick up and a scattering of customers in the seating area.

"Fuckin' A, turkey!" the big man behind the espresso counter boomed, looking extremely pleased, and for some reason, he pointed at the Harley man.

I ignored their bizarre behavior and did another scan of the room.

That was when I saw in the corner next to the espresso counter, Roam and Sniff sitting at a table trying to look inconspicuous even though they were of the age where they should be at school *and* they were wearing homey clothes.

I stalked up to them. "Let's go," I ordered.

"Law," Roam replied, just that, but it was enough.

"Up! Now!" I snapped.

"Law, no one's even come in yet," Sniff told me.

I turned to Sniff, not knowing what he was talking about and not caring. "I've been worried sick and driving all over Denver looking for you two. We need to have a talk. We're going back to King's. Get up. Let's go," I repeated.

They looked at each other and didn't move.

I put my hands on my hips. "Boys." My tone held a warning.

"Law. We been waitin' forever," Sniff said.

Roam was silent.

"For what?" I asked.

"One of the boys to come in. Any of 'em," Sniff told me.

Roam sat back in his chair and threw Sniff a "shut up" look.

I leaned in. "I cannot believe this," I snapped, and shook my head because I really couldn't. "Which one of you started the rumor about last night?" I asked.

Sniff went silent and I got my answer.

"So, you're sitting around waiting for one of the Nightingale Boys to show up, is that it?" I went on.

"Wanna talk to Crowe," Roam finally spoke.

I opened my mouth to reply, or maybe yell (okay, probably yell), but I was interrupted.

"Hey woman," the big guy behind the espresso counter boomed at me and I looked at him. "You wanna latte? I'll make you my special. On the house."

His generosity was a surprise and I looked around the room again.

Most of the customers from around the espresso counter had cleared. The rest of the folks who looked like regulars were all watching me openly and grinning like lunatics. I didn't want to upset the lunatic asylum and didn't know how it'd look if I waltzed in, yelled at a couple of runaways and didn't buy a coffee.

So I said to the big man, "Sure."

"I'm Tex," he informed me, even though I didn't ask, and he started banging on the espresso machine in an alarming way.

"I'm Jules," I replied because I didn't want to appear rude.

"She's called Law," Sniff declared loudly.

Oh crap.

"Law?" The blonde behind the espresso counter walked to our side and looked at us, smiling. Her smile was amazing, and for a second, I was dazzled.

"Yeah. She's Law. Street name. Got it 'cause she's The Law. Gonna bring down all the dealers. She goes out huntin' 'em down at night, just like Batman," Sniff announced.

"Enough, Sniff," I said, my voice low.

The blonde's eyes turned to me. They'd grown round.

In fact, the whole place had gone silent and there was a tremor in the air that was almost physical.

Then the big man pointed at me and boomed, "Fuckin' A, darlin'!" Then he threw his head back and shouted, "*Yee ha!*"

Yikes.

Indy, the blonde, and the Dolly Parton lady had approached us.

"Seriously?" the blonde from the book counter asked, staring at me.

I glared at Sniff.

"I'm Indy." The redhead came up to me and shook my hand, saving me from having to answer.

"Jet," the blonde behind the espresso counter said and waved.

"I'm Roxie," the blonde from the book counter put in. She shook my hand, too.

"Daisy. Sugar, I like your boots," the Dolly Parton woman offered, also shaking my hand, but she was looking down at my shiny, black cowboy boots. They were a Christmas present from Nick the year before.

"Me too," Indy said. "They're the shit."

"Um… thanks," I replied as the bell over the door went.

"Holy fuck," Roam breathed from behind me.

I twisted to look at him, but he was staring, eyes wide, at the door. Slowly I turned around to the door, feelings of dread seeping through me.

Three men had walked in and at the sight of them my breath left me in a whoosh.

All tall, all dark one looked like the All-American boy gone wrong, but in a good way (a *very* good way). Another had close-clipped black hair and killer facial hair, his mustache trimmed to razor sharpness down the sides of his mouth. If it had been on anyone else, it would have looked ridiculous, but on him it was quite simply *hot*. The last was taller than the other two (which meant he was seriously tall). He had coloring and eyes that I knew, from the stories I'd heard about him, were from his Hawaiian ancestry. They all had fantastic bodies, clearly noticeable under their clothes, and they all looked like the badass mothers I knew them to be.

These men were Lee Nightingale, Luke Stark and Kai "Mace" Mason, in that order.

"Goddammit," I muttered under my breath.

They approached and instinctively I moved in front of the boys.

All of their eyes were on me and they noticed my movement. One side of Stark's lips went up in a sexy half-grin, Nightingale's eyes crinkled at the corners and Mace smiled flat out.

They thought I was some silly woman, the jerks. My back went straight and my chin went up.

"Law," Nightingale said when he arrived at our group.

"Shit, Law. He knows who you are!" Sniff piped up behind me, his voice filled with excitement.

"Quiet, Sniff," I said, not taking my eyes from Nightingale.

"You got business here?" Stark asked, positioning himself beside Roxie and telling me not so subtly that I *didn't* have business there.

"I've just come to get my boys," I assured Stark. Then, eyes still on Stark, I said to Roam and Sniff, "Let's go guys."

I didn't hear chairs scraping so I turned to them. They hadn't moved.

"I said, *let's go.*" And I used my word-is-law voice.

They both immediately stood.

"Don't forget your coffee," Tex boomed.

I nodded to the big man, but said to the boys, "Hazel's down the street. Get in. I'll be there in a minute."

"But, Law," Sniff whined.

"I'll be there in a minute," I repeated, walking over to take my latte.

I wrapped my fingers around its heat, ready to offer to pay when the bell over the door rang. I looked toward it and saw Vance walk in.

"God *dammit*," I hissed under my breath.

His gaze locked on me and he walked to our group and stopped, his eyes never leaving me. I felt his stare like he was touching me, and my mind, working against me, flashed on this morning, and my body, also working against me, reacted.

Roam and Sniff had frozen.

I shook off the Crowe Effect. "Boys, get to the car."

"I wanna work with you," Roam said to Vance and Vance's eyes left my face and sliced to Roam, but he didn't say a word.

"I wanna be, like, your trainee or somethin'," Roam went on, and you could tell just by looking at him that this was taking everything he had.

Crowe's face was blank and he showed no reaction, not even to Roam's obvious mixture of discomfort and longing. I felt my heart squeeze and my breath freeze, worried that Crowe would make a fool of him. There was nothing in Roam's life that he ever wanted that he actually got, and you could see, quite plainly, that there was likely nothing in Roam's life that he wanted more than he wanted this.

"Roam——" I started to break in.

"You on the street?" Vance asked Roam and my eyes swung to Vance. He was not blank anymore, he was watching Roam closely.

"Sometimes," Roam said. "At King's," he went on.

"Stay at King's," Crowe returned and that was all he intended to say. I could tell because his eyes cut to me.

I could feel Roam's disappointment. It filled the air.

"We need to talk," Vance said to me.

"I'll do what you say!" Roam continued, and everyone looked at him because his voice had gotten louder, higher, more desperate. His body was tense, solid, and I felt my throat close. "Anything you say. I won't mouth off. I'll just do it. I won't be a problem, I swear."

"Roam?" Crowe asked and Roam nodded, confirming that was his name. "Get your diploma, get smart. Once you do that, I'll think about it."

Roam shook his head, not letting it go. "Has to be now."

"Roam, we'll talk about this in the car," I said to him.

Roam's body swung to me.

"*It has to be now!*" he shouted, and my body jerked.

I'd never heard him shout.

His face was distorted with something, an internal battle, the physical manifestation of which could be seen in his expression.

"Be dead in three years," Roam continued and my heart stopped.

"Roam, don't say that," Sniff put in quietly.

"I'm gonna get 'em. All of 'em, and I gotta know how to do it. If I don't, they'll kill me."

49

I started to walk along the front row of the crowd to get to Roam and was just passing Vance when Roam started to back up. Vance stopped me with an arm around my waist and he pulled my back to his front. I didn't fight Vance and didn't try to get to the retreating Roam.

Roam backed up until he was against the wall.

"Roam, we'll get back to King's. We'll talk," I said softly.

"No. You're after them. You're doin' it. I'm gonna do it too. They killed Park. They didn't shoot 'im, but they might as well have. Park was..." he stopped, his voice went hoarse. "Park wanted..." he tried to go on, but stopped again.

I leaned away from Vance to detach his arm from me so I could get to Roam, but Vance's arm tightened and he pulled me deeper into his body.

"Best way to get them, Roam, is not to become one of them," Nightingale cut in, his eyes sharp on Roam and I could tell he'd taken in everything.

"You don't know," Roam spat at Lee, taking (I thought) his life in his hands. I didn't expect many people talked to Lee Nightingale like that, certainly not fifteen year old boys. "You have no fuckin' clue."

"My best friend is Darius Tucker," Lee told him.

Roam's body went still and his eyes grew wide. Mine did too.

"I do know," Lee said with finality.

This hit Roam, I could tell, but he didn't give up. His eyes went to me and Vance.

"I wanna be you," he said to Vance quietly.

"You can't be me. You gotta be you. And right now, you're a kid. Be a kid," Vance advised from behind me.

"I'm not a kid," Roam protested.

"That ain't a bad thing, sugar," Daisy put in.

"I'm not a kid!" Roam yelled at her.

All right. Enough was enough.

"Roam, don't speak that way to people. It's rude," I put in and shoved forward, detaching from Vance and going to Roam. "We'll get some hamburgers and we'll go somewhere and talk. The three of us."

"Done talkin'," Roam said.

"Roam, let's talk with Law. Come on," Sniff approached him too.

Roam looked down on me. "You saw him lyin' there, in a fuckin' alley, fuckin' shit and trash all around him. Trash, Law. *Trash.* You and me and Sniff, we all saw Park lyin' in the fuckin' trash," he said to me, and I knew the vision of Park's dead body was burned on his brain too.

I swallowed then said, "Yeah, Roam, I saw him."

"We was gonna go to California, learn how to surf. We was gonna go to Alaska and wrestle polar bears," Roam told me, for the first time confiding the teenage boy dreams he shared with Park.

"Polar bears are mean motherfuckers. I saw that on some nature channel," Sniff informed Roam, trying to be helpful.

"Stop saying motherfuckers," I said to Sniff, then turned again to Roam. "Let's get a burger. Come on."

"Park'd do it for me," Roam said, still not letting it go.

I wanted to touch him, hold him, put my arms around him, but I knew he wouldn't want it. He was a teenage boy and he was a street tough standing in front of a posse of the biggest badasses in Denver. He'd freak if I tried to mother him. Not to mention he'd never had a mother who'd touched him, held him and put her arms around him in a loving way. He wouldn't know what to do.

So instead I smiled at him. "Yeah, Park would do it for you, and I'd be just as pissed at him, nagging him and getting in his face because it just isn't smart." Roam took a deep breath, maybe to say something, but I didn't let him. "And then he'd listen to me and let me help him get his life sorted out."

Roam stared at me.

"You know he would, Roam. Think about it. You know it," I told him.

"He would. He thought Law was the shit, even before she actually was The Law," Sniff added.

Roam kept staring at me.

"For God's sakes, are you boys hungry or what?" I asked, throwing my arms out and pretending to sound exasperated.

"I'm hungry," Sniff said.

"You're always hungry," I told him.

Sniff grinned. "I'm a growin' boy."

"I hope so. You need to fill out. The inspectors come to the Shelter and look at you, they'll think we're starving you all to death," I said.

"'Specially if they look at May. I swear, she eats most of the pudding cups," Sniff returned.

"That's not nice," I admonished.

"It's true," Sniff retorted, his grin growing into a smile.

"Okay, maybe it's true," I relented, giving him a subtle wink.

"Would you two shut up? I want a double beef burger with cheese, giganto-sized," Roam cut in.

I nodded to Roam immediately, trying my damnedest not to look as happy and relieved as I was that whatever it was that had a hold of him, he'd let go.

I turned to take the boys out and stopped dead.

Everyone was watching us, including and especially Vance.

His eyes were on me and there was something in them I couldn't read. Something familiar, even precious. Something I remembered from a long time ago, but hadn't seen in so long, I didn't remember where I saw it in the first place. Before I could figure it out, the look disappeared.

I nodded in the general direction of everyone.

"Nice to meet you all," I said then started to shove through, but Vance caught my bicep and stopped me.

"Your place, six thirty," he reminded me, his eyes serious.

I just gave him a look. He released me and the boys and I walked away.

"What was that about?" Sniff stage-whispered to me.

"They got a date," Roam answered, too quick for his own good (and mine).

"No shit? You got a date with Crowe? Holy fuck!" Sniff yelled.

I rolled my eyes. Now *this* would be all over the street in an hour.

"Keep your voice down, Sniff. And don't say shit or fuck. Don't you boys ever listen to me?"

"No," Roam said and grinned at me.

For the first time that day the sky of my life brightened and I grinned back at him.

Just as the door closed behind me, I could swear I heard, "Now *I'm* thinking Law's the shit." This was said in an unfamiliar man's voice so it had to be Mace who hadn't spoken.

"You ain't wrong about that, sugar," this was obviously Daisy.

I ignored their words, got the kids in the Camaro and we went to get burgers.

It wasn't until after we were sitting eating burgers that I tasted my latte and, even cold, it was the best flipping thing I'd ever tasted in my life.

Chapter 5
Nick's Third Degree

At six thirty, when I was supposed to be nervously anticipating Vance's arrival at my duplex, I was in Heavy's garage, wearing silvery-gray sweatpants with two black stripes running up the sides and a white t-shirt with the arms cut off with Gold's Gym on the front in black. I was jabbing a punching bag and sweating like a pig.

"Jab, Jules, fuckin' *jab!*" Heavy shouted at me, sitting on a bunch of boxes stacked at the side of his garage, working through his second double pack of Ding Dongs. "You jab like a girl. Keep your leg back, aim for the kidneys. *Jab!*"

"I'm jabbing, Heavy!" I shouted through my panting, then quit jabbing and started roundhouse punching the sides of the bag, then I quit doing that too. I hugged the bag and stared at Heavy. "How long do I have to do this?" I asked.

"You only been at it an hour," Heavy answered and then shoved an entire Ding Dong in his mouth.

I glared at him. "Don't you think an hour is enough?" I asked. "I'm not exactly going to be boxing with drug dealers for a whole fifteen rounds."

"Don't do fifteen rounds anymore, the sissies, only do twelve," Heavy informed me.

"Well, I won't be going twelve rounds with them either."

"You gotta be in shape. 'Specially now that you're goin' up against the Nightingale Boys. Fuck, girl, you... are... loco."

I used my teeth to yank at the strings of my boxing gloves, shoved one under the pit of an arm and tugged it off. "I'm not up against the Nightingale Boys," I said.

Heavy shook his head. "Got a friend, he's a cop, says Hank Nightingale and Eddie Chavez pulled up all sorts of shit on you yesterday. Searchin' your name and findin' it all over your kids' records."

So *that* was how Vance knew everything.

I found this annoying. The whole bedroom interrogation that morning was bullshit. Vance knew the answers to most of his questions before he'd even asked them. This meant his "making me talk" was just an excuse to kiss me.

I didn't know what to do with that so I didn't do anything with it. I'd have time to think about it, maybe when I was eighty.

Heavy was watching me closely as I tugged off the other glove.

"Unh-hunh," he read my face correctly and went on. "Nightingale and Chavez searched you and Lee's got a big nerd workin' for him who could hack into the computers at the Pentagon. By now, they know everything about you, even your panty size."

This gave me pause for reflection. I didn't like the idea of Vance knowing *everything* about me. Though I didn't care about my panty size, unless he felt like buying me a present for my birthday, which was only a few days away.

What was I thinking?

Vance was not going to be in my life, thus no birthday present. And certainly not panties.

I looked at Heavy. "My birthday is Thursday," I told him.

"Well, happy fuckin' birthday," Heavy grinned, white cream and chocolate cake in his teeth.

I dropped my gloves to the floor, sat next to him on the boxes and pulled back some tendrils of hair that had come loose from my ponytail.

"Not today, Thursday," I took a deep breath and then went for it. "You want to go out for a drink or something?"

Heavy stared at me. "Don't you have girlfriends?" he asked.

I pulled in my lips and hit him in the shoulder.

"Forget it," I said and smiled. "I gotta stretch."

I got up and walked over to a mat that Heavy had put out for when he showed me moves to defend myself against attack. I dropped down on it and started to stretch.

"You goin' to the range after this?" Heavy asked, still staring at me.

"Yeah."

"You goin' out after that?" he went on and I knew what he meant. Was I going out after bad guys?

I'd been giving it some thought, especially after what Roam had done. I wasn't exactly being the best role model.

Still, I was an adult. I was being smart and I was getting trained. I wasn't a kid pelting a drug dealer with rocks (I had to admit, though I'd never tell Roam, that was a good one).

I looked at Heavy. "I'm going home for food, and then, yeah, I'm going out."

"Be safe," he said, got up and went into the house.

I stretched, and when I was finished I pulled on my black zip-up sweat-shirt and grabbed my bag. I walked into the house and I could see the back of Heavy's blond head. He was sitting in front of Monday Night Football.

"I'm outta here, Heavy," I called.

"Cool," Heavy called back.

I walked to the front door and I heard Heavy say my name, so I turned.

"What?" I asked, peering around a column to look into the living room.

He'd twisted around the side of his reclining chair to look at me. "I'll go out for your birthday, but not to one of those girlie bars with martinis or any of that shit. American beer. Televisions. Women wearing tight t-shirts. You doin' that for your birthday?"

I smiled at him. "I could do that."

"Great. I'll be there."

Then he twisted around again and stared at the football.

$\rightleftarrows$

I went to the range and shot for half an hour, then gabbed to Zip for half an hour, then went home figuring Vance would be long gone. It was well after eight and I didn't think Vance was the kind of guy who hung around for long after it was obvious his date had stood him up.

I let myself into the duplex and listened to Boo telling me about his day for a few minutes before I shut him up with some treats. Then I listened to Boo complaining about lack of treats for a few minutes before I shut him up with a kitty cuddle.

I dropped him and took off my clothes, got in the shower and cleaned off the sweat and gun smoke.

When I stopped the shower, Boo was sitting on my toilet seat, staring at me, and then he told me how he felt about me stopping his cuddles and taking a shower.

"Oh Boo. Shut up," I said.

Kristen Ashley

He gave me a look and jumped down off the toilet seat. He did a little graceless skid on the bath mat, corrected himself and flounced out of the bathroom, all haughty.

"Damn cat," I muttered, smiling to myself.

I slathered with lotion that smelled of cucumbers and melon and pulled a comb through my hair. I put on underwear then I yanked on a pair of faded navy blue fleecy sweats with a drawstring waistband that I let ride low on my hips. The sweats had loose hems that had a small notch on each side at the ankle. They were too long and rested over most of my feet and dragged under my heels. I pulled on a white thermal long-sleeved shirt, scooped up Boo and headed over to Nick's for leftovers. I knocked on the backdoor and stuck my head in.

"Nick?" I called.

"In the living room," Nick yelled back, sounding impatient. "Monday Night Football," he finished, explaining the impatience. You didn't interrupt Monday Night Football at Nick's. Or Saturday collegiate games. Or Sunday NFL day.

I walked in, dropped Boo and he pranced into the living room, big bushy black tail straight up. Then I heard him immediately complain to Nick about the lack of treats and cuddles on the other side of the house.

I opened Nick's fridge. "You got any leftovers?" I shouted, head in the fridge.

"In here," Nick yelled again.

I pulled my head out of the fridge, straightened, closed the fridge, turned and stopped dead.

Vance was standing in Nick's kitchen in the exact same pose he'd been standing in mine that very morning, arms crossed, hip against the counter.

My eyes narrowed and I crossed the room in a flash, getting in his face.

"What are you doing here?" I hissed in a whisper, forgetting for a moment about our date and thinking he'd broken in, just like he had on my side. I was angry but also a little amazed. He hadn't made a sound.

"Oh, Jules?" Nick called from the other room. "We got company. Seems you're a little late for your date. I let him in so he could wait over here."

Then I heard Nick chuckle to himself.

I closed my eyes and took a deep breath.

When I opened them Vance was grinning at me.

I clenched my teeth.

56

Vance's eyes scanned my face. "Murder is illegal," he said to me.

"I'm willing to do my time. I just don't know which of you to kill. How much more do you get if it's a double homicide?" I asked.

His hand shot out and wrapped around my neck then he pulled me to him and I hit his body, full-on. I put my hands on his chest and pressed back with both my neck and my hands, but I didn't move so I gave up.

Vance got close to my face. "You don't want me dead, you want me to fuck you. You can kill me after," he said.

My eyes rounded at his bluntness, then I pressed again and his other arm wrapped around my waist and he pulled me deeper into him. I tilted my head back and opened my mouth to say something smart, but he got there before me.

"Be careful, Jules," he warned, voice low so Nick wouldn't hear, his eyes flashing with an anger that I hadn't noticed before. "I'm bein' patient here. I'm not overly fond of bein' stood up."

Unfortunately, since Vance hadn't made anyone levitate recently and I was standing in the kitchen of the only family I had, I felt safe so I decided to spit in the eye of the tiger.

"I didn't agree to go on a date with you. If I remember, you *told* me we were going out," I said in a quiet voice too.

"We have things to talk about," he returned.

"No, we don't. You already know everything. Your cop friends were searching my name yesterday and you have a computer guy at the office who's been looking into me. You just used that as an excuse to make me talk."

He got closer, apparently unsurprised I knew all of this. "Okay, we don't have things to talk about. We have things to *do*," he said.

My belly fluttered.

"Like what?"

"Like finish what we started this morning."

I knew that was what he was going to say.

"That's not gonna happen."

"Yes. It is."

"No. It... is... not."

"You gonna come in here and get some food or what?" Nick shouted.

"Yeah," I called.

Vance's arms tightened.

"Let me go," I said to Vance, going back to my quiet voice.

Kristen Ashley

His hand fisted in my wet hair, held my head steady and he kissed me.

Oh crap.

This was not good.

I resisted and it worked for a few beats then his mouth opened over mine. Mine automatically opened to let in his tongue, and the minute it slid inside my mouth I melted into him and kissed him back.

Almost as quickly as it began, it ended and I felt of surge of disappointment.

His head came up and he looked down at me.

"I'm gonna have you, Jules," he promised, and at his promise tingles rushed across my skin in a very a pleasant way. Then he let me go, turned me and gave me a little push toward the hall.

I walked into Nick's living room. Nick was lying full out on his couch.

"Hey Jules," Nick said, grinning at me.

"Would you like your hemlock now or should I put it in the Thanksgiving turkey?" I asked Nick, throwing myself in an armchair. Boo jumped up in my lap and out of habit I began to stroke him. He settled in and began to purr.

"Like you're cookin' the Thanksgiving turkey. Please," Nick returned, his eyes sliding to the TV.

Vance settled into another armchair. He nabbed a can of pop from the coffee table that he'd obviously been drinking and sat back, crossing a scuffed cowboy-booted ankle on his knee.

"Jules doesn't cook. You should know that. Kitchen plus food plus Jules equals disaster," Nick told Vance.

"I'll keep that in mind," Vance responded, his eyes cutting to me, and there wasn't any anger there anymore, just amusement.

"Nick. Shut up," I said, and I was sure my eyes still had anger in them.

"She can be rude sometimes too," Nick shared, his gaze never leaving the TV.

"I've already learned that," Vance replied.

I leaned forward and grabbed a slice of pizza from the open box sitting on the coffee table. I took a big bite, chomping on it and deciding to watch the football and ignore both of them.

"She makes a killer margarita though," Nick went on, a font of Juliet Lawler information and happy to impart it on anyone.

"I don't drink," Vance said.

This was such a strange comment that both Nick and I looked at Vance.

"No?" Nick asked.

"Recovering alcoholic," Vance said, now his eyes were on the TV.

I moved my eyes back to the TV, too, shocked at this knowledge and not wanting to make a big deal of it.

I couldn't imagine Vance as a drunk or out-of-control in any way. He seemed to be totally on top of every situation.

I took another big bite of pizza, chewed, and pulled off a bit and fed it to Boo, who was staring at my slice of pizza with desperate kitty eyes.

"How long you been dry?" Nick asked.

"Ten years. Dried out in prison," Vance replied.

Nick and I looked at Vance again.

"Prison?" Nick asked.

"Two years. Grand theft auto."

I swallowed hard and turned back to the television.

"Christ, man," Nick said softly. "You must have been what, a teenager?"

"Sent down when I was twenty," Vance replied.

I took another bite of pizza and gave another piece to Boo.

Boo was in heaven. I was freaking out.

"Close with your folks?" Nick asked.

"Nick…" I decided to cut in. He was getting a bit nosy.

He was the only father I ever knew and any father's duty was to be hard on his daughter's dates, especially when they informed you they were recovering alcoholics and ex-cons. But this wasn't high school and this was a bit much.

"Haven't seen 'em since I was ten," Vance answered without hesitation.

My head swung around and I looked at Vance. He was leaned back in his chair, eyes on the TV, casual and laidback, seemingly unaffected by Nick's third degree.

I looked hard at him, an expert at reading people, it was part of my job, but he gave no indication he was uncomfortable in any way.

"Why not?" Nick asked, giving up on football and turned fully to Vance.

"Father turned me out. Wasn't a good place to be so I didn't go back."

I took another bite, forced my eyes to the television and fed Boo another tidbit. I tried to take my mind off a ten year old Vance turned out of his home, but I couldn't. I couldn't imagine any ten year old being turned out of their home, even though I did what I did. It still surprised me, practically every day.

And I didn't even want to consider the idea that it happened to Vance. In fact, I hated the idea so much it caused me physical pain. My stomach began to hurt, like I was going to be sick, but I forced myself to eat the pizza like nothing was wrong.

"Well, there you go." Even Nick couldn't go on after that piece of information was shared.

"Can we watch football?" I asked the television.

"Yes ma'am," Nick answered.

The room went silent. I finished my pizza and found my mouth was dry, probably for more reasons than just eating a slice of pepperoni pizza. I picked up Boo, got up and dumped him on Nick's stomach.

"I need a beer. Nick?" I asked.

"No, Jules. I'm fine."

My gaze moved to Vance. He was looking up at me and I could read nothing in his eyes.

"Another pop?" I asked.

He shook his head but kept watching me. I looked at the floor and started from the room.

I had to pass Vance's chair to get to the kitchen. As I did I slowed, and as if it had a mind of its own, my hand came out and I ran the backs of my fingers along Vance's jaw.

Do not ask me why I did this. I couldn't tell you. When I was done, I didn't look at him. I didn't stop, I just kept on walking to the kitchen and I didn't look back.

And when I got into the kitchen I filed my touch in my memory filing cabinet and locked the door.

⌐×⌐

After Monday Night Football was over, we said goodnight to Nick. Vance, Boo and I walked through the back room and over to my side. I opened the backdoor. Boo shot in, I turned and stood in the door, showing Vance he was not invited inside. There was a step up from the back room to my kitchen so I was looking down at Vance and he was looking up at me.

"Well, nice date. I had a good time. Thanks," I said, even though I'd screwed up the date totally, so much it really wasn't even a date. However, my intention was to make my message clear. No entry.

Vance looked at me a beat, then his shit-eating grin spread on his face. He put a hand to my belly, pushing me back as he stepped up and walked in, clearing the door. He shut the door behind him, took his hand from my stomach and turned to my alarm panel. He hit a four digit code and I heard the sequence of buzzes that meant my door and window sensors were armed.

I had the fleeting feeling of anger that he shoved inside, but this was swept away by surprised admiration when I watched him set my alarm.

"How do you know my code?" I asked when he turned back to me.

Vance just kept grinning at me and then he started walking toward me.

My admiration cleared.

Um... not good.

I started backing up.

"Erm... Crowe, the date's over," I told him.

He shook his head and kept advancing.

I kept retreating.

"Really, it's late. I'm tired." I wasn't. I was going out that night and I needed him to get gone.

"You have two choices," Vance told me.

I stopped in the doorway to the hall and put my hands on my hips. "And those would be?" I asked.

"We can talk or we can fuck."

My eyes rounded. Then they narrowed.

I didn't answer.

"Though," he went on, "I should tell you even if you pick talking, after we're done, we're still gonna fuck."

I frowned at him and leaned in. "You are *too much*," I snapped.

He ignored my threatening posture. "You don't chose, I will and I'll pick fucking. We can talk after."

I was right, he was too much.

"I'm not going to sleep with you," I told him.

He just smiled at me.

"Excuse me, but didn't we just meet yesterday? I'm not that kind of girl."

At that, he threw his head back and laughed.

"What's so damned funny?" I asked, frowning and just stopping myself from giving him a big old girlie shove.

He looked at me. "You were that kind of girl this morning."

He was right, I was. Another ten minutes and I'd have been screwed, literally. I wasn't sure that was a good thing for a number of reasons. At the moment, most especially, I didn't want him to know I was a virgin. That might have an adverse effect on my street cred.

"Temporary insanity," I retorted.

"Jules, choose."

"No."

His hands shot out and grabbed me, yanking me forward. Then his arms wrapped around me, pulling me into his body. I should have been smart enough to learn, after seeing it enough times, how quickly he could move.

"How about this?" he suggested looking down at me. "We talk, but we save the fucking until later, maybe after our second date when I actually take you out somewhere."

There wasn't going to be a second date so I took this as a boon.

"Agreed," I said.

He smiled at me in a way that made me think he knew my thoughts.

He let me go. I walked down the hall, but he grabbed my hand when we were walking by the bed platform and stopped me.

I turned to him.

"What?" I asked.

His eyes shifted to the bed. "Climb up," he said.

My mouth dropped open. "I thought we were going to talk."

"Yeah, we're gonna do it up there."

Was he crazy?

"We're not going to talk on the bed!"

"Climb up, Jules."

"We can talk in the living room."

"Climb up."

"No one talks on a bed."

"Jules, climb... the fuck... up."

I whirled to make my way into the living room. I didn't get even a step. Lightnin' Crowe grabbed my hand again, spun me around, then bent, twisting his body and lifting me so he was carrying me around his shoulders, one hand on my arm, his other arm around my thighs.

"Holy shit! Crowe, put me down!" I yelled.

I figured he was going to hurt me. No way was he going to climb up steps and get me into my bed without slamming me into the ceiling. The hallway ceiling was low, the bed area was an elevated alcove, the ceiling high. There was only a small gap to get in and a lot of that was taken by the bed. Even I, after living there five years, still conked my head on the hallway ceiling at least once a month.

I shouldn't have worried. This was Vance Crowe we were talking about. He climbed, bent nearly double, shoved his torso through with me around his shoulders, not even scraping the ceiling. He released me, rolled me in and came up behind me, snagging me under my armpits and hauling me up the bed. He lay down on his back and pulled me up over his body.

I was too shocked to move and staring at him in disbelief.

God, he was good.

"Now we can talk," he said, his arms wrapped around my waist.

"Why do you want to talk up here?" I asked.

"I like it up here."

I rolled my eyes.

Whatever.

Time to get this over with so I could go out and annoy bad guys.

"How do you know my alarm code?" I asked.

He didn't answer, just smiled.

"Crowe! I want to know."

"You wanna know, I'll show you. Later, not tonight."

I blinked at him. "Seriously?" I asked, so wanting to learn that I completely forgot that tonight was our only night and tomorrow I was going to figure out a way to get Vance Crowe out of my life for good.

"You wanna know, I'll show you," he repeated.

"Wow. Thanks." I was still forgetting.

"I like Nick," he stated conversationally.

I couldn't help myself. I smiled. "I do, too."

"What do you call him?" he asked what I thought was a strange question.

"I call him Nick." I replied.

"No. He isn't your Dad, but he is, so what do you call him?"

I stared at him. "How do you know that?"

"He and I talked."

I went still. "About what?"

"About him raisin' you, about your family dyin', your granddad dyin', your aunt dyin'."

I gasped. I did this partly because Nick had apparently shared a great deal of information about me, but mainly because Nick never talked about Auntie Reba, not to anyone but me.

"He told you about Auntie Reba?"

"Yeah."

I didn't know what to do with that because I felt it said something about Vance, that Nick would trust him enough upon first meeting him to mention it. It freaked me way the hell out.

I shirked off my freak out and forged ahead.

"What else did he tell you?" I asked, feeling uncomfortable with the knowledge that he knew way too much about me.

"He told me I was your first date in five years."

"Oh my God," I whispered, horrified. I was going to *kill* Nick.

"And he told me your birthday is Thursday."

I decided to be quiet and hoped that our talk wasn't going to be a long one. After two minutes I was over it and wanted to shut down, move on, fill my mind with something else, anything else, but Vance.

Vance watched me. I kept silent.

"Tell me about Park," he demanded softly.

"No," I said instantly and pushed away. The conversation was officially over.

His arms tightened. He came up, twisting me to my back and his body rolled into me so he was half on me, his thigh thrown over both of mine, pinning me to the bed.

He looked down at me. "You already know we investigated you," he said.

"Yeah."

"You're a busy woman."

I stared at him and kept silent.

"Even before this shit went down with Park your name is all over police records. You worked at a battered woman's shelter, got involved in a couple of messy cases. You got mentions in a number of kids' files, comin' down to the station when they got into trouble, puttin' in a word for them. Got 'em out and into King's."

I stayed silent.

"Park was different," Vance said in a way that I knew wasn't a question.

I sucked in my lips and stayed quiet.

"So are Roam and Sniff, aren't they?"

I couldn't keep it up. "They're my boys."

He watched me, his eyes scanning my face, and something came over him. Not the sexy something, something else. Something that looked an awful lot like concern.

"Jules, you know, you gotta keep a distance. You don't, it'll destroy you."

"I can keep a distance."

"Yeah? Like spendin' your nights puttin' your ass on the line, makin' drug dealers pay for what they did to Park?"

My eyes slid to the side.

"Um…" I mumbled.

"And runnin' around lookin' after two teenage runaways like they were your own flesh and blood?"

I brought my eyes back to him and stayed silent.

"That shit with Roam today at Fortnum's… Jesus, Jules, you aren't his sister, you're his social worker."

"I know that."

"Didn't look like it to me."

"Don't tell me how to do my job," I clipped.

"I'm tryin' to talk some sense into you."

"You don't know these boys."

"Yes I do. I grew up with kids like them."

This shut me up because that night I learned he had. It was somewhere I didn't allow my mind to go because I hated the thought of someone as magnificent as Vance Crowe living on the street, but now he said it straight out, it forced my mind to go there.

I felt my discomfort edge away and I just stopped myself from touching him.

"I'm sorry," I whispered.

He shook his head and his eyes got hard. "Jules, listen to me closely. I'm not another one of your causes. I survived. It was shit and I nearly didn't, but

I came out the other side. What I went through, it made me who I am. You do your job, only your job, those boys'll come out the other side too."

Then I whispered—don't ask me why, but I did—"I love them."

He watched me a beat then his eyes changed again. Not to the concerned look, or the sexy look, but the look he'd given me that day at Fortnum's.

It touched me somewhere deep. Somewhere I'd forgotten I had.

"They're good kids. They make me laugh," I went on, unable to stop myself. "They're smart, sharp as tacks and not just street smart. All that and they've had no love, Vance, no love in their lives at all. Only abuse. They didn't leave home because of teenage rebellion or family misunderstanding or minds not meeting. They left home because they had to to survive or they'd go crazy or get hurt. The only people in their lives they can trust, ever could trust, are each other... and me. Now Park's gone, it's just the three of us. Park was their leader. He was the best of them, keeping them safe and straight even as he searched for release for himself. Without him, I don't know if I can save them."

Vance watched me while I talked, but at my last words, he broke in. "They gotta save themselves."

"They're kids!" I protested.

"They've learned enough to know their lives are in their hands."

"They're kids, Vance."

"Jules."

"No," I shook my head. "No. They're special and if I don't do anything else in my life, I'm gonna make sure *they* have one."

"Jules."

"No!" I shouted.

Vance stared at me then I could tell he came to a decision.

"I'm not gonna change your mind, am I?" he asked.

I shook my head.

"Then you gotta stop what you're doin' at night so you can be around to take care of them."

I went back to silence.

Vance stared at me again. Then he muttered, "Shit."

I couldn't help myself. I knew he was giving up so I grinned.

He caught the grin and his eyes flashed. I stopped grinning.

"You go out, I'm your shadow," he said. "Someone has to keep you safe."

Um... no, I thought.

"No," I said out loud.

"Yes."

"No!" I yelled. "I know what I'm doing."

"You don't have a fuckin' clue."

I frowned at him. "Leave it alone, Vance. I know what I'm doing. I know you and all the boys think that I'm some kind of idiot female, but I'm not. I know what I'm doing."

He dropped to his side, taking me with him so we were face-to-face.

"I'm keepin' you alive," he said.

"Vance——"

"You're gonna stay alive. At least until we have a second date."

I rolled my eyes.

It was my turn to give up. It was his turn to grin.

Okay, then I was going to get something out of it.

"I want a favor," I declared.

His grin deepened and the change happened, this time it *was* the sexy change. "Yeah?"

"You'll get a second date if you come into King's tomorrow and talk to Roam."

The change vanished. "I'm not takin' him in."

I shook my head. "No. I don't want you teaching him. I just want you to walk up to him, talk to him in front of the other kids like you know him, like you respect him. Roam *and* Sniff. All the kids know about you, they respect you. You act like Roam's your boy, it'll enhance his reputation. It'll mean something to the other kids. It'll give him confidence."

It would do more than that. It would give him just a tiny smidgen of what he wanted. It would be the first time he got even a taste of a life's desire.

To Vance, it was taking thirty minutes and talking to a kid.

To Roam, it could change his life.

Vance didn't answer. He just looked at me.

I leaned in a bit, not much, and then I whispered, so low you almost couldn't hear it, "Please."

Vance's eyes changed again. They went soft and sexy and I felt my breath catch.

"I'll do it."

I didn't realize my body was so tense, but when he agreed I relaxed into him. His arms got tight and his hands drifted up my back, pressing me to his body.

"One condition," he said.

Oh crap.

"What?" I asked.

"This second date is tomorrow night. You'll be here and you won't stand me up."

"Okay," I agreed instantly.

"That's not the condition."

Fuck.

"What?" I repeated.

"I take you out, after, I spend the night here. You don't go out huntin' drug dealers. You stay in, all night, with me, in this bed, naked, and when I make you come you say my name."

My stomach plummeted again. It felt good again, but still, I just stared at him.

I couldn't promise that.

"Crowe——" I started.

"Take it or leave it."

I could just not believe this.

"I'm asking you to do something nice for a kid and you're asking... you're... I don't *believe* you."

"Maybe I should tell you somethin' about me. I learned early you don't do somethin' for nothin' and you get the best deal out of your end as you can. I want you. I want to taste you. I want to fuck you. I want to make you come and I want to hear you moan my name when you do so I know that you know it's me who made you come. You don't agree, I don't see Roam."

I frowned at him. "I think you might just be a bastard," I snapped.

"Get over it," he returned.

I stayed silent, trying hard not to scratch his eyes out or knee him in the balls.

"Jules, you want it, too," he told me, and even though he was right, it still pissed me off.

"All right, fine," I clipped. "Tomorrow night."

God, the things I did for my boys.

He rolled into me again, pushing me to my back, and I glared at him.

"Is our talk over?" I asked irritably.

"Yeah," he said, but the change was over him and he was smiling at me. It was a small smile, but a satisfied one.

"Good, then you can go."

"In a minute." His face was coming toward mine.

"No. Now," I ordered.

"Not until I've had another sample."

"Crowe!" I got out before he kissed me.

I pushed against him and tried to pull away, but he rolled fully on top of me, pressing me into the bed and insisting with his tongue that I open my mouth. I resisted, trying to twist my head away, but he didn't stop. His hands were moving on my body when his head finally came up.

"Tomorrow night," I said.

He didn't say anything. He just looked at me with his eyes soft and sexy. His hand went under my shirt, sliding up the skin of my midriff and my body froze. It did this mainly because the tingles had started and the warmth of his hand felt nice, but I was still trying to resist.

His head came back down again and his lips hit mine at about the time his hand cupped my breast.

My mouth opened in a gasp. His tongue slid in, my body melted, the tingles took over and Vance got his sample.

Chapter 6
Superheroes

After Vance got his sample, he kissed my mouth lightly a few times then lifted up and kissed my forehead, then he was gone.

I lay in bed for a while, recovering.

Then I lay in bed for a while wondering how in *the hell* I was going to get out of tomorrow night.

I couldn't sleep with Vance. Not only would he find out I was a virgin, I had no idea what I was doing (mainly because I was a virgin).

He was obviously good at it. I even knew a few women who knew first-hand he was good at it. How embarrassing would it be when I was *not* good at it?

I decided to think about it later, much later, after I'd jumped a plane to Nicaragua tomorrow afternoon and disappeared off Vance Crowe radar.

I jumped down off the bed, scattering and ticking off Boo, who thought we were in for the night. I put on a chocolate brown turtleneck (as in, *dark* chocolate, almost black), matching cords, a deep brown belt and matching boots. The boots had low heels, they were comfortable and I could run in them. The best thing about the boots, though: even with all that, they still looked killer (you couldn't be a badass mother without killer boots; it was a rule).

I pulled back my hair in a ponytail and I was ready to roll.

Then I turned out the lights and I waited.

I didn't put it past Vance to watch the house and then follow me.

After I figured he'd given up (if he was out there at all), I gathered my weapons, went out to Hazel and I took on the night.

⋙⋘

My plan was simple.

Wreak enough havoc on the dealers and the suppliers of the dealers who made their sales in the places where the runaways hung out so that the dealers would eventually give up and find some other place to do business.

If the runaways followed the dealers, I would move to new turf.

Kristen Ashley

I wasn't taking on all Denver dealers, trying to shut down their business. I just wanted them to leave my kids alone.

I knew driving Hazel was stupid, and I was considering dipping into the ever growing mortgage fund that Nick never touched and buying something for patrol that was less conspicuous than a red cherry-condition 1983 Camaro. I just couldn't find the time.

I patrolled and kept my eyes peeled for a tail. There wasn't one.

Things were quiet. Some kids were out. It was cold, so not many. There weren't any dealers around.

I was considering going to the bar where I'd seen Darius last night and watching him, or just giving up, packing it in and getting some needed shuteye when I saw them.

Martin and Curtis, two runaways from King's. They were brothers, fourteen and twelve. They'd come in about a month after Park died and I knew it was because they heard about me (because of Sniff, everyone had heard about me).

They hit my caseload, so I was working with them. They hadn't told me much and didn't spend the night at King's, but I was hoping for a breakthrough soon.

I watched as they ran out of an alley and down 15th Street. They were being followed by two dealers. I knew the dealers. They weren't small time. They were serious players.

My heart started thumping and I followed them. The kids ducked into another alley and the dealers followed.

If I followed in Hazel, they'd see me. I wasn't sure if that was good or bad so I made a split-second decision.

Quickly, I parked on the street. I had my mace in my pocket, my stun gun and Glock on the seat. I grabbed the Glock, exited the car and left it unsecured. I ran into the alley and hoped I wouldn't pee my pants.

By the time I got to them, Martin, the older brother, was stand up wrestling with one of them, grunting and losing. The other one had Curtis against the wall.

Fuck.

I aimed my gun at the dealer on Curtis.

"Back off!" I shouted.

72

His head whipped around. The other one got Martin in a headlock and twisted him around violently so he could look at me.

Their names were Clarence and Jermaine, no street names that I knew of. Clarence had Martin. Jermaine had Curtis.

I kept my gun and eye on Jermaine and channeled my internal badass mother.

"Back off," I repeated, low.

"Holy shit!" Jermaine laughed. "It's The Law."

He pulled Curtis forward by his collar and slammed him viciously into the wall and I heard Curtis's skull crack against the brick.

Um...

I... did... not... *think*... so.

My eyes narrowed and my head cocked to the sight of the gun.

In a serious, pissed-off voice, I said, "I'll say it one more time. Let him go."

To my surprise, he let him go. To my despair, he only did it so he could come at me.

Martin was still struggling against the headlock, intermittently groaning and whining. His feral noises of fear were spurring me on by pissing me off even more.

Curtis was standing frozen, likely partially dazed, partially scared stiff.

"Watcha gonna do Law? Slash my tires? Throw a smoke bomb? Light some shit on fire on my doorstep? You're a fuckin' joke," Jermaine taunted.

Excuse me, I never lit poo on fire on someone's doorstep. That was immature.

"Go. Now," I returned, ignoring his words. "Leave the kids alone. If you go, no one will get hurt."

"Fuck you, bitch," Jermaine snarled and then came at me.

When he came at me, I switched my gun to the other hand knowing he'd get physical just to prove a point. The big man subdues the silly woman.

Fuck him.

Right away he gave me my opening, throwing out his arm to grab me. So I took it.

When he arrived at me, I grabbed his wrist and leaned down, ducking under his arm. Using my leverage, his momentum and bulk, I twisted his arm and flipped him up and around. He landed with a sickening thud on his back.

Without hesitation, I aimed and kicked him savagely between his legs. He let out a ferocious howl and curled into a fetal position. I put my boot to his neck and leaned my weight into it (maybe a little more weight than I needed, but I told myself that I was new to this and allowed myself some leeway).

I lifted my head, my eyes slicing to Clarence. I switched my gun to my right hand, cupped it with my left and aimed.

"Let him go," I ordered.

Clarence was staring at me in shock, so much so he didn't let Martin go.

I dropped my aim and fired. The bullet hit next to his left foot. He felt the impact and jumped but he didn't let Martin go.

I lifted my gun, aimed it at his head and cocked my own to the gun's sight. "I said, let... him... *go*."

He let Martin go.

Martin ran immediately to Curtis.

I stood aiming at Clarence, my boot still at the writhing Jermaine's neck, and I wondered what the hell I should do now.

Then Clarence's eyes moved from their study of my gun to look over my shoulder.

"Holy fuck. It's true," Clarence whispered, but loudly so I could hear.

Like a sixth sense, I felt rather than saw Crowe coming up behind me. He got up beside me and stopped, his eyes on the man at my boot.

I guessed I was wrong about not having a tail.

God, he was *good*.

Out of the corner of my eye I saw a shadow move from behind Clarence. I focused and Mace arrived at the scene. He was looking at Vance. At the sight of Mace, I got over my admiration of Crowe.

This is just great, I thought with mental sarcasm.

"Did I see what I think I just saw?" Mace asked to Crowe.

"You saw it," Crowe replied then he looked at me.

It was dark. I couldn't read his eyes and didn't try. I looked back at Mace and Clarence.

Mace's eyes had cut to me. He stared at me a second and I could tell by the white flash in his mouth area that he grinned. Then he grabbed Clarence's wrist, twisted it around to his back and shoved him face first against the brick wall. He pulled some cuffs out of the back of his cargo pants and slapped them on Clarence.

"Stay," he said to Clarence as if he was a dog.

I dropped my gun and put it in the back waistband of my jeans.

"You can take your boot out of his neck now," Vance said to me.

I looked down. Jermaine was still curled up in apparent agony and not going anywhere.

"Whoops," I muttered and lifted my foot.

Vance crouched and cuffed Jermaine. Mace had pulled a phone out of his pocket and he'd connected.

"Luke. We got a pick up. Yeah, another couple from Law." He faded into the shadows and I heard him say, "You are not gonna fuckin' believe this…"

I walked to Martin and Curtis. "You guys okay?"

They didn't speak, just nodded, mouths open in disbelief.

"Curtis, your head?" I asked.

He just kept nodding.

"Why were they chasing you?" I asked them.

They kept staring at me.

"Come on boys, spill. These are bad guys, worse than most. What were they doing chasing you?"

"We thought we'd help you go after the drug guys," Curtis told me.

"Yeah, we been followin' them two for a while," Martin threw in with pride.

Oh crap. Not this again.

"All the kids are talkin' 'bout doin' it. We got sick of talkin' so we decided just to do it," Curtis went on.

"It's so fuckin cool you're workin' with Crowe," Martin said and turned to his brother. "Told you she was workin' with Crowe."

Curtis nodded but was silent, overwhelmed by the excitement of it all. His eyes moving between me and Vance, who had pulled up Jermaine and was positioning him against the wall next to Clarence.

My eyes returned to the kids. "Don't say fuck, and I'm not working with Crowe."

"Yeah you are. I heard he's, like, your man and you're, like, his woman," Martin replied.

"Yeah, Sniff said that, today, you two were huggin' at that bookstore where they all hang out," Curtis put in.

Damn Sniff and his mouth.

I looked at Vance and noticed he had turned to us. I didn't know him well enough to guess his reaction to this latest fiasco, but if I'd had to guess, it wouldn't have been him smiling wide like he was pleased about something, which was exactly what he was doing.

I sent him a look and turned back to the boys. "All right, kids, let's get this straight. You two do not go out on the street and get in the faces of bad guys. Anyone else you hear talking about it, you tell them I said the same to them. Do you hear me?" I said in my word-is-law voice.

"We hear you," Curtis replied.

"No need. You workin' with Crowe, and that Mace guy in on it too..." Martin added, trailing off, awe still in his voice.

"Streets'll be clean in no time," Curtis finished, like we were superheroes.

I looked back at Vance and he was still smiling.

I rolled my eyes.

Headlights came from behind me. I turned and saw a black Ford Explorer heading down the alley. It stopped close to us and Stark swung out of the driver's side. A huge blond guy that looked like a relative of the big man at Fortnum's got out the passenger side. They walked up to us. Both of them were grinning.

Martin and Curtis's mouths had dropped open again.

"Goddammit," I hissed under my breath.

Just what I needed, Super Dude Stark and Paul Bunyan sweeping up the trash. The kids were going to talk about this until Christmas.

Mace re-emerged from the shadows just as the huge blond said, "Jesus, Law, you ever take a night off?"

"The Law never takes a break," Curtis offered.

I looked skyward. As I was doing so, Vance approached me and curled an arm around my neck, pulling me into the side of his body. Martin and Curtis had trained their gazes on us, and again their mouths dropped open, but now their eyes were bugged nearly clear out of their heads.

"Knew you were his woman," Martin finally said.

I'd had enough. "You two know Hazel?" I asked.

More awestruck looks.

"Your Camaro?" Curtis breathed.

"Yeah. She's parked on the street. Lock yourselves in until I get there. Tonight, you're sleeping at King's."

"We get to ride in Hazel?" Martin asked.

"Move!" I snapped.

They both ran.

I turned toward Vance, which only succeeded in me curling into his body. I pulled back at the neck, but his arm didn't go anywhere so I gave up.

He was grinning down at me.

"Take your arm away," I demanded.

He didn't. Instead, he leaned in and kissed my forehead. This was such a strange thing to do in the current situation, and I was so shocked by it, I blinked at him.

"What was that for?" I asked.

"I'm just relieved that when you told me you knew what you were doin', you actually knew what you were doin'."

It wasn't a well-lit alley, but I was pretty sure he was looking at me with new respect. I felt a rush of warmth, starting at my belly and going outwards. I didn't know what to say, so I didn't say anything.

The big blond guy and Mace were pushing Clarence and Jermaine toward the Explorer.

"Where are they taking them?" I asked.

"Don't know. We still got Shard in the holding room. You're challenging our capacity," Vance replied.

"You... you... what do you mean you still have Shard? What's a holding room?"

Vance was watching them load up Clarence and Jermaine. His eyes came down to me and his arm loosened, sliding from around my shoulders. I pulled back, but he kept me close with his fingers curled around my neck.

"I didn't like the way Shard was lookin' at you last night. We took him to the holding room in the offices to talk to him, convince him he didn't want retribution. He's being difficult."

"Oh my God," I breathed. That did *not* sound good.

"Don't worry, he won't touch you," Vance assured me, and I figured either they would talk him out of it or Vance would stop him. One way or the other, he wouldn't touch me. Something about the thought of that made that rush of warmth intensify.

"So what about Clarence and Jermaine?" I asked.

"They aren't low level. We'll need to talk to their people. Lee's already taken his side in this. Whatever happens, you won't feel it."

My head jerked in surprise and I stared at him in the shadows. "What do you mean, Lee's taken a side?"

"I mean he's made it known where he stands," Vance replied.

"And where does he stand?" I asked.

"By you."

My breath caught and it was my turn for my mouth to drop open. "You're joking."

"Nope. Not a popular opinion. Hank and Chavez both want you shut down. They think you're gonna get hurt and vigilantism isn't a big hit with them. You aren't real popular with Darius, either. Still, Lee decides somethin', that's it," Crowe said.

"Where do you stand?" I asked.

"Got your back when you're on the street. The rest of the time I'll be tryin' to talk you out of it."

I put my hands to my hips. "I thought you just said I knew what I was doing?" I asked.

"He gave you a classic opening and you took advantage of it. He thought you were a joke. You kept your cool and did well, but word'll get around. Somehow, with your shit, it gets around faster than most. People will begin to take you more seriously. Maybe take you as a challenge and look for you. You won't get the same opening again."

"I'll be ready for it," I said. "That's not my only move."

Vance's shit-eating grin made an appearance.

"So what you're sayin' is... you *wanted* to lose this morning when we were wrestling in bed?" Vance asked.

I opened my mouth to speak (or probably yell) when Luke materialized at our side.

He was smiling huge, no half-mouthed grin this time, and I knew he heard what Vance said. Vance dropped his hand from my neck.

"Hate to break up this lover's chat, but we gotta take these boys in. You gonna speak for Law or you want me to do it?" he asked.

"Speak for me?" I asked.

"I'll do it," Vance said, ignoring me.

"Speak for me?" I repeated.

"You givin' her your protection?" Luke asked, ignoring me too.

"Speak for me?" I said again, then I hesitated, my eyes narrowed and I went on. "Protection?"

"Yeah," Vance answered Luke's protection question.

"Um... protection?" I asked.

Mace arrived at us. "Tell them she's got mine too," he said.

"Excuse me... boys?" I cut in.

Vance looked at Luke. "What about you?" he asked.

"I'm in," Luke replied.

"Helloooooo?" I called.

"You want to call Lee, make it official?" Mace asked.

I gave up, crossed my arms on my chest and tapped my toe.

"Yeah," Luke answered on a short laugh. "He's at dinner with Indy, Roxie, Hank, Ally, Tex and his parents. Welcome to Denver for Roxie. He's probably ready to murder someone about now. He'd kill to get a high priority call."

The guys looked at each other with amused faces.

"Um, pardon me, but it *is* after midnight. I doubt they're still at dinner," I informed them.

They all looked at me.

"Shit," Mace muttered.

"Probably shouldn't call him then," Luke half-grinned.

These guys.

"Does someone want to tell me what you're talking about?" I asked.

"We'll leave that to Crowe. Later," Luke said, then he de-materialized, poof, gone.

Same with Mace.

I didn't ask how these boys seemed to appear and disappear without apparently moving. I had more important things on my mind.

"What's that mean, speaking for me and protection?" I asked, turning fully to Vance.

"Jermaine and Clarence work for the same guy. Not good to have your boys in a showdown with a white woman in an alley and they get bested. Normally, Princess, you could expect retribution. Someone's gotta talk to him to convince him not to send someone to put a bullet in your brain. That someone is me."

I didn't say anything, partially because I didn't want to think about a bullet in my brain, and partially because he called me "Princess".

"At the same time I make this rumor of you and me bein' partners true. I give you my protection and they'll take that into consideration before they, or anyone, thinks to move on you. It'll mean a fuck of a lot more with Mace and Luke in. It'll mean even more if Lee throws down."

I knew he was saying serious stuff, but the only thing I could think to say was, "Princess?"

He got close, his hands went to my hips and pulled them to his and he looked down at me.

"You understand what I just said to you?" he asked softly.

I nodded but said, "Princess?"

He grinned and got closer, his shadowed face blocking out the small amount of light.

His voice still soft, he said, "You sleep in that big bed, wearin' soft, lacy nightgowns, all those fancy sheets and pillows and fancy furniture in the living room. You live like a fuckin' princess."

"I'm not a princess," I whispered.

"You are to me."

Oh my *God*.

I didn't say anything, *couldn't* say anything. I just stood there and stared at his shadowed face.

He kissed my forehead and murmured, "Get your kids home."

And then he, too, vanished into the night.

Chapter 7
Wear Something Nice

The minute I swung into King's the next morning I knew the night's escapade had already made the rounds.

There were twice as many kids there than yesterday. They all looked at me when I walked in and the room went wired.

"Goddammit," I muttered under my breath.

"Hey Law!" Curtis shouted from across the room.

I walked to him, ignoring the eyes that followed my progress. "How's your head?" I asked.

"Good," he answered, grinning at me like a fool.

"You have a headache, dizzy at all?"

"Nope, nothin'."

"You feel dizzy, you tell someone, yeah?"

He nodded.

I turned to Martin, who was standing beside him. "You okay?" I asked.

"Definitely," he nodded, pleased as punch to be a central character in my crusade.

I shook my head, shoved his shoulder, turned and saw May bearing down on me like a storm cloud. Without a word, she grabbed my arm, dragged me across the room and into the quiet hall.

"Thought you said you weren't partnered with Crowe?" she asked, eyes bright again. But this time her excitement was mixed with a shade of anger at not being in the loop.

"Um…" I mumbled.

"And what's this I hear 'bout you two havin' a date? You go out on a date with Crowe last night and didn't tell me?" she kept on.

"It wasn't a date, as such," I hedged.

"You spend time with him last night, outside of kickin' black boy dealer ass, that is?"

"Well… yeah," I admitted.

"He get in your panties?" she was relentless.

"May!"

"Well, did he?"

"No," I answered.

"Did he try?" she went on.

My eyes slid away. This was none of her business, of course, but one didn't really go up against May. She might be a soft touch, but she was also a mother hen, and a nosy, straight-talking one at that.

"Hon," she started and I noticed her anger was gone, "this is the best news I've heard all month, maybe all year."

My eyes came back to her. "What?" I asked.

"You need a man. Don't know why the boys aren't crawlin' all over you, way you look. Hate to see you lonely, livin' your life for a bunch of kids, most of 'em won't give you the time of day. Every girl needs to get her some and get it regular if she can. You need a life outside this place, and what I hear of him, you settle him down a bit, Crowe might be just the boy to give it to you."

I thought for a second about the herculean task of "settling" Crowe down a bit. It almost made me laugh, and then I looked at May's face and decided against it.

"May, it isn't like that."

She just looked at me.

"May it was just one, kind of, date," I told her.

"He ask you out again?"

"Um…" I hesitated and May leaned threateningly closer. "Yeah, tonight," I admitted.

"Mm-hmm," she mumbled, crossing her arms and nodding at me.

I stared at her a beat.

Whatever.

Time to move on.

"I have work to do," I said.

She stopped me as I tried to move away. "You really flip Jermaine on his back and kick him in the balls?" she whispered.

Slowly, I nodded.

"Girl, you're workin' on becomin' famous." She smiled and let me go.

Famous was not what I was going for, but I figured infamous was more where I was headed.

I went in search of Sniff and Roam and found them in their bedroom.

I stuck my head in and said, "I want you both here all day. Later, we're going to talk."

"Hey Law," Sniff called. "Fuckin' cool what you did last night."

I gave him a look. "Stop saying fuck," I ordered.

Sniff grinned.

I looked at Roam. He was smiling at me.

I couldn't help myself. I smiled back.

⊰⊱

It was nigh on impossible to get any work done. Kids and colleagues alike approached me. Some asked flat out if what they'd heard about last night was true (those were my kids). Some skirted the issue and looked at me like I might be a touch crazy (those were my colleagues).

I did my best to talk it down, making it sound like your normal, average, everyday drive through town in the middle of the night when you coincidentally find yourself running into two drug dealers and confronting them in an alley with a Glock (though I didn't mention the Glock).

Furthermore, my mind kept racing forward to that night, when I was going out with (and then getting laid by) Vance Crowe. I still hadn't come up with a delay tactic, and the flight to Nicaragua was looking more and more appealing as the day wore on.

I took two appointments with kids. I called a couple parents, did some paperwork, and along with the talk of my adventure last night, I heard the whisperings that the kids thought it was so cool some of them wanted to try it out for themselves. This was regardless of my warning to Martin and Curtis.

I wanted to ignore it and hope it was all talk, but it was beginning to become clear that I wouldn't get that choice.

May approached me after lunch. "Hon, you're gonna have to say somethin'. You can't ignore this. You tell them not to do it, they won't do it. They look up to you. They'll listen to you."

I looked at her, not certain she was right. The kids never listened to anyone. My word might be law in the Shelter, but it didn't hold the same weight when it came to the street.

Then I looked across my cubicle to Andy, the other full-time social worker. He heard May and silently nodded his head. That was when I knew May was right.

Damn.

I pushed back my chair.

The rec room was still packed when May and I entered it, and again, everyone's eyes swiveled to me.

May clapped her hands and announced, "Quiet, ya'll. Eyes on Law. She's got somethin' to say. Clarice, you turn off that TV. We need your full attention." When Clarice, a heavyset, sixteen year old black girl that I'd pulled from The Mall a few months ago flipped off the TV and all eyes had locked on me, May turned to me and said, "Go on, hon. Tell it like it is."

I didn't know how to tell it like it was, but I looked at the kids staring at me and I knew I had to try.

"All right, folks, listen up," I began. "We hear you talking about going out, thinking to avenge Park. But I'm telling you right now you're not going to do it. I see any of you kids on the streets, getting into different kinds of trouble than you normally find, I'll shut you down myself. Got me?"

I was channeling Crowe Speak to make my point. Nothing gets the word across like talking like a badass mother when they thought you *were* a badass mother.

They all just stared at me.

"Got me?" I snapped.

The door opened, but I ignored it, thinking that it was just more kids arriving.

"Where's Shard?" someone called to me. "He ain't on the streets. Is Nightingale torturing him?"

"Yeah, you bring 'em down and the Nightingale guys take 'em in and make 'em pay. Is that how it is?" someone else threw in.

I looked at the ceiling, then I looked at May, then I looked back at the room. Where did they get this shit?

"No, the Nightingale Investigation Team is *not* torturing Shard," I answered.

At least, I didn't think they were.

"Where is he then?" another kid called out.

"I don't know, maybe at church, praying for his sins," I replied.

Some kids laughed. One kid called out another question.

"You flip Jermaine like they said? Kick him in the nuts?"

"I'm not discussing what happened last night," I said in my word-is-law voice.

"She did, it was fucking awesome," Curtis called out, ignoring my word-is-law voice.

"Yeah and she shot at Clarence, right by his foot. Swear to *God*, he jumped like a spider. He was *all* freaked out. Thought he'd shit in his pants," Martin added.

"Boys, quiet. Curtis, don't say fuck. Martin, don't say shit." Then I addressed the entire room. "This conversation is over."

I was losing their attention. Something had caught it and several of the kids were looking toward the door.

I forged ahead to finish my point. "I'll say it one last time. Not one of you goes on the streets looking for trouble. You do..." I hesitated, not used to badass threatening. Then I remembered what Vance said to me when I aimed at his Harley, "There'll be consequences."

They weren't paying attention at all anymore. Most of the kids were staring at the door, some with wide eyes, some with mouths hanging open.

"Sweet baby Jesus," May breathed from beside me.

I looked at the door. Vance, Lee and Luke were all standing there.

Vance was wearing a black turtleneck, faded jeans, black cowboy boots and a black leather jacket that hung over his hips. His hair, as usual, was pulled back in a ponytail at the base of his neck, and above all, he looked *hot*.

He also looked like he was about ready to burst out laughing.

Lee was standing next to him, wearing an olive drab v-necked sweater, a white t-shirt under it, jeans, boots and a clay-colored suede jacket.

Luke was next to Lee wearing head-to-toe black, a tight black t-shirt that you could see stretching across his pecs under his black motorcycle jacket, black cargo pants and black boots.

Lee and Luke also looked highly amused. It was clear they'd heard every word.

"Goddammit," I muttered under my breath.

The boys advanced into the room coming at me. The kids watched, mesmerized, their heads moving with the progress of the Nightingale Men.

"Hi boys," I said when they arrived.

Luke half-grinned. Lee's eyes crinkled. Vance smiled at me flat out.

"Law," Vance replied.

I rolled my eyes at him for using my street name. If it could be believed, he looked even *more* amused at my eye roll.

"Hon," May said from beside me, sounding slightly breathy. I looked to her and she was taking in the boys. "Hon," she repeated. "Oh my, *hon.*" Now she was just looking at Crowe.

"May," I said sharply to break through the Crowe Effect.

She blinked and looked at me. "What?"

"Snap out of it," I whispered to her.

She shook her head. "Yeah, yeah, right."

I introduced her. "Boys, this is May. May, this is Vance Crowe, Lee Nightingale and Luke Stark."

They all turned amused looks to her.

She opened and closed her mouth a couple of times and then said in a breathy voice, "Hi ya'll."

I looked at Vance and shook my head. He just gave me one of his grins. This made my belly flutter, especially when my mind took that unfortunate moment to fast forward to what was supposed to happen later that night. It was like he read my mind and his grin turned wicked. I frowned. When I did so, I wasn't sure, but it looked like he was again trying hard not to laugh.

"We need to talk," Lee cut in to Vance's and my bizarre nonverbal exchange, but he was looking around at all the kids watching us. "You have somewhere private?" he asked when he turned to me.

May threw up a hand. "I'll go check. See if one of the counseling rooms is open. Won't be a minute." Then she whirled and trotted off.

I looked back at The Boys. "What's up?" I asked.

"Private," Luke said, and at this single word I sucked in my lips thinking this was not good.

"Hey Crowe," Sniff greeted, as if Crowe was his best friend and they hung out all the time. He came up on one side of me.

Roam silently moved in at my other side.

"Sniff," Crowe replied then he looked at Roam who was standing between Vance and I. "Roam," he said.

Roam nodded his greeting.

"Throw rocks at any dealers lately?" Crowe asked.

Roam's body jerked, not sure if Crowe was fucking with him in a good way or a bad way, and I watched them both closely.

"No," Roam answered hesitantly.

"Too bad," Luke put in. "Shard won't forget *you* anytime soon."

Roam's eyes swung to Luke and I saw hope fill them for a second before he hid it. "Yeah?" Roam asked, trying to be cool.

"Yeah," Luke answered. "Not sure that's a good thing, kid. We let him go, he may come lookin' for you."

Roam's body went stiff, whether from fear or what he thought was an admonishment from Stark, I couldn't tell.

"That won't happen," Crowe offered casually, but there was a fierce undercurrent to his words as if he would personally be looking out for Roam.

Roams eyes skidded to Vance, and the hope in them lasted longer this time. I felt what was becoming a familiar warmth start to spread through me as I looked between Vance and Roam.

"You studyin'?" Vance asked him.

Roam nodded.

"You are not, Roam," Sniff put in, ever the big mouth.

"Shut up, Sniff," Roam hissed, then looked at Crowe. "I'm gonna get my diploma. Then I'll come lookin' for you."

Vance's eyes moved to me. "Likely you won't have to come lookin'," he said.

Oh my *God*.

What in *the hell* did that mean?

I stared at him. The warmth had turned to fire and I stopped breathing.

Sniff was looking between Vance and me.

"You guys gonna get married or somethin'?" Sniff asked.

My eyes unlocked from Vance's and my head snapped around to glare at Sniff. I let out my breath in a whoosh, using all my strength not to strangle the life out of him.

"Sniff!" I clipped, my body burning for an entirely different reason. "Why on earth would you say such a thing?"

"What?" he asked, all innocent, looking at me. "It could happen. I could be, like, your pall bearer or something."

I heard Luke chuckle. I knew it was amusing. However, I thought it would be a lot more amusing if it was happening to someone else.

"Ring bearer, stupid. A pall bearer carries a casket," Roam told him. "And anyway, you're too old to be a ring bearer. You could be an usher. They seat people."

"How you know all this shit about weddings?" Sniff asked, and then didn't wait for an answer but kept right on talking, as usual. "Just as long as I get to wear one of them fancy suits. Those are *the shit*."

"Stop saying shit," I cut in, having had enough. "Don't you boys have an appointment with the tutor about now?"

Sniff grinned at me. "Yeah."

"Well then, go." I took a deep breath and turned back to the Nightingale Boys.

As I guessed, they were all looking at me with their amused faces.

Whatever.

I looked to Roam to tell him to go to the tutor, but he was looking at Crowe.

"See you around?" Roam asked, not quite able to hide the craving in his voice, and I sucked in a breath.

Crowe just looked at him and I felt my heart begin to pound. Then he lifted his hand, and palm out, he shoved Roam's head to the side in one of those macho-man to mini-macho-man head-cuffs.

Crowe's hand dropped and he murmured, "Yeah."

Roam's face split into a huge smile. His glance skidded along Luke and Lee and he turned. His smile hit me and he walked away, but before he did he purposefully bumped me with his shoulder in a teenage boy shoulder bump that was meant to show affection without really showing it. Then he moved away, throwing an arm around Sniff's neck, putting him in a headlock and taking Sniff with him before Sniff could say anything (else) stupid.

I looked at Vance and felt the clouds that followed my life crack open for once, and gorgeous sunlight beamed down on me.

I'd asked him to be nice to the kid, show him some attention. He had, but he went way beyond the call of duty.

I could have kissed him. Of course, I did not.

May jogged up to us. "Blue room's free," she announced.

"Thanks May," I said, pushing down my thoughts of kissing Crowe, thinking maybe simply thanking him was a better way to go, and leading the Nightingale Boys to the blue room.

I opened the door to the blue room and let them precede me. I caught Crowe by the arm before he went inside and whispered, "After this, I want to talk to you."

He looked at me closely for a beat trying to read me, but I kept my face as blank as I could. Then he nodded. Crowe and I went in and I closed the door behind us.

There was a couch and a table with some chairs around it. No one sat so I didn't either.

"What's going on?" I asked Lee.

"Darius wants a meet," Lee told me, not leading into it, just saying it straight out.

My mouth dropped open. Then I snapped it shut because I figured a badass mother wouldn't stare with her mouth open.

"With me?" I asked stupidly. They hadn't come all the way to the Shelter to tell me Darius wanted to meet with the Queen of England.

"Yeah. It'll be you and Vance, Darius and me. Tomorrow night. Can you fit that into your ass-kicking schedule?" Lee inquired.

Luke chuckled again. I frowned at Luke and he quit chuckling, but he gave me one of his sexy half-grins. I turned back to Lee.

"What's this meet about?" I asked.

Vance was standing at my side. Close to my side. Not close-close as in loverly close, but close enough.

"He's got an offer he wants to make you," Lee answered.

"What kind of offer?" I pushed.

"Don't know. He hasn't shared. He wants you off the street and he's willing to negotiate," Lee told me.

I stared at him. This was an interesting turn of events.

"What does that mean, negotiate? Is he going to offer me money?" I pressed.

"Likely," Luke said and my eyes cut to him. Then they went back to Lee.

"Forget it. I'm not taking money," I declared and I felt Vance get tense beside me. In fact, the entire room got tense.

"Law——" Lee started.

"No way. Forget it," I stated in my word-is-law voice.

"Take the meet. Listen to what he has to say," Lee advised.

89

"I'm not going to sit down with a drug dealer and listen to him offering me money he's made by destroying people's lives. No. That is *not* going to happen," I stated.

"Law, this is a game," Lee informed me. "You entered the game, now you have to play it. You don't take the meet, it's disrespect. Darius won't like that."

"Do I care?" I asked.

Vance came closer and turned his body into mine, cutting Lee off from sight.

"Take the meet, Jules," he said.

I looked up at him and opened my mouth to speak, but he got there before me.

"Take the meet. Listen to what he has to say. You can say no. Then you can tell him what you want. Maybe we can come to a compromise, maybe not. You don't take the meet, everyone will lose," Vance went on.

"What do I have to lose?" I asked.

"You don't want to go up against Darius. You do, since we made our positions clear last night, that puts us against him. That means war with you caught in the middle, and the middle is an uncomfortable place." He got closer and his voice dropped. "Jules, we're talkin' war between Lee and Darius. You don't want to be the cause of that."

Again I opened my mouth to speak, but he kept going, voice even lower, eyes intense. I'd never seen him so intense (well, he was normally always a trifle intense, but this was something else). So I stared at him.

"It'd be like Sniff goin' bad and Roam challengin' him to a death match. In that situation, nobody wins. Do you understand what I'm sayin' to you?"

I kept staring at him and it came to me. Eddie Chavez, Lee Nightingale and Darius Tucker, all friends, all close, just like Park, Roam and Sniff. I guessed that somewhere along the line, Darius turned, went bad. Regardless, Eddie and Lee stayed close to him, such was their bond. It was precarious. Something would eventually test it, something just like this was bound to happen. You couldn't have a cop, a PI and a drug dealer remain friends without it going sour somewhere along the line.

But I didn't want it to be me that made it go sour.

I nodded to Vance. "I'll take the meet."

He lips turned up at the ends and I knew he approved. I got that warm feeling again, but kept my face blank and he moved away from me.

Lee and Luke were watching me, not amused anymore.

"Is everything okay with Jermaine and Clarence?" I asked.

"Vance took care of you," Luke answered. "You need to be safe, though."

"You get in a situation like last night, you call backup before going in," Lee added.

"Backup?" I asked.

"Vance will give you the number," Lee stated, but didn't answer my question.

I turned to Vance. "Backup?"

"You call the Nightingale control room," Vance explained. "One of us will take your back."

Oh my God.

Were they serious?

"That isn't necessary," I announced.

Lee was making a move to go.

"You've been smart so far. Don't be stupid now," he warned, then our talk was over. He jerked his head to Luke and Vance, and Luke made a move.

"In a minute," Vance said.

They glanced at him. Lee nodded. Luke grinned. They closed the door when they left.

Vance turned, and with his eyes on me and us being alone, I totally forgot why I asked to talk to him in the first place.

"Jules?"

With effort, I cleared my head. "Um, I just wanted to say..." I lost it then got it back again. "Thanks. You didn't have to go that far with Roam, and I appreciate it."

The air changed. Vance's macho man forcefield clicked on, and I could swear, my body leaned into him a bit.

Then his eyes got soft and sexy. My belly fluttered.

His voice came at me, smooth as silk. "You want to thank me, you *ever* want to thank me, you don't say it to me. You show me."

I stared. "Sorry?"

He didn't explain, he just said, "Come here."

Without hesitation, I went to him, such was the power of the forcefield.

When I made it to him, one of his arms went around my waist. His other hand twisted around and around in my ponytail, fisted, and he pulled my head back gently.

Then he said, "Kiss me."

My belly plummeted.

"Sorry?" I repeated, this time in a whisper.

His face came so close I could feel his lips against mine. "Kiss me," he said there.

Oh crap.

I wasn't sure I even knew how to kiss someone.

"Vance——" I breathed.

"Kiss me. Now," he ordered.

I kissed him. I had no idea what I was doing, but I just went for it. I figured it was better to get it over with because I was learning fast that Vance wouldn't let it go.

I put my arms around his neck, grasping my right wrist in my left hand. I lifted up on my toes a bit, just as I put pressure on his neck. I opened my mouth under his, going for the gusto, but in the back of my head wondering if I should start small.

Apparently I made the right choice. His mouth opened immediately, my tongue slid inside and that was all I had to do. That was the extent of "my" kiss.

Vance walked me back quickly. I slammed against the wall, his fist tightened at my hair and his other hand slid down over my bottom and pressed me against him. He forced my tongue out of his mouth and slid his in mine.

It felt so damned good I fit my body to his, pressing in close, one hand curling around his neck and the other hand pushing inside his jacket. My arm wrapped around his waist then it went tight.

It got a little hot and heavy after that. There was some groping (on Vance's part) and maybe a few throat moans (on my part) and then his mouth tore free.

He pulled back, just an inch, and he stared at me, his eyes intense. Something strange there, almost like surprise.

I stared back. We were both breathing heavily.

Finally he muttered, "Jesus."

He could say that again.

I felt hot, everywhere, and I was pretty certain my stomach had evacuated my body.

"I should have broke in last night, woke you up, fucked you until you couldn't breathe. I thought about it. I should have fuckin' done it."

Oh my *God*.

He said this like he was talking to himself. Still, I heard it and it flipped me out.

"Vance——" I whispered.

"Save it," he cut me off. "Tonight. Six thirty."

Then the tractor beam switched off. His chin lifted, he kissed my forehead and he said, "Wear something nice."

He let me go, but his hand wrapped around mine. The warmth of his hand in mine, the strength I felt there, the intimacy of the gesture took me off-guard.

Okay, so we'd necked, groped, laid in my bed (of all places) and talked. I'd held him at gunpoint and he'd beat me at wrestling. Even though this had all passed between us, his holding my hand made a statement that went beyond the cat and mouse game we seemed to be playing since we laid eyes on each other.

I didn't know if you held hands with a woman you intended to sleep with and then leave, which Crowe had a reputation for doing. He saw, he conquered, he left.

Furthermore, I had no girlfriends to ask. I didn't expect this was a topic of conversation that either Zip or Heavy would be delighted to get into with me.

Though, if I were to guess, my answer would be no.

I didn't know what to do with this and I was struggling to process it when he turned us to the door, and in the window to the room that faced the hall we saw several kids (and I could swear May as well) quickly move away. We heard movement and giggling and then nothing.

"Goddammit," I muttered under my breath.

Vance just looked down at me, wearing his arrogant, shit-eating grin.

And all of a sudden I had new things to worry about. This made my list include my soon-to-be-fucking by Vance Crowe, everyone at King's hearing about our make out session, what it meant that Vance held my hand, and the fact that I had absolutely nothing "nice" to wear on our date.

〜※〜

Later that afternoon I cornered Roam and Sniff. Roam was looking at me funny. Sniff was grinning.

"Hey Law," Sniff said.

I pushed his shoulder and then swung my gaze between the both of them. "I got a favor to ask you two."

"Anything Law," Sniff said immediately.

"Depends on what it is," Roam said cautiously.

I sat down on the arm of the chair that Sniff was sitting in. "You hear anyone talking about going out at night——" I started.

"We ain't snitchin'," Roam broke in.

I shook my head. "I don't want you to snitch. I want you to tell them it's a bad idea. Talk them out of it. They'll listen to you."

"They'd listen to Park," Sniff put in.

I turned to Sniff. "Now they'll listen to you."

Sniff looked like he didn't believe me and he threw a glance at Roam.

"Like it or not," I began, "Park left you something. You two have been around longer than most, been on the street longer than most and seen a lot more than most, including finding Park and knowing the Nightingale Boys. You can ignore that, use it the wrong way or use it the right way. I'm asking you to do the right thing. That's it. Now it's your choice."

They both looked at me and didn't give anything away. I waited for something, anything, but they gave me nothing so I gave up.

"All right, I said my piece." I got up from the chair, preparing to go, but Roam stopped me from leaving.

"Law," he called.

I looked down at him. He and Sniff exchanged another glance and he hesitated like he didn't know what to say or didn't want to say what came next.

"Yeah?" I prompted.

Roam took a breath. "Careful of Crowe."

Sniff looked at his feet.

"Sorry?" I asked.

Roam got up and looked down on me. Sniff got up too, but he was inching away.

"He's a player," Roam told me. "Heard about you two. Everyone's talking about it. He's movin' in fast."

I could tell he was uncomfortable. So was I, so I cut in. "Roam, don't worry about me. It's not——"

"He's a player," Roam interrupted me.

"Roam—"

"He's a player," he repeated. "Everybody knows it. He wants a piece of your ass."

"Roam!" I snapped.

"That's all he wants." Roam was a dog with a bone.

"I think I know what I'm doing," I said, even though I didn't, but I still could not believe I was getting a talking to from a fifteen year old boy. So he had more earth-shattering life experiences than your average adult.

Still.

"Don't say I didn't warn you," Roam finished and before I could say anything he and Sniff moved away.

I watched them go and I was trying to get my mind around what just happened when I heard an exclamation from across the room.

"Sugar, I just *love* that sweater! Where'd you get it?"

I turned to look at the front door, and Indy, Jet, Roxie, Daisy and a beautiful brunette who looked like a female version of Lee Nightingale were standing there. Daisy was addressing Clarice, who was wearing a big, fluffy pink sweater.

"Stole it," Clarice declared boldly to Daisy.

Daisy didn't even blink. "Okay then, where did you steal it?" Then she turned to Indy. "Gotta get me one of those. It'd go *perfect* with my new pink cowboy boots." She turned back to Clarice. "You steal another one, darlin', my size is medium."

"Daisy!" Jet exclaimed.

"What?" Daisy asked.

Clarice stared at her like she'd dropped to earth from another galaxy. I walked up to them.

"Hey Jules," Indy said when I arrived.

"Hi. Um…" I didn't know what to say.

Roxie smiled at me. "Thought we'd pop by, say hi."

"I'm Ally Nightingale." The brunette offered her hand and I shook it, not surprised by her last name.

"Hey," I greeted then turned to Daisy. "Sorry about this, but you probably shouldn't encourage the kids to steal. We try to talk them out of that kind of thing."

Daisy looked at me for a beat then turned to Clarice. "What's your name, sugar?"

"Clarice," Clarice told her.

"Well, I'm Daisy. You go back to that shop, you let me know and I'll meet you there. You have a cell?"

Clarice nodded.

"Give it to me, I'll program in my number," Daisy told her.

I stared, and so did Indy, Roxie, Jet and Ally.

Street tough Clarice, looking a little dazed, gave Daisy her cell and the whole time Daisy punched in numbers, she talked. "We won't steal anything, we'll just browse. Then maybe go get a coffee. You drink coffee, sugar?"

"Um…" Clarice mumbled.

"I'll get you a soda. That pink really suits your coloring. You got flair," Daisy went on.

Clarice continued to stare and only blinked when Daisy handed her back her phone.

Then Daisy turned to me.

Obviously ready to move on, she asked, "You got a place to talk?"

I nodded, thinking maybe this was the weirdest day in my life. "Sure," I replied.

"What's goin' on?" May trundled up to us looking amongst the hot chicks and being clear she wanted in on the ground floor of any new event that rocked my life.

I introduced her. "May, this is Daisy, Ally, Roxie, Indy and Jet. Guys, this is May. She's a volunteer here."

They all did their greetings and Daisy repeated, "We gotta talk, girl. You got somewhere private?"

"Blue room's still open," May put in immediately, and I added May to the top of my ever growing mental list of people I wanted to murder.

"Well, what are we waitin' for?" Daisy asked and then shoved forward like she owned the place and knew exactly where she was going. May pushed up next to her and we all followed.

When we got to the blue room, May closed the door behind us and this time everyone settled into a seat like they were going to spend the day doing girlie talk in a counseling room at a shelter for runaways. Daisy, Ally and Roxie sat on the couch. Indy, Jet and May pulled chairs around to face it. Daisy patted the arm of the couch next to her, and with no other option (like running, screaming, from the room, which I wanted to do, but thought might be rude), I sat on it.

"What's up?" I asked.

"We just came to see how you're doing," Indy answered. "You okay?"

I looked at her confused, not knowing what she was really asking.

"Yeah," I said.

"We heard about last night... and, um, the night before," Jet put in.

I switched my gaze to Jet. "What'd you hear?"

"That you're one kickass bitch, that's what we heard. You crazy or some-thin'?" Daisy asked, clearly not in the mood to beat around the bush like the other women.

"No," I replied, my eyes narrowing as I looked down at her.

Daisy took my narrowed look and it bounced off her like she was made of Teflon. "All right, sugar, I believe you," she said then giggled and it sounded like tinkly bells.

"We hear you're going out with Vance," Ally put in.

My eyes moved to her. "Not exactly," I replied.

They all looked disappointed.

"Yes you are," May threw in. "You had a date with him last night."

They all perked up.

"You had a date last night with Vance?" Indy asked.

I opened my mouth to say something when Roxie cut in. "That is so *cool!*" Then she leaned toward me. "What's a date with Vance like?"

"It wasn't exactly a date," I told her, feeling weird, mainly because this *was* weird. "We watched Monday Night Football with my uncle and then talked."

They all looked disappointed again.

"You were necking with him like a teenager in this very room just a couple of hours ago. I saw you my damned self," May carried on, spilling all my secrets.

I widened my eyes in a "shut up" look at her and noticed the hot chicks had all gone perky again.

"I bet he's a good kisser," Ally said.

"I bet he's a good everything," Daisy put in. "You get anything else from him?"

Was this really happening? I didn't even know these people.

"Um…" I muttered. It wasn't any of her business, but I didn't want to appear rude.

"Oh come on, share. You're among friends," Ally told me, even though I knew her less than the other four, and I didn't know the other four at all.

I didn't do girl talk, or at least I hadn't really done it since college. I didn't know where to begin, and anyway, it was important to note (again), I didn't even know these people.

"Maybe you should understand something," Indy said, watching me closely. "Lee and I are getting married."

I just looked at her. I didn't know how that information made anything more understandable.

"Congratulations," I said.

"Eddie and I are living together," Jet put in.

I looked at her, guessing she was talking about Eddie Chavez and wondering why she shared this information.

She kept talking. "We met, like, five months ago. Then I had this situation where a loan shark was after my Dad but came after me, then some other guy tried to rape me and then——"

"I'm still sorry about that, sugar," Daisy interrupted.

"It wasn't your fault, Daisy," Jet assured her, taking her hand and giving it a squeeze.

"Still, he was workin' for my husband. I feel responsible," Daisy went on.

"Don't," Jet said on a dazzling smile.

I watched this conversation wondering if maybe *they* were a little crazy when Roxie butted in.

"I'm living with Hank, Lee's brother. We met each other less than two months ago. I moved from Chicago. My ex was kind of a jerk——"

"Kind of? He was a first class jerk," Ally threw in. "He was more like a grade A prime asshole."

Roxie smiled at her. "Yeah, well, anyway," she looked back at me, "the point is he kidnapped me and then, after I was rescued, he stalked me. It was a nightmare. Vance was the one who rescued me. Tracked me down and found me handcuffed to a sink in a sleazebag motel in Nebraska. He was very cool about it, took me to an outlet mall on the way home and everything, and I didn't even have to ask."

I nodded, not knowing what to say. Stalking ex-boyfriends, kidnapping, rapists, outlet malls. It was too bizarre for words.

Indy smiled at me. "We know you know Lee. Well, Lee, Eddie and Hank, they're all part of our tribe. Vance is, too. What we're saying is you get sucked in by one of the boys, you're part of our tribe too."

"We're the Rock Chick Welcome Wagon," Ally noted on a grin.

"See, these guys move kind of fast," Jet added.

"It can make you dizzy," Roxie said.

"So you need your girls around you," Indy finished.

I looked to May to see how she was taking all of this and she was smiling at me like a loon. Maybe she *was* a loon. Maybe *all* of them were loons.

"So, what's goin' on with you and Vance? Spill, sugar. We're here for you," Daisy told me.

My eyes settled on her and it struck me immediately that she wasn't just saying that. I realized with some intuitive clarity that they weren't here to be nosy and interfering. They meant all this shit.

I opened my mouth to tell them it was none of their business, to guard my heart like an emotional Rottweiler, when, just like I did with Zip blurting out my plan to save all the runaways from drug dealers, I told them everything.

Everything.

From the minute Vance cornered me in the alley to when he was holding my hand. I held nothing back. I even told them I was a virgin.

When I was done, they were all staring at me with wide eyes and open mouths.

"Shit," Daisy breathed then swung her head to Roxie. "He moves even faster than Hank."

"You can say that again," Roxie replied.

"You're a virgin?" Ally asked, eyes still huge.

"I can't think about that right now," I said to Ally. "It's one thing at a time. He told me I should wear something nice. I don't have anything nice. The only nice thing I have is a dress I wore to a colleague's wedding two years ago, and it's a summer dress and it's November. I can't wear a summer dress in November. And anyway, I don't even know what 'nice' means."

"Well, I can help with that," Indy announced and looked at Ally. "We'll call Tod and Stevie."

"I'll help with the outfit," Roxie put in, and Indy nodded.

"I'll do your makeup," Jet said on a smile.

"I'll do your hair," Daisy offered.

"*No!*" Indy, Ally and Jet all cried in unison, making everyone else jump.

"*I'll* do your hair," Indy declared firmly.

"She gives good hair," Ally informed me.

"You got her outfit," Daisy complained. "You can't have her hair, too. What am I gonna do?"

"You can take the virgin part," Indy offered.

Daisy's blue eyes swung to me and they were bright. "Oh yeah. I can do that."

"Where do you live?" Ally asked.

I wasn't keeping up, and before I could think better of it I gave them my address. They all got up.

"She's in the 'hood," Indy noted to the group and then looked at me. "I live two blocks away from you."

I nodded, still not keeping up.

Indy turned to the group again. "Five fifteen, we all meet at Jules's. Bring what you can," Indy ordered.

"I'm comin', too," May threw in and looked at me. "Moral support."

"Works for me," Ally replied.

"Me, too. See you there," Roxie said to me.

Then they were gone. May and I stared at the door.

"What just happened?" I asked the door, and felt, rather than saw, May's eyes on me.

"What just happened was, just like I said, Crowe's offerin' you a life. If you're smart, which I know you are, you're gonna reach out and grab it."

Then she was gone, too.

Chapter 8

You Like Bikes?

"She needs more sparkle," Daisy announced, and I could see her out of the corners of my eyes, to which Jet was applying shadow. Daisy had her hands on her hips and she was staring at me assessingly, and I could tell she did not like what she saw.

"She doesn't need *any* sparkle. She's going on a date with Vance, not ballroom dancing at The Ritz," Indy returned, standing beside me and holding a curling iron in my hair.

"Tod, she needs sparkle. Every girl needs sparkle. Find some goddamned sparkle, comprende?" Daisy ordered, ignoring Indy.

The gang had descended on my house about five minutes after I arrived home from the Shelter. They came in carrying hangers full of clothes, curling irons, hairdryers, cosmetics bags stuffed with makeup, accessories and boxes of shoes.

They had two gay men in tow. One, Tod, was a tall, lean, effeminate white man with a brown crew cut. The other, Stevie, was shorter, more butch, handsome and Hispanic. Tod, they told me, was Denver's top drag queen, his alter ego known as Burgundy Rose. Stevie, they also told me, was his long-suffering but nevertheless obviously-loving partner.

"Sparkle," Tod muttered, digging through piles of clothes, belts, scarves and shoes. "Gotcha."

"I'm not sure about sparkle," I whispered to Jet.

"Don't worry," Jet replied with a small smile to me, then she glanced worriedly at Indy.

I figured this worried glance was not good. Really not good. The butterflies in my stomach started fluttering, and not in a good Vance-said-or-did-something-sexy way, but in an oh-my-God-get-me-out-of-here way.

Roxie was sitting on my couch drinking a margarita, Boo in her lap. His yellow eyes were closed and she was stroking him full body.

He was in heaven. I was in hell.

"We already decided. She's wearing the black," Roxie put in.

"*You* decided," Daisy returned. "Black is boring. I think we should do the sequins."

My eyes swung to May, who was lounging in my chaise. She lifted her margarita glass at me and winked.

"Daisy, give it up. No sequins, for God's sake. This is Denver, not the fucking Oscars. Talk to Jules about Vance popping her cherry," Ally ordered. She and Stevie were re-hanging clothes that Tod was tearing off hangers.

At Ally's comment I sucked in breath and I was pretty sure I experienced a heart palpitation.

"Ally Nightingale. Don't be crass. You've scared the poor girlie to death," Tod admonished, and Ally threw him a look.

"I think you should just tell him you're a virgin," Jet suggested. "He'll understand and be gentle."

"Oh. My. God. Do *not*, whatever you do, tell him you're a virgin." Daisy sat down next to Roxie on the side of the couch which was closest to the armchair I was sitting in and she leaned into me, full-on cleavage hanging over the arm of the couch. "Go with the flow," she advised. "He does something you like, you do it back to him. You want to touch him or use your mouth on him, just do it. Whatever you do, he'll like it. Men aren't very discerning. All that touching stuff just gets in the way of the real thing. He won't care, long as he gets some."

"Daisy, that's just not true," Roxie put in. "Men like foreplay just as much as women." Stevie made a noise and Roxie turned to him. "Don't they?" she asked.

"Don't look at me. I'm not getting into it," Stevie said.

"Stevie—" Roxie started, but he shook his head.

"You two've been foolin' around. He seem to notice you don't know what you're doin'?" Daisy asked me.

"Um," I mumbled, my eyes sliding again to May.

May just sucked back more of her margarita.

"Don't do that," Jet said to my eye slide. "I've got to do your mascara. Wide eyes, open mouth, look up," Jet demanded, and I did as I was told.

"Well?" Daisy pushed, and I blinked, repeatedly, as Jet applied mascara.

"I don't think so," I answered, trying to talk and keep my mouth open at the same time. "Though the only thing I ever did was um..." I stopped, wondering how I'd gotten into this mess with this gaggle of women I didn't even know, sharing stuff so private I wouldn't have even told Auntie Reba about it. "Touch my tongue to his neck and ran my hands up his back."

"What'd he do when you did that?" Indy asked, twisting the curling iron around another lock of hair.

"Well, he kind of... groaned, and then things kind of... escalated," I fought for the words.

"He liked it," Roxie declared, and I could hear a smile in her voice.

"Just pay attention, listen and learn. He'll have hot spots and you'll find them. Just explore," Daisy advised.

"Hon," May butted in, speaking for the first time since everyone got there other than to say, "I'll take one of them margaritas." "Folks have been doin' this since folks have existed. It's instinctive. Just relax. What I saw today, that boy's so into you, you got nothin' to worry about. He'll lead the way."

I took a deep breath and nodded (slightly, Jet was still doing my mascara).

"What does she do when he, um..." Jet started, but didn't finish.

"It'll hurt," Roxie said.

"Mine didn't hurt," Ally stated and went on. "Just a twinge. Hardly any blood at all."

My wide eyes widened further and I looked at Jet, who was so close to my face she was all I could see. She pulled back, her hand went to my knee and she squeezed.

"Mine hurt like a mother," Roxie muttered.

"Jules is old enough maybe she doesn't have a cherry anymore. You go horseback ridin', sugar?" Daisy asked me.

"That's an urban myth," Indy cut in before I could answer. "I didn't feel mine at all," she finished, then she unraveled a new curl.

"You were drunk off your ass," Ally reminded her.

"Was not," Indy retorted.

"You were too," Ally returned.

"Gettin' drunk may be a good thing. Loosen you up a bit," Daisy suggested.

"Can we stop talking about this?" I asked suddenly. "I'm sorry but it's freaking me out."

"I'm with Jules. Let's stop talking about this. Blood and pain. Ick. It's making me squeamish," Tod said.

I glanced his way and he did, indeed, look pale.

"But—" Daisy protested.

"Daisy," Stevie started quietly, "Jules asked us to stop talking about it."

Daisy leaned back, crossed her arms on her massive chest (no mean feat) and started pouting, clearly denied the likely gory details of her own deflowering.

"Just a little cherry lip balm. Don't want color just in case he kisses you," Jet muttered to herself, swiping my mouth with balm. Then she announced, "Done with her makeup." She leaned back and took in my face with a discerning eye.

Tod moved in behind her. "Girlie, you are the Mistress of Makeup. She looks like a goddamned movie star."

Everyone came around to look. They all nodded approvingly, except Daisy.

"Needs more sparkle," Daisy muttered.

"Shut up, Daisy," Indy said, unwrapping another curl. Then she gouged some gunk from a jar, rubbed it in her hands, ran her fingers through my hair and mussed it. She stepped back, pulling some tendrils here and there away from my face. Then she looked at the finished product and smiled. "Hair's done."

"Um, hate to tell you this, hon," May broke into the Check Out Jules Fest, "but you got fifteen minutes to get dressed and get this place cleaned up or he'll be here and see your posse givin' you the works."

"Holy crap!" Indy shouted. "Unplug the curling iron," she ordered no one and everyone.

"Get me that cosmetic bag," Jet snapped her fingers at Stevie. "Now!"

Roxie pulled me out of my chair. "Let's get you dressed."

She shoved a pile of clothes in my arms and pushed me toward the bathroom.

I walked into the bathroom with my pile. They'd even picked out my underwear, and on top was a new bottle of perfume that Roxie stopped by the mall and bought me on the way over.

I bought some sexy underwear as a side obsession to my sexy nightwear since they sold the stuff in the same department. I didn't have much, but they'd found the sexiest. A pair of black, lacy, Brazilian-cut panties and matching demi-cupped bra.

Over this I put on a pair of Roxie's black slacks, which looked normal until they were on. They rode way low; even lower than my cords and jeans, exposing the small of my back in a serious way when I bent even slightly. They had a straight front and wide leg.

On top of this they gave me Indy's plain black t-shirt. Again, it looked normal until I put it on. It was stretchy with a hint of spandex and fit like a glove. It came down over the waistband of the trousers, but again, if I sat, the trousers went down, the shirt rode up and the small of my back was exposed.

"Shit," I whispered, the butterflies exploding, and I sat on the toilet seat to put on the high-heeled shoes which had a half an inch platform sole, peek-a-boo toe and ankle strap.

I spritzed with the cologne and put on Roxie's jewelry. A wide silver cuff bracelet and some wide silver hooped earrings.

Then I looked in the full-length mirror on the back of my bathroom door.

"Oh my God," I breathed.

I looked like a girl. My hair was in curls. Not masses of them, but subtle and pretty. My eyes were done up smoky and, even I had to admit, sexy. And the outfit was simple, but kick-fucking-ass.

Especially the shoes (which were Tod's).

I took a deep breath, opened the door and walked down the hall. The place was cleaned up and tidy. All paraphernalia had already been loaded in cars and there was not a margarita glass in sight.

Everyone looked at me when I walked in and they stared.

Then they smiled.

And I felt for the first time all day that maybe I could pull this off.

"Told you she didn't need sparkle," Indy said to Daisy.

"Sugar, you got *that* right," Daisy replied.

"Hon," May said, smiling at me, "don't you worry about gettin' laid. Trust me. You got *nothin'* to worry about."

　　　　　　　　　　　⚜

Ten minutes later everyone was gone, giving out hugs, air kisses and well wishes for a successful cherry popping as they went.

Before she left, May hugged me tight and looked me deep in the eye and whispered, "Nothin' to worry about."

Even with May's encouragement I'd just sucked down a shot of tequila, winced as it hit my throat and decided again that there was no way I was going to pull this off.

I shoved the tequila bottle to the back of the counter, behind the margarita glasses that someone had washed and were resting upside down on a kitchen towel. I put the shot glass in the sink and was wondering if they had any red-eye flights from Denver International Airport to Nicaragua when my backdoor opened and Vance walked in.

I stared at him. He stared at me.

I was pretty certain I was looking at him like a deer caught in headlights.

He wasn't looking at me that way. He was looking at me in an entirely different way. A way that made the butterflies come back. This time the good ones seemed to be at war with the bad ones and it was up in the air which ones would win.

He hadn't changed clothes, which was one for the side of the bad butterflies. I worried that I looked like I was trying too hard.

Finally I said, "Both doors were locked. How did you get in?"

He started walking toward me but didn't answer.

I was right by the counter. I backed up a step and my hips ran into it.

"You don't have to break in, you know. You could knock on the front door like a normal person," I told him as he arrived at me.

I thought he'd stop but he didn't, not until he got into my space. *Way* into my space. So into my space I could feel the heat from his body, and he leaned into me, putting his hands on the counter on either side of me.

I leaned back and tilted my head to look up at him. "Hello? Crowe? Are you in the room?"

"Shut up," he said, and I blinked, then my eyes narrowed.

"What did you just say?"

Then his head dropped, his mouth hit mine and he kissed me. He didn't touch me, not with his body or his hands, though I was acutely aware of the position of both.

No, he touched me only with his mouth, and kept me locked to him there using his macho man tractor beam in cahoots with his talented tongue, and the good butterflies got an advantage.

His head moved away an inch and he murmured, "Tequila."

Fuck.

Sucking face with a recovering alcoholic after a shot of some serious spirits was probably not a good thing.

"Crowe——" I began.

His head dropped again and he ran his tongue across my lower lip.

I stopped breathing.

"I like it," he said low. He moved back a fraction and looked at my body, then up to my eyes. "I like all of it." Then he came in close again and his face did the same. "You look good, you taste good." His mouth came closer and his eyes stared into mine. "I bet other places taste even better."

Oh my *God*.

The good butterflies started to beat the shit out of the bad butterflies.

I pulled back a bit. "I'm sorry about the tequila. I had some friends over..." I partially lied, not about to impart the information on him that I needed liquid courage for our date.

"Jules, people drink. I don't. Don't worry about it," he said like he wasn't worried about it at all.

"Okay," I replied softly.

Then he did something strange. His hand lifted and he ran his fingers through my hair at the side of my head all the way down the back. Then he pulled some over my shoulder and started to play with it, twisting one of Indy's curls around his fingers just above my breast. All the while he watched his hand as if his mind was somewhere else.

It felt nice. It sent tingles along my scalp and skin. Sexy tingles, but something else, too. Something warmer, sweeter.

"Vance?"

His eyes came to mine and I realized his mind was *not* somewhere else.

I swallowed.

Then I asked, "Are we going out or what?"

He grinned, his fingers still playing with my hair, and I could feel the heat from his hand on my chest.

"Yeah," he answered.

"Shouldn't we, like, go?" I went on.

He kept grinning. "Yeah," he repeated.

I waited. He didn't move.

"Well, *are* we gonna go?" I asked.

"You got a jacket? We're on the Harley."

My stomach fluttered. Not butterflies, just excitement. I loved motor-cycles.

His forcefield intensified when he caught sight of my obvious excitement, and he moved in so our bodies were now touching.

"You like bikes?" he asked.

I nodded, trying to be cool (but probably failing).

"You got a jacket?" he repeated.

I nodded again.

He grabbed my hand and moved away.

"Let's go," he said.

⟨⟨⟩⟩

Vance took me to The Broker Restaurant.

I'd been there only once before. Nick had taken me there for my sixteenth birthday.

The Broker had been around for years. A fancy restaurant built into the bank vault in the basement of the old Denver National Bank building. You even had to walk through the cage and round steel door of the old vault to get into the seating area. It had burgundy leather, button-backed booths and rich cream tablecloths and napkins. They gave you a big bowl of huge steamed shrimp as a complimentary appetizer.

I was pleased that I was wearing something nice. One didn't do jeans at The Broker, unless one was Vance Crowe, who looked in jeans like most men looked in a tuxedo.

We were shown to a half-oval booth. I stared at it and bit my lip. This meant we'd be sitting side-by-side and I wasn't sure this was a good thing.

I didn't say anything and slid in. Vance came in after me and settled, arm along the back of the booth behind me. I leaned forward, slipped off my blazer style black leather jacket and threw it to the side of me with my purse. I kept my body forward, the better to stay out of reach.

The waiter asked what we wanted to drink. I wanted tequila neat with a side of Valium and a time machine that took me back to that moment when I shot out Sal Cordova's tires so I could rethink my actions.

I ordered a cosmopolitan.

"Sir?" the waiter asked, his glance going to Crowe.

Vance didn't reply. I looked over my shoulder at him. His eyes were looking down and toward my bottom. I glanced around and saw my skin exposed. My torso shot straight and I leaned back against the seat.

Fuck.

Vance's eyes came to mine. They were soft and sexy and a little amused. His look scored one for the good butterflies.

Then his gaze moved slowly to the waiter. "Cranberry juice."

The waiter nodded and walked away.

Vance turned back to me. I snatched my napkin out of the wine glass and arranged it on my knee with obsessive attention to its placement and smoothness.

"Jules."

"Mm?" I asked, still smoothing at my napkin.

"Jules."

I looked at him.

"Relax. I'm not going to tear your clothes off in a booth at a steak joint."

I stared at him.

The Broker Restaurant was hardly a "steak joint". It was a well-established, highly-rated gourmet restaurant. They had more than just steak; they had fish and lamb and pasta, too.

And complimentary steamed shrimp. No one gave you complimentary steamed shrimp. They weren't rinky-dink shrimp, either. They were the good shrimp, the big meaty ones.

I shook off thoughts of defending The Broker's greatness.

"I came here for my sixteenth birthday," I told him in an effort to lead the conversation away from tearing my clothes off.

He got closer and gave the impression he was supremely interested in this trivial comment. I didn't realize that it was the first time I'd shared anything personal with him that he hadn't had to force out of me.

"Yeah?" he asked.

I nodded. That was it. The extent of my conversation.

"What are you doin' this birthday?" Vance asked.

I was so nervous, without thinking I blurted, "Going for drinks with Heavy and Zip."

It was his turn to stare at me, and he did so as if I'd just announced I was going to hula dance on the moon.

"Heavy and Zip," he said.

Damn. Not good.

"They're——" I started, thinking fast for a lie. I didn't figure there were dozens of men in Denver nicknamed Heavy and Zip, but I was going to make two of them up, no doubt about it.

"A retired PI and a gun shop owner. I know who they are. Jesus, Jules." Vance shook his head.

Too late for the lie.

"They're my friends," I said.

"They're in on this with you."

"They know what they're doing," I told him.

"Yeah, Heavy knew what he was doing about five years ago when he should have retired. Instead, he retired last year when he was well past it. Zip's just a lunatic," Vance returned.

I felt my blood pressure rise. "Zip is *not* a lunatic. He's a good shot."

"It all comes out," he muttered.

"And Heavy used to be a cop before he was a PI. He still has friends on the Force and his ear to the ground. Not to mention, he was a semi-pro boxer."

"And his wife was a speed freak and he couldn't get her clean so he scraped her off to save himself, even though he didn't want to, and it fucked with his head. Now he's using you to exact vengeance."

Wow. I didn't know that.

I didn't let Vance in on the fact that this was a revelation.

"That isn't true," I protested.

"Which part? Her bein' a speed freak or you bein' his instrument?"

I turned my body to him and my eyes narrowed. "Me being his instrument."

Vance's head went around and he watched the waiter putting down our shrimp bowl. Then, without a word to the waiter, he turned back to me when the waiter moved to leave.

"Jules——"

"Vance, we're not talking about this," I declared.

"We are. You want to get serious, you come into the office. Mace or Luke will work with you."

That was not going to happen.

"I'm fine with Zip, Heavy and Frank," I said, not wanting to work with Mace and Luke, mainly because they'd kick my ass.

I looked at Vance and saw his expression had changed from just disbelief to disbelief mingled with anger.

"*Frank?*" he said low.

Whoops.

"Um…" I stalled.

"Please tell me you are not working with Frank Muñoz."

"He's a good guy," I defended Frank.

"He makes Zip look adjusted."

"Okay," I gave in a smidge. "So he's a little intense."

"A little? He has stockpiles of arms, water and canned goods in his basement."

"He does?" I asked.

Vance nodded.

See? I knew Frank was thinking about destroying the world.

Damn.

"From now on, you're workin' with Mace and Luke," Vance stated as if that was that. He moved away from me and leaned back as our drinks arrived.

"I'm not. I'm fine where I am."

"Are you ready to order?" the waiter asked.

I looked down at my menu, which I hadn't even opened.

"No," Vance said shortly.

"*Thank you,*" I finished for Vance.

The waiter moved away.

Vance turned to me again and got even closer than last time. "Jules, Zip's son OD'ed in the eighties. Heavy's wife was a speed freak. They're out for revenge and using you to get it. Frank is just a nutcase."

I didn't know Zip's son OD'ed, either. I hated it that Vance knew more than me.

"Crowe—" I started.

"You keep this up, you need to work with people who have their heads in the game."

"Like Mace and Luke aren't their own kind of crazy," I said.

His eyes flashed.

Yikes. Again, not good. I'd definitely said the wrong thing.

"Mace and Luke know their shit, understand their limits and play to their strengths. They do what they do because they're good at it. They could teach you a few things."

I was sure they could. Still.

I looked away, picked up my menu and started to read it like it was the most fascinating novel ever written, nonverbally making the point that our discussion was over.

Vance pulled the menu out of my hands and tossed it on the table, nonverbally making the point that our discussion was *not* over.

"I was reading that," I protested.

"In a minute."

"Now. The sooner we order, the sooner this date is over, the sooner *we're* over."

At my words, I watched, fascinated in a kind of passing-a-car-accident way, as he leaned in and his eyes went hard. If I thought I'd made him angry earlier with my (admittedly stupid) comment about his friends, I'd thoroughly made him angry now.

"We're not over because of an idiotic fight."

"We haven't even begun, Crowe, and this isn't an idiotic fight. You're trying to tell me what to do."

"I'm tryin' to help you."

"Then maybe you can find a better way to communicate that than saying nasty things about my friends."

"I haven't said anything that isn't the truth."

"They aren't using me."

"Jules, they are."

"Then they are, but still, they like me," I said, and I said it in a way that made it sound like I desperately needed to believe it. And if it was anatomically possible, I would have kicked myself.

His chin dipped, his head went back in a slow jerk and he stared at me a beat. Then something happened to his face. The anger just disappeared. Vanished. Gone. In its place was something else. Something softer, something I couldn't read.

"Jules," he said quietly.

I grabbed my menu, entirely unable to deal with the something else in his face.

112

"Let's just order," I snapped, opened the menu and studied it.

After the waiter had taken our orders, I sipped my cosmo and stared at the tablecloth of the booth across from us. Vance allowed this for a few seconds then his arm came from the back of the booth, wrapped around me and his hand cupped my shoulder. He curled me to face him and (*again*) got in my space.

"Excuse me," I said, all haughty.

"We *have* begun," he said, his eyes staring into mine.

"No," I stated.

"I don't know what shit you're workin' through, but I know it's there. I know you'd rather not even acknowledge it, and definitely don't want me to be a part of the process. I don't care. Princess, this is happening between you and me."

"What, exactly, do you mean by 'this'? You fucking me?" I snapped, being nasty. It wasn't me and I didn't like it, but I couldn't stop myself, either.

"Yeah. Me fucking you. In your bed, on your couch, in *my* bed and any-where else I can think of. I'm gonna do you on your back, on your knees and you're gonna ride me. And when I've exhausted you and you don't have those fucking shields up, I'm gonna make you talk to me and tell me what this shit is about and then, maybe, I can help you with it."

What he said stunned me, shocked me and made me feel funny, but not exactly in a bad way. In kind of a good-but-scary way.

My emotional Rottweiler started barking and drooling and I pulled away from Vance, but his arm tightened keeping me where I was.

"You've got tonight. Then that's it," I announced.

He shook his head. "You have no idea what you're dealin' with."

"I know exactly what I'm dealing with," I told him.

He let me go and grabbed a shrimp.

Then he said, "We'll see."

Chapter 9
Stop Chuckling

It had to be, officially, the worst date on record.

We ate, we drank and we didn't speak.

Well, Vance spoke. I didn't speak. After we ate the shrimp, he pulled my hair off my shoulder, leaned into my ear and whispered, "Stop bein' angry, Jules."

I just threw him a look. He gave me an arrogant grin.

He seemed unaffected by my snit. In fact, he carried on like nothing was wrong and I wasn't emanating Go-To-Hell-Vance-Crowe Death Rays. Between the salad and main course his arm came around me, tucking me into his side, while his hand played with a curl in my hair. I allowed this because to struggle would be tacky, and we were in The Broker, the least tacky place in Denver. Between the main course and dessert, when I'd forgotten about the dip in my slacks again and had leaned forward, he ran his fingers across my exposed skin.

After we were done, he paid. We walked to his bike and he got on. I got on behind him, thinking that a motorcycle was *the worst* form of transportation when you were holding an angry grudge against its driver. He started the bike, leaned back into me and grabbed my wrists, pulling them around his waist, which pressed my torso into his back. Before I could disconnect, he rocketed from the curb and I hung on so I didn't go off the end of the bike and to a scary, body-skidding-on-pavement-tearing-skin-off death.

He parked behind my house and I let us in. Even though I wanted to see him break in, I wasn't in the mood to ask. Once in, I switched on the light.

Boo walked into the kitchen as I shrugged off my jacket and threw it and my purse on the table. Boo then immediately started complaining about my absence and other imagined kitty insults. I scooped him up, walked down the hallway and wandered around the living room, turning on lamps, Boo in my arms.

Boo talked through this. "Meow, meow, meow."

I finished with the lamps and looked at Vance, who was leaning against the hall entryway, watching me.

I really wished he wasn't so good-looking. It would make sustaining being pissed-off at him a lot easier to do.

"Shut up, Boo," I said, eyes on Vance.

"Meow," Boo replied, eyes on me.

I looked at Boo. "You already had your treats."

"Meow."

"No more, you're too fat."

"*Meow!*"

"I don't want to hear it," I told Boo.

"*Meooow!*" Boo returned.

"Are you talkin' to a cat?" Vance asked.

I looked at Vance but didn't answer him. I gave Boo a cuddle, bent over a bit and dropped him.

"Meow," Boo said after he landed on his feet, always one to get in the last word.

He went over to Vance, rubbed against his ankles and then walked down the hall, likely heading to his dry food bowl.

"How long you gonna stay pissed at me?" Vance asked. Throughout Boo's exit his eyes never left me.

"Until the end of time," I answered.

For some reason, my snotty comment amused him.

Whatever.

"That should make tonight interesting," he said, pushing away from the wall and coming to me.

I turned away from him, pulled off Roxie's wrist cuff and dropped it on the pub set. Then I brought my hands up to take off my earring. My heart was beating like a jackhammer, and the butterflies, which had gone away to struggle valiantly elsewhere throughout our terrible date, came back, clearly prepared to put up an epic battle of good versus bad in the pit of my stomach.

I felt Vance behind me and he swept my hair from one shoulder and over the other. I bit my lip, put the back on the pierced earring and dropped it to the table then went after the other one. His arm wrapped around my middle and he pulled my back to his front. His lips went to my neck.

This felt nice. Too nice, melt-your-anger nice, and I stiffened my body in response.

I got the earring out and put the back on it and Vance said quietly against my neck, "Stop bein' angry, Jules."

"You can't tell me to stop being angry. You can't tell me who to spend my time with. You can't break into my house and get into bed with me while I sleep. And you can't make me have sex with you in return for you doing something nice for a kid who's had no nice things happen to him in his life," I declared. I dropped the earring and turned and looked up at him, or more appropriately, *glared* up at him.

He watched me for a few seconds, one arm still around me, then he said, "I can see you aren't in the mood. We'll sleep on it tonight. Tomorrow, after we meet with Darius, we'll talk. Then we'll do what we should have done two days ago."

Damn.

I'd forgotten about the meet with Darius.

Was I ever going to get Vance Crowe out of my life?

I took a deep breath and nodded, grasping onto his out like a lifeline. "Perfect. Wonderful. Sounds good to me," I agreed, deciding that tomorrow I'd definitely be in Nicaragua by dinnertime.

He watched me again and then said, "We sleep together though."

Hmm.

Maybe it was not so much of a lifeline as a noose.

"I don't think so," I returned.

I could tell he was making a decision. I watched him as he made it.

His face came closer to mine and he said, "Then tonight we do what we should have done two days ago."

"Crowe—" I started to pull back against his arm but his other one wrapped around me.

"Jules, I'll tell you now what I would have told you at dinner if you'd been speakin' to me. This," he said, one hand dropping to my bottom and pulling my hips into his, one going up my back to press my torso to his chest, "is the sweetest thing I've had in my life and I haven't even fucked you yet. I never expected to get a chance at anything so sweet, and now that I got it I'm not gonna let it go. If you think you can act like a bitch and make me back off, you're wrong."

Was I being a bitch?

Okay, so the "until the end of time" comment was a wee bit bitchy, but he was telling me what to do and saying bad things about my friends!

"You were telling me what to do," I said quietly, still fighting my corner.

"I know what I'm talkin' about."

This was true. He knew more about Zip, Heavy and Frank than I did and he certainly was more of a badass mother than I was.

"They're my friends," I said.

"I'm your friend," he told me, and I couldn't help it. I stared.

At his words, the good butterflies trounced the bad butterflies and the bad ones retreated to Siberia.

"Vance," I whispered, my emotional Rottweiler deciding to take an inappropriately timed nap, and my anger started to melt away.

"Stop bein' angry." He repeated his earlier command, but in his soft, silky voice.

I kept staring at him a beat. Then it wasn't just my anger melting away. My body melted into his.

"Okay," I whispered.

At my whisper, his lips turned up, his head came down and he kissed me. I kissed him back.

I wound my arms around his neck and pressed into him and his hand at my bottom came up, then went down again, this time inside my pants. I liked the feel of it there, as in *really* liked it.

My mouth opened under his and his tongue slid in. I realized in some hazy recess of my mind that somehow managed to be unaffected by his kiss that this was actually going to happen.

His mouth moved away from mine and slid to my jaw, then to my neck, and his hand at my behind went deeper.

"Vance," I whispered against his neck.

"Yeah?"

"We have to talk about something," I said, thinking perhaps I should share my virginal status. It might turn him off, and if that was the case I had nothing to lose, because if it did, and he didn't understand, then I didn't want to be with him anyway. If it didn't turn him off, it might make things go easier for the both of us.

His head came up and he looked at me, his lips still turned up at the ends.

"Princess." He pressed his hips into me at the same time his hand pulled mine to him and I felt his hardness. It freaked me out and made my belly flutter at the same time. "The time to talk was at dinner."

I opened my mouth to say something but he kissed me again, lots of tongue, his other hand going up my shirt and sliding along the skin at my back. It felt good, good enough for me to go with it.

He ended the deep kiss and kissed me lightly; once, twice, again. I pulled the ponytail out of his hair and slid my fingers in. His hair was silky thick and that felt good, too.

"Vance, seriously—" I whispered, my fingers tangled in his hair, then I lost my train of thought when his hand came out of my pants. He pulled away and then both hands slipped my t-shirt up. My fingers untangled from his hair, my arms rose with the t-shirt and then it was gone.

Um...

Yikes.

"Two seconds," I said, beginning to feel the edge of desperation.

He wasn't listening to me. He was staring at my body. One of his arms held the bottom half of me to him at my waist while his other hand explored my side, my ribcage and then up. He cupped my breast over the bra, his eyes watching his hand, then the tips of his fingers traced the lace across my breast.

My desperation disintegrated, and with it my ability to breathe in a normal rhythm.

All right, well, whatever. So he discovered I was a virgin at the last possible second. Who cared? People were starving in Africa. There were bigger things to worry about.

But I'd worry about them later.

I leaned into him, pressing myself against him with his hand between us at my breast, and I kissed him.

May was right. People had been doing this for ages and instinct kicked in. It went from slow and sweet to hot and hungry in a flash.

Our lips disengaged, my mouth moved along his jaw, my tongue tasting under his ear. I put my hands in his jacket, pushed it off his shoulders and it dropped to the floor. Then I did the same as he did with my t-shirt and tugged off his turtleneck.

"Dear Christ," I whispered when I caught a look at his chest and abs, his stomach muscles tight and defined, "maybe I *will* work with Luke and Mace if I can get as ripped as you."

He pulled me into him then his hands began roaming my skin and his mouth went to my neck.

"Jules?" he called there, and a thrill shivered across my skin at his voice vibrating against my neck.

"Mm?" My hand had moved between us, fingertips exploring the ridges of his abs. I felt them tighten at my touch, and at his reflex a pleasant jolt shot between my legs.

"Not a good idea to mention Luke and Mace right now."

"Oh," I muttered, my fingers halting and I felt like an idiot. "Sorry."

He kissed me again. I forgot about feeling like an idiot when he pulled his hips back and undid my pants. He pushed them down my hips and they fell away. Before I could feel weird about standing in my living room in nothing but underwear and high heels his arm went around my waist. He lifted me clear of my slacks and set me down, leaned back and looked at me, full body.

That was when I started to feel weird about standing in my living room in nothing but underwear and high heels.

This lasted two seconds then he yanked me into him. My body slammed against his and he kissed me again, hotter and hungrier than he'd ever kissed me before. Then with light kisses and hands sliding down my ass, he walked me back, toward the couch.

"You do anything to change your body, I'll shackle you to the bed," he murmured against my mouth.

"Really?" I asked, just because I felt what he said needed a response. I was too occupied by trying to figure out how I could get his pants off to care about his answer.

"Why does it take superhuman effort to get anything out of you, but while we're havin' sex you won't shut up?"

The backs of my legs hit the couch and I went down. Vance came down on top of me. His weight and warmth felt good so I put my arms around him and looked at him.

"You were the one who said something."

"Shut up, Jules."

I rolled my eyes.

He grinned at me and moved partially to the side.

All of a sudden his hand slid down my belly and I felt his fingers press between my legs. This invasion came quickly and I probably should have been shocked. Instead it felt good. So good, my hips bucked involuntarily and my lips parted.

Wow.

His fingers pressed deeper and that felt even better.

I hooked my leg around his hip instinctively, giving him easier access, and I lifted my head and kissed him, our mouths open, my tongue slid inside. At this, his hand went away but came back inside my panties this time, and he touched me. The first time anyone touched me there (other than myself, of course). It felt so damned good, incredibly good, otherworldly good, I stopped kissing him and moaned into his mouth.

His fingers moved, my hips moved. His fingers moved more, my nails scraped his back, and after a while of this, I felt something begin to build inside me, something exciting and beautiful, and my neck arched with the sheer pleasure of it.

"Look at me Jules," he commanded softly.

I dropped my chin and with effort opened my eyes and looked at him.

The moment I did, his finger slid inside me.

My bones turned to water.

"Vance," I breathed.

The second I muttered his name his eyes went so intense it felt like they burned into me. His finger slid out and then back in again, and I pulled him to me as I pressed up toward him.

Then his body stilled. His finger froze and his head came up.

I stared and it was as if ice water had been poured over my skin.

He'd figured out I was a virgin.

Goddammit, I thought.

"Vance—" I began.

"Quiet, Princess," he whispered.

It was my turn to freeze.

Gently his hand moved away and he jackknifed off me, but once he gained his feet he leaned in and brought me up with him.

He kissed me swiftly then said, "Get dressed. Get your gun. After I leave, arm the doors and windows and call the control room."

Then he let me go, went across the room, tagged his sweater off the floor and pulled it on. I stared at him, stunned immobile, as he pulled his hair back into a ponytail.

He looked at me. "Now, Jules. Someone's out there."

121

My body came unstuck and I dressed quickly. I had my pants on when he made a noise like a half-whistle. I looked up at him and he tossed me his phone. He had his jacket in his hand.

"Control room," he said low and then he pulled his gun out of his jacket, dropped the jacket on the armchair and took off on silent feet.

I yanked my shirt on, following him down the hall. By the time I made it to the kitchen, he was gone.

I locked the door, armed the alarm and went to the dresser under my bed platform and got my gun. I stood in the hall and I started to scroll his phonebook, but it was the first choice. I hit the green button.

It barely rang.

"Yo," someone answered.

"This is Jules," I said into the phone.

"Shit. Do you have another pick up?" It was Mace. "I thought you and Vance were out tonight."

"No. Listen. I'm at my house and Vance says someone's outside. He's gone—" I stopped talking and my body went stiff when I heard gunfire. It was close.

Just as quickly I unfroze, started talking again and I bent down to pull at the buckle of the ankle strap of one of my shoes. "Gunfire, Mace, fuck."

"We're on it," Mace's voice wasn't teasing, it was all business.

"Do you need my address?"

"No. Stay inside, stay safe—"

I heard more gunfire as I kicked off a shoe.

I interrupted him, "More gunfire."

"Stay inside. Keep your house armed."

"I'm going out there."

"Stay inside, Law," Mace ordered. "We'll be there in five."

I kicked off the other shoe. "We don't *have* five," I snapped, flipped the phone shut and threw it on the bed.

I ran to the closet, pulled out my Pumas, yanked them on and tied them as quickly as I could. Then, with my gun, I ran through the house, unarmed the alarm and went out.

I barely cleared the backdoor when Sal Cordova careened into me. I went backward and his arm went around me.

"Fuck, he shot me," Sal groaned, looking up at me and leaning deep into me. I took on most of his weight and staggered with it. "Your fuckin' partner shot me in the ass."

With the arm not locked around me, Sal was holding onto his backside.

"Jules. Goddammit," Vance was standing a few feet away. I spared him a glance and he had his gun trained on Cordova.

I bent at the knees, taking Sal down with me and planting his ass on the ground. He gave out a howl and rolled to the side. I shrugged off his arm and bent down to yank his gun out of his hand, then took a step away.

"You shot me. You shot me in my goddamned ass," Sal whined to Vance, and any worry I had for him was lost. His voice was strong; strong enough to whine. I figured he'd be okay. "You didn't have to shoot me," Sal went on.

Vance grabbed me around the waist and pulled me back so I was behind him.

"You shot first," Vance returned sharply. "What the fuck were you thinkin'?"

Um… Vance sounded pissed right the hell off. Then again, he'd been working at getting in my panties for a few days now. He was probably not pleased that five minutes after achieving his aim he'd been interrupted by having to shoot someone.

"You're movin' in on my action," Sal explained.

It was my turn to be not pleased.

I turned to Sal. "Oh, for God's sake. Seriously, Sal?" I asked, not believing my ears.

"You got the hots for me, I know it. Sat right across from me and—" Sal started.

"I sat across from you and threatened you," I told him.

"Playin' hard to get. You women always play hard to get," Sal replied.

"Maybe it isn't because we're playing hard to get. Maybe it's because we don't want to get got in the first place," I explained.

"Naw. It's not that."

Yes, Sal was that stupid.

"Do we need to call an ambulance?" This came from somewhere to Vance and my left then Luke materialized and came to stand by Vance. He looked down on Sal.

"Yeah," Vance responded. "Although I'd rather let him bleed to death."

"Shit," Sal moaned.

Luke pulled out his phone. I listened to Luke calling the control room and asking for the ambulance and the police. While I did this I thought about the current situation.

The good news was Vance hadn't figured out I was a virgin.

The bad news was Vance had been stopped at a really good part.

I turned to Vance. "How long is this gonna take?" I asked impatiently.

I felt his eyes on me in the dark. Then I saw the flash of white as he smiled. His arm came around me and he pulled me to him. I could focus on him better at closer range and caught his arrogant grin close up.

"Probably a while, Princess. Longer 'cause I'll have to get stitches."

My breath fled my body.

When I sucked in air, I asked, "Why?"

"He tagged me. Thigh, just skimmed. I'll need to have it looked at."

"You're hit?" Luke asked from beside us.

"It's nothing," Vance answered, and I saw Luke nod. Apparently that was good enough for him.

"Crowe," I said, weird feelings going through me, feelings I never felt before and feelings I didn't like.

"It's nothing," Vance repeated.

"Crowe! It is not nothing! You've been shot!"

"I've been shot before, Jules. Trust me, this is nothing."

This time instead of my breath fleeing, I sucked in air on a gasp.

"You've been shot before?" I asked on the exhale.

"Yeah, last time wasn't pretty," Luke volunteered.

"Luke's had worse," Vance informed me. "Gut wound."

"Survived," Luke said casually. "You got it in the lung."

Oh my *God*.

"Stop talking," I snapped, cutting into their gruesome, macho trip down memory lane.

I heard Luke chuckle.

"Stop chuckling," I clipped.

He didn't stop chuckling, but luckily the sirens heading our way drowned him out.

The outside light came on, the backdoor opened and Nick stood there. He took us all in, wearing a real life rendition of his Morgue Face.

"What's going on?" he asked.

"Goddammit," I muttered under my breath.

⌐≈⌐

I was in my bathroom washing my face.

Vance was somewhere in my duplex, doing whatever he did before going to bed.

I didn't know how I got talked into letting him spend the night with me, though I had to admit, it didn't take much. I figured it was partially payback for the favor to be nice to Roam, partially the fact that I felt responsible for him getting shot.

Earlier, outside, before the ambulance came, I'd explained things to Nick and his mouth got tight. He looked like he was ready to tie me up in an attic room and leave me there until I died so I wouldn't get anyone else shot in one of my fool crusades. But luckily, we didn't have an attic room.

The ambulance came and carted off the moaning, whining Sal. The police came at the same time and talked to everyone, including me.

I finally got a chance to see, though not meet, Hank Nightingale and Eddie Chavez.

Hank looked like a Nightingale, tall and dark, except he was the handsome All-American boy stayed good. Chavez was just as freakishly good-looking as the rest of The Boys.

They did flybys, likely hearing that Vance got shot and coming to check he was okay. When they came Vance was sitting on my back stoop. A paramedic had cut away the thigh of his jeans and was checking his wound. I was standing several feet away with Nick. Both Hank and Eddie glanced in my direction, and they didn't look like they were card carrying members of Indy and the girls' Welcome Wagon.

Lee swung by, too, another flyby to check on Vance. He didn't stay long, then he was gone.

I talked with a police detective named Jimmy Marker. I gave him a slightly tweaked version of the Sal Cordova story making Sal sound like a garden-variety stalker, which, in a way, he was.

When I was done talking, Detective Marker looked at me and asked, "You Law?"

I kept my eyes on him, my face blank and my mouth shut.

"Know you're workin' with Heavy," Marker noted.

I was surprised but kept silent.

"Heavy's a good man," Marker went on.

I nodded once, not sure where this conversation was going.

"What you're doin' is stupid and unsafe," he continued.

Now I knew where this conversation was going and I kept quiet.

"You should stop or you'll get yourself killed," he advised, and his voice was both sharp and concerned.

I figured they taught this in cop school.

I didn't reply.

"Or you'll get someone else killed," he finished.

It took a great deal of effort, but I stayed silent and didn't bite my lip like I wanted to.

He watched me, shook his head and then strangely muttered under his breath, "These boys need to get their heads examined."

Then he walked away.

I drove Vance to the hospital in my Camaro.

He was right, it wasn't that bad. He got cleaned up and stitched up. He came out of the treatment room with his jeans on, the thigh cut away, and I could see a white bandage there.

We went back to Hazel.

"Where do you live?" I asked when we were standing by Hazel.

Before I knew what he was talking about, he took the keys from my hand.

"Spendin' the night with you," he replied.

"What are you doing? Give me my keys." I made a grab for them, but he yanked them out of reach.

"Get in the car," he ordered.

"No one drives Hazel but me," I told him.

"Hazel?" he asked.

"My Camaro," I replied.

He stared at me for a beat then grinned and shook his head as if I was downright adorable. This caused me to feel that sweet warmth again, but I shook it off and focused on our current verbal tussle.

"Crowe," I said warningly.

The grin faded. "Please don't argue, Jules. Just get in the car." This he said in a weary voice.

I sucked in my lips, his weary voice getting to me. I walked to the passenger side and Vance took me home.

Upon entry he locked the door behind us and turned to arm my alarm. I went directly to my dressers, rooting through them to find my least sexy night apparel (I had none). I settled on a baby blue silk nightgown that looked like an old fashioned slip. It was tight against the midriff, had an a-lined skirt that skimmed my knees and a thick rim of ecru lace along the top and bottom edges. I stalked to the bathroom, leaving Vance to do whatever he wanted to do, which was what he'd do anyway.

Now *I* didn't know what to do. The heat of the moment was over. My emotional Rottweiler had woken up and was on the alert.

I put my hair in a sloppy bun at the back of my head with a ponytail holder and stared at my face in the mirror. I took a deep breath, squared my shoulders and left the bathroom.

Better to get it over with, whatever "it" might be.

The house was dark when I got out of the bathroom except a dim light came from the bed platform. I went to the steps, climbed up one and saw Vance under the covers, comforter up to his waist, a bunch of my pillows behind his back so he was sitting up.

His chest was bare. Boo was lying smack in the middle of it, his tail sweeping in a wide arc along Vance's abs and waist. Vance was stroking him and I could hear Boo purring from where I was standing.

Clearly Boo didn't object to a new presence in the house.

Vance's eyes moved to me and I climbed into bed as gracefully as I could (which I feared wasn't graceful at all). Then I crawled to the opposite side, as far away from Vance as I could get, and got under the covers.

I laid back, stared at the ceiling and wondered what Vance had on under the covers, or if he had anything on at all.

At the final thought, my breath went funny.

"Jules."

"What?" I said to the ceiling.

"Come here."

I thought about fighting it and decided against it. Don't ask me why, but it had been a weird day. In fact, it had been a weird four months. With my work, my training and my nightly patrol—and now my head-to-head battle with Vance—I was tired and I simply didn't have it in me.

I scooted closer. Vance's arm came around my back, curled me into his side, and I had no choice but to rest my head against his shoulder. I laid there, body tense. I didn't know what to do with my hands so I tucked one arm underneath me and stroked Boo's side with the other.

"How's your leg?" I asked.

"I'll live," he answered.

"I'm sorry. It's my fault you got shot."

"It isn't your fault Sal Cordova is a moron."

This was true.

I went silent.

Vance reached up and turned out the light. In the darkness I felt his heat seeping into me and my body began to relax.

I laid there for a while and listened to Boo purring. I stopped stroking him and rested my hand on Vance a few inches below my face. I was getting the impression that nothing was going to happen at this juncture to continue the night's sexual activities. Vance was action man. If he meant to make a move he would have done so by now.

I took a deep breath, let it out and my body relaxed more.

"I ruined our second date," I whispered.

Vance didn't say anything.

I went silent again.

Then for some bizarre reason, I started talking.

"I told you I went there for my sixteenth birthday. Nick took me."

Vance still didn't say anything.

I kept talking. "It was five and a half months after Auntie Reba died. We had been…" I hesitated, "it wasn't good. She died sudden, unexpected. It seemed the clouds over our lives would never clear."

Vance still stayed silent.

I went on, "Nick wanted to make the day special. The sixteenth birthday, for a girl, is important. He bought me a dozen pink roses, because they're my favorites, and gave them to me in the car. Made me take them with me to the restaurant so people would know it was my day. He had them bring me a cake with sparklers on it."

Somewhere along the line, while I was talking, Vance started stroking my back.

I relaxed deeper into him. "We had fun. It was the first time since Auntie Reba died that we forgot the hole she left for a couple of hours and enjoyed ourselves. We even laughed."

Boo got tired of being petted, walked across my waist and settled in a kitty curl at the base of my spine.

"As a present, he gave me a diamond necklace made from Auntie Reba's engagement ring."

Vance stopped stroking my back, his arm went tight around me and he rolled to face me. This trapped my hand between us and his other hand went to rest on my hip.

There was a small window at the head of the bed, and I could just barely make out the planes and angles of his face in the moonlight.

He still didn't say anything, but I could see he was looking at me.

"I'm sorry about the tequila," I whispered, changing to a different subject.

Finally he spoke but quietly, "Don't worry about it."

"You licked my lip," I reminded him.

"You tasted of cherries," he told me.

Oh right, Jet's lip balm.

"I forgot."

"Drinking is my problem. I won't make it yours," he told me. His deep voice was relaxed, even sleepy, but there was still that fierce undercurrent that he used when he was talking to Roam.

I didn't say anything.

I waited. A few minutes passed and then I went on, "I can't believe you shot Sal Cordova in the ass."

I couldn't help myself. I thought it was funny, even though I knew I shouldn't, so I smiled at him in the moonlight.

"Seemed a good place to aim," he told me, and I felt my body go slightly stiff.

"You *meant* to shoot him in the ass?" I asked.

"He *is* an ass," was Vance's reply.

"That's true," I told him and then relaxed again.

I sighed and was silent for a few beats.

"What did you mean when you told me you never expected to get the chance at something so sweet?" I whispered in a voice so low I thought maybe he wouldn't hear it.

His hands slid along the silk of my nightgown, down over my bottom, then I felt the fingers of one hand curl into the material. He pulled it up and then one of his arms went tight at my waist. The other hand skimmed over my bottom and pulled me deeper into him.

What he didn't do was answer.

Or, maybe, that *was* his answer.

I held my breath through his movements, my belly fluttering, but then his hand and arm went still.

"Vance? Did you hear me?" I asked a little louder.

"I heard you." That's all he said.

"Um…" I started, knowing it was likely rude, but finding courage in the dark and saying it all the same, "From what I hear, you've had a lot of sweet things."

"No. I've had a lot of easy things."

"I know a couple of girls you've——"

"None of them smelled of melons, tasted of cherries or ended up worth the effort," he said bluntly.

I blinked at him in the dark. "Are you saying I'll be worth the effort?" I asked.

"Yeah," he responded immediately.

I blinked again, stunned and feeling weird. Good weird, bad weird, scary weird, Rottweiler snarling weird.

"How do you know I'll be worth the effort?" I asked.

"I know."

"How?" I pushed.

"I just know."

"How?" I didn't let it go.

"You eat shit most your life, work, sweat and bleed for anything you could get the rest of it, you know sweet when you taste it."

Oh my *God*.

I didn't know what to say to that so I didn't say anything at all and fell silent.

"You done talkin'?" he asked after a few minutes.

130

I nodded.

His hand at my waist slid up my back to my head. He tucked my face into his throat and he held me.

I laid there awhile.

Then, when I thought he was asleep, I took my hand from where it was pressed against his chest and I wrapped it around his waist.

When I did this, his arms went tight. He yanked out my ponytail holder and my hair spilled over his hand. He ran his fingers through it, then I felt him twirling a tendril somewhere in the area between my shoulder blades.

I guessed that meant he wasn't asleep.

Whatever.

I closed my eyes and settled in.

He kept playing with my hair.

Before I knew it, before I even would have thought it possible, I fell asleep.

Chapter 10

Mine

I woke up with a belly in the state of advanced fluttering. In fact I was pretty certain in the recesses of my deep sleep I'd already experienced some significant flutterings and thought they were a dream.

I knew by now, with Vance's relentless pursuit of me and all that had happened during that pursuit, that what I was feeling was very, *very* turned on.

This had to do with the fact that Vance's body was pressed close to my back.

It also had to do with the fact that Vance's hardness was pressed against my bottom.

But mostly, it had to do with the fact that Vance's hand was at my breast and his thumb was stroking lightly back and forth across my nipple.

I moved slightly and so did Vance, pressing into me.

With his mouth at the back of my neck, he said, "Mornin'."

At the same time his thumb stopped stroking. It was joined by his finger and they pressed together. Also at the same time his other hand slid into the front of my panties and went deep.

I felt a shockwave shoot from my nipple and detonate between my legs.

"Oh my God," I whispered.

He didn't stop. Both his hands worked me, and I pushed back into his body, nestling my bottom into his crotch. I started breathing heavily, my still sleepy mind completely muddled.

I tried to turn, to touch him, but his arms tensed and he held me where I was.

I gave up, giving into the sensations. I felt his teeth nip my shoulder, catching the strap of my nightgown. His body moved as his mouth pulled down the strap, exposing my breast. He was now skin against skin at my breast. One of his fingers slid inside me and I felt heat slice through my body.

I tried to turn again, but he kept me where I was, finger moving in and out, and instinct made my hips move with it, riding his hand.

"Jesus, Jules," he said at my neck, his voice hoarse, and his finger slid away and touched me again, moving, swirling and I felt it coming.

I'd had orgasms before, self-induced, but it was nothing like this. Nothing at all. It overwhelmed me. I sucked in breath and Vance knew it was going to happen.

He rolled me to my back, his hand still between my legs. I wrapped my arms around him, bucked my hips, his mouth came to mine and it hit me.

And when it did I moaned his name.

The minute I finished his name, he moved away. I made a detached mew of protest at the loss of his heat and hand, but he wasn't going anywhere.

I was still in the throes of my orgasm when he tore my panties down my legs, spread my thighs, came up between them and filled me.

It didn't hurt, not at all. Instead it felt beautiful.

I whispered his name again. He pulled up my legs at the knees, pushing deeper, moving rhythmically and my hips matched the movements of his.

"Jesus Christ, you're tight," he muttered into my neck and I wrapped my arms around him, pulling my knees back further so he could slide deeper.

He went up on his hands. Grinding into me, looking down at me, his eyes dilated and his hair around his shoulders.

Looking up at him, at that moment, he was the most beautiful thing I'd ever seen.

"Come back to me," I murmured, and the minute I asked he did, his hand moving between us, touching me, pressing into me. I was sensitive there, ready again. I started panting. It was too much. I thought it would shatter me.

"Vance," I whispered in an urgent voice.

"Let go," he told me, deep voice husky, eyes staring into mine.

I did.

A few minutes later, he did too.

⌘

I used to go to summer camp in the mountains for two weeks, and when I got older, I became a camp counselor.

We did a lot of horseback riding.

Maybe Indy was wrong and it *wasn't* an urban myth.

Whatever. It didn't matter.

What mattered was the fact that I just discovered that sex was great. Sex was wonderful. Sex was *the best* thing ever invented.

Vance's weight was on me, pressing me into the bed. He was still inside me, my arms wrapped around his waist, thighs tight against his hips, and I was thinking stupid thoughts, my mind racing, my body spent.

Vance slowly, gently slid out of me and shifted to the side, taking me with him. I lifted my chin to look at him, maybe even smile at him, but with one look I knew something was definitely not right.

Damn.

Maybe I'd done it wrong.

"Vance…"

His eyes were intense, more intense than his normal intense. Something was in his face, something not right, and I didn't know if it was good or bad, but whatever it was, it was immense.

"Did I hurt you?" he asked.

So that was it.

I shook my head.

His hand moved between us, then between my legs, touching me gently. My hips jerked at his touch because I was still tender.

The whole time he looked into my eyes, staring at me in that intense way.

"What are you doing?" I whispered.

"Checkin' for blood."

My breath caught.

Oh crap.

He knew. He knew I was a virgin.

How did he know?

It was my turn to stare at him.

"Are you on the pill?" he asked.

I shook my head again.

His hand went away, his eyes went to it then he moved to the bottom of the bed and dropped over the edge silently. I stared at him while he did this, stunned immobile, then his hands wrapped around my ankles and he dragged me down the bed. He caught me when I came over the side and put me on my feet.

"What are you doing?" I asked, unable to keep up.

He grabbed my hand and pulled me into the bathroom.

"Am I bleeding?" I went on.

"No."

"Then, why—?"

He stopped in the bathroom and nabbed a rolled washcloth (mint green, Egyptian cotton; my towels were *lush*) out of a basket on the back of the toilet. He threw it into the sink and turned on the tap.

"Vance, for God's sake, what are you doing?" I snapped, my patience spent.

He came at me, face clouded.

I took one look at his face and retreated. Without far to go in the small room, my back hit the bathroom wall and his body came up against mine.

"You were a virgin," he stated.

I opened and shut my mouth three times, not knowing what to say.

"Don't deny it," he warned.

"How did you know?" I whispered.

"No one's that fuckin' tight. Jesus, Jules, why didn't you say anything?"

"Turn off the faucet," I ordered in an effort to stall. I did *not* want to have this particular conversation.

"Answer me," he demanded. Vance was apparently intent on having this particular conversation.

I gave in to get it over with. "I tried, last night, but things got..." I started then stopped, "and this morning things were advanced—"

He interrupted me, "I didn't use protection."

I blinked at him then my eyes got wide.

"*Fuck!*" The word was a gentle explosion under his breath and then he got further into my space, his face close to mine. "I didn't expect it to go that far."

This was not good.

"What did you expect to happen?" I asked.

"I expected to make you come with my hand and have time to get protection before I fucked you. But Christ, your face when you came..."

He stopped speaking and I stopped breathing.

Then he went on, "I also expected you to be the kind of woman with enough experience and brains to keep herself protected."

My mouth dropped open then I snapped it shut and said, "You make it sound like my fault."

"You didn't tell me you were a virgin. Things would have gone differently if you had."

I didn't know what that meant and I didn't get the chance to ask.

He kept talking. "How in *the fuck* does someone who looks like you remain a virgin until you're twenty-six fuckin' years old?"

Okay, so I was getting the impression that my virginal status was a turn off.

Instead of this making me angry, it hurt me someplace private, someplace there was no way in hell I'd ever let show.

I pretended his words didn't affect me and looked for an excuse.

"I've been kinda busy," I told him.

"That's not it."

"I'm a lesbian?" I tried.

He stared at me like he thought it might be a good idea to call a certain kind of doctor.

Then he twisted his torso around, turned off the faucet, came back and put his hands on the wall on either side of me.

"No one has ever touched you?" he asked, his voice still sounding angry, intense, and I didn't know how to react.

I mean, this wasn't exactly the end of the world, was it?

Was I that bad?

"No one's ever touched me," I answered softly.

"No one?"

I shook my head.

"Put their mouth on you?" he continued.

"Vance!" I exclaimed.

"Answer me, goddammit!" he clipped, his eyes flashing, the intensity escalating, and my heart began to race.

"No!" I yelled. I was confused and beginning to get freaked right the hell out.

When I said no, he moved quickly, yanking my body to him, then his arms went around me tight and his mouth came down on mine in a hot and heavy, full-on-tongue-action kiss.

It took my breath away.

He pulled away, but only to yank my nightgown over my head and throw it aside. I noticed his nakedness then, forgetting my own, and stared in amazement at his body for the second he gave me before it was against mine, pressing me to the wall, hands everywhere, mouth on mine.

My belly was fluttering again, wildly, and I went with it, exploring his skin with my hands.

Okay, so maybe I was wrong about my virginal status being a turn off.

It was out-of-control. Even though we'd just finished we started again, and it was not like before. I thought that had been intense, but *this* was. It was violent, unrestrained. We were all over each other and it was fucking amazing.

Within minutes I was alternately panting, kissing him, tasting his neck, his collarbone, his shoulders. My hands were running over his ass when he bent, lifted my leg, swung it around his hip and slammed into me.

My head went back when he filled me and cracked against the wall.

Vance heard it, picked me up with his hands at my behind, still inside me. I wrapped my legs around his hips and my arms around his shoulders. He moved us into the hall, his head tilted back and mine tipped down, our mouths locked together.

He fell to his knee on the floor and dropped me to my back. He moved over me. I kept my legs and arms around him and he started immediately moving inside me, hard, fast, deep, my body jolting with his thrusts. It felt good, beyond good, straight to magnificent.

His hands went to the sides of my head, fingers in my hair, and he looked down at me while he moved. I tried to kiss him, but he dodged my mouth.

"Never," he said, his voice gruff, his hips stopping their thrusts and grinding into me.

"Never what?" I murmured, one of my hands sliding down his back. The other one went into his hair.

"Outside my bike, never has anything important in my life been just mine."

My body stilled. So did my heart, and my eyes locked with his.

He started moving again, slowly, deeply and he kept talking. "Always castoffs, leftovers, used, sometimes even food from dumpsters."

My heart started beating again, only to trip over itself. My breath came fast, not only from what was happening to my body, but what he was saying.

"Vance—"

His lips came to mine. His hands moved out of my hair and went to the sides of my face and he stared in my eyes, pressing deep inside.

138

"Mine," he muttered, his deep voice hoarse, that fierce undercurrent there.

His tone caused a shiver to run through me, straight through to my soul. Then he kissed me.

⚊⚊

"I've got to get to work," Vance said to me, or more appropriately, against my neck.

We were back in bed, comforter up to our waists. Vance had his arms around me. I had my hands pressed against his chest.

Boo was sitting on the end of the bed, staring at us with barely concealed impatience at what he considered the unacceptable delay in the arrival of his morning wet food breakfast.

After we were done on the floor in the hall, wordlessly Vance had carried me up to the bed. Not like last time, but cradled in his arms. He'd managed that feat, too, gracefully. He pulled me into bed, yanked the comforter over us and he held me, still silent.

I was silent, too. My body was completely sated after three earth-shattering, back-to-back orgasms. So much so, I could barely move.

My mind was blank with shock, and if I admitted it to myself, pure unadulterated fear.

I pulled my thoughts together, tossed my emotional Rottweiler a juicy steak and twisted my head to look at Vance. "We have to talk."

And we did. We *so* had to talk.

He kissed me quickly then looked in my eyes. "Is this one of your whisper-sweet-stories-about-your-life-and-smile-at-me talks or something else?" he asked.

"Something else," I told him.

"Then we don't have to talk."

"Crowe."

He kissed me again.

"I'll call you later," he said.

"Crowe—"

"We'll go out to dinner before the meet with Darius."

"Crowe!"

He leaned in, kissed my forehead, let me go, moved swiftly and disappeared off the edge of the platform.

"*Crowe!*" I shouted.

I scrambled to the end of the bed, wrapping the comforter around my naked body. With effort and absolutely no grace I threw my legs over the side of the bed. I stumbled, corrected myself and jumped down, pulling the bulk of the king-sized comforter with me.

I went charging into the living room, Boo hot on my heels, but Vance was gone.

"Goddammit!" I shouted at the empty room.

"*Meow!*" Boo concurred.

⊰⊱

I arrived at King's nearly an hour late, and the minute I came through the door May bore down on me like I was a clueless tourist wandering into the street in Pamplona and she was the bull.

She was followed, to my complete surprise and absolute mortification, by Daisy and Roxie.

"Well?" May asked after she arrived, looking at my face closely.

"I don't want to talk about it," I stated, walked right by the trio and stomped across the room, ignoring the kids who were staring at me.

The ladies caught me at the entry to the hall and hustled me, protesting all the way, into the yellow counseling room. Roxie shut the door and May drew the blind on the window to the hall.

"Oh sugar, what happened?" Daisy asked, eyes on me, her voice gentle.

I faced off against Daisy and ignored her soft look. "I said I don't want to talk about it."

And I didn't. My emotional Rottweiler was straining against his chain, snarling and barking, teeth bared.

I didn't need this shit. I didn't need these people.

I didn't need to think about the fact that I'd had unprotected sex, *twice*, with Crowe. If his swimmers were anything like him they were gonzo and had probably already fertilized at least one of my eggs, and as I stood in the yellow counseling room were likely creating a beautiful baby with dark hair, dark eyes and amazing bone structure. This would mean I'd *never* get Vance Crowe out of my life.

Furthermore, I didn't need to think about what he said to me, how he said it or how it made me feel.

I needed to think about my mission. I needed to keep my head in the game.

The door flew open, and Roxie, who still had her hand on the knob, went flying.

Indy, Ally and Jet stormed into the room. I looked to the ceiling and fought for patience, deliverance, or the ability to beam myself to Nicaragua.

I came back into the room when I heard Indy say, "Sorry Roxie."

"What'd we miss?" Ally was staring at me.

Jet closed the door.

"I have to get to work," I announced, stalking to the door, but Daisy got in front of me and stopped me.

"He hurt you?" she asked, her voice still kind.

"No," I answered. "I'm late. I have appointments."

"Does anyone know if they did it?" Jet whispered to May.

"We haven't got that far," May replied.

"Sugar, talk to us." Daisy grabbed my hand.

I looked at our hands then at her then I pulled my hand out of hers. "Listen, I don't mean to be rude, but I have work to do and this, really, is none of your business."

Daisy's head jerked and she took a step back.

I went to walk by her, but a strong hand wrapped around my upper arm, ultra-long fingernails (I noticed at a glance they were painted frosty pink with swipes of silver across the tips) biting into my flesh, and Daisy turned me back around. I was now facing a Daisy without the kind and gentle look on her face. This was a serious Daisy, serious as a heart attack.

"Girl, I know you're a kickass, head-crackin' mamma jamma, but whatever happened with Vance you ain't ever gonna get through if you don't talk to your girlfriends, comprende?"

"You aren't my girlfriends," I told her.

Her eyes narrowed.

"Excuse me, but we held the goddamned Sacred Girlfriend Ritual last night in your very own livin' room," Daisy declared. "Complete with margaritas and makeup."

"Sorry, Jules, but you aren't getting rid of us," Indy said.

"If he hurt her, I'm gonna kick his fuckin' ass," Ally said to no one.

"Vance wouldn't hurt her, no way," Roxie said quietly, watching me.

May pushed through everyone and grabbed onto my upper arms.

"Talk, girl," she said quietly in her Mama's-Gonna-Make-It-Better voice, and even I, head-crackin' mamma jamma (whatever that meant), was no match for May's Mama voice.

I took a deep breath and let it go.

"The date was terrible," I told them. May's hands dropped and she stepped back, her face falling with disappointment.

"Oh no," Jet whispered.

"We fought," I explained.

"About what?" Roxie asked.

"He tried to tell me what to do," I answered.

"Well, *that* wasn't the way to go," Indy muttered.

"When we got back to my house, we made up," I went on.

"That's good," Jet put in, her expression brightening.

"Then we started to… um, you know…" I faltered.

"Go on," Ally encouraged.

"Then, at a good part, Vance had to stop and go outside to shoot Sal Cordova, who was stalking me."

Daisy started to giggle.

"He shot him in the ass," I told Daisy, and I had to grin because I still thought it was funny.

"What kind of good part?" Ally asked, bringing me back to the matter at hand.

I looked at her, grin still on my face now for a different reason.

"A *really* good part," I told her.

"What we talkin' about here? Hands and fingers or mouth and tongue?" Daisy demanded to know.

"Or fingers and tongue?" Ally threw in an alternate combo.

"Hands and fingers, mainly fingers," I answered.

"Oh my," Roxie breathed.

"Vance got shot, too," I said.

"No!" Indy exclaimed. "Lee didn't tell me."

"He's okay. Just a graze, some stitches in his thigh," I assured Indy.

"So, you didn't do it," May said.

I looked to May. "Yes. We did. This morning. Twice."

Their eyes grew round and they leaned in.

"How was it?" Indy asked.

"What's his body like?" Ally asked.

"Did it hurt? Are you okay?" Roxie asked.

I closed my eyes, bit my lip, and then opened my eyes again and told them the rest. All the rest. Everything. When I was done talking, they were staring at me, mouths open.

"Holy crap," Indy breathed.

"I knew that horse ridin' thing was no urban myth," Daisy said to Indy.

I looked at Roxie and she had tears in her eyes. I watched her a second, and forgetting about my travails, I walked to her.

"I'm okay," I assured her, and she nodded, tears still threatening. Then I asked, "Are you okay?"

"Vance. We…" she stopped. "Jules, remember I told you yesterday he was the one who rescued me when my ex kidnapped me?"

I nodded.

Roxie nodded back and kept going. "Well, after he brought me back, he went after my ex, Billy, when Billy got away. Tracked him for days. In the end, during the big facedown when Billy caught up with us at Daisy's party, Vance shot him in the hand."

I stared. I'd heard the story but I didn't know it was Roxie's boyfriend or Daisy's party.

Wow.

I shook off my wonder at this news and focused on Roxie.

"You said 'us'," I told her, getting closer but not touching her. "Did you see that happen? The shooting?"

She nodded.

"Roxie, that must have been tough," I said softly.

She blinked at me. "I'm not crying because of *that*."

This surprised me.

"Why are you crying?" I asked.

"I'm crying because of something Hank told me, the reason why Vance went after Billy. See, when Billy kidnapped me, he beat me up pretty badly, broke some ribs. When Vance found me, I was a mess. He didn't take to that very well, said any man who raised his hand to a woman had to pay. Hank told me he went after Billy because Vance came from a violent home. His Dad put him out of the house when he was ten because Vance tried to get in between his Dad and his Mom when his Dad was beating her. This all fits together and it makes me happy he found you, but it also makes me sad that he had to live through that before he did."

"My God, I didn't know that," Ally said from behind me.

"I did," Indy replied quietly.

"You went through a lot with this Billy," I said to Roxie, ignoring her words about Vance.

That was another thing I didn't need. Knowing why Vance was turned out. Knowing he'd witnessed his mother's abuse. Knowing he'd had enough strength of will, sense of self and capacity for love at age ten to go against his father in an effort to protect his mother.

I didn't need that at all.

So I rolled it up in a big old ball and threw it in the high, chain link fenced compound that stood behind my emotional Rottweiler.

"Jules, did you hear what I said about Vance?" Roxie asked, taking me from my thoughts.

"I heard you. I know about Vance. I know he was a street kid and he's an ex-con and recovering alcoholic."

"Holy shit. I didn't know that either," Ally said again.

"I did," Indy repeated.

"How do you know all this shit?" Ally asked.

"Lee told me," Indy replied.

"That boy has a big mouth," Daisy put in.

"He does not," Indy defended Lee.

"He tells you everything," Jet entered the conversation.

"Of course he does. We don't have any secrets," Indy replied.

"Oh, please. You lie to him all the time," Ally returned.

"Okay then, *Lee* doesn't have any secrets," Indy retorted.

"Excuse me girls, but can we get to the topic at hand here?" May cut in and looked at me. "When're you gonna see him again?"

144

"I'm breaking up with him tonight," I announced.

May gasped.

Daisy looked at the ceiling. "Here we go again," she said.

"What?" I asked.

"Jet tried to break up with Eddie," Daisy told me.

"Didn't work," Jet said on a smile.

I turned to Jet in surprise. "Why did you try to break up with him? I saw him last night. He's hot."

Jet just stared at me like she thought maybe I'd recently sustained a head injury.

"And Roxie tried to break up with Hank. That didn't work either," Daisy continued.

My eyes swung to Roxie. "You did? I saw him last night, too. He's lush." I took them both in. "Are you two nuts?"

"Um... have you *looked* at Vance?" Jet asked me.

I shook my head. "It's not the same thing. Anyway, it's not about the way they look. It's about how they act."

"Sugar, how... exactly... is Vance acting like someone you'd wanna break up with?" Daisy queried.

"He said 'mine', like he was claiming me. Like I was a possession or something," I argued.

This was true. It was just like I was a possession, a highly-valued family heirloom with treasured, precious memories attached that had gone missing and was thought never to be found, but all of a sudden, it was back.

I didn't tell the girls that though.

"Our boys can get kind of possessive," Indy shared, but she didn't sound too upset by it. "You get used to it. I just try to ignore it," she advised.

I persevered.

"And he tells me what to do. All the time," I informed them.

"Yeah, they can be bossy too," Indy said on a sigh. "I just go my own way and ignore that, too."

"Wait until you're branded. Eddie branded me," Jet added.

I blinked at her. "Branded you? Like they do to cows?" I asked.

She smiled. "Not exactly like that. He just made it known that if anyone touches me, they'll answer to him or any of his friends."

"Lee did that with me, too, in a way," Indy threw in.

"Hank too," Roxie said.

Damn.

"Vance has already done that. The whole Nightingale Investigation Team has thrown down on my side," I shared.

Indy smiled. "I knew that, too."

"I didn't! Dammit! Why am I so out of the loop?" Ally snapped.

May broke into Ally's rant. She sounded exasperated too, but at me.

"Oh for goodness sake, Jules, you break up with that boy you're off my Christmas card list."

I just stared at her, keeping my mouth shut.

She took my stare and then pulled out the big guns. "And no birthday cake for you. I know you like your cake and your birthday is tomorrow, and I had a good one all planned to make for you. But you let go of Vance Crowe, forget it," May went on.

"May, that's not fair!" I protested, and it was true, it *wasn't* fair. It was cruel. I loved her birthday cakes. Everyone loved her birthday cakes. She made the best birthday cakes ever, even better than Auntie Reba (but I'd never tell Nick that). Last year, she made me German chocolate cake with that delicious condensed milk frosting with pecans in it. It was amazing.

I carried on my argument to May, "It's my life. I know what I'm doing!"

"Mm-hmm," was all May uttered.

The rest of the girls were looking at each other.

"Your birthday is tomorrow?" Jet asked.

"Let's have a party!" Ally yelled.

"Great idea," Indy said.

"No!" I broke in. "No party."

"Too late, sugar. Ain't no stoppin' the Rock Chicks when there's a reason to party," Daisy told me.

They started smiling.

Oh *crap*.

I took a deep breath.

Whatever.

Time to move on. It was obvious I wasn't going to get anywhere with this pack.

"I have to get to work," I told them.

"We'll get together tonight, plan the party," Ally decided. "Eight o'clock. Brother's."

"We should go together, since we live close," Indy said to me. "I'd love to ride in your Camaro."

Daisy was watching me closely. She was also smiling.

I sucked in my lips. I really didn't need this shit.

"I'll pick you up, quarter to eight," I said to Indy. "After I get back from the shooting range."

"The shooting range?" Indy asked, eyes wide with excitement. "Cool! Can I go with you?"

I stared at her. Then I sighed.

"Yeah, give me your cell. I'll program in my number."

Told you I was a fool.

Chapter 11

We Sleepin' at Your Place or Mine?

Indy and I pulled up to Heavy's house at five thirty.

The Rock Chicks and I had all exchanged phones and numbers and Indy had called me that afternoon. When I told her I had to train with Heavy before the shooting range, she asked to come along to that, too.

I'd said yes.

More fool I.

I pulled my exercise bag out of the backseat and led Indy into Heavy's house.

"Heavy!" I called. "We're here."

"Who's fuckin' 'we'?" Heavy came out of the kitchen and stared at Indy.

"Uncle Charlie!" Indy yelled when she saw him.

"India Savage!" Heavy yelled back, a huge, goofy smile spreading on his face. "Get over here, girl, give your Uncle Charlie a hug."

They hugged each other.

I stared.

"What's going on?" I asked.

They ignored me.

"I didn't know you were called Heavy," Indy told him, leaning back in his beefy arms.

"Long story, girl. God, I haven't seen you in ages. Not since that FOP picnic, what, two years ago? Hear you're shacked up with Nightingale," Heavy replied.

Indy got all girlie and showed him her ring, wiggling her fingers for effect. "We're getting married," she said.

"About fuckin' time you two got together," Heavy replied, letting her go. "Luckiest boy on the planet."

I was still staring.

Kristen Ashley

Heavy had never given any indication at all, whatsoever, that he was the kind of man who would allow anyone to call him "Uncle Charlie" without a swift upper cut leading directly to a KO.

Boy, I really did *not* know Heavy.

I should probably learn a lesson from this and research my benefactors a bit more in future.

"Helloooo?" I called.

Heavy grinned at me. "This is Indy Savage, Tom Savage's daughter," he said this like I didn't already know it already. "Tom and I worked together when I was on the Force. I've known Indy since she was yay-tall." He held up his hand to about thigh level.

Then something occurred to him, his grin fled and he blinked at Indy.

"What're you doin' with Jules?" he asked, morphing into Father Bear at the thought that Indy was turning vigilante and joining my crusade.

"We're going out tonight for dinner after she trains and shoots," Indy told Heavy. "I heard she's good. I wanted to watch."

Heavy kept staring at her.

"Honestly, Uncle Charlie," Indy assured him. "I'm not getting involved with Jules's other business. Lee would handcuff me to the bed again."

Again?

I didn't get to ask the "handcuff to the bed *again*" question because Heavy's stare sliced to me and it was my turn to get the Father Bear treatment.

"Speakin' of that, what's this I hear of you goin' hand-to-hand with Jermaine and Clarence?"

"I took Jermaine down," I told Heavy.

"Word is you went in after 'em, confronted 'em. What I train you, girl, is for defense, not offense. Got me?"

"They had a couple of runaways," I explained.

"Shit, Jules. Now you're gonna have every fuckin' asshole on the street callin' you out. It'll be like the Wild Fuckin' West. You learn quick and you're gettin' strong, but you go up against one of them motherfuckers without surprise on your side, they're gonna wipe the floor with you."

My back went straight. "Heavy, don't worry about it," I said.

"I *do* worry about it," he retorted.

"Well, don't," I told him.

"I know you got Nightingale's team at your back. They're good, but they got business to attend to. They can't protect you every minute of the fuckin' day," Heavy went on.

"Vance won't let anyone hurt her," Indy decided to share, her face happy. Then she confided, leaning toward Heavy, "They're going out."

I looked to the ceiling, took in a deep breath and let it out on a loud, long sigh.

Damn.

When I looked back at Heavy he was staring at me again.

"He fuck you yet?" Heavy asked.

"Uncle Charlie!" Indy snapped.

"Heavy!" I said at the same time.

Heavy kept his eyes on me. "Girl, that boy is a player. P-l-a-y-e-r. It wears a skirt, has a pretty face, long legs and a sweet ass, he'll charm it then he'll fuck it. You got all 'a those in abundance."

Indy was glaring at Heavy with her hands on her hips.

My eyes narrowed on Heavy. "Do *not* refer to women as 'it'," I warned. "This conversation is over."

Heavy opened his mouth to speak.

"Over! O-v-e-r," I snapped in my word-is-law voice, using his own word-spelling tactic against him to make my point and then I walked toward the garage door. "Let's train."

My phone rang in the car while I was pulling the keys out of Hazel's ignition. Indy and I were parked in the lot outside of Zip's.

The display said "Unknown caller". I flipped it open.

"Hello?"

"Where are you?" It was Vance.

My heart did a funny flip. I mentally told it to behave.

"Well, hello to you, too," I replied.

"Where are you?" he repeated.

"At the library," I lied.

"You're sittin' outside Zip's."

At his words I looked around, but didn't see any Harleys or black Explorers.

I caught Indy's eye and she mouthed, "Who is it?"

I mouthed back, "Vance."

"Jules," Vance said in my ear.

"Where are *you?*" I asked.

"I'm standin' in your living room, waitin' to take you out to dinner."

Whoops.

"Um..." I mumbled.

"What'd I say about how I felt about bein' stood up?"

"You said you'd call," I told him.

"I got busy, but our plans didn't change."

"Vance, I hate to tell you this, but they were *your* plans."

He was silent. I didn't take this as a good sign.

Finally, he warned in a low, quiet voice, "Don't make me come after you."

Yikes.

I bugged my eyes out at Indy. She bit her lip on a smile.

"How did you know where I was?" I asked, deciding to change the subject.

"I planted a device in your car," he told me.

I sucked in breath and this time, my eyes, still on Indy, went wide in shock.

Her smile faded and she mouthed, "What?"

"You planted a tracking device in my car?" I said slowly.

Indy put her hand to her open mouth.

"And in your bag," Vance said.

"I do not believe you," I hissed.

"Jules, get home."

"I'm shooting then I'm going out for drinks with the girls," I told him.

"Jules—"

I cut him off, "When's this meet with Darius?"

"Goddammit, Jules—"

"Forget it, I'll ask Indy to call Lee. I'll see you there." I flipped the phone shut and looked at Indy. "Can you call Lee—?" I started.

She was nodding, already digging through her purse.

"I'm on it," she said.

When we walked into Zip's, Indy had her phone to her ear and she stood just inside the door while I approached Zip who was behind the counter.

"Girl, you are *loco!*" Zip shouted at me the minute he saw me.

"Now... Zip," I said placatingly, arriving across the counter from him.

"Do not 'Zip' me. You're fuckin' loony tunes. It's like you sent out an engraved invitation to every fuckin' asshole on the street, 'You are cordially invited to try and kick my ass.' Shee-it."

"Zip, let me—"

"And you got the Nightingale Boys backin' you. Christ Almighty, girl. Those boys're crazier than you." His eyes went beyond me. "Fuck, is that Indy Savage?" Zip asked, staring at Indy.

"Yes—" I began.

"Oh no. No, no, no. I don't want Lee Nightingale on my ass. You are not draggin' her into this. She'll recruit Chavez's woman and Nightingale's sister and it'll be the Rock Chick Renegades against the Denver Drug Dealers. I see rivers of blood and pissed-off bad boys denied their pieces of ass and they'll come after *me*. No fuckin' way, I won't be a part of it."

I couldn't help it. He was being so dramatic I had to smile. "Zip, listen to me. Indy just wants to see me shoot. She's not 'into this'. Please, Zip, she's just..." I hesitated and stared at him. "A friend," I finished.

Zip went silent and watched me. He knew enough about me to know the importance of what I'd just said.

Then he asked, "Crowe fucked you yet?"

"Zip!" I snapped.

"Well, has he?"

"That's none of your business."

He dropped his chin and shook his head.

"He has," Zip muttered to the display case like I was his twelve year old kid and he was disappointed in finding me in the garage stealing a smoke. Then he looked up at me again. "Girl, you're cruisin' for a broken heart and a bullet-ridden body. Goddamn." He reached into the case, pulled out a box of ammo and slammed it on the counter, indicating my tongue-lashing was over. "Get her glasses and ear protectors. Three's open. Goddamn."

Kristen Ashley

Indy took her phone away from her ear, flipped it shut and approached us, smiling at Zip.

"Hey Zip," she said.

"Goddamn," he replied.

Indy threw me a look. I mouthed "not now" and I walked her back to the range.

"What was wrong with him?" she whispered as we stood in the small soundproof antechamber, putting on glasses and wrapping ear protectors around our necks.

"Nothing. He just gets a bit... overprotective," I explained. "What'd Lee say?"

She scrunched her nose. "Lee said that you go to the meet with Vance."

"Goddammit," I muttered. I was worried those boys would stick together.

"I tried to get it out of him. I even offered naked gratitude. But he didn't bite," Indy told me.

"Naked gratitude?" I smiled at her.

She linked her arm in mine and turned us to face the door to the range. "Why do you think I know everything? Naked gratitude. Works every time." She winked at me. Then she said, "Well, *nearly* every time."

I was still smiling at her.

We put our ear protectors over our ears and stepped inside the range.

＊

With the target twenty-five yards away, I had both my arms up, gun in hand, the side of my right hand above my wrist held in my left hand. My arms slightly bent to absorb the impact of the recoil, my head tilted to the gun's sight; I emptied a clip in the target.

Seventeen rounds, head for three, then chest for three, and back again until the clip was spent. I dropped my gun and squinted at the target. I saw that I didn't do too badly even with my arms aching, and Indy came up close to my back. Super close, weird close.

Yikes.

I started to turn to tell her to back off, but it wasn't Indy.

It was Vance.

154

Before I could react, he reached low, grabbed my wrist with one hand and twisted the gun out of my grip with his other.

Oh crap.

I stared at Vance's angry face for a beat then my eyes slid to the side.

Indy was sitting on a stool behind me. For the last twenty minutes we'd been taking turns with my gun. Her father had taught her how to shoot and she wasn't a bad shot.

Now she was sitting frozen and throwing me an "eek" look.

Vance's hand was still at my wrist. He dragged me right by Indy without sparing her a glance and toward the soundproof door.

I tried to pull free. This didn't work.

We went through the door into the antechamber and he closed it behind us.

I tore off my ear protectors and goggles and tossed them on the shelf on the wall.

"What the fuck?" I snapped.

He shoved my gun in the back waistband of his jeans, ripped off his protective gear and tossed it on a shelf next to mine.

"What the fuck?" I repeated, thinking he hadn't heard me with his ear protectors on.

Then he looked at me.

Wow.

I didn't have to know him very well to know he was seriously pissed.

"You hung up on me," he said, voice smooth and quiet.

"Vance."

"Don't ever hang up on me."

Most girls would probably hear the way he said those six words and nod meekly.

I wasn't like most girls.

"You put a tracking device on my car," I said in my defense.

"So?" he responded.

"And in my purse," I went on.

"This is a problem because...?" he asked.

"This is a problem because..." I couldn't think why it was a problem with his angry eyes on me. Then it came to me. "It's intrusive," I finished.

"It's intrusive," he repeated.

"Yes," I clipped.

"Then you'll probably not be happy to learn that your house is bugged. The living room and kitchen have cameras, as do the front and back entrances."

My mouth dropped open. "You're joking," I whispered.

"I put them in myself the first night I broke in. The only reason the windows don't have them is because you have protective bars."

Oh my *God*.

I was going to have to learn not to sleep so heavily. I didn't know how to manage that, but I'd have to try. I could not believe he wired my house while I was asleep.

God, he was fucking *good*.

I shrugged off my admiration and pulled back my anger.

"You're watching me?" I asked, narrowing my eyes.

"The team's watching you in the surveillance room at the office."

Oh my God.

My mind flashed to the Sacred Girlfriend Ritual, complete with margaritas and makeup and discussion of popping cherries. Mace had been in the surveillance room last night. He'd picked up my call when Vance had gone after Sal. He'd probably watched and listened to the whole thing.

No doubt about it, I was moving to Nicaragua.

"Goddammit," I muttered under my breath and, embarrassment overwhelming me, I sagged against the wall.

Then my mind flashed to Vance and I on the couch, and my head, which was tilted down to stare at my boots, shot up.

"Last night—" I started.

"They're instructed to turn off the internal cameras when I'm with you," Vance told me.

"What if they don't?" I asked.

"They do."

"What if they don't?"

"They fuckin' do. Jesus, Jules, that isn't the point."

"What *is* the point?"

He moved quick and got in my space.

I was *really* going to have to learn to be prepared for how quickly he moved.

He stared down at me, eyes still angry. "The point is you stood me up and you hung up on me. That's what we're talkin' about."

"No, now we're talking about you and your boys keeping tabs on me."

"We're protecting you."

"I want them taken out. The cameras, the bugs, the tracking devices, all of it," I demanded.

"That isn't gonna happen."

"I'll take them out myself," I told him.

"You wouldn't find them."

He was probably right.

"I'll ask Frank to take them out," I said.

Frank would find them, I was certain.

"Muñoz pulls them, I'll put more in," Vance shot back.

"Goddammit Crowe."

"Jules. The shit stays at your house so I can protect you. No discussion."

That's when I saw red and I snapped, "I *hate* it when you do that."

"What?"

"Make these macho man declarations. It pisses me off."

"If you weren't so fuckin' antagonistic, you'd realize it's for your own damned good."

Again, he was probably right.

Still.

My anger ebbed a bit. I frowned at him but this had no effect.

"We'll take Indy home. Then we're goin' to dinner and we're talkin'," Vance said.

"No, I can't. The Rock Chicks have decided to throw me a birthday party and we're going to Brother's to plan it."

His eyes narrowed. "You wanna explain to me how you're all of a sudden close with Indy and her gang?"

I shook my head, not because I didn't want to explain it, but because I couldn't.

"I have no idea." When he looked dubious I continued, "Honestly. I swear. I actually tried to get them to leave me alone, but I thought Daisy was going to take me down in a bitch-slapping fight when I told her my life was none of her business. Have you seen that woman's nails? I'm not gonna go there."

He shook his head a few times and his hand came to the wall at my waist. He leaned into it and therefore leaned into me, getting way close.

"We got shit to discuss," he said, his face an inch from mine.

"Yes. We do. Unfortunately, I'm moving to Nicaragua after our meet with Darius so we won't be able to do that," I declared.

He stared at me a beat then slowly his anger disappeared and he grinned, just like he did last night, as if I was downright adorable.

"What'll Roam and Sniff do if you move to Nicaragua?" he asked.

With him no longer being angry, the smooth was still in his voice, but it was an altogether different kind of smooth. This had an effect on me, an effect I ignored.

"I'll take them with me," I decided on the fly.

He moved in closer, his free hand coming to my hip, his eyes getting soft and sexy, and I felt my belly flutter in a way I *couldn't* ignore. "What'll *I* do if you move to Nicaragua?"

Immediately I mouthed off. Do not ask me why, but I was going with the Belly Flutter Defense.

"Find yourself a woman who can cook and doesn't mind you ordering her around all the time, being bossy and dictatorial and macho and hyper-intense and actually *likes* it when you get all… whatever… and make her belly flutter."

After I said that, my mouth snapped shut.

Damn.

I'd gotten carried away and went too far.

Vance finished moving in, pressing me back into the wall with his body.

"I do that to you?" he asked, his voice silk.

Like he didn't know.

"Back off, Crowe."

His eyes dropped to my mouth and my heart started hammering in my chest.

"I do it to you," he muttered.

See? I knew he knew.

"Back off," I repeated.

His hand came from the wall to curl around the side of my neck. His other arm went around my waist and he pulled me to him. "Get Indy to show you where the offices are. Meet us there after Brother's."

I nodded, deciding tardily to keep silent.

"We sleepin' at your place or mine?" he asked.

I changed my mind about keeping silent.

"*I'm* sleeping at my place," I informed him.

"That works for me. I like your bed."

I rolled my eyes. When they came back to him, he was grinning again. What... ever.

The door opened and Indy came through. She closed the door and took off her ear protectors.

"Sorry guys, I tried to give you time," she said.

I slid away from Crowe.

"That's all right," I told her. "We're done."

Indy turned to take off her goggles and put them and the ear protectors away. When she did, with an arm around my waist, Vance pulled my back to his front. He slid my gun in the back waistband of my cords and his mouth came to my ear.

"We're far from done," he said there.

Over my shoulder, I threw him a look.

He threw me a grin.

Again.

Whatever.

Chapter 12

Channeling My Head-Crackin' Mamma Jamma

"I think we should have a theme."

"A theme?"

"We're not having a theme."

"We've never had a theme. We should do something, like dress up like James Bond characters."

"It's tomorrow night. We don't have time."

"I am *not* dressing up like a James Bond character."

We were sitting in the back room of My Brother's Bar, a drinking establishment in lower, *lower* downtown that was decorated in "wood". They had no bottled beer, only beer on tap, and had arguably the best bar menu in Denver, including buffalo burgers, hot soft pretzels with jalapeño cream cheese, and fantastic onion rings.

We'd been there over an hour and had dinner (I got the ticky turkey; a hot, shaved turkey sandwich with jalapeño cream cheese and some delicious orange gunk on a fresh hoagie roll).

Most everyone was into their third or fourth beer. I was drinking diet cola. I wanted nothing to impair my judgment when I sat down with Darius.

The conversation was fast and furious, and as far as I could tell no decisions had been made.

I was not participating. I'd never had a birthday party with more people than Nick and Auntie Reba in attendance. I didn't feel I had anything to offer.

Our group consisted of all the girlie gang, including May, Tod and Stevie, and surprisingly Indy's coffee guy, the humongous, hairy Tex.

Tex also didn't participate in the party planning discussion.

Hank brought Roxie. Eddie brought Jet. Hank and Eddie didn't sit with us, but positioned themselves in the front room at the bar by the door. Jet said this was because they didn't have a lot of insight into planning parties. I figured

Kristen Ashley

their presence at the bar at all was because I was there. They thought I was dangerous, I was with their women and they weren't taking any chances. Thus they moved off to stand at the entrance and keep watch.

"Jules, who do you want us to invite?" Indy asked, pulling me from my thoughts.

"Just Nick, my uncle, and Zip, Heavy and Frank," I answered, wondering, if they decided on a theme, how any of those men would take to that idea. Not very well, I guessed, and the thought of Heavy in a James Bond-esque costume made me smile.

I came back into the room and saw they were all staring at me.

"Zip the gun shop guy?" Jet asked.

"Yeah, he's my friend," I told her.

"Anyone else?" Indy cut in.

I shook my head.

She stared at me. "No one?" she went on.

I kept shaking my head.

"Friends form work?" Roxie prompted and I started to get uncomfortable.

"Let's move on," Tex boomed from beside me, saying his first words of the night except, "Give me a Ralphie Burger and a Bud," then, "What do you mean, you don't have Budweiser? Fuck! This is America!"

Everyone jumped at Tex's boom, looked at each other, and then they started a bewildering conversation about cashews.

This went on for a while when Tex leaned into me.

"You wanna blow this joint, go out, crack together some dealer heads?" he asked in a booming whisper.

The group had moved onto whether they should make a bowl of sangria, pitchers of margaritas or personally created mojitos, which was apparently a very important decision that took all their undivided attention, so they missed Tex's boom.

I turned to him. "I don't crack heads very often. I usually slash tires and throw smoke bombs," I told him.

He stared at me.

I went on, "Sometimes I get creative with plastic wrap, and once I doused a dealer's Mercedes with canola oil. Inside and out."

At this he grinned.

"Bet that took a lot of oil," he remarked, sounding impressed.

"Three gallon jugs." I smiled.

He nodded his appreciation. "You ever want to get serious, I know where to get teargas and grenades," he told me.

It was my turn to stare, not knowing if he was serious or trying to be funny. I decided he was trying to be funny.

"I'll keep that in mind."

He nodded again and then turned to the group and boomed, "Sangria! Next topic!"

I got up and announced, "I'm getting a drink. Anyone need anything?"

Lots of shaking heads and then they moved on to decorations. Yay or nay, and if yay, what kind?

I wandered to the bar. When I got to the front room it was packed. The only space available at the bar was next to Eddie Chavez.

Damn.

Just my luck. I took a deep breath, slid in beside him and caught the bartender's attention.

"What 'cha need?" the bartender asked me.

"Diet," I ordered.

He put ice in a glass and pulled out the soft drink gun. I felt, rather than saw, Hank and Eddie's eyes on me.

I turned to them. "Hey," I said.

Yep, they were both looking at me, but neither responded to my greeting. Whatever.

The bartender set the drink in front of me.

"How much?" I asked.

He grinned then winked. "That's on the house."

Pu-lease.

I'd heard that before.

"How much?" I repeated, making my point that I was *not* interested.

He blinked then his face fell. He was cute and probably not accustomed to being shot down.

I felt sorry for him, but I needed to flirt with a bartender like I needed a hole in the head. Firstly, Eddie and Hank were watching, they were friends of Vance's, and even though I was not *with* Vance, everyone, including Vance, thought I was. Secondly, I wasn't into the bartender. I wasn't into anyone, in-

163

cluding Vance (okay, that last part was a lie, but I wasn't averse to lying to myself in extreme situations).

"A buck fifty," the bartender cut into my Romantic Denial Reverie.

I dug in my purse, got out my wallet, gave him two dollars and he wandered away.

"Crash and burn," Eddie muttered under his breath as I threw my wallet back in my purse.

"Sorry?" I asked even though I heard him.

Eddie moved away from the bar to stand beside me and Hank moved forward, both of them effectively fencing me in.

"Word of advice?" Eddie asked, ignoring my earlier question.

I took a sip and glanced at him over the rim of my glass. Then I put the drink on the bar.

I did not want a word of advice from Eddie Chavez.

Instead, so as not to be rude, I said, "Sure."

"Whatever Darius offers, take it. Save face and get off the street."

Hmm.

I was thinking these boys weren't big fans of The Law.

I decided not to answer.

"You have a good reputation for the work you do. People respect you and have for a long time. Until this," Hank said, standing in front of me. "It's understandable. You work hard to keep these kids clean, when one of them goes down you want to do something. But Jules, you're goin' about it the wrong way."

Okay, so even though Hank was being nice, I figured it was time to be rude.

"Thanks for the advice, but you don't know what the fuck you're talking about," I said to Hank.

"We're both Vice," Eddie told me.

"I know what you are," I replied.

"That means we do know what we're talkin' about," Hank explained.

I turned back to Hank. "I know what Vice is."

"It's about the kids," Eddie murmured to Hank.

"Yeah," I said to Eddie, my voice was low and serious and not to be mistaken. "It's about the kids."

Eddie just looked at me, unaffected by my-word-is-law tone.

"Maybe you should know Lee's on his own with this one. Darius wants you off the streets, and so do I," Eddie shared. "I don't agree with Lee, and if I see you on the streets, fuckin' around where you shouldn't be, I'll take you down."

The way he said it made me think this wasn't an idle threat. So now I had the dealers and the cops actively against me.

This wasn't surprising, but it was annoying.

I didn't respond.

"You get caught, taken in, it could mean you lose your job," Hank told me.

"I'll take my chances," I returned.

"We bring you down, we'll go after Zip, Heavy and Frank next. They should know better than encourage you to put your ass out there," Hank went on.

Damn, Vance had been talking.

Now I was beginning to get mad. "Zip, Heavy and Frank don't *want* me out there. They can't control me any more than Crowe can. They're just giving me the knowledge to keep me from getting hurt."

"They don't have that much knowledge," Hank retorted, his voice and eyes hard.

Before I could reply, Eddie leaned in. "Something else, Law. You get Jet involved in any of this shit, and she, or any of them, gets caught up or put in danger—"

"Back off, Chavez," my patience was waning, "they came to me. I'm not recruiting. This is a one woman deal."

"This shit spreads," Eddie warned.

"I'd sooner gnaw off my own goddamned arm than see Jet or Indy or Roxie or any of them get hurt," I told the boys.

To my surprise I meant it, and the looks on their faces told me they believed me.

Finally.

"They're planning a birthday party, not a vigilante drug war," I continued.

This was met with silence.

"Though, Tex did offer me teargas and grenades," I shared.

"Jesus Christ," Hank muttered under his breath.

"Don't take him up on it," Eddie said straight out.

I stared. "I thought he was joking," I murmured.

"Fuck." It was Eddie's turn to mutter under his breath.

Before anyone could say anything else, Indy walked up to us, burrowing in between Eddie and Hank.

"Hey guys." She smiled, then she looked between the three of us. She felt the tension and her smile faded. "What's going on?"

"Nothing," I said immediately. "So, is it cashews or macadamia nuts?"

She looked at me. "Cashews. It's always cashews, and you aren't fooling anyone." Her eyes flashed between Eddie and Hank. "You two, back off."

"Stay out of it Indy," Eddie ordered.

"*You* stay out of it. This is Jules's deal," Indy returned.

"Indy——" Hank started, but Indy cut him off.

"Excuse me, but wasn't it you who went ballistic when Roxie was kidnapped? Lee nearly had to lock you into the safe room."

Hank's eyes remained hard, but he didn't respond.

Indy's gaze cut to Eddie. "As for you, you think you wouldn't go maverick if something happened to Hector?" Indy asked Eddie.

"Hector?" I cut in.

"Eddie's younger brother," Indy told me.

"I'm a cop," Eddie reminded Indy.

"You're a cop who already doesn't follow the rules. You'd lose your fucking mind if something happened to Hector, and it could, and we both know it."

"Hector's my brother. This kid Jules is avenging——" Eddie started.

"He meant something to her," Indy interrupted him.

"Goddammit, Indy——" Eddie carried on and Indy leaned in.

"He *meant* something to her," she said quietly. "You know how it is. You already lost Darius, Eddie, and what happened to him turned you into a cop. You *know*."

I watched, fascinated, as Indy and Eddie squared off.

Neither spoke. Neither moved.

I was beginning to think Indy was a bit of a head-crackin' mamma jamma too.

I realized this could go on all night so I cut in, "Oh, for goodness sakes, it's cool. We're cool. The world is cool. Indy, do you want a drink?"

She tore her gaze away from Eddie's and looked at me. "I can't. Lee called. It's time."

Saved by the call from the badass boy.

"Great," I said, "let's go."

Indy kept glaring at them both, deciding to include Hank in her unhappiness. I grabbed her arm, deciding not to go the way of the glare. I'd already been rude enough. I dragged her to the door.

We were in Hazel and on our way to the Nightingale Investigations offices before I asked about Hector.

"Lee, Eddie and Darius were all best friends for as long as I can remember. As kids they were wild. Serious wild. Crazy wild," she told me, then stopped.

"Yeah?" I prompted. I kept my eyes on the road, but I heard and felt her move in her seat to turn to me.

"It isn't my place to say, but we all loved Darius. We all still do," she said, shocking me.

I didn't respond.

"He was a great guy. I think he still is that guy, somewhere deep. When he was in his late teens, his Dad was murdered. Long story, sad and ugly. Darius had a rough time, fell in with a bad man, lost his way and never found it back."

I nodded. Some people were born bad. Some people were forced into it. It was interesting to know which sort of person Darius was.

"Lee and Eddie had different reactions to this. Lee straightened up and went into the Army. Eddie straightened up and went into the Academy. Regardless, they're all close to this day."

"And Hector?" I asked.

"Hector's a wildcard. No one knows what he's into, and he's gone off the radar. Eddie and Lee are trying to get a lock on him, but they're getting nothing. I told you about Lee, Eddie and Darius because they could get into some big trouble; hotwiring cars, bar fights, shit like that. Rumor has it Hector's giving them a run for their money. We're talking bad shit far beyond hotwiring cars and bar fights."

I pulled in my lips, catching her meaning. I didn't respond and simply drove.

Indy went silent until we got close to Lee's offices and she directed me into an underground parking area. I parked next to Vance's Harley.

The sight of it made my heart skip a beat.

"Vance has a great bike," Indy breathed, staring at it.

"You can say that again," I told her.

She smiled at me. "You ride on it yet?"

I nodded.

"Is it hot?" she asked.

I nodded again, this time on a grin.

"Lee has a Ducati."

"Nice," I said slow.

She started to giggle, and for some reason, so did I.

After we finished giggling, we got out, went into the building and walked up some flights of stairs. Outside the door that had a plaque that said "Nightingale Investigations" on it, I stopped and turned to her.

"I hear anything about Hector, I'll let you know. You can do with it whatever you want."

"I'd appreciate that," she said, then she went on. "So would Eddie."

I figured I could use a favor from Eddie, especially since he intended to "take me down".

We walked into the offices. All the lights were on and I was surprised at the reception area. It screamed money. The place was decorated richly. Cowboy chic, gleaming wood, leather couches and a bronze bucking bronco on a column in the corner. Behind the huge reception desk sat a blonde woman who was so gorgeous, she looked cut out of the pages of a fashion magazine. The woman looked up, her brows drew together, and she stared at us with undisguised dislike as we approached the desk.

Yikes.

"Hi Dawn," Indy greeted, smiling sweetly but supremely fake. I was impressed.

"Hi Indy," Dawn returned the favor and her gaze moved to me. "Who's this? Is it *The Law?*" she asked sarcastically.

Oh my God.

What a bitch!

"My name is Juliet Lawler," I told her, my voice cold.

"Yeah, I know," she said back, her voice arctic.

Wow. She *was* a bitch.

I wondered if it was just us or if this woman was mean to everyone who walked through the doors. If so, Lee needed a new receptionist.

Indy leaned into her and said with false concern for Dawn's welfare, "You *do* know there are cameras and bugs in here?"

Dawn didn't bother to respond, got up and walked around the desk.

"I'll tell Lee you're here," she said.

"I'm sure he already knows," Indy replied.

Dawn disappeared behind a door.

"What a bitch," I spoke my thoughts aloud to Indy.

"She had a thing for Lee," Indy informed me.

I made a face. "You're kidding? Did he know?"

She nodded her head. "Yeah, he didn't care. Not interested. Then she had a thing for Vance."

This information, coupled with the knowledge that everyone (as in *everyone*) kept telling me Vance was a player, made my stomach clench in a very unhappy way.

I couldn't help myself, I blurted out in a whisper, "Oh my God. Did he do her?"

This time she shook her head. "No way."

"Thank God," I breathed. If Vance touched Dawn, well... one word: *ick*.

"Then she had a thing for Luke. No go. Then Mace, then Hank. They all think she's a bitch."

"Why does Lee keep her?"

"Says she's efficient and..." she hesitated, "*cordial*."

After she said this, in unison we both widened our eyes at each other and then burst out laughing. In fact, at the idea of Dawn being cordial, we laughed so hard we bent double with it.

"Having fun?" Lee asked, moving toward Indy, having entered from the doorway.

Vance was coming at me and Dawn was walking behind the desk. I straightened, wiped a tear of laughter from my eye and watched Lee approach Indy, which gave me the opportunity to ignore Vance.

Lee put his hands to either side of Indy's neck and kissed her right on the lips. After he was done, Indy smiled up at him. His eyes crinkled, and watching them, my heart spasmed.

What in *the hell* was that all about?

A heart spasm at the sight of true love?

What kind of head-crackin' mamma jamma was I?

"Law," Vance said beside me.

I turned to him. "Crowe," I returned the greeting.

I held my body stiff. My emotional Rottweiler had woken up and was on guard. Vance watched me closely and I got the impression he saw my Rottweiler and decided he was a cuddly puppy. I got this impression because his sexual tractor beam switched on. His eyes got soft and his arm curled around my waist, pulling me around and into his body.

"Crowe," I said low and quiet, a warning in my voice.

He ignored my warning and his face dipped close to mine.

"Shut up," he said, but he said it through one of his grins.

"Don't tell me to shut up," I flashed.

He just kept grinning.

Whatever.

"Are we going to do this or what?" I asked.

Instantly, his eyes went serious, but he didn't let me go.

"We get there, you let Darius talk first. You let him have his say and you listen. Then you let Lee guide the conversation and you take cues from Lee. Yeah?"

"I'm not stupid," I told him.

"I know you aren't," he surprised me by saying.

I blinked at him.

"Really?" I blurted, then I wished I hadn't because his eyes got soft again and I was having trouble channeling my head-crackin' mamma jamma with his soft eyes on me.

"Really," he said quietly.

"I thought you thought I was a little crazy."

"Crazy. Yeah. Stupid. No."

Hmm.

That was *mostly* good.

What was I thinking? I didn't care if Vance thought I was crazy *or* stupid.

Before I could purposefully kill the mood, Luke did it for me.

"Fuck. You guys havin' a sit down with Darius or an orgy in reception?"

I went up on my toes and looked over Vance's shoulder. Luke was standing in the doorway, arms crossed on his chest. He looked like he didn't know whether to grin or vomit. A glance at Dawn showed she definitely wished she could vomit, and her eyes were on Vance and me.

I smiled brightly at her just because. I felt Vance's body move with laughter even though he didn't make a sound.

I turned my head and frowned at him.

"What?" I snapped.

His mouth came to my ear. "Wouldn't know, don't want to know, but I bet she doesn't taste like cherries."

That got a belly flutter.

I sicced the Rottweiler on my belly flutter and glared at Vance when his head came away from my neck. "Stop talking to me. I'm trying to channel my head-crackin' mamma jamma."

At my words, a hint of surprise passed his face then he got that "you're adorable" look again and even though I knew he heard me, he asked, "Your what?"

Time to stop speaking.

He watched me a beat and then looked at Lee.

"We movin'?" he asked.

"Yeah," Lee answered and his eyes cut to Dawn. "Dawn, thanks for stayin' late. We're done for the day." Then he looked down at Indy and I watched as *his* face went soft. "Luke's takin' you home."

"Lee, if you want, I can take Indy home," Dawn said sweetly, the queen of kindness.

Blech.

It was my turn to consider vomiting.

"I got her." Luke walked forward without sparing Dawn a glance.

Vance let me go and I turned to Indy just as she arrived at me and gave me a big surprise hug. I stood in her arms, uncertain what to do for a second, then I hugged her back.

"Good luck," she said when she let me go. She stayed close and whispered, "Remember, deep down, he's a great guy."

I took a breath and nodded.

Before Indy and Luke left, Luke stopped at the door and sliced his eyes to me. "Tomorrow, five thirty. Here. You and me. Don't be late."

Then he was gone.

I stared at the door but asked Vance, "What did that mean?"

"You're training with Luke tomorrow," Vance told me.

I totally lost any hold on my head-crackin' mamma jamma and my mouth dropped open. "No I'm not."

"I were you," Lee said, coming up to us, "I wouldn't be late."

I stared at the both of them.

Fuck.

⌐⍺⌐

Vance followed me to my house on his Harley. We parked Hazel in the garage. I jumped on his bike and we met Lee at a bar on Colfax, the same bar I'd seen Darius in a few days before.

We got drinks, Vance a soda, me a diet soda (even though I wanted tequila, I was still going for a clear head) and Lee a beer.

We stood at the bar, me and the badasses, surveying the room and not speaking.

Vance didn't get touchy and sexy. This was a different Vance. This was badass Vance. He was relaxed, but alert and very serious. We weren't lovers here, we were partners. How he communicated this, I could not tell you, but he did. I knew it, felt it. Anyone in that bar fucked with me, they fucked with Vance.

And it was pretty clear no one wanted to fuck with Vance.

Or Lee.

Me, now that was probably another story.

Still, we were given a wide berth.

After about ten minutes, Lee murmured, "Let's go."

I had no idea why he said this, if he got some sign, but they moved and I followed. We walked to the back of the bar, down a hall and into a room.

In the room were three people. Darius sitting at a round table with a supplier I'd heard of and seen once or twice (but didn't know his name) on Darius's left, and on his right, a pretty middle-aged black woman with tawny brown eyes and a huge afro.

"Lee Boy! Lookin' good," the woman shouted when we walked in, sounding happy and welcoming, like we'd come to her dinner party.

"Shirleen," Lee said, walking into the room. I followed. Vance followed me.

Lee put his beer bottle down and sat. I put my glass down and sat next to him, thinking this was the right thing to do. I rethought it when Vance positioned himself standing behind me and to my right. Instead of looking indecisive and getting up to stand with Vance, I kept my seat.

The supplier's eyes went to Vance. They got hard and scary and I held my breath.

Vance hadn't allowed me to bring my gun, even though I was pretty certain he and Lee were carrying, though Vance didn't share. He said it would send the wrong message for me to walk in armed. And since I'd never had a sit down with a drug dealer, and expected he knew what he was talking about, I gave in.

At that moment, though, I wished I had it just in case.

Lee felt me tense. His eyes cut to me, and quickly, to my shock, *I kid you not*, he winked at me.

Lee "Badass Mother" Nightingale winked... at... me.

I guessed this meant everything was all right. I let out my breath and tried to relax.

The seating scenario had us facing off against Darius, Shirleen and the other guy.

"So you're The Law," Shirleen said, looking at me. "You're a tiny little thing. How you flip Jermaine on his back?" she asked.

"Um..." I started, thinking I wasn't exactly tiny, but then again she *really* wasn't tiny, so it was all relative.

"Not that I think that's bad, mind," she went on as if I hadn't uttered a sound. "Jermaine is one evil brother. I do not like him *at all*. Got my friend's daughter, Shaneequa, pregnant, then left her high and dry. No child support, nothin'. We was *thrilled* when we heard you kicked him in the balls. He deserved it."

"Shirleen," Darius said quietly.

"Well, he did," Shirleen retorted. "Got his ass kicked by a white girl. A *tiny* white girl. I cannot wait to tell Shaneequa," Shirleen said to me. "Hey, now!" she exclaimed. "Why don't you come with me to see Shaneequa? She'd love to meet you. She'll give you a big, fat kiss."

"Shirleen," Darius said again, sounding more impatient now.

I stared.

I couldn't help it. This was definitely not how I expected this sit down to be.

Shirleen ignored Darius's impatience.

"I hear you work with them kids at that Shelter. Well, I got me another friend. Last year, her boy, he went to the street. So young, that boy. Do *not* know why, but he did. His parents are good people, no reason why he'd take to

173

the street. One of you social workers found him and talked to him, got him to the Shelter then got him back home. Lord knows what was goin' on in that boy's head. Still, they was glad to have him home, I can tell you that."

Darius was now sitting back, his eyes were on Lee. He was looking harassed.

"What was the boy's name?" I asked Shirleen.

"His name was Tye. Who names their child Tye, with an 'e'? What is *up* with that?" Shirleen answered but I leaned forward.

"Tye?" I asked. "I know Tye."

And I did. He *was* young, eleven, and luckily I got to him early before he'd been chewed up and spit out. He'd only been on the streets a few weeks when I talked him into the Shelter. By that time, he'd been scared out of his mind. The reunion had been quick, maybe only a few weeks more.

"You do?" Shirleen was leaning forward, too.

"Yeah. I got him off the street. He wasn't one of my cases, but we used to talk all the time in the rec room. How is he? Is he doing okay?" I went on.

"Got on the A and B Honor Roll last year," Shirleen bragged, as if he was her own son.

"Oh, that's great. Tell him I said hi."

"Will do, girl," Shirleen said to me. "Maybe I'll get him to come over when we visit Shaneequa."

"I'd like that," I replied, smiling at her.

All of a sudden Shirleen's eyes changed. They didn't go scary, like the supplier's had. They went kind. The change was so swift it took me off-guard and I had no chance to respond to it.

"Your time's better spent in that Shelter than on the street," she said.

My smile faded and I felt my head-crackin' mamma jamma coming over me. Luckily, before it got a full hold and I fucked everything up, Shirleen continued.

"Darius and me been talkin'. We're passin' the business on slow like. Too much headache, now with dealers gettin' smoke bombed and plastic wrapped. They're unhappy, want us to whack a social worker. I draw the line at whackin' social workers, un-unh. Not me. So we're makin' deals." She indicated the supplier with a nod of her head. "Boys wanna move up, we'll let 'em. We'll start with passin' off the dealers who deal to the kids. No more. We move on from there. The games are goin' good. We'll stick with that."

I felt my heart racing. I could not believe she was telling me this. I could not believe they were getting out of the drug business.

The room had gone wired. Lee had tensed beside me, waves of something—emotion, disbelief, whatever—were coming off him and bouncing off me. I felt it at my back from Vance too.

I understood what it meant. It meant this was huge.

"You all right with that?" Shirleen asked me (as if I'd say no).

I didn't trust myself to speak, so I just nodded.

"It'll take time. You should know we don't speak for the others. You take on the street, you don't have no protection from us. We're Switzerland when it comes to you. And this deal does not leave this room. Word hits the street before we pull out, it's war. Got me?" Shirleen went on. Her eyes were no longer kind. They were hard and they were sharp.

I just nodded again. She stared at me a beat that turned into two.

Then the sharpness went out of her eyes and she said quietly, "Thank you for takin' care of Tye."

Oh my God.

She'd known all along it was me who got Tye off the street.

I felt something hit my chest. A weight I hadn't felt in a long time, not since Auntie Reba died.

I knew what it was. It was tears.

I swallowed and quickly pulled myself together.

"Tye's a good kid," I said softly.

"They all are," she replied just as softly.

Then abruptly she put her hand on Darius's shoulder and stood. "I need a drink. Who needs a drink?" No one said anything. "Suit yourselves. Shirleen's gettin' a drink."

Then she was gone.

We all stayed where we were and were silent.

Finally, Lee, his eyes on Darius, asked from beside me, "She speak for you?"

Darius shook his head, not in the negative, but instead, partially amused, partially beleaguered.

"You know Aunt Shirleen," was all he said.

"You told Eddie?" Lee asked.

"We've set up a meet after this one," Darius replied.

"This gonna go well for you?" Lee went on and Darius's eyes changed, went hard, scary.

"I had to guess? No," Darius answered.

More waves of something I didn't get started pounding around the room.

"You know——?" Lee started, but Darius interrupted him.

"I know."

Lee nodded then his eyes cut to me. "Let's go."

I got up and followed Vance in order to leave the room. Lee followed me.

Before we got to the door, Darius addressed me for the first time and called, "Law."

I turned and looked at him. He stared at me, his face blank. I stared at him the same way.

Then he said, "Tye's my nephew."

This news hit me like a physical blow. It was a miracle I didn't stagger back, but somehow I found the internal strength and kept myself under control.

Again, I just nodded but didn't say a word.

Lee's hand went to my back, and with a gentle push, he moved me forward.

Without a word, we left the bar. Vance and I got on his bike and Lee got in his Crossfire.

Vance flicked two fingers at Lee, I put my arms around Vance's middle and we shot off.

⫷⫸

Vance parked close to the backdoor of my house and we got off the bike. He grabbed my hand and started toward the house, but I stopped him with a jerk on his hand. When he turned his eyes to me, I realized I was trembling.

"What just happened?" I whispered.

"We'll talk inside."

"It was important, wasn't it?"

"Jules," Vance said softly. "Let's get inside."

Then he tensed and his head swung to the side of the house, his eyes narrowing. Lee materialized out of the darkness. I stared at him as he walked to us, straight to us, straight *to me*.

My body went solid. My hand tightened in Vance's, but Lee stopped close. He leaned in, wrapped a hand around the back of my head and pulled me to him. He kissed my forehead, let me go and then, just as fast as he got there, he was gone.

I didn't realize I was holding my breath and I let it out in a rush.

"It was important," I whispered to the darkness.

Chapter 13

My List

I let us in. Vance locked the door behind us and unarmed the beeping alarm, then rearmed it for windows and doors. Throughout this he never let go of my hand.

Boo pranced into the kitchen, took one look at us and let loose with news of his day and his dissatisfaction at the wait to get his treats.

Vance murmured, "Quiet, cat."

Boo, surprisingly, ceased meowing, though he did it with a kitty pouty face.

Vance curled me into his body and his arms went around me tight.

I didn't resist this. I told my Rottweiler to hush because I needed this just this once, just this time.

I put my arms around him, pressed my face into his neck and held him back. Slowly, I felt his strong, warm body absorb my trembles until they were gone.

Vance's phone rang. He ignored it and kept hold of me.

His phone quit ringing and he said quietly, "You did well."

I nodded against his neck. Vance saying that meant a lot, more than I wanted it to mean, but I sure as hell wasn't going to let it show.

He kept hold of me as the minutes ticked by and Boo started swirling his kitty body around our ankles.

Then Vance's phone rang again. I pulled back, but Vance's arms stayed around me.

I looked at him and whispered, "I'm okay. Get your phone."

He watched me a few beats, read on my face that I wasn't fibbing, so he let me go.

While I got Boo his treats, Vance pulled out his phone, flipped it open and said, "Yeah?"

Boo came with me into the bathroom and watched while I brushed my teeth and washed my face. I slathered on my night cream that smelled of oranges and changed into my blue nightgown. I wrapped my fleecy dove gray robe around me, walked into the living room, lit some candles and a soft lamp and lay on my side on my lilac couch, Boo tucked into the crook of my lap.

I stroked him. He purred, and I thought about what a funny world it was.

I may not have saved Park, but I saved Tye, and with him I may have helped to save Darius, and maybe even Shirleen.

I listened vaguely to Vance talking on the phone in the kitchen and then listened when he stopped talking. Without him making a sound, all of a sudden he was there, his thighs in my line of vision. I followed them up, and just when my eyes hit his face he leaned over, gently gathered up Boo, dropped him in the armchair and turned back around.

Then he gathered *me*.

Picking me up, Vance turned. He sat, twisted, then settled back, lying full-length on the couch with me on top of him. I put my elbow into the seat cushion between him and the back of the couch, lifted up my torso and looked down at him.

"Anything important on the phone?" I asked.

"It'll wait," he said, eyes on my face. The fingers of one hand spread open my robe then slid from my hip and up my side.

"I like Shirleen. She's funny," I told Vance, ignoring his movements even as his hand went from my side to move forward across my ribcage.

"Everyone likes Shirleen," he replied.

"Are they going to be able to get out of the business without getting hurt?" I asked.

His fingers curled, his knuckles stroked feather light against the underside of my breast and my belly fluttered in what I was classifying as a Grade Three flutter (yes, I could classify them now, Grade Ten was an orgasm).

"Don't know," he answered.

I swallowed.

"We need to talk," I informed him, deciding it was time. Definitely time. Way past time. My emotional Rottweiler was growling warningly, telling me if I didn't do something soon it would be too late.

"All right," Vance agreed, his hand moving away from my body, but it came up, then pulled my robe down my shoulder.

"Crowe, seriously," I shrugged my shoulder to try to keep the robe in place, but he already had it down my arm and then it was off on one side.

His hand slid around my waist to my back and he pulled me to him, his mouth going to my neck.

"Talk," he said there, and I admitted to myself that I liked it when he spoke against my neck. It felt good.

"You have to listen," I said to him, feeling Grade Three rise to Grade Four, and being unable to do anything about it when his lips hit my ear and he traced the outer edges with his tongue.

"I'm listening," he murmured in my ear when he was done.

A shiver went through me.

Okay, whatever. I had to move on before I lost the will to move on.

He wanted it this way, fine.

"We have to stop seeing each other," I announced.

I'd lost track of his hand, what with his mouth at my ear, but now I felt it pull my nightgown to my waist. Then his hand slid down inside my underwear and cupped my ass.

Oh crap.

That felt good, too.

"How about we stop seein' each other tomorrow?" Vance suggested.

"Crowe..." I started, getting the distinct impression he wasn't taking me seriously, but he stopped me speaking by kissing me. While he did this, he pulled out my ponytail holder and my hair fell around us.

When his mouth disengaged from mine, I was breathing heavily and his lips slid back to my neck.

"How're you feelin'?" he asked quietly.

I nodded. At that point, with his hand at my ass and his lips at my neck, I was feeling *fine*.

His head came back and he looked at me. His eyes were warm, his face soft and sexy, and his hand at my behind moved to the small of my back. He started stroking me lightly there with his fingertips and tingles were sliding across my skin.

"Are you tender?" he went on and I realized what he was asking.

I shook my head.

One of his hands pulled back my hair and wrapped it around his fist. The other hand went from the small of my back, sliding across my side to cup my breast.

When his thumb stroked my nipple I shot to Grade Five.

He kissed me again, deep and lots of tongue, then soft, sweet, light, quick kisses, then lots of tongue again. The whole time his thumb stroked my nipple and his hand was fisted in my hair.

By the time he stopped kissing me, I was firmly established at Grade Six.

I completely forgot about not seeing him anymore. I shrugged off the other side of my robe and threw it over the back of the couch. Then I yanked his t-shirt out of his jeans. He let go of my hair, did an ab curl, I pulled the tee over his head and tossed it aside. My mouth went to his collarbone and down his chest, exploring, watching the muscles contract, fascinated and so turned on I took myself to Grade Seven.

When I made it to his stomach and was sliding lower, using my lips and my tongue, he pulled me up and kissed me again, hot and to the edge of control.

"I want you to ride me," he murmured against my mouth, and just those words shot me to Grade Eight. His eyes looked into mine. "You think you could do that?" he asked.

I bit my lip and nodded. I was pretty sure I could do that. If not, I was a quick learner.

His hand went back into my panties, sliding them part the way down my behind, and he whispered, lips still against my mouth, "Take off your underwear."

My heart was beating so hard, I thought he had to be able to feel it. I swung my hips and legs up to the side, pulled off my underwear and tossed it to the floor. When I finished, to hide the fact that I felt somewhat embarrassed by what I'd just done, I put my mouth on his and kissed him.

One of his hands was at my ass, the other one between us working at his belt and fly. His mouth and tongue went to my neck, my tingles turned to shivers, the shivers to trembles. I was teetering on the edge of Grade Nine and he wasn't even inside me yet.

"You sat there, facin' a drug dealer across the table, totally in control. Like you were made of ice," Vance whispered against my neck. "I was so fucking proud of you."

Oh my *God*.

He did *not* just say that.

"Vance," I breathed, my heart racing for a new reason, a different kind of warmth spreading through me.

His fingers curled around my wrist, pulled my hand between us and wrapped it around him. My head shot around and I stared at him. I'd never touched a man like that before, nowhere near it.

"Sit up," he ordered softly before I could freak out.

He kept my hand where it was. I positioned myself to sit astride him, pulling up my knees on the couch, lifting up my torso. As I did, our hands together guiding him, he slid inside me and then gently Vance pulled our hands away.

Then I was up and he had filled me.

It was *nice*. Grade Nine nice.

"Wow," I whispered.

His hands came to my hips and he coaxed me to move. It didn't take a lot of coaxing; it came naturally. I moved and found my rhythm, one of Vance's hands at my waist, one cupping my ass. It felt great to be in control. Unbelievable.

I watched him as I moved. His eyes were locked on mine, that intense, possessive "mine" look in them. If anything, it made me breathe faster; my heart tripping in my chest, the trembles gathering, joining forces, gaining momentum and then shooting between my legs.

"Come closer," Vance demanded, and without hesitation I leaned into him. "Hold on to me," he ordered, and I put my hands on his shoulders, and he again looked me in the eyes.

That was when he bucked, slamming inside me. I moaned. I couldn't help it; it felt so good. He did it again and again and I learned what he meant by riding him, and if I thought it was unbelievable before, I was mistaken. *This* was unbelievable.

His hand went between us. He touched me at the exact right spot and my hips jerked. I moved with his hand and his bucking hips. I bent closer, my chest against his, my lips against his, and he kissed me.

I was close, heading toward Grade Ten like a rocket.

"Say my name," he demanded.

I opened my eyes and looked into his. He slammed into me again, his finger pressing deep and moving.

Grade Ten hit me with an overwhelming force, and when it did, against his mouth, I moaned his name.

I found there was an annoying side effect to having an orgasm, a side effect that Vance didn't seem to share.

My body became acquiescent and my mind drifted to ridiculous thoughts, like what I'd wear to my birthday party.

I never worried about what I was going to wear.

Vance held me for a while after we finished, me still astride him, him still inside me, my mind inventorying my closet and deciding I needed to go to the mall.

Then he knifed up so he was seated, me still astride him, and I made a little mew because it felt kind of good. I could swear I felt him smile against my neck when he heard the sound.

He disengaged from me gently, pulling me up at the waist. He turned in the seat and set me on my feet in front of him. He held me steady, hands at my hips, still seated, looking up at me, and I stared down at him.

God, he was beautiful.

He got up, pulled up his jeans and picked me up, again cradled in his arms. He carried me to bed, deposited me on the end of it and I had just enough wherewithal to crawl towards the pillows and collapse.

Vance got fully undressed in the hall and followed me up, pulling the covers out from beneath me and then over both of us. He turned me into his arms, tucking my face in his neck.

"Jules."

"Mm?" I murmured. My mind had wandered again and I was thinking I might need more underwear, and maybe a new pair of ass-kicking boots, from the mall.

As well as my party outfit, of course.

"I didn't use protection."

At his words, my trip to the mall went out of my head with a "poof", and my body went rock-solid. Then I unfroze, pulled back and looked at him.

He was smiling.

Smiling.

I stared at him like he was a lunatic.

"What, exactly, is there to smile about?" I yelled. Visions of Vance teaching a dark haired little boy how to feloniously disable an alarm popped unwanted into my head, and I quit yelling and breathed, "Oh my God." Then I repeated it, "Oh my God."

He rolled me to my back, his body mostly over mine. He came up on his elbow, still smiling.

"Calm down," he said.

"Calm... *calm down?* I'm always lecturing the kids about using condoms. I'm like... why didn't you... oh my *God*."

"I'll use protection next time."

My eyes narrowed. "Next time?"

He kissed me softly then pulled back. "Yeah," he said casually.

"It might be too late," I informed him, deciding to fight the "next time" fight later.

I mean, didn't men flip out about these things, too? His behavior was just bizarre.

He didn't respond.

"What if it's too late?" I asked.

"If it's too late, you'll make a good mother, if you remember to get a baby-sitter before you go out and crack heads."

My eyes bugged out and my mouth dropped open. He was making jokes. *Making jokes.*

He took in my bug-eyed look and I felt his body shake with laughter. Then I *heard* his laughter and my blood pressure skyrocketed.

"This is *not* funny, Crowe," I snapped.

"Yeah it is."

"What's so damned funny about it?"

"You," he replied. "You're very cute, Princess."

Um.

He did *not* just say that.

"Vance..." I said his name in my-word-is-law-and-you-are-in-*trouble* voice.

He ignored my voice. "What's done is done. We can't go back. There's no point getting upset about it."

"Excuse me, but—" I interrupted, but he talked over me.

"Odds are I didn't get you pregnant, but if there's anyone I know who could cope, it's you."

"Maybe I don't want to cope," I snapped.

He grinned. "Too late now."

He thought this was hilarious.

I slapped his arm. "Stop grinning."

He ran his fingers through my hair at the side of my head and then curled a bunch of it around his fist.

"Motherhood won't be a challenge for you," he went on, laughter in his voice.

Apparently he thought he was funny. I frowned at him. I did not think he was funny.

At all.

"Let's see, Sunday night, you saved a runaway from a drug dealer," he started.

"I did not, you did. He was kicking my ass," I reminded him.

He talked over me. "Monday night, you brought down two dealers single-handedly."

"Well, I *did* do that," I allowed.

He kept talking. "Tuesday night, you had to take a break from keeping the streets safe for the citizens of Denver to go out with me."

"Crowe—"

"Tonight, you began the healing process of three brothers who'd been torn apart by tragedy. They're not blood, but brothers all the same."

"Stop talking."

"What're you gonna do tomorrow? Cure world hunger?"

"Crowe, I said *stop talking.*"

He started to laugh again. He let go of my hair, curled his arms around me and rolled to his back, taking me with him. I lifted my head, planted my forearms in his chest and frowned down at him, but he ignored my frown and kept talking. Or, I should say, teasing.

"Discover the cure for cancer?"

"Crowe. I'll say it again, this is *not* funny."

His face changed, went soft. His tractor beam switched on and he finished quietly, almost as if he was talking to himself. "Motherhood won't be a challenge for you."

"Crowe."

"Stop worrying about it, Jules. We'll deal with it if it happens."

"No, *we* won't. We're over. Done. I'm breaking up with you," I announced.

There. I did it.

His hand twisted in my hair again and he brought my face to his. "You can break up with me on Friday. I wanna take you to your birthday party tomorrow."

Well, I guessed I didn't do it and he was still not taking me seriously.

"Stop joking, I'm being serious," I informed him.

He brought my face the rest of the way to his and kissed me. Not softly this time, there was meaning to his kiss.

I was a little breathless and my head was slightly muddled when his lips detached from mine, but I kept at it even when his lips went to my neck.

"We need to talk about this," I told him.

"We'll talk about it on Friday," he murmured against my neck, and I knew the way he said it that he had absolutely no intention of talking about it Friday.

Then his tongue slid from my jaw to my shoulder and I shivered.

"We need to talk about it now," I tried to speak in my word-is-law voice, but it came out breathy.

"Friday," he rolled me to my back again and came over me.

"Vance—"

His mouth against mine, he said softly, "Shut up Jules."

"Stop telling me to shut up."

He kissed me quiet, and while he did his hand went up my nightgown, straight to my breast and his thumb took a swipe at my nipple. I gasped against his mouth, and after my gasp he lifted his head an inch and looked me in the eye. His eyes were now full-on intense. His sexual tractor beam had gone super-powered and all my breath escaped my lungs.

"You wanna talk while I go down on you, be my guest. But I'm finally gonna taste you, and then I'm gonna fuck you again, and it might be distracting."

Oh my *God*.

I was already at Grade Six.

"You wanna talk?" he asked.

I immediately shook my head. Not because I didn't have anything to say, but mainly because I couldn't speak.

He grinned and it was wicked.

Then his mouth came to mine and after that he did as he promised.

But he wore a condom this time.

The house was dark. Boo was snuggled into the small of my back and I was curled into Vance's side, my arm around his waist, his tucked under and curled around me, hand at my hip.

I was thinking that sex was good, but oral sex might be even better. It was a tossup, and I was mentally enumerating the pros (there were lots) and cons (I couldn't find any) of both when Vance said softly, "Tell me about your Aunt Reba."

Still in the throes of post-orgasm mellowness, I didn't clam up.

Instead, I asked, "What do you want to know?"

His fingers were tracing patterns on my hip and I liked the feel of it. It was sweet and relaxing.

"Did she look like you?" he asked.

I shook my head against his shoulder but said, "Maybe a little in the face. I look like my Mom. I have my Dad's hair."

At that, Vance's hand went from my hip. His fingers captured a tendril of my hair and I could feel him twisting it at my back. That was sweet and relaxing, too.

"She was wise," I whispered, smiling against his shoulder and thinking about Auntie Reba. "She was a lot younger than my Mom but very wise. I know a lot of people don't believe in this kind of thing, but I'm sure she had an old soul."

His body heat was warming me. I pushed closer to him and for some reason kept talking.

"She was really young when my family died, probably too young to take me on, but she was all I had left. Nick and her had just started going out when it happened. I think they got married because of me."

When I stopped talking, Vance didn't say anything so I kept going.

"Not that they wouldn't have gotten married anyway. Nick... I've never seen a love like that. He's still lost to this day without her. I used to wish he'd find someone, but he never will. It makes me sad, but I'm glad Auntie Reba still has someone to love her like that. She deserved it because she gave her love like that."

Vance stopped twirling my hair and turned into me, wrapping both his arms around me.

He remained silent and I looked at his face in the moonlight from the window. Then, do not ask me why, looking at Vance in the moonlight, I shared my most favorite memory of my Auntie Reba.

"Nick and I used to listen to music. A lot. Nick was into Southern Rock, but also a big fan of Elton John. I loved Stevie Wonder, and Nick liked to encourage my love of music, so he bought me everything that had anything to do with Stevie. I remember lying in our living room. We lived in a different house then. I had my back on this big, pink beanbag they bought me for Christmas, and Nick and I were listening to Stevie. Auntie Reba came in and lay down beside me, her back on the beanbag with me. Stevie's 'Isn't She Lovely' came on and Auntie Reba grabbed my hand in the middle of the song. After the song was done, she just looked at me."

I sucked in my lips and Vance's hand came to my jaw. His thumb ran across my lower lip when I released it, and his eyes, I could tell, were looking in mine.

I was whispering when I carried on, "I knew what she meant. She didn't have to say anything. Even though I wasn't their child, I knew what she meant. Have you heard that song? Do you know what I mean?"

"I've heard the song," he responded softly.

I took in a breath. It broke in the middle but I kept it together.

Then I stared at him, and with a lot of courage and a little moonlight, I asked quietly, "What was your Mom like?"

He answered immediately, "She was beautiful. She was broken."

I waited but he didn't continue.

"Do you ever think you'll try to find them?" I asked.

"I know where they are."

I blinked at him. "Have you...?" I started, but he knew what I was going to say.

"No," he answered.

"Will you?"

"No."

"Do you want to tell me about it?" I whispered, my stomach clenching, my heart slowing, knowing I shouldn't care, but wanting him to say yes.

"No," he said.

I nodded, letting him have his space, but feeling disappointment running through me like acid. I dipped my chin and pressed my face into his throat so he wouldn't see it.

"Maybe," he said from above me, "if you break up with me on Saturday, I might tell you on Friday."

My body went still.

"Though, I'm thinkin' I'll tell you on Saturday if you break up with me on Sunday."

My head tipped back and he was grinning down at me.

My eyes narrowed on him. "Crowe."

"Shut up Jules."

"Don't tell me—"

His lips touched mine. "Shut up," he said quietly. "Go to sleep."

I tried to force my way out of his arms, but they went ultra-tight and he kept me where I was.

"You're very annoying," I told his throat.

He didn't answer.

"I'm still breaking up with you on Friday," I went on.

"No you aren't."

I went silent.

Whatever.

I tried to hold a grudge, but I was too tired. His body was too warm and I'd had two orgasms. A grudge was physically and mentally impossible.

Instead, my body relaxed, my mind went blank and I fell asleep.

⇥⇤

I was dead asleep when I felt Vance tense then move swiftly. He'd been pressed against my back and I felt the cool air when his body came away from mine.

I turned, got up on an elbow and watched Boo go flying off the bed just as Vance vanished over the side.

I came up to a seated position, confused, then my breath caught in my throat when I heard a knock on the backdoor. It opened, the alarm started beeping its warning and Nick called, "Jules?"

"Hey Nick!" I yelled immediately and rolled forward, taking the sheet with me. I twisted to the side, yanking the sheet around me, frantic now for a different reason. I threw my legs over the side of the bed, missed the steps and went flying.

I would have landed likely painfully on all fours, but Vance caught me at the last minute with an arm around my waist. I doubled over his arm with an "oof". He pulled my torso up and set me on my feet, his arm still around me, my back to his front.

Throughout all of this, Nick kept talking while he punched in my alarm code and walked through the kitchen. "I thought I'd treat the birthday girl to coffee and a muffin. What do you say to——?"

He stopped talking when he hit the doorway to the hall and caught sight of Vance and me. Then he came to a dead halt.

Oh crap.

I really hoped that Vance had some clothes on even though I did not, just the sheet. Somewhere during the second round last night I'd lost my nightgown.

Um...

How embarrassing was this?

"Nick——" I started.

He didn't miss a beat. "Vance can come, too."

"Nick."

"We'll go to Fortnum's. I hear they have a great new coffee guy," Nick continued.

I nodded, deciding to pretend I was dressed, life was cool and I wasn't caught by the only father I remembered standing in an advanced state of undress in the arms of... whatever Vance was to me.

"That sounds good," I said.

"Vance?" Nick's eyes went over my shoulder.

"Yeah," Vance said.

"Great. Just knock on my door when you two are ready."

Nick turned to leave and I sagged against Vance's body. Then he turned back and I went ramrod straight again.

I heard Vance's quiet laughter in my ear and I kept my face perfectly composed and my body still so as not to turn around and gouge his eyes out.

"Just to say... I'll be a little more cautious next time. Don't want to get shot in the ass walking into my niece's kitchen," Nick remarked.

Behind his glasses, Nick was laughing too.

The men in my life. I wanted to murder them all except Roam and Sniff, but they weren't men yet, they were boys. When they became men I was sure they'd get scratched onto Jules Hit List just because men on the whole were vastly annoying and they wouldn't be able to help themselves.

Before I could say anything, Nick was gone.

The minute I heard the door close, I whirled on Vance and saw that luckily he had his jeans on. Unfortunately, he had his gun in his hand.

I ignored his gun and the sight of his chest (very hard to ignore, seriously) and clipped, "What's funny now?"

Instead of answering, he snatched me into his arms and kissed me, full-on, full tongue. Even in a snit, I had to admit, it was delicious.

When he lifted his head, he said in his silky voice, "Happy birthday, Princess."

Um…

Wow.

He looked at me with sexy eyes and stated, "Let's take a shower."

I could do a shower. I could do a lot of things after a "happy birthday" like that.

He let me go and twisted to put the gun on the side of the bed platform by the mattress.

That was when I saw his back.

"Oh my God," I breathed.

Vance came back around to me, but my eyes didn't move from the space where I'd seen it, even though I was now staring at his chest.

"Jules?" I heard him call.

I walked around him and he came with me, but I put my hand to his waist and whispered, "Stand still."

Surprisingly, he did as I asked.

I got to his back and saw the puckered scar of the gunshot wound. I put both my hands on him then, my arms tight against my sides to hold up the sheet. One hand went to his belly, one hand at the small of his back.

I leaned around and looked at his chest.

Nothing.

I looked to his back again.

Gunshot wound.

I went back to his chest then to his back and again.

Then...

I lost my mind.

"They shot you in the back?" I yelled.

He turned to face me. "Jules."

I lifted my eyes to his face.

"*The back?*" I shouted.

His arms started to come around me but I jerked away.

"What kind of asshole shoots someone in the back?" I was still shouting.

"Jules, listen——"

"That is just... I cannot believe... no one shoots anyone in the back. Only gutless sissies would shoot someone in the back." My brows drew together and I frowned at Vance. "What happened?"

Correctly reading that there was no way he could interfere with my rant, Vance leaned against the bed platform and crossed his arms.

"I can't tell you. When it happened, we were workin' a contract with the Feds."

I put my hands on my hips. The sheet started unraveling so I compromised and put one hand to my hip while the other one held the sheet around me.

"How did you get shot in the back?" I asked.

"I can't tell you that, Jules."

I looked to the ceiling.

"I just cannot believe this shit," I told the ceiling like it would respond. Then I looked back at Vance. "I want a word with Lee. Government contracts where you go up against cowardly assholes that would shoot his men in the back, I... think... *not.*"

"I'm fine," Vance assured me.

"I know you're fine. I can *see* you're fine. I do not *care* if you are fine." I ended my tirade enunciating every word like my life depended on that particular communication.

In the face of my anger, Vance started laughing.

Laughing!

My body prepared to have a stroke.

"This is not fucking funny!" I shouted.

He moved fast. His hands came to my hips giving me a swift yank. I flew forward and slammed against his body.

His shaking-with-laughter body.

His arms went around me. His face went to my neck and I felt his laughter there, too.

Finally he said, "You wanna break up with me now?"

Oh my *God*.

He did *not* just say that.

"What's your middle name?" I snapped.

His head came up and he was still smiling. "Why?"

"Tell me your middle name," I demanded.

He kept smiling but he told me. "It's Ouray."

I blinked. "Ouray? Like, the town?"

"Yeah. It's Ute. It means 'arrow'."

"Okay, then," I took a deep breath and let loose, "Vance Ouray Crowe, do not fucking piss me off. It's my fucking birthday and when I say this is not funny, it is not fucking funny!"

Vance stared at me a beat, that Jules-is-downright-adorable look in his eye.

Then he asked conversationally, his arrogant grin replacing his smile, "Do you think Nick'll wait for coffee long enough for me to fuck you?"

My eyes narrowed.

"You've just moved to the top of my list," I informed him snottily.

His grin didn't waver. "Your list?"

"My 'Men in My Life I'm Going to Kill' List. You're at the top."

This time he threw his head back and laughed, full body, full throated, full-on laughter.

When he was finished, his eyes came back to me and he said, "You can kill me after I fuck you."

"Vance!"

His mouth came to mine and he gave me a soft kiss. "Shut up, Jules. We need to shower."

"It's my birthday. Don't tell me to shut up."

"Nick's waiting. You can keep yellin' at me later."

This was true, Nick was waiting.

I pulled out of his arms and stomped to the kitchen, grumbling under my breath and tightening the sheet around me. "I have to feed Boo. *Then* we can

194

take a shower. *Then* we'll go to coffee. *Then* I'm gonna call Lee and give him a piece of my mind."

I heard the bathroom door close and I realized Vance wasn't listening to a thing I said.

I yanked Boo's food bowl out of the cupboard and slammed it on the counter.

What*ever*.

Chapter 14

Your Real Family

Nick walked into Fortnum's ahead of Vance and me. We walked in (I kid you not) holding hands. Or Vance was holding my hand and I was giving myself a secret birthday present by letting him.

Yes, the badass mother and the head-crackin' mamma jamma holding hands. The dealers would probably piss their pants laughing if they saw us.

The place was packed.

Tex, Jet and Ally were working the espresso counter. Indy was clearing used cups from the seating area. The big, gray-haired, gravelly-voiced Harley guy was behind the book counter next to a woman I hadn't seen the first time I was there. She was dark-haired, painfully thin and very tall.

"Oh fuck," the Harley guy said loudly when he saw me. "Batten down the hatches."

Nick's eyes moved to the Harley guy and then narrowed when Nick saw that he was talking about me.

"What's his problem?" Nick asked just as loudly, turning to Vance and me.

Um.

Uh-oh.

"I've no idea," I replied, feigning innocence.

"She's my problem," the Harley guy answered, still looking at me. "We've had the works. Indy's kidnappings and murder. Jet's kidnappings and rape attempt. Roxie's kidnapping and stalking. Car bombs. Grenades. Knife fights. Female wrestling at Chinese restaurants. Mayhem at a haunted house. Gunshots at a strip club. Showdowns at society parties. Now we got a vigilante on our hands." The man looked at Vance while the tall woman edged away from him and disappeared into the shelves which I thought was a smart move. "What is it with you boys?" he asked Vance. "I really wanna know."

Everyone was staring at us, and there were a lot of everyones. Nick and I were staring at the Harley guy, both of our mouths open.

"Excuse me, I've gotta talk to Duke," Vance murmured, face blank, which I didn't figure was a good sign. He let go of my hand and walked to the book counter.

Nick's arm went around my shoulders and he dipped his head to my ear. "You think he knows about you?" he whispered.

"Yeah," I nodded, "I think he knows about me."

"Do you know what he's talking about? Mayhem at a haunted house? Gunshots at a strip club?" Nick asked.

"Some of it," I answered.

Nick looked closely at me. He was wearing a rendition of his Morgue Face with a little bit of "Oh my God" thrown in. Then he shook his head.

"Don't tell me. I don't wanna know," he said.

"Gotcha," I replied, thinking he really didn't want to know.

"Shee-it, it's the fuckin' birthday girl," Tex boomed from behind the counter, a crazy-man grin on his face. "Get up here, Law."

"Hey Tex," I called.

"Do you know these people?" Nick was still whispering as he led me toward the coffee bar.

"Um... yeah. We've kind of become friends. Vance hangs out here," I answered.

"Ah," Nick said slowly, though his expression showed that he didn't know if that was a good thing.

"Get outta the way. Get... the fuck... outta the way. There's a birthday girl here. She comes to the front of the line," Tex was booming at the customers. They were looking at each other. Some of them seemed taken aback. Others, likely the regulars, just did what they were told.

"I'll make you today's special. Vanilla and spice. It's a knockout and it's on me," Tex told me as we approached him then. When we arrived at the counter, he asked, "Who's this guy?" His eyes were on Nick.

I introduced Nick to everyone. Indy came up and gave me a birthday hug and Jet and Ally wished me a happy birthday while they completed coffees.

We placed our orders and moved to the other side of the counter to wait for our drinks. Vance met us there. When he did I looked back at Duke. Duke was frowning at me. I looked at Vance again.

"Everything okay?" I asked.

Vance just smiled at me. I decided to take that as a "yes", though Duke's face said it was a "no".

"What're you havin'?" Tex boomed at Vance.

"Sorry, but I was next." The male customer at the front of the line, clearly having a death wish, spoke up.

Tex's eyes cut to the customer and his brows drew together.

Um.

Yikes.

"Oh yeah? You are?" Tex asked the customer.

"Uh… yeah," the customer answered, now sounding not so sure even though he was standing at the front of the line.

"You a badass motherfucker who hunts down drug dealers at night?" Tex went on.

The customer stared at Tex, then he stared at Vance, then he stared back at Tex.

"Er… no," he replied.

"You a badass motherfucker *at all?*" Tex continued.

The customer looked at Vance. Then he looked at Tex. The customer had thinning sandy-brown hair, was an inch or two shorter than me, was wearing a suit and was perhaps ten pounds underweight. He was no badass motherfucker. He looked like an accountant.

The customer decided belatedly to keep his mouth shut.

"That boy is a badass motherfucker. Badass motherfuckers get their coffee first. It's a rule at Fortnum's. You become a badass motherfucker, you get to go to the front of the line. You got me?" Tex declared.

The customer nodded, perhaps the only thing he was able to do, which I figured was why he didn't turn around and leave.

Tex turned back to Vance. "Now, what'll it be?"

"Americano, room for cream," Vance said. His lips, I noted, were twitching. I could tell he wanted to grin, but he was trying really hard not to.

"You got it," Tex returned.

I waited. Then, when nothing else happened, I took a deep breath and relaxed, thinking that our dramatic entrance was over.

I was wrong. Very, very wrong.

All of a sudden Tex boomed again. This time he pointed at the couch in front of the window with a wide arc of his arm, the espresso filter in his hand. A pot of used, soggy grounds went flying across the room to splat on the floor in front of the couch. The people preparing to sit on the couch jumped away from the splattering grounds.

"What now?" Nick muttered from beside me.

"You! Yeah you!" Tex boomed, shaking the filter at a couple standing frozen in front of the couch. "Do not put your asses on that couch. The Law is sittin' there with her uncle. Move!"

"Tex, we're fine," I said, my eyes on the scurrying customers.

"Stop scaring the customers," Indy snapped over my words. Her hands were on her hips. "And stop tossing the portafilter around. You're getting coffee grounds everywhere. Do you ever clean them up when you do that? *No!* I clean them up. Jet cleans them up. Jane cleans them up. Does Tex clean them up? No, Tex does *not* clean them up!"

Jet was giggling, hips leaned against the back counter, arms wrapped around her middle. Ally was grinning like a loon while she grabbed a towel and hustled towards the couch to clean up the grounds.

I was thinking if I had one birthday wish, I would start the day again and miss Fortnum's and getting caught by Nick wearing nothing but a sheet. Though I'd keep the shower with Vance. It was fast but it was *nice*.

"That's the best goddamned seat in the house," Tex explained to Indy, cutting into my thoughts, "and Law's sittin' there."

"Tex—" Indy began.

"No lip!" Tex slammed down Nick's cappuccino next to my special and the foam sloshed over the sides. Then he looked at me. "Sit!"

"All right, we're sitting," I said, smiling at him, hopefully placatingly. "Calm down, big man."

Tex glared at the next customer, the unfortunate who'd opened his mouth. "She's a badass motherfuckeress. She'd kick your ass soon as look at you. You've clapped your eyes on The Law. Count yourself lucky, sucker. Now, what'll it fuckin' be?"

I looked at the ceiling. Then I looked at the customer who was now staring at me and shook my head with an apologetic wince.

"I see you've given up on keepin' a low profile," Nick remarked, walking with me to the couch.

I decided to keep my mouth shut. I heard Vance laugh softly beside me. I threw him a frown. Then his laughter became not-so-soft.

Whatever.

We settled on a couch, me by the arm, Vance on the arm next to me, Nick on the seat on my other side.

Nick took a sip of his cappuccino. His eyes got big and he stared into his paper cup. "Now I understand why they put up with him. This coffee is great."

I just nodded and took a sip of my own and decided "great" didn't do it justice.

Nick's hand went into his jacket and he pulled out a long, thin box, wrapped with pink paper topped with a little pink bow

"Happy birthday, sweetheart," he said, his eyes warm on my face, handing the box to me.

I slammed my special on the table in front of me and clapped. I couldn't help it, I loved presents and Nick's presents were *the best*.

"What is it?" I asked stupidly.

"Open it." Nick smiled at me.

I took it and ripped into it like a girlie girl (I did have a reason; seriously, his presents were the best). I tore off the paper and threw open the box.

Then I froze.

In it was a silver bracelet, a beautiful silver bracelet. It was made of hammered, matte silver squares each about an inch wide held together by small links. Each square was different. Some had etchings, some pieces of gold or copper soldered on to them. Four of them had stones of varying shapes, sizes and colors.

"I had it made special," Nick told me and started pointing. "That one's blue topaz, your mother's birthstone. That one's garnet, your father's. That's peridot, for Mikey. The last one's amethyst, for Reba."

At his words, the weight hit me in the chest again so hard my body moved with the force of it. I leaned back and I felt Vance's warm thigh against my back. My throat closed and my vision got blurry.

"Nick," I whispered.

Nick looked at me then started talking fast. "Now, Jules, don't start. If you start, I'll—"

"Where's your birthstone?" I asked, my voice soft, and it sounded croaky.

"That bracelet represents your family," Nick explained.

"Yeah. I know," I replied, my voice still sounding funny. "Where's your birthstone?"

"Your real family, Jules," Nick said softly.

I stared at him a beat then I slowly leaned into him, put my hand on his knee and looked in his eyes.

"Yeah. I know," I repeated. "Where's *your* stone?"

Nick just looked at me, and the way he did made me start blinking, fast.

I was not going to cry, I wasn't. Not in front of Nick, who would cry with me. I knew it and I didn't want that for him. Not in front of Vance (no way in hell). And not in front of everyone at Fortnum's who thought I was a head-crackin' mamma jamma.

"Here," I said, pulling the bracelet out of the box and throwing the box on the table. "Put it on me." I handed it to him and then gave him my wrist. I forced brightness into my voice and continued as if the emotional moment had never occurred, "I want to know where you got it. Your stone is emerald, right?"

"Yeah, sweetheart. That's right," Nick murmured, his voice sounding funny, too.

"You'll take me there. We'll get them to put in another square. Okay?"

"Okay," he whispered.

He fastened it on me and I shook my wrist around.

"Beautiful, Nick. Perfect." I leaned in and kissed his cheek. "Thanks."

"You're welcome, Jules."

I turned to Vance and shook my wrist at him. "See? Isn't it pretty?"

Vance grabbed my wrist, which was shaking too hard for him to see anything, and he held it fast. My eyes, which were avoiding his, moved to look at him.

He was staring down at me. He had that "mine" possessive look on his face, but that other look was there, too. The look that clawed at my memory and made my heart skip every other beat.

I stared at him, captured by the look, flipping through my memory cabinets to find the memory, but before I could the look was gone.

His hand twisted so that his fingers laced in mine. He gave my hand a gentle yank and I came forward. He leaned down and kissed me softly.

"It's beautiful," he said when he was done kissing me, and I was stuck staring at him again.

"Well!" Nick said from behind us and Vance let me go. That moment was lost, too, and I turned to Nick. "I gotta get to work. You two goin' out tonight?" he asked, standing up.

I stood up with him and felt Vance move to his feet behind me, then he got close.

"No. The gang here is having a party for me. I'm not sure when and where, but when I find out, will you come?" I asked.

Nick watched me a second, not able to hide his surprise at any gang throwing a party for me. I had a slumber party once when I was thirteen. That was it. I wasn't Johnny-no-mates. I had friends and went to their parties, but had only ever had that one party for me.

Then Nick's eyes moved to Vance. He stared at Vance for a few beats, did a slow smile and looked at me.

"Wouldn't miss it for the world." He leaned in and kissed my cheek. He shook Vance's hand, grabbed his cappuccino, then he was gone.

I watched the door close behind him then I turned to Vance.

"I have to get to work, too," I told him, feeling weird at what he'd witnessed; weird as in exposed.

He nodded, his arm came around me and pulled me to his body. Clearly Vance didn't feel weird.

"Don't forget, you're trainin' with Luke at five thirty," he reminded me.

I shook my head. "I can't."

"Why not?"

"I have to go to the mall. Buy a party outfit."

Vance grinned. "Not sure Luke will accept the mall as an excuse."

"I'm not sure I care if Luke will accept it or not."

"Five thirty," Vance said, still grinning.

"Crowe, I need to go to the mall." It sounded almost, but thankfully not quite, like a whine.

Vance didn't respond to my whine.

Instead, he said, "I'll meet you at your house in time to take you to the party."

"We don't know when or where that'll be."

"I'm sure we'll find out."

I was sure he wasn't wrong. Most of the party planners were in the very same room and he worked with their boyfriends.

"All right," I gave in.

"Pack a bag. I want you at my place tonight."

That got a Grade Three flutter right off the bat. I wanted to see where Vance lived. I knew I shouldn't want to, but I did. I also wanted him to "want" me at his place. I knew I shouldn't want that either, but I did.

And it was my birthday so I should get what I wanted.

It was then my emotional Rottweiler started panting and whining.

Damn.

"Vance—" I started.

"Pack a bag."

My eyes narrowed. "Seriously, you're going to have to do something about that macho-speak."

"Jules, pack a bag."

I frowned at him. He stared at me.

Then I gave in.

"All *right*," I said.

He kissed me again, softly, and I was a bit disappointed at getting a soft, sweet kiss. Not that it was a bad kiss, not at all, but it *was* my birthday.

When his head moved away, he was wearing his shit-eating grin like he knew my thoughts.

"Later, Princess," he said.

Then he was gone.

No sooner had he vanished than the Rock Chicks descended.

"Let me see that bracelet," Indy demanded, grabbing my wrist. "That's gorgeous! I want one!"

"I see you didn't break up with Vance last night," Jet said, smiling at me.

"I did," I told her. "He just kinda ignored me."

She was still smiling.

Whatever.

"I have a problem," I told them. "I need to go to work and I need to train with Luke at five thirty, and then there's the party, and somewhere in between I need to go to the mall and get a party outfit."

"You have a lunch hour?" Indy asked immediately, dropping my wrist.

"You're training with Luke?" Ally asked, eyes wide.

"Yeah, but it's only an hour," I told Indy. "And, yeah, but against my will," I told Ally.

"Doesn't matter," Indy said. "Meet us at Cherry Creek Mall. By Aveda. Noon. We'll sort you out."

"But——" I started.

"Noon," Indy repeated.

"I wanna train with Luke," Ally put in.

"Everyone wants to train with Luke," Jet replied.

We all looked at each other. Then we all started giggling.

Once we were done giggling, Indy and Ally went back to work, but Jet walked me to the door, checking out my bracelet.

I looked at her.

I wanted to ask, but I didn't want to ask. I wanted to know but I didn't want to know.

Oh hell, I just went for it.

"Jet?"

Her head came around to look at me. I stopped and so did she.

"Yeah?"

"What's it mean when a guy holds your hand?" I asked.

Her fingers were around my wrist. They moved to wrap around my hand.

"It means he likes you," she replied.

"What's it mean when he's a guy like Vance?" I went on.

Her hand squeezed mine.

"It means he really likes you," she repeated.

"What's it mean when he's a known player and a guy like Vance?" I kept at it.

She reached out and grabbed my other hand. "Jules, it means he really, *really* likes you," she said softly.

I sighed. "I was afraid of that."

She smiled at me. "I told Roxie and I'll tell you: trust me on this, don't fight it," Jet said.

My voice got low. "I have to."

"Why?"

"I don't know, I just do," I lied. I knew perfectly well, I just didn't want to share.

She nodded. "I understand."

I blinked at her. "You do?"

"I'll tell you about Eddie and me sometime. Actually," she said, her eyes getting bright, "I take that back. Fight it. It's much more interesting that way."

"For who?" I asked.

"All of us," she grinned, "including you."

Hmm.

That did *not* sound good.

⋙⋘

The girls (and boys) and I swung into the doors at King's only ten minutes late from my lunch hour.

We'd just conquered Cherry Creek Mall and in the trunk of Hazel I had a new party outfit with shoes, a new nightie to take to Vance's on my sleepover, two new sets of very sexy underwear; a cute pair of cords I didn't really need, a couple of t-shirts I really didn't need, a fantastic new blouse I really, really didn't need, and a serious new pair of ass-kicking boots.

This was accomplished because it wasn't just Indy, Jet and Ally who met me at the mall. Roxie, Daisy, Tod and Stevie had come with.

I stood in different fitting rooms in different stores and they threw clothes at me. In came clothes, out went clothes. Some would go scout other stores and whisk me away on the trot if they saw something I *had* to try on.

I didn't need to train with Luke that evening. I'd had the workout to end all workouts at the mall.

But my party outfit was killer and the shoes were *amazing*.

We'd all just made it through the door when May came trotting up to us, hands moving around in circles at her side, highly agitated about something.

Oh crap.

The minute she made it to us I asked, "Where are Roam and Sniff?"

"What?" she asked, her eyes bright. "They're in with a tutor, you gotta—"

"They're okay?" I went on.

"Yeah, hon, you gotta—"

"You look like something's wrong. What's wrong?" I pushed.

"I'm tellin' you, you gotta—"

"Is it one of the other kids?" I cut in.

She put her hand to my mouth. "Hush, girl. You gotta come with me." Then she grabbed my wrist but stopped and stared down. "Ooo, look at that pretty bracelet!" she exclaimed.

"May! What's going on?" I clipped.

She snapped to and said, "Right." Then she dragged me through the rec room, turning around towards my posse. "Hey ya'll," she greeted as if she wasn't acting bizarre in the extreme.

"Hey May," they replied, almost in unison.

May took us down the hall into the shared office space. When the nine of us burst through the door, everyone in the room looked up and stared.

I wasn't paying attention to anyone. On my desk was a beautiful bouquet of the most exquisite pale pink roses.

I smiled. May let go of my wrist and I walked forward.

"Holy crap," Indy breathed.

"Good God," Roxie whispered.

They all followed me to my desk and we stood staring in silent awe at the roses, such was their magnificence.

I dumped my purse on my desk, breaking into the Rose Stupor, and Jet said, "I would never have thought Vance was a flower type of guy."

"Me either," Ally put in. "More like edible undies."

"Ally!" Tod snapped. "Get your mind out of the gutter."

"I'm just saying what everyone's thinking," Ally defended herself.

"They're not from Vance," I told them.

Everyone looked at me.

"They're not?" May asked.

I reached for the card and shook my head. "They're from my Uncle Nick. He knows pink roses are my favorites."

I was a little surprised. Nick was super generous, but a specially designed bracelet must have set him back a whack. A dozen pink roses, especially roses like this, perfect, so pale pink they were blush, every bloom total perfection, must have cost some serious cake. They weren't even a traditional bouquet with all that baby's breath in a heavily cut glass vase. There were just the roses with thin spikes of green shooting out here and there bending around the blooms and a simple, cylindrical vase that was pure class. The bouquet was a work of art.

"Well, that's damned disappointing," Daisy muttered from beside me as I gently touched a rose.

"Your uncle is feeling generous this year." Indy smiled at me.

"Probably thinks she won't see another birthday," Stevie murmured.

"Shh, Stevie," Jet shushed him.

I slid my fingernail under the heavy cream paper of the card's envelope and pulled it out.

Then I froze.

There was only one letter on the card, nothing else. In black, bold pen it said, "V".

"Oh my God," I breathed.

"What?" someone asked (I was too freaked to distinguish voices).

"What is it?" someone else asked.

I swayed a bit, suddenly lightheaded, and someone else yelled, "Grab her! She's going down!"

I was pressed into my office chair. My mind started clearing and I heard Roxie say, "Get her some water."

Tod picked up a manila folder from my desk and started fanning me with it. "Deep breaths, girlie. Deep breaths. Do you think she should put her head between her knees?" he asked Jet.

May swiped the card from my fingers. She looked at it and a slow smile spread on her face.

"These ain't from her uncle. Praise be to Jesus."

"Let me see that." Daisy snatched the card out May's hand. "It just says 'V'," she told everyone, her eyes big and happy. She looked around the gang. "How hot is that? That boy's got *class*."

They were all looking at me grinning like fools.

"I told him," I whispered and then stopped talking.

"What's that, sugar?" Daisy enquired.

I cleared my throat and looked up at them. "I told him about Nick giving me pink roses on my sixteenth birthday and how they were my favorites. It was a few months after my Auntie Reba died and how Nick and I had the first good night since she..." I stopped again and looked around them. "I told him," I repeated.

"Righteous," Ally said softly.

I felt something hit me then. Something terrifying, a delayed reaction. I grabbed my purse, pulled out my phone and shot out of the chair.

"Jules—" Indy said my name, her grin had gone uncertain.

"I need his number," I announced.

"What?" Roxie asked.

"Give me his cell number!" I shouted. "Who's got his number?"

Everyone started pulling out their phones.

"I have his number," Indy told me.

"I don't have his number," Daisy said, but she was still digging through her purse as if she could help.

"I *wish* I had his number," Tod put in.

"Here it is," Indy said and recited the number.

I punched it in then walked out of the room, down the hall and saw the blue room's blind was closed. I went to the yellow room. It was free so I walked in, shut the blinds, closed the door and put my back to it. Then I hit the green button.

It rang, once.

"Yeah?"

"Vance?"

"You called me, Princess, who else would it be?" he asked, his amused voice was silk.

"We have to stop seeing each other," I told him.

Silence.

I waited. Then I waited some more.

My emotional Rottweiler had torn free of his chains and he was barking, snarling, drooling, jumping around and ready to attack.

When he still didn't say anything, I called, "Vance?"

"Why?" he asked.

"What?"

"Why?" he repeated. This time there was impatience in his tone.

"This isn't going to work," I said, as if that was an explanation.

"Why?" he obviously realized it wasn't an explanation.

Because I like you a lot. Because you're beautiful and strong and make me feel things I can't allow myself to feel. Because you listen to me in the moonlight like every word I say forms a drop of nectar. Because you've lived a shit life and come out the other side to be someone amazing. Because now you live a dangerous life with a scar on your back to prove it and I can't afford to lose anyone else that means something to me, I thought.

"I can't explain it," I said.

"Try." His voice was beyond impatience now. It was short and clipped.

"Okay then, I'm *not* going to explain it because I don't have to. It just isn't going to work."

More silence, and I could actually feel the anger coming through the phone.

Then he said, "You're mine tonight."

My belly fluttered. "Vance."

"Tomorrow it's over. Tonight you're mine."

"That isn't smart."

"I don't give a fuck."

"I really don't think—"

"I'll be at your house at five to eight. We're on the Harley tonight. Pack a bag."

"Really, I think, after the party—"

"You're in my bed tonight. I want your scent on my sheets."

Oh my *God*.

"Vance," I said again. This time it sounded like a plea.

"Five to eight," he repeated.

Then he disconnected.

I stood there, back to the door, and kept the dead phone to my ear.

Then I slid down the door, ass to the floor, knees pointed to the ceiling, hands on my knees. I stared into space, forcing my mind blank, telling myself I could do this and tomorrow it would be over and my life would be back to normal.

Myself didn't really believe I could do this and it didn't much like the idea of normal.

Chapter 15
You Got a New Partner Now

I was on my back on the mat on the floor in the "down room" at the Nightingale Investigations office.

It was a big room with a couch, TV, treadmill, weights and an exercise bike. The guys used it for down time or when they were hanging around on call (only the bad boys at Nightingale Investigations would call a room with workout equipment the "down room").

And of course the mat on the floor where Luke was kicking my ass.

"You're not focused," Luke said.

He was standing over me, staring down at me, hands on his hips.

He was right, I wasn't focused. My mind was everywhere but there. Heavy would be disappointed.

Luke was good. He knew far more moves than Heavy, was stronger, faster and constantly surprising me. Still, even as a novice, I knew more than I was showing.

"Get your head in the game," Luke continued, bending and offering me his hand to help me up for about the twenty-fourth time.

I nodded mutely, locked my fingers around his wrist, put my other hand to his forearm and then I gave a solid jerk, hoping to take him by surprise and take him down just once for the sake of my pride.

His feet were planted. He stood strong, only his arm and shoulder moving with my jerk, which was disappointing. The corner of his lip went up on one side. He yanked me up and I found my feet. I immediately shifted my weight to one leg, threw my other calf around the backs of his and tagged him behind the knees. They buckled but he released my hand, his other arm went around my waist and he twisted.

We both went down. His arm tightened around my waist, the other hand went out to shield our fall. I landed in a poor strategic position, on my back, him on top of me, his full weight pressing me into the mat. My legs were incapacitated, and if he hadn't cushioned our fall my head would have slammed against the mat and his weight would have knocked the wind out of me.

His head came up and he gave me a half-grin. "Better," he said.

"Thanks," I said back.

"You're still fucked."

"I kinda noticed that," I told him.

"Don't go out on the street with your mind on the mall."

"My mind isn't on the mall. I've already done the mall and my party outfit is brilliant."

He just stared at me, looking like he might laugh, and I noticed his dark eyes weren't brown or black like I thought. They were a deep, dark blue.

Wow.

"You wanna get up?" I asked, pushing thoughts about his eyes to the very back recesses of my mind so as never to pull them up again, and placing my hands on his biceps to push him.

"Not particularly," he said casually, like he could lie on top of me all night, which he probably could.

Hmm.

Not good.

"Well, I want you to get up," I said.

"It's good to want things."

"Luke, get off me."

"How solid are you and Vance?" he asked.

It was my turn to stare. "Why?"

"Just answer the question."

"Why?"

"'Cause I'm thinkin' not many men want their woman roaming the streets at night lookin' for trouble, no matter if she can handle a gun and herself. I don't see a good future for you two unless you get your ass back to that Shelter and your mind on what you really can do to help those kids."

One thing you could say for that: it sure was honest.

"Well, then you'll be pleased to know we broke up today. We're only going to the party together because we made a deal."

I passed the torch and it was his turn to stare. Then for some strange reason he started to look a little angry.

"That didn't take long," he murmured as if to himself.

"Shit happens. Now, get off."

The door opened and both of our heads twisted to it. Vance was standing there. He stood frozen for a beat, hand on the doorknob.

Then his arms crossed on his chest, his eyes went hard and his face got scary.

"What... the... fuck?" His voice was low and as scary as his face.

Luke looked at Vance then he looked at me. Luke's face was blank, but his eyes were active and I could tell he was thinking about something.

I looked back at Vance.

"He's showing me some moves," I told Vance.

"Yeah, I can see," Vance replied.

Um.

Yikes.

Luke knifed off me, grabbed my forearm and pulled me up to stand close to him. I didn't move away because there were crackling-not-happy vibes floating around the room and I didn't want to do anything to set them off. And anyway, I was feeling very weird around Vance. I'd broken up with him, he'd kind of accepted it, yet we weren't through. I'd become used to him being around, getting in my space, descending into what had become a familiar banter. This was just weird. It felt foreign, uncomfortable, *wrong*.

We all stared at each other.

Then Luke asked, "You two over after the party?"

Vance's eyes sliced to Luke. My lungs squeezed painfully, my eyes widened and moved to him, too.

Vance didn't answer. Neither did I.

"You're through with Law then you won't mind me movin' in," Luke said, clearly not worried about fanning the flames of the crackling not-happy vibes.

Oh my God.

I continued staring at Luke with wide eyes, but my mouth had now dropped open.

"You move in, we have problems," Vance returned softly.

"You move out, don't seem like it's much of your business."

The crackling vibes got red-hot.

It was time for me to say something.

"Excuse me, but I *am* in the room," I snapped. "I thought you said not many men like their women roaming the streets looking for trouble?" I pointed out to Luke.

"Yeah, I did. Though *I* think it's kinda cute," Luke replied.

Oh my God.

"Well hurray for you, but come tomorrow, you boys are off the job. I'm a single-act show again," I returned.

"You're in for trainin' tomorrow, same time," Luke shot back.

"No fucking way."

"Only a girl would turn her back on a good deal just because she got fucked in the process."

"News flash, Luke. I *am* a girl," I returned heatedly, hands going to my hips.

"Yeah," he grinned, leaning back. "I noticed that."

Vance moved. Luke and I swung our eyes to him and I realized too late the red-hot vibes went white.

His movement wasn't distinguishable. He was still standing, arms crossed on his chest, but something about him went hostile.

I waited. Luke (thankfully) was silent. The room burned.

Then Vance said, eyes on me, "Five to eight."

Then he was gone.

I whirled on Luke. "What in the hell was that all about?"

He just grinned at me.

"Stop grinning," I demanded.

"Tomorrow, after training, you and I patrol."

"I don't think so."

"I do. You aren't going to learn shit on a mat. You gotta learn in the field."

"I said *no.*"

He kept grinning. "You got a new partner now."

I rolled my eyes to the ceiling.

These guys.

I wore a little black dress to the party.

And it was *little*.

It seemed like a good idea at the time, before the flowers, before my freak out, when I was in a happy birthday daze.

It wasn't a good idea now.

I'd gone home from training, packed a backpack (better for the Harley), showered and done the whole makeup and hair bit. Subtle makeup; it was all I knew how to do, and my hair was up in a messy twist, which I didn't know how to do, but luckily, after five tries, it worked.

During the mall extravaganza, as birthday presents, Roxie bought me this lotion that made my legs look shiny and ultra-smooth. Jet had given me three kinds of flavored lip gloss (I'd made the mistake of telling her about Vance's "you smell of melons and taste of cherries" comment and she got a bit overexcited): bubble gum, grape and, of course, cherry.

I went with grape for the evening.

My dress was clingy black jersey, to the knee, halter-necked. The front fell in a drape, low on my cleavage. The back also had a drape, super-low, exposing most of the small of my back. My shoes were spike-heeled, pointed-toe, open sides, but with a full back and a thick strap across the very top of my foot, just under the ankle.

I went with bare Roxie-lotion-shiny legs, my new bracelet on my wrist and Auntie Reba's diamond at my neck.

I was filling Boo's food bowl, telling him he had to be a good kitty until I got home the next day, when Vance walked in the backdoor.

I straightened and stared at him.

Hair back, leather jacket, black cowboy boots, thick black belt with a heavy silver buckle, jeans and a crisp shirt with subtle stripes of wine, navy, midnight and charcoal patterned into it. The shirt was opened at the throat.

At the sight of him my mouth went dry.

"You gonna be able to ride on the Harley in that?" he asked.

I decided a snotty, "Well, hello to you, too," was no longer in order. I wasn't sure, as I'd had no experience, but I figured I'd lost the right to bicker when I told him we had to stop seeing each other.

I also decided to ignore the clench in my gut that he didn't rush me against the counter and kiss me like last time.

"It's stretchy," I answered.

His eyes moved the length of me then came back to mine. I couldn't read them.

"Get a jacket," he replied. "Where's your bag?"

I put on my black leather blazer and the backpack and we rode to Fortnum's.

The lights were blazing in Fortnum's windows and I could see the place was already packed. I was a little shocked. They'd only planned the party the night before and spent most of the afternoon with me at the mall and the Shelter.

I hopped off the back of the bike, rearranged my skirt, and Vance slid the backpack down an arm. I whirled with it as he pulled it off the other side and I ended up facing him. He threw it over one of his shoulders.

I looked up at him. His face was blank. My stomach had decided to settle into a permanent, painful twist.

I turned away, biting my lip and feeling the weight in my chest that threatened tears.

The sooner we got in there, the sooner the party would be over, the sooner the night would be over, the sooner I could face whatever challenge the next day brought.

Or move to Nicaragua.

Vance caught my wrist and swung me back around, his body moving toward me at the same time so I collided with it.

He dropped my wrist, his arm went around me inside my jacket and his hand dipped straight into the drape at my back.

My lips parted and his other hand went into my hair, pulled out the clip and my hair fell over his hand and my shoulders.

"Crowe! It took me five tries to twist that thing in my hair."

I forgot about not bickering.

He ignored my comment. "You get the idea to experiment with flirtin' in front of me, think again. I won't like it and you'll be the one who'll pay."

I closed my eyes, sucked in a breath, then opened them again.

"Can we just get through the night?" I asked.

"We'll get through the night," he promised, and something in that promise made me shiver.

He stared at me, hand at my behind, the other one in my hair.

I became conscious of the fact that anyone could see us from the windows.

"Can you take your hand off my ass?" I asked, allowing myself a little shade of snotty. We *were* standing on a public street and in full view of the windows and Nick might be in there.

Instead of doing as I asked, he pulled me deeper into him and kissed me. This wasn't a soft, sweet kiss, but deep, hard and full-on tongue.

When he quit kissing me, he whispered, "Grape," against my lips and his eyes looked in mine.

My stomach lurched painfully into a tighter knot at the memory of a better time.

I held my breath, wondering why I gave into tonight; to the party, Vance, everything. I was so much better on my own. Dinners with Nick, Boo as my bed partner and my music to keep my company.

Before I could find an answer to my mental question, Vance released me, grabbed my hand and we walked in.

Everyone yelled happy birthday.

Even though I felt like crying, I did my very best to smile.

⋙⋘

"Methinks, even with the mini-make-out-session on the sidewalk, all is not well in paradise," Tod remarked, standing beside me, both of us holding glasses of champagne.

It was an hour into the party and I was trying to have fun (and not succeeding).

They'd decided on baked Camembert and crackers, fruit trays, crudités, champagne and truffles. All the men, including everyone from Nightingale Investigations (except a guy I hadn't yet met named Ike, who had night duty in the control room), were there and wearing jeans and nice shirts or sweaters. Tod and Stevie wore casual suits and Tex wore one of his normal flannel shirts. All the women were dressed to the nines; little dresses, lots of hair and makeup.

Nick was there and seemed to be enjoying himself. Heavy and Zip were also there, and both seemed a bit uncomfortable. Frank was a no show. Not exactly the most sociable person one-on-one, he might have been able to do beers at a bar, but parties were a no-go.

Tex surprised me because he was with a pretty blonde lady and they looked close. I wouldn't have expected Tex to have a date, especially not a pretty blonde lady. I was further surprised (a nice way to say absolutely floored) to find out she was Jet's mother, Nancy.

Duke surprised me by showing up at all. He brought his wife, Dolores, and she was a cracker.

Jet and Eddie had yet to arrive.

I was avoiding Vance like I'd forgotten to wear deodorant (I hadn't) and I didn't want him to find out.

I was avoiding Luke because Luke was a wildcard. I didn't want him to flirt with me then me be the one to pay.

Vance looked seriously unhappy. Luke looked seriously amused.

I looked to Tod and he was watching me closely.

"Everything's fine," I assured him.

"Liar, liar, pants on fire," Tod said.

"No really, it is."

"Girlie, pu-lease. I had a hot guy like that I'd be all over him, embarrassing my friends enough to leave early so I could *really* be all over him."

"You do have a hot guy like that," I told him.

"Not the same ten years on. You two are in the first blush of romance. You should be going at it like rabbits."

"I broke up with him," I blurted. Do not ask me why. I shouldn't have and I knew it.

Tod blinked at me, face shocked.

See? I knew I shouldn't have.

"What?" he asked.

"I broke up with him when I ran out of the room after I saw the flowers. I called him and broke up with him. We made a deal. He gets tonight then we're over."

"You said you phoned to thank him," Tod told me.

"I kinda... um... fibbed."

Tod looked at me. He opened his mouth, then closed it and looked away. Then he looked back, opened his mouth again and yelled, "*Are you fucking nuts?*"

Most everyone turned to stare including, to my horror, Vance.

I turned to Tod, my back to the room (and Vance). "Tod! Keep your voice down."

"Girl, that boy is hot for you, not to mention that boy is just plain *hot*."

"Tod—"

"You need a doctor. You need an intervention. You need Daisy," Tod said and started looking around the room.

"No! Do not call Daisy over here. Why do you think I fibbed to you earlier today? I didn't want this kind of reaction."

"What's going on?" Roxie hissed from beside us. She looked gorgeous, wearing a figure-skimming strapless little black dress of her own, and her shoes were nearly as amazing as mine.

"Jules broke up with Vance. It's over. Done. Kaput," Tod announced.

"*What?*" Roxie screeched.

This time I felt the room's attention on my back at Roxie's outburst.

I closed my eyes (I really shouldn't have told Tod) then I opened them.

"Please, be quiet," I begged.

"Why did you break up with him?" Roxie asked in a low voice.

"It's too complicated to explain."

"But... he's macho, he rides a Harley and he bought you flowers. Macho men who ride Harleys don't buy women flowers. They take them to a roadhouse, get them drunk and get in their pants," Roxie explained.

"What's happening?" Ally asked. She and Indy had arrived together.

"Don't tell them," I said quickly.

"Jules broke up with Vance. It's over," Roxie said over me.

Both of them turned to stare at me.

"That's what she did after she saw the flowers," Tod shared.

"I thought you said you were thanking him," Indy said.

"She lied," Tod told them.

"Why on earth would you do that?" Ally (kind of) yelled.

"Because I didn't want this exact same thing to happen," I said in a soft clip, giving up on getting them to be quiet.

"Ya'll, what is goin' *on?*" May asked, pushing close, and I could see Daisy on her heels.

Damn.

Daisy. Not good.

And May. Worse.

"Jules broke up with Vance. It's over," Roxie, Tod and Ally said together.

"You are jokin'," Daisy said, her eyes narrowed and I moved back, not wanting to be in bitch-slapping, nail-scratching distance.

"Where's that cake? I'm takin' back the cake. Lettin' my grandchildren eat it. They aren't crazy fools. They deserve it," May announced.

"Please don't make a big deal if this. This is not a big deal. We've only been together a few days," I told them.

"A few days for these boys is a few months for normal men. He's in deep, you're in deep and you damn well know it," Daisy snapped.

"Yes. I do," I snapped back, leaning into her and having... had... enough.

It was my fucking life and it was my fucking birthday and I could do whatever the hell I wanted.

At my tone, and what I didn't know was the look on my face, everyone leaned back a bit.

"My whole family died in a car crash when I was six. My Mom, Dad and older brother. I was with them, got really hurt, spent a lot of time in the hospital, but I survived. When I was ten, my new puppy was run over by a truck. Splat!" I clapped one palm on the other and everyone jumped. "When I was eleven, my grandpa, the only living grandparent I had left, died of Parkinson's. When I was fifteen, my Auntie Reba died after having knee replacement surgery. *Knee replacement surgery*," I hissed the last three words. "Four months ago, Park died. I found him in an alley. He was the best kid I'd ever met and I've met a lot of them. This morning, I saw the scar of the gunshot wound Vance got during some business he was doing for Lee. He was shot again a few days ago, protecting me. I will *not* lose another person in my life. I will *not* lose someone else I care about. *I will not*."

"Girlie—" Tod said softly.

My eyes were blurry again and I just hated that.

"I will not," I repeated, turning to Tod.

"What on earth is going on?" Stevie asked, coming late. "Everyone is staring."

My eyes moved to Stevie and my stomach twisted tighter to the point where I thought I might be sick.

"Could they hear me?" I whispered after I'd swallowed back the nausea.

Stevie took one look at my face and blinked. Then he looked at Tod. Tod shook his head.

Stevie's eyes came back to me. "No, they couldn't hear you. Are you okay?"

"No, I'm not okay," I said to Stevie and then looked at May. "Can you please, please," I grabbed her hand and leaned into her, "please, just serve the cake? I really need that cake."

She didn't argue. She nodded her head and her hand squeezed mine. "Sure, hon, I'll serve the cake."

I closed my eyes again, let out a deep breath and then looked at May. "Thank you."

May peeled off to serve the cake.

I looked around at the concerned faces. "Can we quit talking about this and just enjoy this wonderful party?"

Daisy came forward, her arm went around my waist and she held on tight. "Sure, sugar." Then she looked back at the gang. "I think we need more champagne."

"That'd be good," I whispered, blinking a few times until my vision cleared.

That was when Jet arrived. She was smiling so huge it lit up the room. She walked up looking somehow dazed and completely unaware, oblivious to the undercurrents of the recent drama.

"Hey guys," she said then smiled at me and gave me a kiss on the cheek. "Happy birthday Jules."

On closer inspection she didn't look dazed. She looked dreamy.

"Jet," I began. "Are you okay?"

"I'm okay. I'm way okay. I'm so okay it's worth the fucking f-word. I'm fucking, *fucking* okay."

"What's going on?" Ally asked.

Jet turned to her. "Eddie told me he loved me tonight. That's why we're late. I, um… kinda pounced on him when he did it."

Everyone stared.

My stomach twisted further, hateful jealousy I wished I didn't feel causing the pain even as my heart warmed for Jet.

Daisy let me go and hugged Jet.

"That is *so* sweet," she said when she broke the hug. "Champagne! We need champagne! Right here!" she shouted, though who she was shouting at I did not know. There weren't any waiters. It was a help-yourself kind of deal.

"I'll get the champagne," Indy offered with a hand squeeze for Jet and a quick, worried look at me.

I ignored the worried look. I didn't need any worried looks. I needed this night to be over.

Jet moved beside me as Tod, Daisy and Roxie formed a huddle close by (likely to talk about me; I ignored that, too) and Ally wandered away, scarily in a direction that would lead her to Vance (I ignored that, too).

"Did you tell him you love him?" I asked Jet.

"I told him ages ago when I tried to break up with him."

I couldn't help it. Even with all the emotion, what she said made no sense and thus made me smile.

"As you know I'm no expert, but that sure as hell doesn't sound like the way to break up with someone," I told her.

She grinned at me, still in her dreamy daze. "It wasn't, though I didn't know that. I moved in during my troubles and he didn't let me break up with him when they were over and never let me move out. This past weekend I even painted his bathroom this really cool shade of deep, deep lavender, a really rich color, but Ally said Eddie'd lose his mind to have a purple bathroom. Still, he told me he loved me. Even a purple bathroom didn't faze Eddie."

She was gazing across the room while she talked and I followed her gaze. I looked across the room and saw Eddie, his eyes on Jet. His lips were twitching, his thoughts clearly private, but in a seriously sexy, public way.

I put my arm around her waist and she did the same with mine. "I think you could have painted the bathroom flamingo pink and it wouldn't faze Eddie."

She looked at me. Her face had settled, lost its daze, and was now just plain happy.

"I know," she said softly.

Don't ask me why, but I touched the side of my head to hers and gave her waist a squeeze. She squeezed me back.

Then May came out with a birthday cake loaded with lit candles, singing happy birthday and everyone joined in.

A couple of hours later, the party was winding down and Nick walked up to me.

With a polite smile, he pulled me away from talking to Zip and Heavy.

"I'm leavin', Jules," he said to me, walking me to the door where he stopped.

"Did you have fun?" I asked, smiling up at him.

"Yeah. They're good people."

He was right, they were.

"Got somethin' to say, Jules."

I cocked my head to the side, not sure I liked his tone but having had just enough champagne to be able to ignore that, too.

"Noticed you gave Vance a wide berth tonight. Don't know why, and it's none of my business."

I held my breath, knowing from experience he wasn't done talking, and I was right.

Nick continued, "Been scared stiff these past four months, you doin' what you're doin'. You know that. The only two good nights of sleep I've had in those months have been the last two, with his Harley sittin' outside the backdoor."

Oh crap.

Vance had Nick's approval. I knew that, but I'd been trying to ignore it. I also knew that he worried about me a lot and I'd been trying to ignore that, too.

What I didn't need to know was that Vance made him feel like I was safe.

"Nick, his Harley won't be out there anymore," I told him softly.

Nick didn't even try to hide the disappointment on his face. I tried to ignore that, too.

I failed.

"The way you two are tonight, was worried about that," Nick said.

I took a breath and forged ahead. "I won't be home tonight. Can you feed Boo in the morning?"

Nick stared at me a beat, clearly confused at this contradictory information. I didn't enlighten him.

Then he said, "I hope you know what you're doin', Jules."

"I do," I replied with fake brightness. "Don't I always?"

"Yeah," he said, but he shook his head. "You always know what you're doin'. Just can't say you've always done the right thing."

"Nick—"

"It may almost always be the right thing for others, but it usually wasn't the right thing for you," he told me. "Life ain't worth livin', Jules, if you don't take a few risks, and I'm not talkin' about puttin' your ass on the line to save the world. I'm talkin' about puttin' your ass on the line to save yourself."

I didn't have anything to say to that and I didn't have a chance to find anything to say. Vance walked up beside us, approaching me for the first time that evening, although, I'd seen him talking several times with Nick.

"Time to go," he said, eyes on me. The look in them sent a shiver up my spine, and not in the usual good way.

I nodded.

His eyes cut to Nick and his hand came out.

"'Night, Nick," he said.

"Vance," Nick shook his hand and then they broke off. "You two enjoy the rest of your evening."

Then Nick went out the door.

"I'll get your jacket," Vance said and peeled off.

While he was gone I lifted my chin, squared my shoulders, mentally prepared for what was to come, and in the middle of that I caught Indy's eye.

She was standing next to Lee. He had his arm around her shoulders and was talking to Eddie. Indy had her arm around his waist and she was looking at me. She put her head to his chest and smiled encouragingly.

Vance came up, my backpack over one of his shoulders, my jacket over his arm.

"Thanks everybody!" I yelled.

They turned, called their goodnights and happy birthdays.

I waved with pretend happiness. I even blew a few kisses, which was not good for a head-crackin' mamma jamma to do, but for once I was amongst friends.

And then we were gone.

Chapter 16
You Wanna Talk Now?

We took Sixth Avenue west to I-70, Vance riding fast. Me pressed against him from crotch to shoulders (dress stretched to the max), arms tight around his waist, backpack on my back, Harley roaring between my legs, hair flying behind me, my legs freezing in the cold. I alternately pressed my cheek into his shoulder or gazed over it, not quite sad, scared or cold enough not to enjoy the ride.

We went into the foothills, past the end of the city lights, strip malls and suburbs where the skies became a bit clearer and you could see the stars a whole lot better.

Vance exited I-70 and I memorized our route, just because, letting myself pretend that I might take it again one day. It was major thoroughfare left to minor thoroughfare. Minor thoroughfare right to a one lane road. One lane road left to a dirt road. I was guessing we were somewhere between Golden and Evergreen. What I did know was that we were in the middle of nowhere.

Finally, he pulled off into a gravel lane and his headlight flashed on a small, one-story log cabin surrounded by pine trees, except for a clearing to the north where there was a major outbuilding.

In the drive there was an oldish Ford pickup truck. Not ancient, but it had at least ten years on it. It was blue, it was dusty and you could tell it was well-used. Next to that was a horse trailer.

Vance stopped the bike, and cut the light. I got off and pulled down my skirt. So did he, without the skirt part. We did the whole backpack whirl thing again. He grabbed my hand and walked me to the house. All this was done in silence.

I was finding it hard to deal with silence.

"Do you have horses?" I asked.

"One. Stable two for my neighbors in exchange for them feeding, watering and exercising mine when I'm in town, which is most of the time," he replied in a way that didn't invite further questions.

He walked right up to the house, hand wrapped around mine, and opened the unlocked door.

"You don't lock your house?" I asked, shocked. Vance, security expert, didn't lock his own house. He was in the middle of nowhere, but still.

"Got nothin' to steal," he said.

We walked in and he flipped on a light, and with one look around I realized he was right. He indeed had nothing to steal.

He dropped my hand, closed the door and walked through the house, leaving me at the door and disappearing down a dark hall. Then a light came on from there.

I looked around more, came forward and took my blazer off, wrapping it around the back of a chair.

It could be cute, his cabin. Definitely cozy. The walls were made of well-sealed logs. The floors were wood with some rugs thrown over them; mostly multi-colored and braided, not tatty, but not designer-cabin-chic either. The front room was one biggish room incorporating the dining room, living room and kitchen. There was a big stone hearth on the side wall of the living room, a smaller one on the opposite side, next to the dining table.

To the right was the living room. He had a couch, and over it was thrown a colorful Native American blanket. A coffee table in front, cluttered with books; some opened and placed facedown, some stacked even on the floor and under the table. A floor lamp made of a twisted branch was beside the couch, buffalos dancing across the shade. The back of a beat-up leather armchair faced the dining room/kitchen area.

And that was it. No television, no stereo, no pictures, nothing.

The kitchen was a u-shape. The back and side walls had top and bottom cabinets, a counter delineating it from the dining area with only bottom cabinets. The cabinets were made of a fantastic knotty-pine. They'd look great refinished and with a gleam to them, especially if granite or concrete countertops replaced the old worn brown one he had. A coffeemaker and a toaster were the only things on the counter except for a stack of mail. The dining area held an old round oak four-seater. Like everything else, it was in good condition, but worn. Maybe bought secondhand because it was old enough to pre-date Vance's ownership, and too worn for stuff that had little use if he wasn't home very often.

Vance came back into the room and I looked at him.

226

He stopped in the entryway to the hall and leaned a shoulder against it, eyes on me.

"If you don't stay here very often, where do you stay when you're in town?" I'd asked out of curiosity, not able to help myself. Mostly because I wanted to know.

It wasn't a good decision.

He stayed silent for a beat after my question, then his face changed and not in a good way.

"You wanna talk now?" he asked, voice low. "Get to know me a little better?"

Um.

Not good.

Someone was not in a happy mood.

"Crowe, I'm just trying to make conversation," I said quietly, deciding not to spit in the eye of the tiger at this juncture.

He pushed away from the wall and started toward me.

"I don't wanna have a conversation. I wanna fuck."

My body prepared to flee, but my mind stopped it and I held my ground.

"I'm beginning to hate it when you say it like that," I said sharply.

I didn't really hate it, not before. It was kind of a turn on. But I did hate it now, especially the way he just said it, which was not nice.

He stopped in front of me and just at the edge of my space. The whole time he approached me, his eyes were on mine.

"I work when I'm in town. If I need to sleep, I sleep on the couch in the down room. If I need to shower, I use the shower there. I keep clothes in my locker. A lot of the time I'm out hunting and not in town at all. I come up here when I have time off, which isn't very often," he answered my question.

"Why do you work so much?" I asked, but wished I hadn't. Again I couldn't help myself. I just wanted to know.

"It's what I do," he replied.

"But why?"

He stared at me a second, leaned forward and took my hand. "Question time is over."

Oh crap.

He turned and pulled me across the room and down the hall.

It was undignified to struggle, especially in high heels and a little black dress. So I didn't, but my belly flutter, coupled with the stomach twist, made me feel a little queasy.

He pulled me into a room off the left of the hall. His bedroom.

The lamp was on by the bed. It was an old iron bed, painted black, a double. The mattresses, though, looked firm and new. There was a down comforter on it covered in a dark brown twill, and another Native American blanket thrown over the comforter. Light brown pillowcases over the pillows. There was a dresser, two nightstands, both with lamps and more books on them, and an old wardrobe because there was no closet. On the outside wall was another stone hearth fireplace nearly as big as the living room. The only thing on the walls was a hide stretched across and stitched tight to a bent piece of wood, an image of an eagle shaved into the fur.

Vance stopped by the bed. He'd already taken off his jacket earlier and now he started to unbutton his shirt.

"Crowe—" I started.

"Take off your dress," he interrupted me, his voice sharp.

I blinked at him, shocked at his tone.

Then I rallied. "Can we please talk, just for a few minutes?"

I wasn't beginning to get freaked. I was full-on freaked.

It didn't take an experienced relationship expert to realize he was pissed-off, and I didn't understand. If he was pissed-off why did he want me there at all? It was like he wanted to make this hard on me, and I didn't like that, not about him.

Furthermore, why *was* I there? I'd never agreed to it. I hadn't even agreed to going to the party with him.

Before I could answer my questions, his hands came away from the last button, he shrugged his shirt off his shoulders and it fell to the floor. Then he captured me by the hips, pulled me closer, and with a swish he had my dress clutched in his fingers and up over my head. Then it was gone.

I was wearing a pair of red satin panties with a little black bow under my navel (one of my new pairs) and no bra.

For a second, shock hit me and I stood frozen. Then I covered my breasts with an arm and bent to retrieve my dress.

I'd decided that it was time to *fuck this*. My head-crackin' mamma jamma was coming out.

There were a lot of things I didn't need that had come at me in the last few days, but Vance being a complete asshole was the biggest one of them all.

Vance caught me as I bent over and pulled me back up.

"Take your hands off me, Crowe. I'm going home," I snapped when I was straight and looking at him. His arms were wrapping around me and pulling me to him.

I tried to push back. They went tight with a jerk and my body slammed into his.

"You aren't goin' anywhere."

"I don't like this. You're making me uncomfortable," I informed him.

"You'll be comfortable in a second when my mouth is between your legs."

Oh my *God*.

He did *not* just say that.

"You're an ass!" I shouted. "This is *not* happening."

"It's happening Princess. I have one more night of your sweetness and I'm gonna take it."

"You're gonna have to *take* it because I'm not *giving* it."

"You'll give it."

"Fuck you!" I was still shouting, and now I was pushing away from him.

"Yeah," he returned. "Exactly."

Then he twisted me. We went down on the bed, him on top, and his weight hit me hard.

I struggled, I swear I did, but he got my wrists to the sides of my head and his mouth was on me everywhere and I couldn't keep it up. I wanted to. I fought it, but I didn't win.

He kissed me hard and deep then his mouth moved over my neck, to my collarbone, between my breasts, doing amazing things to my nipples. It was just too much. I hated him at first, then I hated myself for giving in, and then I couldn't think of anything (certainly not hate) when his mouth kept at me.

He knew when I quit fighting. He let my wrists go and I pushed him to his back, too turned on to think of running. I did the same to him, just as Daisy told me to do. If he did something I liked, I should do it back.

I went further, though. Out-of-control turned on, yanking his belt loose, undoing his fly, pulling his jeans down. I took him in my hand, and I kid you not, no experience, nothing but instinct, I took him in my mouth.

I had no idea what I was doing, but I just winged it. I did what I liked and I liked what I did, and I knew he liked it, too, because after a while he started to make low, growling noises.

Then he pulled me up and to the side. He sat up, yanked off his boots and socks, stood up and pulled off his jeans. I used that time to push the soles of my shoes against the heels, shoving them off. He bent over me, feet still on the floor, one hand to the bed beside me. He reached down and dragged off my panties. When they were gone, he spread my legs and then he was there, slamming inside me.

"Vance," I breathed when he did.

"Say it again," he demanded against my mouth.

I did.

It was like it was in the hall of my house; hard, fast, deep, and I was coming close to orgasm just from the velvet violence of it.

Suddenly his hand glided down the back of my leg, lifted it at the knee and he slid out of me. He rolled me to my belly, repositioned between my legs and, hands at my hips, he pulled me up, just the lower half of my body, and then he was inside me again.

I felt a moment of being stunned then it melted away. He could go deeper that way, harder, and God, it felt good. I pushed my hips into him, curled my fingers into the covers at the sides of my head and little mewing noises came from my throat that I couldn't control.

It would seem impersonal, him being so far away, but he didn't let it. His hands went from my hips, fingertips brushing my behind, the small of my back softly then back to hold my hips.

That was all nice, even fantastic, but better yet the position felt naughty and it was simply downright *hot*.

I was close. The noises I was making were getting urgent and he pulled out and flipped me around again. He dropped to his side, his arms went around me then he went to his back, taking me with him, rolling me on top.

"Don't stop!" I cried (kind of loud and snappish), but he just stared into my eyes. He pulled my legs up on either side of him, guided himself inside and sat up.

Um.

Wow.

His head was tilted back, eyes still on me and I looked down at him.

"I wanna see your face when you come," he murmured.

Um.

Wow again.

My arms went around his shoulders and immediately I started to move, my mouth at his. We were both breathing hard, not kissing, lips just touching. It didn't take long before my Grade Nine and Three Quarters bypassed Grade Ten and went straight to Grade Thirteen and a Half.

⌖

I shivered.

"I'm cold," I whispered, face in his neck, lips at his ear.

He reached across the bed and pulled the blanket over us. I was still on top, still astride him, my torso against his, my knees pressed against his sides.

I was trying to quiet my mind.

Once he covered us, his arms went back around me and he held me pressed tight against him.

We hadn't used protection again, which was another thing I *did not need*. This time I understood that it was out of either of our control. But we were playing Russian roulette with my ovaries and eventually my ovaries were going to succumb to the bullet.

Gently he rolled me to the side, still under the blanket, and he moved away.

"Furnace," was all he said, and he was gone.

I lay there alone, under the blanket, while he went to turn on the furnace. I hadn't realized how cold it was inside, but then again it was colder outside and I'd been half frozen when I walked in.

At this though, my mind finally stilled, and that side effect that I thought before was annoying now seemed charming because the ridiculous thoughts didn't hit me. What just happened came over me in a humiliating rush.

Everyone told me he was a player. He'd get into my panties, and even as pissed-off as I was and *he* was, he did, and I'd let him. I hadn't begged him with words, but my body had done it and I hated myself for it.

I got up, wrapped the blanket around me and was trying to pull my underwear on when he walked in.

231

He was naked, apparently oblivious to the cold, looking beautiful (as usual). His ponytail had come out somewhere along the way. There was a clean, white bandage wrapped around his thigh where he'd been shot, and behind him the house was dark.

"Don't do that," he said to me.

"I'm going home," I told him, still trying to get the panties up under the big blanket. I was no longer looking at him, but anywhere else. "Can I borrow your truck? You can pick it up from the Shelter tomorrow. I'll give May the keys."

He came forward as I was still fighting with my panties, and he hustled me, moving me gently but firmly back, around, over, his arm coming around my waist to hold me to him. He leaned down and flipped back the cover. I wasn't much use fighting him and trying to keep the blanket around me and my panties in place at the same time.

My hands gave up on my underwear and they dropped to the floor. I was trying instead to keep hold of the blanket at the same time I was slapping at his hands. I lost that battle, too. He pulled the blanket away from me and tossed it on the bed. He leaned into me and we went down.

I tried to roll away while he pulled the comforter back, but he caught me and rolled me to him face-to-face, his arms going around me.

I stilled and stopped fighting. I knew I wouldn't win, no matter how many moves I knew.

"I'm going home," I said, looking at him.

He didn't say anything.

I closed my eyes tight and dipped my chin so I wouldn't see his face. Then I opened them again and said what I had to say.

"Please, Vance. I can't stay here now," my voice was barely audible, "not after that."

"What was wrong with that?" he asked.

"It was humiliating."

It was his turn to still. "How was it humiliating?"

"Just let me get dressed and go home."

His hand went into my hair and he tugged at it until my head came back.

"Tell me what was humiliating about what we just did?" His voice was quiet, low and I knew he was pissed-off again.

232

"I gave in. I barely fought. You just had to... I don't know... kiss me and that was it. It's humiliating."

At my words, his body relaxed and his hand smoothed over my hip. I knew right off that he wasn't pissed anymore, but he wasn't going to smooth away the Return of the Major Freak Out.

"I don't even know what I'm doing here!" I cried suddenly. "I broke up with you this afternoon. Hell, I broke up with you last night!"

"Think hard, Princess. You might come up with an answer."

"I don't want an answer," I said truthfully, shocking myself with my words.

Damn and double damn.

I didn't need *that* either, so I mentally pushed it to the side.

"I didn't think so," he murmured, making me think, and making me freak out more that he had my number.

"I need to go home," I said, pulling back, but his arms got tight again.

"I know you need to go home, Jules, but you're not gonna go home."

I gave up pulling away.

"Why are you doing this?" I asked, looking at him.

"You want to stop seeing me then you'll stop seeing me, at least this way. I'm not gonna play that game."

"I'm not playing games," I snapped, interrupting him, now getting pissed-off myself.

"Yeah. You are. You just don't have enough experience to know you are."

My mouth dropped open.

He did *not* just say that.

"I'm not playing games," I repeated, a little more heatedly this time.

"What were you doin' with Luke this afternoon?"

"I wasn't playing a game."

"Well Luke was, and is, and will continue to do it. And you didn't get it and won't get it until you get your head out of your ass."

No...

Wait.

He did not just say *that*.

"I don't have my head in my ass. He was *kicking* my ass!"

"He was fuckin' with your head."

I pulled free saying, "I'm going home."

He caught me, rolled me to my back and rolled on me, full body. His hand came down, pulling out one of my legs until his hips were settled between both of them.

"Get off me, Crowe," I demanded, squirming underneath him.

"Stop fightin', Jules."

"Get *off* me!"

"Stop fighting!" His voice had risen. I'd never heard his raised voice and my body froze at his tone.

"Don't yell at me," I whispered, feeling that weight in my chest again, knowing he was that angry with me, and I hated that, too.

It felt like these days I was always on the verge of crying, and I couldn't remember the last time I cried.

What was up with that?

He talked over my secondary freak out, further fuelling the fire of my first. "For Christ's sake, I'm givin' you what you want. I don't know what's in your fuckin' head, *you* don't even know what's in your fuckin' head. Until you're ready to sort it out, it's gonna stay fucked up and I know enough to know there isn't a fuckin' thing I can do about it. So you want this to end, it ends. But tonight is mine. You want to fuck it up further, keep fightin' me, but I'm gonna have you fightin' or sweet. I don't care. But Jules, I'm tellin' you, I'd rather it be sweet."

I didn't know what to say to that so I didn't say anything. I just stayed silent.

He watched me for a while then he said, "I'd be happy with fightin', too. If what happened ten minutes ago is any indication, maybe I'd rather it be fightin'."

I didn't know if he was joking or being serious.

I decided to go with joking.

"Stop joking," I said quietly.

"I wasn't joking."

Okay then, he *wasn't* joking.

That got a belly flutter.

"Well, I've decided to be sweet," I said, just to be contrary.

He grinned, and his grin was so at the ready it made me wonder if he'd used reverse psychology on me. Then his face came down and disappeared in my neck and I felt his lips there.

The belly flutter escalated to Grade Two.

"I've changed my mind," I told the ceiling, "I'm going back to fighting."

His hands went down my sides to my hips and he lifted them. And then, I kid you not, he slid inside me. Slowly, gently, but I could feel he was again rock-hard.

My breath went out in a rush at the surprise of it and the fact that I moved from a Grade Two to a Grade Six in about three seconds.

"Vance," I said softly, and his lips moved from my neck to my mouth.

"That's it, beautiful. Every time I slide inside you, I want you to say my name," he muttered there.

He'd started moving and I started moving with him.

"I thought it was every time I came," I whispered, and his hands moved on me, a thumb sliding across my nipple as my hands roamed his back.

"I want you to say it then, too."

"Why?" I asked.

"I like it."

"But why?"

"I don't know why. It doesn't matter why. I just do."

That seemed plausible to me.

"Okay," I said agreeably, my hands going over his ass, and either my word or my hands (or both) made him grin again. He kissed me and started moving faster.

When he stopped kissing me and his mouth went to my ear, I said in his, "You have to get a condom."

"In a minute."

"Vance."

"In a minute."

I rolled my eyes.

He drove in deep.

When he did, it felt so good I whispered his name low into his ear.

Then I slid my hands in his hair, pulling it back, and I traced the outer edges of his ear with my tongue just like he'd done to me last night, and I'd liked that too.

After the second time, when it was dark and I was curled into Vance's side, his fingers drawing on my hip, the moonlight coming in from the two windows on either side of the fireplace and the one at the back of the room, I asked him in a whisper, "Were you mad at me when we got here?"

"I wasn't happy to walk in the down room and see Luke on top of you. I wasn't happy that you ignored me at the party. And I wasn't happy you were breakin' up with me. So yeah, I was mad at you when we got here."

I went silent because I knew the answer already. I didn't even know why I asked. I supposed if that was the way he took out his anger it wasn't all that bad.

The minutes ticked away.

Then I asked, "Why do you have so many books in the living room?"

"I like to read when I'm here," he answered.

"Why don't you get a bookshelf?"

"Don't need one."

I supposed he didn't. Still, he could use one.

For some reason I went on advising him about the décor of his cabin. "You should put new countertops in and refinish the cabinets in the kitchen," I told him.

"Why?"

"It'll look nicer."

"It doesn't have to look nice. It needs to keep me dry and warm."

"But it's your home," I said.

"It's just a cabin."

Something about that hit me somewhere deep. If this wasn't what he considered his home and he had no place in Denver, where was home?

I decided not to ask. He wouldn't answer anyway, and considering we were breaking up I had no right to know.

Instead, I said, "I like my space to be special."

His hand went still and he rolled into me.

"Yeah," he said, "I noticed."

I stared at his face in the moonlight, not sure if what he said was good or bad. Considering the way his space was, I decided it was bad.

"You don't like it."

He looked me in my eyes for a moment, then he kissed my forehead.

"I like it," he said softly when he was looking at me again.

I stared at him, memorizing his face when it was like it was now. Beautiful and gentle.

"The moon seems brighter here," I whispered.

"It is." His hand came up and he started to play with my hair.

I pressed in closer to his warm body.

"It's been a weird birthday," I told him, my voice still quiet.

He didn't answer.

I kept silent for a few minutes, then, knowing I should tell him, needing to tell him and knowing I'd only have the courage in the dark, I said, "I don't know if you saw the roses but they were beautiful."

His arm came tighter around me and fitted me to his body, but he didn't say anything. He just looked at me in the moonlight.

"They were perfect, each one of them. I've never seen anything like it."

He still didn't say anything.

"You should know that everyone was there when I saw them. Indy, Ally, Jet, Daisy, Roxie, even Tod and Stevie."

He kept quiet.

"Daisy said you have class."

He finally spoke. "I'm not certain how to take that, comin' from Daisy."

I smiled at him. "Believe me, she meant it as a compliment."

The smile was still on my face when his hand came to my jaw, and even though I couldn't see it in the dark, I just knew his eyes had changed. I felt them warm on my face.

Then he kissed me. It was long, slow and sweet. He carefully pulled the covers down our bodies. The air in the cabin was no longer bitter cold, but it still hit me.

"What are you doing?" I asked as he rolled over me.

"I'm gonna fuck you in the moonlight."

"It's cold," I told him.

"You'll get warm."

He wasn't wrong.

Chapter 17
Give It a Week, with Me

Luke and I walked up to my house after a night of patrol.

Patrol, I decided, was boring as hell.

I'd much rather be pouring canola oil on a Mercedes Benz or throwing smoke bombs than driving around town looking for trouble when there was none to be found.

It had been one of the worst days of my life (and I'd had a few), and truly the most boring night.

⌘

Vance had woken me up by making love to me, slow, sweet, taking his time. It was a new experience and one that I liked (a lot).

We'd taken a shower, gotten dressed and he drove me to my house.

Without a word he walked me to the back stoop, kissed me (also slow, sweet and taking his time), then he walked back to his bike and roared off.

Gone. Just like that. It was done.

I stared at the spot where I last saw him as my stomach twisted tight and my heart squeezed.

Then I went inside and listened to Boo telling me that Nick hadn't broken up his wet food with a fork like I normally do.

I picked him up and gave him a cuddle.

"Be quiet, Boo," I whispered with my cheek pressed to his fur.

Boo was quiet.

⌘

I'd spent the day waiting for Vance to call, walk into King's, do something Vance-like to invade my space and my life.

Nothing.

Kristen Ashley

May was openly worried about me and talking constantly in her Mama's-Gonna-Make-It-Better voice. May was a love, a good friend and a kind heart, but no Mama in the world would make me feel better.

All the gang phoned me. Roxie phoned twice. They were checking in and checking up and offering me everything to keep my mind off Vance. Yahtzee and sparkling wine (Tod and Stevie). A movie (Indy and Jet). A drunken night of debauchery (Ally). A day at the spa (Daisy). And a shopping spree (Roxie).

I'd turned them all down and mentally licked my wounds while my emotional Rottweiler sat next to me, tongue lolling, tail wagging, happy.

I was thinking I needed a new emotional guard dog. Something cute and cuddly with a smushy face that I could carry around in a purse and dress in ridiculous doggie clothes. Something like a pug.

The only bright spot had been when I'd called Nightingale Investigations and asked to speak to Luke. Without hesitation the guy named Monty who answered gave me Luke's cell number.

When I called, Luke answered by saying, "You're not gettin' out of trainin'. I don't care if he dumped you."

"He didn't dump me!" I (kind of) shouted. Then I realized he knew it was me who was calling. "How do you know my number?" I asked.

"Everybody's got your number. You're an unofficial member of the team."

Oh. I didn't know that. An unofficial member of the Nightingale Investigation Team. That was *way* cool.

I shrugged off the way coolness of being a member of the team, even if it was unofficial.

"I want to bring Roam and Sniff—" I started.

"Not gonna happen," Luke interrupted me.

"Luke! I don't want you to train them. I just want them to come and watch. Maybe they'll learn something. And they'll be impressed by the offices. And I want them to hang around good male role models."

Silence.

"Luke?" I called when the silence stretched.

"Good male role models?" Luke asked. I could tell by his tone he thought that was funny.

"Can I bring them or what?" I snapped, losing patience.

"Don't be late."

I guessed that was a yes.

Roam and Sniff walked into the offices trying to be cool, but I was right, they couldn't hide it. I knew they were impressed.

I walked into the office, scared to death I'd run into Vance.

Dawn smiled at me sweet-as-pie and informed me Vance was not in the building.

Bitch.

Then Roam and Sniff watched me get my ass kicked by Luke and they'd laughed themselves stupid. I told myself when their eyes weren't closed with laughter they probably learned something, so it was worth it.

After training, I took Roam and Sniff out for burgers then back to the Shelter. Then I went home to Boo and listened to him complain about my constant absence. Mostly I ignored him.

I took a shower, dressed in my take-on-the-night uniform. My new burgundy cords, black belt, black cowboy boots, black, stretchy, tight, long-sleeved tee, and black leather blazer. I waited for Vance to break in, say he wasn't going to let me go, like Eddie had done to Jet, and apparently Hank had done to Roxie, and also Lee had done to Indy.

No Vance.

I told myself this was good. I didn't believe myself and was beginning to think myself was a big, fat moron.

Luke picked me up. We drove around for two hours, doing mostly nothing and saying absolutely nothing (Luke, I found, wasn't a big conversationalist). We stopped a couple of times so I could talk to some kids and that was it.

⌖

At my door I pulled my keys out of my pocket.

Luke pulled my keys out of my hand.

"What the...?" I started, but with a Super Dude super-door-unlocking-power he was already pushing open my door. When he was inside, he turned to my alarm and punched in a code.

"How do you know my code?" I asked, coming in behind him.

He threw my keys on my chaise and walked into the house.

"Everyone knows your code," he told me, still walking across the living room.

I stared at his back.

So much for my life going back to normal.

I closed the door, turned on a lamp and followed him. I saw the light go on in the kitchen and heard Boo talking to Luke.

Luke was making himself at home and opening a bottle of Fat Tire beer when I arrived. Boo was asking him who the hell he thought he was and also could he spare a few kitty treats for a poor, abused house cat?

"What are you doing?" I asked as he leaned his hips against the counter and took a pull off the beer.

"Havin' a beer," he answered when he was done swallowing.

"I can see you're having a beer. *Why* are you having a beer?"

"I'm thirsty."

Oh for goodness sakes.

"Luke. It's late. I'm tired. I've just been bored out of my mind. I don't even know what patrol *is*. All I know is, so far, fieldwork sucks."

"Fieldwork is the business."

"My business is plastic wrap and canola oil," I told him.

After I was done with my statement he gave me one of his half-grins and I realized what I said sounded like.

"Go home," I ordered, deciding to get snippy instead of blush.

"If you're worried Vance can see us on the cameras, don't. He's after a skip."

With everything that happened, I'd forgotten about the cameras.

I did a mental review of my time in the house without Vance and realized with relief I'd been clothed through all of it and hadn't done anything embarrassing like dance around singing "Sir Duke" with Stevie Wonder, which I was prone to do.

I decided to ignore the cameras, for now. "A skip?"

"Someone who skipped bond. Vance is in Wyoming."

For some strange reason, knowing that and finding out from Luke slid in deep like a knife to the chest, and it hurt like hell.

He pushed away from the counter, index and middle fingers around the neck of the bottle, and walked up to me, like Vance did, overpowering and right in my space.

Then he put the hand not holding the beer to my neck, thumb at my jaw. I had no idea what he was up to, but I stood my ground, head-crackin' mamma jamma that I was, no retreat.

I rethought my decision when I looked in his face.

This was not badass, Super Dude Luke. His look was gentle, and if he was kickass hot normally, gentle would have taken me to a serious Grade Three belly flutter if I wasn't hung up on Vance.

"He shouldn't have fucked a virgin," Luke said to me.

Oh my *God*.

Any hint of a belly flutter disappeared. Mace had heard the cherry popping discussion and talked.

I tried to jerk my head away, but his fingers tightened around the back of my neck and I felt the warmth of his body as he got closer, *way* closer, but still not quite touching me with his body.

"Nothin' to be embarrassed about, Jules." His voice was soft.

"Maybe you should go home now," I suggested, deciding he was wrong. There was indeed something to be embarrassed about, but I didn't want to have this discussion with him, or anyone for that matter.

"It's sweet as hell and every fuckin' guy at the office wished they'd gone after you and trapped you in that alley after you shot out Cordova's tires. Including me."

Oh… my… *God*.

These guys gossiped like a bunch of women.

"I wouldn't have fucked you and left you, though. No fuckin' way," he went on, still talking softly, but sounding like he meant it.

Um.

Wow.

I swallowed and straightened my shoulders. "You don't know what you're talking about."

"I know Vance."

"You don't know what you're talking about," I repeated, and he didn't, and I wasn't going to tell him.

He stared at me a beat.

Then he said (luckily deciding to switch topics), "Tomorrow, training early. I'm takin' you out to dinner then we're going on patrol."

"Tomorrow's Saturday. No training and I'm going to annoy some dealers tomorrow night. I haven't done it in days. I don't want them—"

"Training at four. Dinner. Patrol. You need to take a break from the dealers," he interrupted me.

"Luke, I'm not going to stop."

"I'm not tellin' you to stop. I'm tellin' you to take a break, make them think Darius negotiated you off the streets. Get some action where you can try what you've learned. Then you can go back after them."

"Luke—"

"Give it a week, with me."

I didn't know what he was asking and I didn't want to know, mainly because I was afraid of what he *might* be asking.

He knew what I was thinking. "Just training, just patrol, just ride-along when I'm workin'. Anything else you can think of that doesn't have to do with that, I'm open to it."

I couldn't help myself. A ride-along while he was working was too good to miss.

Anything that didn't have to do with that I wasn't going to think about.

"Okay, training and patrol tomorrow... no dinner," I gave in partially.

"Dinner."

"No dinner."

He got closer and my breasts brushed his chest.

Um.

Yikes.

"Dinner," he said softly.

Time to retreat.

I pulled back. "Training and patrol. If I'm hungry, dinner."

"You'll be hungry."

Whatever.

Time to stop talking.

I frowned at him. He gave me a half-smile.

Then he touched my nose with his finger and was gone.

I stood in the kitchen and wondered what in the hell just happened.

Then I decided not to wonder. Best to leave it alone and book my flight to Nicaragua first thing in the morning.

I got ready for bed, making certain I did it in the bathroom where Vance told me there were no cameras (and I hoped he wasn't lying).

I climbed in bed and waited for Vance to break in. Wyoming wasn't that far away, just a few hours. He could make it back in time. From what I heard he was a good tracker.

244

I tried to stay awake so I could hear him when he came in and be ready to give him a piece of my mind before I jumped his bones.

Then, when I dozed, I tried to do it lightly.

Then I fell dead asleep.

⊰⊱

I woke to the phone ringing.

I didn't open my eyes and did a body scan, feeling for extra heat, the weight of an arm on me.

Nothing.

I opened my eyes and saw Boo staring at me.

"Meow," Boo said.

I slept on my side in the middle of the bed. Even though it was a big bed it wouldn't give Vance much room to sleep and not touch me if I was in the middle.

Still, I turned to my back and twisted my head to look.

No one there.

Boo walked onto my chest, sat down and stared at me.

"*Me... ow,*" he repeated.

My answering machine clicked on.

"In a second, Boo," I whispered, waiting for a voice to give a message and hating myself because I was holding my breath.

The voice came.

It wasn't Vance. It was Ally.

"Girl, wake *up*. We're all doing mimosas and eggs benedict. Dozens. Meeting in an hour. Be prepared, Tod's bringing the Wedding Planner Book. It might get hairy." She paused. "By the way, 'in an hour' means nine thirty."

I listened to her disconnect.

I laid there, stared at the ceiling and stroked Boo. Boo liked breakfast, but he liked stroking better so he settled in and waited.

I wondered if I could do mimosas and eggs benedict with a gaggle of Vance's friends. I wondered how, if I *did* do mimosas and eggs benedict, I would go back to a normal life. I wondered what the Wedding Planner Book was.

I curled my arm around Boo, threw back the covers and Boo and I slid off the bed.

I got Boo breakfast.

Then I got ready for Dozens.

〰️

After another boring, useless, action-free night of patrol, Luke and I walked up to my house.

I told him he could just take off, but he insisted on walking me up to the door.

I'd had another shit day. No calls, no space invasions, no nothing from Vance.

I shouldn't be surprised. I *did* break up with him and I wasn't playing games.

Still, I didn't expect him to give up so easily.

〰️

I found out at breakfast that Tod had declared himself Indy and Lee's official wedding planner and thus had created The Wedding Planner Book. Indy hadn't actually made this officially official, but was letting Tod live the dream.

For some reason though, throughout breakfast, Tod argued with Roxie (not Indy) about all things wedding. This argument took the form of Tod saying what was going to happen and Roxie saying whatever Tod said was going to happen *wasn't* going to happen with a lot of, "We've been here before, Tod."

Indy ignored them and gabbed with the rest of us about her and Lee's plans to go to Lee's cabin in Grand Lake for Thanksgiving, whether something big was going to happen between Tex and Jet's mom (apparently Tex was Roxie's uncle and that would make Jet and Roxie related by marriage; I was learning this was an incestuous group), and a lengthy discussion about Luke and my conversation last night.

Indy confirmed that all the guys on the team knew about my cherry popping.

At this news I ordered another mimosa.

"Men think virginity is hot," Ally assured me after I'd given the waitress my order.

"Maybe for eighteen year olds. Not for twenty-six, nearly twenty-seven year olds," I told her.

"No… um, they just think it's hot," Indy put in. "Even Lee thought it was hot."

I stared at her.

"Yeah, Eddie thought it was hot, too," Jet shared.

I turned my head and my eyes bugged out at Jet. "How does Eddie know? He's not even a member of the team."

She just looked at Indy and kept her mouth shut. Lee had told Eddie.

These guys.

"Hank knows too," Roxie decided to stop arguing with Tod and enter our conversation. I actually felt the blood drain from my face when I looked at her. "For the record, he also thinks it's hot."

That was it.

"I'm moving to Nicaragua," I announced.

"Oh sugar, it ain't that bad," Daisy threw in. "Vance thought it was hot."

That was true, Vance thought it was hot—for about a day (okay, maybe two).

I caught the waitress and doubled my mimosa order.

"You should know pretty much everyone is pissed at Vance for leaving you," Indy said after I finished my bid for a drunken stupor.

"He didn't leave me. I broke up with him," I reminded her.

"They don't look at it that way. They figure if he wanted you, he could have, you know, talked you out of it," Indy went on.

I was thinking, deep down inside where I didn't want to go, they were right. Any thinking about Vance made my heart hurt so I pushed it aside.

"It's better this way," I told them all.

They just stared at me, and I knew they didn't believe me.

Whatever.

Time to talk about something else.

I turned to Tod.

"I like tangerine and chocolate for wedding colors," I lied.

Tod's eyes got wide and happy.

"Oh shit," Ally muttered.

"Do not *even* go there," Roxie warned, eyes narrowing on Tod.

The discussion soon got heated.

Kristen Ashley

I was off the hook.

I went to training with Luke, and nearly at the end of our hour's session, I dropped him to his back with me on top.

"Yee ha!" I shouted in his face, sitting astride him, chest pressed to his.

"What do you do now?" Luke asked, hands at my hips, mini-half-grin on his lips.

"I don't know," I sat up, "maybe this?" Then I swung my arms out in front of me in a continuous loop and chanted, "Go Jules, go Jules, go Jules."

The door opened, my head swung to it in an oh-my-God-not-Vance panic, and I saw Mace walking in wearing a white tee with some surfer design on the front and black track pants with white stripes up the side. He looked at us on the floor, face blank like every day he walked into the down room and saw a woman astride Luke.

Maybe he did.

Then I was flipped onto my back and Luke was on top.

"Hey!" I snapped. "I was celebrating."

"Probably you should celebrate after you've incapacitated your target," he told me.

"I was thinking you might want to have a family one day," I returned.

He laughed in my face. I frowned in his.

"Babe, you weren't even close. Though, you wanna be, I'd give it a shot."

"Stop flirting with me," I snapped.

"Stop bein' so cute," he shot back.

The treadmill came on and both of us looked to it and saw Mace jogging. It was then I realized I was lying on the floor with Luke on top of me, having a conversation.

Damn.

"Don't mind me," Mace said, face no longer blank. I didn't know him very well, and he normally looked like he was in a bad mood (Mace was Mr. Seriously Broody Hot Guy Badass), but now he looked like he was going to laugh.

"You have a big mouth," I told him, turning my snit on him.

He jacked up the speed on the treadmill and the jog went to a run. He was completely unaffected by my snit.

248

"Too good not to share," was all he said, knowing exactly what I was talking about.

"You're on my list," I said to Mace and then looked at Luke. "You too."

"What list?" Luke asked.

"My Annoying-Men-I'm-Going-To-Kill List."

Luke rolled to his side and came up on an elbow. He was flat out smiling now.

"Why me?" he asked.

"Just because," I retorted and got to my feet.

I looked at Mace. "If you told Dawn, I'm going to torture you before I kill you."

"Dawn doesn't know," Mace said, amused look gone.

"Dawn's not gonna know," Luke said, on his feet, too.

Well, that was something.

Luke threw his arm around my shoulders.

"Let's get a beer," he said, and walked me out of the room.

I didn't argue, mainly because I could use a beer.

⌖

We went to Lincoln's Road House for beer and dinner. It would seem Luke had been right, I *was* hungry.

Lincoln's was a biker bar on a slip road facing I-25. It had great food, a broken-in feel, hot guys, women wearing chaps and slick bikes of every make, model and color lined up on the side road that flanked the bar.

They had a band so we watched it for a while.

Then we got in a big fight about who was going to pay, because I figured if he paid it'd be a date, and Luke figured he was a man with a significant over-abundance of testosterone so he was going to pay no matter what (this wasn't exactly his argument, more my take on the underlying message).

People started staring.

I shut up.

Luke paid.

Then we went on patrol.

⌖

This time at my door after patrol, keys held firmly and at the ready, I shouldered up to the door and let myself in.

Before I could claim the doorway and keep him out, Luke shoved me in with a hand at the small of my back, closed the door behind us and unarmed the alarm.

Then he walked through my living room.

"I'm tired, Luke," I told his back.

He disappeared into the dark hall.

I sighed and turned on a lamp. I shrugged off my blazer, threw it on the chaise and followed him into the kitchen.

The light was on and Boo was telling on me because I'd run out of kitty treats and hadn't been to the grocery store. Luckily, Luke didn't speak Cat and seemed to have the Super Dude super-power to be totally oblivious to Boo's meows.

Luke handed me an opened beer when I walked in and then he settled his hips against the counter, arms crossed on his chest, lifting his forearm to take a pull off his beer every once in a while.

We didn't speak.

For my part, this was mainly because the only thing I could think to talk about was whether Vance was back in town or not. And I wasn't going to do that.

For Luke's part, on the whole, he didn't talk much.

Finally Luke spoke. "Tomorrow, you're off. Monday, I'm workin' and you're ride-along."

I nodded, drank some of my beer, settled my hips against the counter and looked at my boots. I was happy about ride-along. It was something to look forward to in a future that, all of a sudden, seemed kind of bleak. I never thought about my future. I lived life day-to-day. I thought a lot about everyone else's future—Roam and Sniff, Nick—but not my own.

Luke's boots came into my line of vision and I looked up. He was close. He set his beer bottle on the counter beside me, pulled mine out of my hand and put it next to his.

Then, before I knew what he was talking about, his fingers curled around my wrists. He lifted my arms, got deep into my space, wrapped my wrists around his neck and his face started coming toward mine.

"What are you...?" I started then stopped.

His hands slid down the undersides of my arms and a thrill shot through me before (I kid you not) he kissed me.

I felt his hands glide down my sides, around my back low and he pulled me to him.

It was a great kiss. It was a hot kiss. There was a goodly amount of tongue, and Luke seriously knew what he was doing.

But it wasn't a Vance kiss.

I participated. I didn't know why. Maybe because I thought it was safe, but also because it felt really nice.

Luke's head came up and he stared at me.

Then he muttered, "Fuck."

"What?" I asked, keeping my arms around his neck. He still had his around my back.

"You taste like bubble gum."

My stomach went into a painful twist and I slid my hands to his chest, putting my arms between us and pushing back a bit. He allowed this, but his arms got tight when he was done allowing it, his message clear, and I stopped.

"Vance told me you're playing games," I said to Luke.

"Vance would know about games," Luke said back.

"Please don't talk about him like that," I whispered. "You don't understand what happened."

"I understand."

"You don't."

"Babe."

The way he said that made me shut up.

"I'm thinkin' you should train with Mace from now on," he said.

Um.

Yikes.

What did *that* mean?

I decided I didn't want to know, and this was mostly denial because I *did* know.

"I'm thinking that maybe training is a waste of time," I told him. "I'm hardly going to get into hand-to-hand combat with these guys doing guerrilla maneuvers."

"You're on the street you need to be ready for anything."

I rolled my eyes. Drama.

"It wasn't like it was before, Jules. They're gonna be gunnin' for you now," he said to my eye roll.

I had to admit, he was probably right.

"All right," I said, giving in.

"You still do ride-along with me."

"Okay," I agreed immediately.

At that, he grinned.

I realized his arms were still around me and my hands were still on his chest. I pushed back and he let me go, touched my nose, then he was gone.

I did the getting ready for bed gig, promised Boo I'd buy him treats tomorrow (and mentally added beer to my grocery list) and lay in bed waiting for Vance to break in.

He didn't.

The longer I waited, the more my chest got tight, the more I had to practice deep breathing in order not to cry.

It was my decision to break up with Vance. I made it. I carried it through. It was better for me, I knew it.

The problem was, lying in bed, alone in the moonlight, I didn't believe me anymore.

Chapter 18
Pizza, Football and Facials

From somewhere far away I heard my phone ringing.

With effort I dragged myself out of a deep sleep to hear the voice after my answering machine message.

"Babe, pick up the phone."

Luke.

I rolled over, reached up to the high alcove next to the bed and dragged down the phone.

"What?" I said into it.

"Get dressed. We got a takedown. Be there in five."

Disconnect.

I laid there with my phone to my ear for a second then blinked up at the clock. It was after two in the morning.

Luke had a takedown. That meant they were going after a bad guy. That also meant that Luke wanted me to come with them.

I threw back the covers, Boo screeched, "Meow!" and I swung off the bed.

~*~

It was Sunday night (Monday morning, really) and I'd had a day of no rest.

It was another shit day, post-Vance. Still no word, no sign, nothing.

I'd woken up that morning after the Luke Kiss, dragged myself out of bed, dragged on my clothes and dragged my ass to the grocery store to get cat treats and the makings for quesadillas.

I had no idea what was in a quesadilla or how to make one, but I guessed. I bought a bunch of other stuff, too.

While rolling my cart through the grocery store I decided to learn how to cook. I was going to take a new lease on life. I was going to be the New Jules. I was going to learn to cook. I was going to be a better Mama to Boo. I might even learn to knit. I was going to be a domestic goddess, super-social worker by day and a drug dealer ass-kicker by night. I was going to fill every second with new, golden opportunities. I was going to take on the kitchen, make my cat the happiest cat on the planet, buy myself some knitting needles and then take on the world.

On the way home, I stopped by the liquor store and bought more Fat Tire.

I went home and gave Boo enough kitty treats to send him into a kitty treat coma. He got all purry and then flopped down in a sunbeam on the chaise lounge and didn't move for hours.

I was cleaning the house and baking brownies from a box (starting small) when a knock came at the door.

It was Daisy.

It wasn't just Daisy. It was Daisy carrying an overnight bag.

"Are you moving in?" I asked, staring at the bag.

"Home facial!" she shouted. She shoved me aside and walked in.

She dumped the overnight bag down on my couch and started to pull out jars, bottles, towels, sprays and all sorts of stuff.

"Put on a camisole, I'm doin' the neck, too," she ordered.

"Daisy, I'm in the middle of cleaning the house."

"You can clean the house any ole time. Now's a special time. Now's *facial* time."

"I've never had a facial," I told her.

Her head snapped up from looking at the bag and her eyes bugged out at me.

"Never had a facial?" she asked, like I said I'd never breathed oxygen outside of my little bubble room.

I shook my head.

She snapped at me with her fingers. "Camisole. Now."

I put away the window cleaner and put on a camisole.

I was lying on my couch, a big pillow from my bed under my head and shoulders, a towel draped over the pillow, mud-colored gunk smudged all over my neck and face, cotton wipes doused in lavender water on my eyes, when there was another knock on the door.

I sat up and the cotton wipes fell into my lap. Daisy was sitting in my armchair, foot on my pub set, painting her toenails. I was supposed to be relaxing and letting the facemask dry.

"Get that, will you, sugar? I'm wet," Daisy said, not looking up.

I rolled off the couch and tossed the wipes on a towel on the pub set. I walked across the room and opened the door.

"Fuckin' A, Law. What's all over your face?"

Tex was standing at my door.

I stared at him. "What are you doing here?"

"Came by with these," he replied, indicating an old, beat-up workout bag he was carrying and he shoved inside. "Yo, Daisy," he called to Daisy.

"Yo, Tex," Daisy called back then she stuck her tongue to the side of her mouth and concentrated on her toenails again.

"What's this?" I asked as Tex dumped the workout bag by the chaise.

"Teargas. You don't have to use 'em, but they ain't goin' nowhere at my place. Thought I'd drop 'em by, just in case. What's that smell? Somethin' burnin'?"

Damn.

"My brownies!" I yelled and ran to the kitchen.

The brownies were burned to a crisp. Total disaster. I set them on the stovetop and walked back into the living room.

Tex was lying on the chaise stroking Boo, who was lying smack in the middle of Tex's big, barrel chest. They both looked like they were going to stay a while.

"You got a cat," he told me like I didn't know.

"That's Boo."

"Hey Boo," Tex said to Boo.

Boo purred.

"You ever need a cat sitter, call me. I got a business on the side," Tex offered.

"I'll keep that in mind," I told him, thinking it was a bit strange Tex was a cat sitter on the side. But then again, he'd just dumped a bag full of teargas in my living room. Pretty much everything about Tex was strange. "I never go on vacation," I went on.

"Vance'll take care of that. Indy and Lee are goin' to Grand Lake for Thanksgivin'. Jet and Eddie are goin' to Cabo for Christmas. And Hank and Roxie are goin' to St. Thomas in January."

"Vance and Jules broke up," Daisy put in.

Tex made a noise that sounded like "puh" then he said, "That'll last, like, a minute."

"She broke up with him two days ago. They're over," Daisy shared.

Tex's big head swung to me.

"Over?" he asked, like the concept of two people ending a relationship was foreign to him.

I nodded.

"Shee-it," he muttered.

There came another knock on my door.

"What now?" I mumbled as I walked to it and opened it.

"Fuck," Roam said, standing outside next to Sniff. They were both staring at me.

"Don't say fuck," I told him. "What are you doing here? You okay?"

"Yeah, what's on your face?" Sniff asked.

"A facemask," I answered.

Both of them kept staring at me. I knew it hurt my street cred, The Law walking around in a facemask.

"It's important to take care of your skin," I defended myself.

They blinked.

"Crowe around?" Roam asked. The first to get over the severe blow to my reputation, he was looking past me.

"They fuckin' broke up," Tex boomed from the chaise.

Roam and Sniff stared at me again. Sniff looked disappointed. Roam's face went hard. I knew what he was thinking.

"Roam, it isn't…" I started.

"Get in here boys, we're orderin' pizza," Daisy called over me.

"We are?" I asked when I'd turned to Daisy.

"Sure. Pizza, football and facials. What else do you do on a Sunday?"

Roam and Sniff pushed in.

Daisy stood up, twisting the top back onto the nail polish. "Time to wipe off the mud. Lay down, sugar. You, Sniff, go wet this cloth, hot water. Hot as you can get it," Daisy ordered Sniff and threw him a pale pink washcloth.

Sniff stood staring at the cloth a second, then, without a word (small miracle), he walked down the hall.

I lay down. Roam turned on the TV.

Thirty minutes later, slathered with face lotion and glistening from shoulders to hairline, facial done, enough pizza on the pub set to feed an army, the boxes sitting next to the jars and bottles of the facial debris, another knock came at the door.

Daisy, Tex, Roam and Sniff were all watching the game. I walked to the door.

It was Heavy and Zip.

"What are you guys doing here?" I asked.

"Came to see if you're still alive," Zip replied, pushing in.

"That the Broncos game?" Heavy asked, pushing in, too, and staring at the TV.

"Naw, Broncos don't start until three," Tex answered.

"You want pizza?" Daisy asked.

"Fuck yeah," Heavy replied, already sitting on the couch and reaching for a slice.

I stood by the door, staring at my ever-growing company, and wondering how this had happened. I wanted a quiet day. I wanted to learn how to cook. I wanted to spend the afternoon at a hobby shop perusing skeins of wool.

"Crowe here?" Zip asked.

"They broke up," Sniff informed him, eyes never leaving the game.

Zip hadn't moved into the room. He was still standing by me at the door and his eyes turned to me.

"Girl, I told you," he said.

"I don't want to hear it, Zip," I replied in a soft voice.

He stared at me a moment then he looked to the floor and shook his head. To my surprise, when he looked up again he also lifted a hand and patted me on the shoulder. Then he got himself a slice of pizza and a seat on the couch.

Heavy wasn't watching at the game. He was looking over the back of the couch at me.

"I don't want it from you either, Heavy," I told him.

He watched me a beat, nodded slowly once, then looked back at the TV.

My cell phone rang. It was Ally telling me that she was coming over.

"Bring beer," I said to her and stared at my living room, "lots of it."

"Gotcha," she replied.

"And some pop, Roam and Sniff are here."

"No problem."

"Indy, Jet and Roxie coming?" I asked.

"Negative, sister. They're spending the day with their men."

I felt a stomach twist.

"See you in ten," she said in my ear.

I flipped the phone shut, beginning to get good at ignoring the stomach twist, and I sat on the floor beside Heavy. He pulled at a lock of my hair. I looked up at him. He winked at me.

My stomach twist felt a little better at the wink, but my eyes got blurry.

Then a knock came from the backdoor.

"Jules?" Nick called from there.

"We're in the living room," I called back.

⊱≋⊰

I swung into the black Explorer next to Luke.

Luke stared at me.

"Ready," I informed him, buckling in.

"You wearin' purple pants to a takedown?" he asked, eyes on my thighs.

I looked down at my cords. They weren't purple, as such. They were more like a lavender-ish gray. I also had on my black cowboy boots, a black belt, a dusty gray, thick knit, long-sleeved tee with a hood and my black leather blazer. The hood of my tee was over the back collar of my blazer.

I thought my outfit was kickass, especially putting it together after two in the morning with only five minutes to do it.

One look at Luke said he didn't agree.

"Just drive," I said.

He drove, but he drove with a grin on his face.

We went to the old Stapleton airport area. Not the ritzy part that had been redone; the shitty part that hadn't.

"What's the deal?" I asked on the way.

"Skip. High bond, means the bondsman's out a whack if we don't pull him in. Name's Warren. Total scum. He's a dealer and a pimp. More the second, keeps his girls high and workin' for him doin' the first. You know him?"

I shook my head. "No."

"I got a Taser for you," Luke told me. "Please tell me you got your gun somewhere in those purple pants."

I pulled it out of my back waistband and showed it to him.

"You need a holster," he said to me.

I nodded, thinking of going shopping at Zip's tomorrow night. A holster would be dead cool.

"Ike's on him. Says he went into a house and hasn't come out. Called backup. Warren's a mean motherfucker and usually not far from his gun."

I nodded again, rethinking my excitement at a ride-along for a takedown.

We stopped in a not-so-good neighborhood. The second Luke cut his lights, my door was thrown open. I jumped and twisted in my seat.

"Calm, Law," the man said, and since Luke didn't shoot him or anything I figured he was one of the good guys.

He was Vance's height. Bald, lean and wiry, and from what I could tell in the dark, black with light skin. He had a killer tattoo slithering up his neck from the collar of his black tee.

"I like your tattoo," I told him.

"You haven't seen it all yet," he told me.

He'd said "yet".

Hmm.

"Do all of you guys flirt rather than just talking like normal people?" I asked who I assumed was Ike.

"Mace doesn't flirt," Ike told me, stepping out of my way so I could get down.

"I don't flirt either," Luke added coming around the back of the Explorer, attaching a fully loaded gun belt to his hips.

I whirled on Luke. "You're the King of Flirt! You flirt all the time."

Luke's eyes sliced to me. I could feel them hot on me in the dark.

"Maybe you wanna call Warren. Tell him we're waitin' out here to take him down. Give him a good chance to load up his gun so he can blow our brains out?" Luke asked after my outburst.

Okay, so maybe I was a bit loud.

"Sorry," I whispered.

I looked at Ike. Ike was smiling.

Damn.

I was screwing up my first takedown.

"He's got a couple women in there and Barry White's playin'. He can't hear a thing," Ike informed us.

Ike and Luke looked at each other. All of a sudden they seemed pleased about something.

Luke's eyes cut back to me. "Keep quiet and stay behind me," he ordered. I nodded and he handed me a Taser. "We try for alive when we're bringin' 'em in. Dead is a last resort," Luke went on.

Yikes.

I nodded again. Then we moved in.

As we approached a house a couple doors down from where Luke parked, Ike disappeared, vanishing into the night. Luke walked right up to the door, bold as brass, and something about the way he did it was way fucking cool.

I could hear Barry White crooning inside the house.

Luke shoved me to one side of the door. I had my gun stuck into my waistband at my left hip and the Taser in my hand.

Luke pounded on the door and shouted, "Bond enforcement."

After waiting about three seconds, Luke put the sole of a boot to the door by the handle and it popped open. He disappeared inside. I followed him.

It was dark and I could barely see, but Luke moved through the house liked he'd been there hundreds of times before. I kept my eyes on his back and moved behind him.

There was dim light coming from a hallway, the source of Barry White. We went down the hallway and into a room lit with candles and lamps with scarves over them. Luke stopped just inside the door, silent, still, watching.

I moved to his left to look.

"*Euw!*"

Yes, that was me, and I said it loudly. I couldn't help it. On the bed were two skanky, skinny women. So skinny, their ribs showed. Both needed to shampoo their hair in a *major* way. They were naked and working on a big, fat, hairy, naked white guy. Hairy as in *hairy*. He was covered in hair to the point that you could call it fur.

The inhabitants of the bed ceased their writhing and groaning, sucking and kissing and looked up at us.

"Bond enforcement," Luke announced, but I could tell, even though my eyes were riveted to the bed in frozen horror, that Luke was laughing.

Before I knew what was happening, the big, hairy, *naked* white guy moved. He was fast for a big man and he came off the bed like a shot.

At me.

I didn't have time to blink. I just lifted up my Taser and shot him.

He immediately went down with a thud, and I was pretty certain most of the furniture in the room jumped when he landed.

Wow.

I added a Taser to my mental Zip's Gun Emporium shopping list.

Breaking into my mental list-making, one of the naked skanks shouted at me, "What the fuck you doin'? You can't come in here and Taser Warren. Who the fuck you think you are?"

Then *she* came at me, body parts jiggling, lanky hair flying.

My Taser prongs were in Warren so I dropped it. She gave me the same opening as Jermaine had done, ready to scratch my eyes out. I grabbed her wrist, flipped her and she landed on her back. I heard her breath escape in a whoosh when she hit the floor.

"Aiiiiyeeeee!" the other skank screamed, coming at me, too.

I hadn't recovered from the first skank. So I planted my feet, dropped my shoulder when she got close and rolled her over my back. She flew over me, arms and legs pumping and landed on the floor.

I pulled my gun out of my waistband and trained it on them two-handed.

"Don't move," I ordered.

They stared, eyes wide, at my gun.

I glared back. "Stupid skanks," I muttered under my breath.

I felt a presence beside me and I looked over at Luke.

His eyes were on the skanks. Then he looked at me and a slow smile spread on his face.

"Babe," was all he said.

Ike moved in on my other side. He was looking at the skanks and the prone body of Warren. Then his eyes moved to Luke.

"Lee's recruitin'. Should we get her an application?"

⊰⊱

Luke told the skanks to dress Warren, and without a word they did as they were told. Then Ike cuffed and shackled him. They loaded him up in Ike's Explorer and Ike took him to the station.

Luke and I went to my house. I let us in.

My blood was still pumping at my triple takedown. I wanted to be cool about it, but I was pretty fucking pleased with myself.

I switched on a lamp, dumped my blazer on the chaise and smiled at Luke.

"Want a beer?" I asked brightly.

He watched me. "Jazzed?" he asked, one side of his mouth going up in his sexy grin.

I nodded.

His eyes cut to the ratty workout bag that was still where Tex dropped it, incongruous in my fancy-ass living room.

"Teargas," I answered his unspoken question.

Luke looked at me again then he shook his head. "The smell?" Luke asked when he was done shaking his head.

"Burned brownies. I'm trying to teach myself to be domesticated."

"Smells like you're failing."

I shrugged, still smiling at him.

He kept looking at me.

"Beer?" I offered.

Slowly, eyes still on me, Luke's grin faded.

"I don't want a beer," he said.

"Coffee?" I asked, cocking my head to the side.

"No," he replied.

Something had changed in the room. The air had started crackling. Before I could put my finger on it or do anything to disburse it, Luke was so in my space he *was* my space, arms around me, mouth on mine, kissing me.

Instinctively I put my arms around his neck. He walked me back, hands moving up my sides, across my back, over my ass, all this time his tongue in my mouth. I felt my thighs hit the arm of the couch and we both went over and down, Luke controlling the fall with an arm out. Then his body settled on mine.

My heart was pumping with adrenalin and excitement, both at the night's activities and the couch activities.

He was good with his mouth. Different than Vance, less intense, more titillating, almost teasing. His lips were always there, but his tongue was playing with mine, giving me a taste of something hot then disappearing when I wanted more, making me go after it. Eventually his mouth disengaged from mine and went down my neck and his hands went up my shirt. I shivered and returned the gesture, liking the feel of the skin and muscle of his back.

His tongue was doing things behind my ear that felt good and I liked it, wanted it, wanted him.

And then just as quickly as I realized that, I *didn't* want it.

Then, I kid you not, I started crying for the first time since Auntie Reba died. I couldn't have helped it if I tried, but I didn't even try. I was just too tired of holding them back.

I turned my head, put my lips to his neck and said quietly, "Luke."

At the sound of his name, his tongue stopped and he turned his head to look at me. He watched me for a few seconds while the tears slid down the sides of my eyes.

Then he said, his voice soft and not angry, "Not normally the reaction I get, babe."

My hands left the inside of his tee and one arm wrapped around his waist, the other hand went to the back of his head.

"I'm sorry," I whispered.

He didn't answer. He rolled to the side, back to the couch, and pulled us up so we were full-on the couch. He kept his arms around me and I pressed my cheek to his chest. I took deep breaths and after a few minutes controlled the tears.

One I'd done that, I tilted my head back to look at him. "You want a beer?" I asked, voice still quiet.

He used his thumb to wipe the tears from my face, and when he was done, he kissed my nose.

Then he answered, "Yeah."

I nodded, pulled away, got up and got us both a beer.

When I walked back into the living room, the TV was on. The sound low, some action movie with explosions was playing. I gave him the beer, sat down beside him and yanked off my boots. When I settled back into the couch, he pulled me into his body, arm around my shoulders.

Boo jumped up and I lifted my legs to the couch and curled into Luke's warmth, head on his shoulder. Boo settled in the space between us and I stroked him.

I wasn't afraid I was giving mixed messages. Instinctively I understood that Luke knew the score, knew I needed not to be alone and was offering me that and nothing else.

It was kind. It was huge. It was as un-badass as it could get and therefore even more badass than ever.

I'd never forget it and I'd always be thankful for it.

I drank my beer. Luke drank his. I put the empty bottle on the pub set and watched the movie.

Then I fell asleep cuddled into Luke.

⚔

"Babe," Luke said low.

I opened my eyes and looked up.

He'd reclined on the couch and I was tucked into his side, my back against the couch, my head on his chest.

"Bed," Luke said.

I nodded.

We got up and he walked to the door taking me with him, arm around my shoulders. He stopped at the door, kissed my nose and looked at me a beat. I bit my lip.

"Jules," he said.

"Yeah?" I answered.

He stared at me a moment before answering. "I *was* playin' a game," he told me.

It was my turn to stare at him. Somehow that hurt and I didn't need any more of that. I had way, way too much of that.

"Now," he went on, "I don't know what the fuck I'm doin'."

Oh my *God*.

Neither of us said anything. There wasn't anything to say.

Then, without another word, he was gone.

I locked the door behind him, armed the alarm and got ready for bed in the bathroom.

I settled in bed, Boo curled into the small of my back.

I felt sadness seep through me; no anticipation, no hope. I knew Vance wasn't breaking in.

I worried about Luke and me. I liked him. He was cool and he was funny, and in an alternate universe I knew something would have happened.

It couldn't, not now.

I was in love with Vance.

How did *that* happen?

I lay in bed knowing I was hugely fucked. Somehow my life had gone totally out-of-control. The Fortnum's gang of Rock Chicks had adopted me. The Nightingale Investigation Team had accepted me. Luke wanted me. And all of this had Vance tied up in it and that hurt me.

I definitely needed to round up Roam and Sniff and get my ass to Nicaragua.

I pulled a pillow to my stomach, hugged it close and tilted my head to stare at the moonlight.

With effort I forced my mind to still.

Then I fell asleep.

Chapter 19

Hush

I was certain I was awake, though I hadn't opened my eyes, and I knew with a sleepy body scan that I couldn't be.

There was heat at my back and a weight on my hip. It was full-on heat, definitely not Boo. I snuggled backwards into it, figuring if I was going to have a good dream, I was going to go for the gusto.

The weight at my hip moved, slid up to my waist then down, curling around my belly. The heat behind me was solid. Both I knew were no dream.

My eyes opened.

Then I turned.

Vance was in bed with me.

He was awake, *very* awake, and staring at me, face blank. I was also now *very* awake and staring at him, face probably not blank.

My heart had stopped. I felt something crawling through my system, something weird, good mingled with bad.

Fear and hope.

"What are you doing here?" I whispered.

I had turned within his arm. It was still around my waist, hand curled into my hip against the bed. When I asked my question, his fingers bit into my hip as they tightened.

"Had duty in the surveillance room last night," was Vance's mysterious answer.

I blinked at him. Then I remembered.

Oh my *God*.

The cameras.

How in *the hell* was I always forgetting the cameras?

"Crowe—" I started, my heart beating now, double time.

"I did *not* like what I saw," Vance interrupted me, his voice underlining his words, and a shiver slithered across my skin at his tone.

"Crowe—" I began again.

"He touches you again, there's gonna be a problem." The tone of his voice, if it could be believed, was deteriorating, and I got the distinct impression there already *was* a problem.

Um.

Yikes.

"Crowe—" I tried again.

"I want to know you understand me," Vance kept going.

"Crowe—"

"Do you understand me?" he asked. He sounded supremely pissed-off now and edging toward impatient.

"Please listen to me—" I started.

"None of it. Watchin' TV together. You curled up to him on the couch, and definitely not his tongue in your fuckin' mouth and his hands up your fuckin' shirt." His voice was getting dangerous, or I should say, *more* dangerous, and his face was no longer blank.

"If you'd just—"

"Jules, do you fucking understand me?" He was keeping his control, but I could tell just barely. I could tell this because his eyes had gone hard and his mouth had gone tight.

That was it.

I sat up and shouted, "Shut *up*, Crowe!"

He came up with me, face like thunder, eyes flashing, and I knew he was ready to blow.

One look at his face and I thought fuck it. It was now or never.

I stood next to my barking, snarling Rottweiler, ripped the plastic off a big, huge, juicy steak with a thick, meaty bone in and threw it to him. He nabbed it in midair, settled down and started gnawing.

Then I pounced.

And finally I surprised Vance Ouray Crowe.

In the beginning he thought I was going to fight him.

Couldn't really fight someone with your tongue in his mouth.

Well, you could, but it wasn't my style.

I was all over him. My hands were all over him. My mouth was all over him.

He was naked, which, if I wasn't in desperation mode to get him to shut up and pay attention to me, I would have thought was kind of brazen, considering the fact that we were over.

Instead, I thought it was good. A time saver.

When he realized I wasn't attacking him, his arms went around me with a force that squeezed my breath out of me, and that was it.

It was hot, heavy, lots of everything like we hadn't seen each other in three years rather than three days. I got astride him and lifted up, pulling my nightie over my head while he watched. When I was done, he rolled me over and tore off my underwear.

Then we went back at it.

Within minutes I was at Grade Nine.

"I want you inside me," I said breathlessly in his ear.

He started to pull away.

"Where are you going?" I was no longer breathless but sounding loud and a little bit shrill.

"Condom," was all he said.

Oh.

That.

I yanked him to me and rolled on my back, opening my legs and his hips slid between them. "In a minute," I said.

"Jules—"

"In a minute."

His head came up and he looked at me, hair around his shoulders, just as beautiful as ever.

I could swear I saw a hint of a grin before his face disappeared in my neck.

Then he slid inside.

After we were done, and once Vance had come back to me after going to the bathroom and dealing with the condom, which he did finally use and showed me how to put it on (which gave a new dimension to birth control that I liked very much, and I got the impression that he liked even better), I laid in his arms. We were side-by-side, my face tucked into his throat.

I had no ridiculous thoughts about my wardrobe or summer camp because my Rottweiler had looked up from his bone and had begun to growl.

Hush, I whispered.

My Rottie cocked his head, whined a bit then went back to his bone.

Through my mental turmoil Vance was silent.

I was wondering about his mood. Okay, I was worried about his mood. Okay, I was scared to death about his mood.

"I need to go to work," I whispered against his throat.

The fear and hope were back. The longer he stayed silent the more the fear was winning.

Vance's arms went loose and he moved a bit away.

The fear took further hold. I couldn't remember a time when Vance so easily let me go.

I looked at him and couldn't read his face.

Damn it all to hell.

"You going to work?" I asked in an effort to force him to speak.

"Been up all night. I'll go to the down room and crash."

I kept watching him, but my throat was beginning to feel funny, like it was going to close up on me.

I knew how important what just happened was to me. I didn't know what Vance was thinking, and from the look of him it wasn't good. Wasn't good as in wasn't anything, which was definitely not good.

"Okay," I said and it sounded kind of croaky.

I sat up, taking the sheet with me and holding it to my chest. Vance moved, getting ready to exit the bed. I grabbed his hand. Do not ask me why but I did. He stilled and looked at me.

And before I could stop myself I whispered, "You can crash here."

Vance didn't speak.

"You can shower here, too," I went on quickly so as not to arouse my Rottie.

He kept looking at me.

My jaw started hurting with the effort to keep the fear and the tears at bay.

"Whenever you want," I said. "Crash, I mean. And... um, shower."

I thought what I just said was huge.

Vance gave me nothing.

"I'll give you a key," I told him, the last ditch effort to get my point across. That was super-huge.

More nothing from Vance.

Not... one... thing.

That was when I nodded.

There you had it.

The fear changed from being scared of not getting Vance back to what my life would mean knowing I couldn't have him back.

Time to move on.

I'd deal with it later. A lot later. When I was making quesadillas like a pro while wearing a sweater I knitted for myself in Nicaragua.

"Okay," I said, my voice sounded higher and I let go of his hand. "I'm gonna get ready for work."

I moved toward the end of the bed, but his arm came around my belly and he threw me back against the pillows and settled his body on top of mine. My breath went out of me at his movements and I stared at him with wide eyes.

"Was it that hard?" he asked, looking down at me, face still showing me nothing.

I could no longer speak so I shook my head, nonverbally lying. It had been harder than hell.

"I don't need a key," he said.

I blinked, not sure how to take that.

"You don't?" I asked, finding my voice.

He shook his head. "Though it'd be easier than breakin' in all the time," he told me.

I felt relief start invading, washing away the fear.

"Probably," I whispered, still a little scared because he was still being blank; not intense or a different kind of intense, but not giving me anything to go on.

"Do you understand about Luke?" he asked.

I nodded.

He got closer, his face got closer, his body pressing me deeper into the bed. "Then we'll make sure you understand it all."

Uh-oh.

I didn't like the sound of that. I didn't share this and just watched him and waited.

"You're mine, Jules. That means no one puts their hands on you and no one puts their mouth on you. I almost came out of my skin watchin' that last night. You're with me and that means we're exclusive. I do not share. Which means no one touches you. Not again. You got me?"

I nodded. I couldn't imagine what I'd do if I saw him that way with another woman, but I was a head-crackin' mamma jamma. I probably would have lost my mind. A macho man badass was even worse.

I decided not to say anything. It was bad enough and saying something would likely just dig my hole deeper. I knew I was already skating on thin ice. I sure as hell wasn't going to go under, not again.

It was cold down there, freezing.

"You got your head straight?" he asked, breaking into my icy reverie.

I nodded again, though I was a little confused at his question.

He kept talking. "We're not playin' this fuckin' game. You try and push me away, I'm takin' you to the cabin and chainin' you to the bed until you got your head sorted once and for all. What we have genuinely doesn't seem like it's gonna work, we'll talk it through and come to an understanding. But when it's good and you get freaked, you aren't makin' the decision for both of us because you're scared out of your mind and don't have the guts to talk about it."

Wow.

I knew Vance was a straight-talker, but, um… yikes.

I thought it was time to cut in. "Vance—"

"I'm talkin' now."

At his tone I shut up. Definitely not the time to cut in.

"You lie in bed in the moonlight when you think it doesn't count and you let me in. I'm tellin' you now… it counts, Jules."

I kept silent.

Vance kept talking. "I don't want you sweet after I've made you come and you don't have your guard up. I want you sweet all the time. You don't start trusting me in the daylight this isn't gonna work."

I stayed silent.

"You go out into the night makin' trouble, fearless. With everything else that means something in your life, you're shit scared. You're gonna have to find a way to get the fuck over it."

I pulled my lips in and bit them to stay quiet. He was right and that was *so* annoying.

"You're mine," he repeated like I didn't get it the first time.

I let my lips go and said, "Okay."

He stared at me.

"Can I say something now?" I asked when he seemed to be finished.

"Just don't piss me off," he warned.

Like I'd do *that,* especially at this juncture.

I waited a beat, then took in a breath and then did something that made my Rottweiler go berserk. I ignored my Rottie. It took all I had but I did it.

"I know it counts," I whispered.

Vance didn't move, didn't speak, didn't do anything.

Then, drool flying everywhere in white globs, jumping up and down, tearing free from his chains, my Rottweiler came at me and I ran like a mad woman, taking my life in my hands. I passed him, threw open the door to the chain link fenced box and ran inside. I slammed the door closed behind me and locked it, keeping my Rottweiler at bay.

Then I ran my hands up Vance's back, stopping when I felt his scar and to make my point, I left my fingers there.

"You're right, you scare the hell out of me," I said it so low I wasn't sure if he heard it.

I didn't have to wonder long. He heard it and he understood it.

He rolled to his side and took me with him, arms going around me tight. He didn't need to say anything because that was enough.

I put my face in his throat again. "I need a boyfriend with a safe job. Like checkout guy at King Sooper's," I told Vance's throat.

He stayed silent.

"The worst thing that could happen is he'd fall off his rolling stool behind the cash register. Maybe hit his head or something. Sprain a wrist."

Vance still didn't speak.

"They have good benefits there, I heard. Great insurance."

More silence.

"That could be a rumor though," I muttered to myself since Vance was obviously not listening.

"Jules."

"What?"

He pulled my hair with a gentle tug and I looked up at him. His eyes were soft and sexy when I looked into them, and when he spoke his deep voice was silk. "Shut up."

Looking at him, the fear moved out of me and I melted into him because, one look at him, I just *knew* and the clouds over my life parted and I felt the warmth of sunshine.

"Don't tell me to shut up," I whispered.

That was when he gave me one of his grins and I knew I was right. Everything was going to be fine. Then he kissed me; slow, sweet, long, like we had all day, and I knew everything was *really* fine.

When he was done, there were no clouds in the sky. None at all. Just sunshine.

"I'm sorry about last night," I said quietly, because I had to.

"You need to talk to Luke," he told me.

I nodded. He was right. I needed to talk to Luke. I didn't want to, but I sure as hell needed to.

"Are you two gonna be okay?" I asked.

"He keeps his distance, yeah. He keeps at this game, no."

Hmm.

That didn't sound good. That sounded like I was Yoko Ono to the Nightingale Investigation Team's Beatles. I didn't want to be the woman who fucked up the band.

"I'll talk to him," I said, then went for another, much safer topic (at least I thought it was safer, but I was very, very wrong). "How long have you been here?"

"About an hour. The minute Bobby walked in, I took off."

"Why didn't you wake me when you got here?" I asked.

"I was pissed. I needed to calm down before I talked to you."

"You could calm down lying naked in bed with me?" I queried in disbelief.

"Lots of ways to work through anger, Jules, and I'm learnin' that I like the way *you* work through it a lot."

I blinked at him. Then I remembered the grin I thought I saw before he slid inside me.

"You knew we were going to have sex," I breathed as the realization hit me.

I caught the grin this time, full-on.

My body tensed and my blood started pumping through my veins.

"How could you know we were going to have sex? We were broken up!" I shouted, trying to pull away, but his arms got tight and his brows drew together.

"We weren't broken up. I was givin' you time to get your head sorted," he said.

Um.

What?

"We were broken up," I repeated.

"We weren't," he repeated right back at me.

"We most certainly were," I snapped.

"Jules, for fuck's sake, you don't kiss a woman that you've broken up with good-bye."

This gave me pause for reflection because it made sense.

Still.

Before I could say anything, he went on, "At the cabin, we made up."

"At the cabin, we were saying good-bye."

He stared at me for a beat then his brows unknitted and he started laughing.

Laughing!

I yanked back and gained some space. He yanked me forward and took it away.

"This isn't funny, Crowe," I snapped.

"You think you fuck four times to say good-bye?" he asked through laughter.

This gave me pause for reflection, too, because I had to admit, it sounded pretty ridiculous.

I didn't tell him that.

I tried a different tactic. "Why didn't you call me if we were still together?"

"Hard to give you space and call you."

Then something else hit me and my eyes narrowed. "You thought I'd let Luke kiss me when you and I were together?"

"You let Luke kiss you *and* put his hands up your shirt," Vance corrected me.

"Whatever," I said.

His eyes flashed. "Not whatever."

275

"I thought we were broken up." Now my voice was louder.

"I know that *now*. I thought you were workin' through shit, experimenting."

Oh my *God*.

He did *not* just say that.

"Experimenting?" My voice was no longer loud. It was quiet, soft and seriously pissed-off.

I'd just gone through all sorts of hell, nearly got emotionally chewed to shit by my Rottweiler, and through all that, he thought we were still together and he was just giving me space. Not only that, he thought I was the kind of woman who'd "experiment" with another guy.

I took a deep breath to calm myself.

Then...

I lost my mind.

I pulled out of his arms and sat up, wrapping the sheet around me and twisting toward him.

"I'm not fifteen years old, Vance, experimenting with every hot guy who comes along! Why didn't you tell me you were giving me space?"

He came up after me and twisted to face me. "Calm down, Jules," he ordered.

"Fuck calm and answer me."

"Jules—"

I forgot I demanded an answer and kept ranting, so in a snit that I forgot to think about what I said.

"I've been *freaking out* for three days. I thought I'd broken up with you and you'd *let* me. I thought we were over and you weren't going to try and get me back. Everyone thinks it!" I yelled.

His arms came around me, pulled me to him and I pulled back. We tussled. This, of course, ended with me flat on my back, head on the pillows and Vance's body pinning mine to the bed.

"Get off me!" I shouted in his face.

"Quiet, Jules, and listen to me."

"I don't want to listen to you," I snapped.

His eyes flashed. His face changed, his hands went to either side of my head and he held my face to look at him.

"Quiet," he ordered low, and my whole body stilled at his tone and the look on his face.

When he had my attention, he started talking. "You freaked when you got the flowers, and the way you told me it was over, I knew you needed that and was willin' to give it to you, but I was takin' one last night. You agreed. I used that night to get you to stop thinkin' crazy and pushin' me away and it worked."

"It didn't."

"You started redecorating my cabin, you thanked me for the flowers, you let me make love to you in the moonlight and again in the morning. You showered with me, you held on tight on the bike when I brought you home. Is that the behavior of a woman who's just broken up with you?"

Hmm.

He had a point.

I kept at it. "You didn't call me for three days."

"I was workin' and it's been intense between us. You freak out any time I get close. You needed space to get your head together. I backed off for a few days and gave it to you."

Okay, that made sense. It was even nice.

Still.

"I do not freak out," I snapped.

He raised his brows.

Fuck!

I was freaking out as we talked.

I glared at him because I didn't have a leg to stand on and I knew it, but my pride wouldn't let me admit it out loud. He watched me, then his face started to go soft and sexy and I knew that he knew my thoughts.

Vance Crowe *totally* had my number.

Damn.

Time to move on.

"All right, well… whatever." It was weak, but I didn't know what else to say.

I caught his grin definitely this time before his face disappeared into my neck. He knew he'd won in more ways than one.

"Next time I give you space, I'll tell you," he said into my neck.

I didn't want there to be a next time. This last time was bad enough.

I didn't share that with him, however.

His mouth moved on my neck and then came to mine and he kissed me, soft and quick and my freak out started to melt away. Then he lifted his head.

"Go to work. I'm tired and need sleep," he said quietly, his face an inch from mine.

"That didn't take long," I replied, kind of snotty, but not really meaning it. "We're back to macho-speak."

"Go to work," he returned, knowing I didn't mean it.

I stared at him.

I started to move away, but his arms got tight. I looked at him and he kissed me again, this time slow and sweet, but with lots of tongue.

That was more like it.

When he was done, my freak out had disintegrated.

Gone.

I looked him in the eyes for a beat then said against his mouth, "Sleep well."

He kissed my forehead and I grabbed my nightie and pulled it over my head. I turned off the alarm so it wouldn't wake Vance, swung off the bed and went to feed Boo.

I showered, got ready as quietly as I could and chanced a glance up at the bed before I left.

Vance was lying on his stomach, sheet down to his waist, and I could see his brown-skinned, muscled back, which looked even browner against my cream sheets. Boo was curled into the side of his waist and didn't even look at me when I peeked.

I had to hold on to the bed platform, not because of a belly flutter, but because my knees went weak. There were all sorts of reasons for this, none of which I had the time or inclination to explore at that moment.

I pulled myself together and walked outside.

Nick was standing in the yard staring at Vance's Harley, which was parked close to the backdoor.

Nick's eyes swung to me, but he didn't say a word.

"Um… seems Vance and I are back together," I informed Nick, explaining the bike.

Nick watched me a beat then dropped his head, stared at his shoes and muttered something under his breath I didn't catch.

I walked closer to him.

"Sorry?" I asked. "I didn't hear that."

He looked at me. "These are the times I hate," he said louder.

I just stared at him.

Then I asked, "What times?"

"The times when I don't know what Reba explained to you and what she didn't."

Oh crap.

Not one of *those* times. Those times were always embarrassing for both of us. Always.

"Nick——" I started, but Nick interrupted me and I could tell it was in an effort to get what he had to say over with and quick.

"Don't fuck with this guy, Jules. This is not the type of guy you fuck with. I figure he's got a lot of patience, and to be honest, no offense sweetheart, he's gonna need it with you. But don't use up his patience. Does that make sense?"

I was still caught at Nick dropping the f-bomb. Nick didn't tend to use the f-word very often.

Nick took my silence as confusion, came closer to me and explained, "What I'm sayin' is, don't jack him around."

"Nick!"

"I'm just sayin'."

"I'm not jacking Vance around!" Okay, maybe I was, but I didn't realize it at the time. "I'm just…" I went on, "working through some issues."

"Well, don't tease him while you're doin' it, that's all I'm sayin'."

"Tease him?" I whispered.

Oh my *God*.

Was I teasing Vance? Was I teasing Luke? Was I teasing both Vance and Luke?

Oh… my… *God*.

How did I go from virgin to slut to tease in a week?

"Do you think I'm teasing him?" I breathed, beginning to freak out.

"Uh…" Nick mumbled, watching me freak out and then lifted a hand to scratch the back of his head. "Maybe you should talk to one of the girls at the bookstore about it."

"I think I'll do that," I agreed quietly, and I was damned certain I would. If there was ever a time for a girlfriend, *this* was the time.

Nick came forward and kissed my cheek, then he was gone.

I got into Hazel and freaked out.

Then I thought of Vance sleeping in my bed and I freaked out more (but in a good way).

Then I felt something funny, sweet and wet, nudging around in my memory filing cabinets. I looked through my chain link fence and saw a cute, fawn-colored pug puppy with a black face pushing his nose through the fence and giving me sloppy, puppy kisses.

I looked through the fence.

My Rottie was nowhere to be seen.

I wondered if I'd miss him.

Chapter 20
Yoko Ono

I sat in the parking lot at King's and pulled out my cell phone. I scrolled down to Luke's number, took a deep breath and hit the green button.

"Yeah?" he answered after the first ring.

"Hey, it's Jules."

"I know who it is and I know why you're callin'. I'm lookin' at the monitors and I see Vance's Harley sittin' outside your house."

Whoops.

"Um, seems there was a misunderstanding," I told him.

"Bet there was, especially with him doin' surveillance room last night."

"He kinda saw us," I explained unnecessarily.

"I know where the cameras are positioned, babe. He more than kinda saw us."

He'd said "cameras", plural. It was a big room, but still.

I decided it was best not to think about it.

"He wasn't happy," I went on.

Silence, but I heard a door close.

"Seems that we weren't broken up after all," I kept going. "He was just giving me space."

More silence for a beat then quietly, "I hope that's it. I find out he threw away his nice shiny toy then got pissed when he saw someone else playin' with it, *I'm* the one who's not gonna be happy."

Um.

Yikes.

"I'm not sure I like being described as a toy," I said, feeling the head-crackin' vibe coming over me.

"I'm not the one treatin' you like a toy," Luke shot back.

I decided this wasn't going very well. "There are things you don't understand."

"Right."

Time to play peacemaker. "Luke, seriously, I don't want to be Yoko Ono."

"Come again?"

"I don't want to be the one who breaks up the band."

More silence then, "Babe."

I felt relief sweep through me. His "babe" was amused. He understood.

Then he continued talking, "Mace heard how you took down Warren and his girls and saw you floor Jermaine. He and I agree, you're ready to be full-time in the field. No more training. It's showtime. You're ride-along with me tonight."

He wasn't asking. I didn't know how Vance would feel about this, but I hoped I could talk him into it because I really, *really* wanted to do ride-along.

"What time?" I asked.

"Pick you up at nine."

"Gotcha."

"Out."

He disconnected.

⚊⚊

I had a morning from hell. Phone ringing off the hook, kids all over me wanting dirt on my now-famous takedown of the furry pimp and his whores, word, as usual, traveling fast (the two skanks obviously had been talking), appointments stacked up. I didn't have a chance to breathe.

May had been busy in the kitchen and I didn't have the opportunity to corner her to ask her opinion about Nick's "teasing and jacking Vance around" concerns.

I escaped at lunch, doing a run at Chipotle for Andy and me. I stormed through the doors at King's carrying a bag full of two fat, foil-wrapped burritos.

"Hey sugar!" Daisy called.

My head swung toward the couches and I saw Daisy sitting with Clarice. They both were wearing identical fluffy ice-blue angora v-neck sweaters, black (Clarice) and white (Daisy) cleavage bursting forth in abundance.

"Please tell me you paid for those," I said, walking up to Daisy and Clarice.

"I quit shop-liftin' when I was thirteen. It lost its allure after a three month stint in juvie. Gettin' Clarice here to turn over a new leaf. That right Clarice?" Daisy turned to Clarice.

"Unh-hunh," Clarice answered.

I wondered about Daisy's ability to be a mentor to a sixteen year old runaway. I didn't know that much about Daisy, but with what I did know, I decided she'd probably be a kickass mentor.

I looked at Daisy. "I need a powwow," I told her.

Daisy and Clarice stared at me.

"What kind of powwow?" Daisy asked.

"Apparently Vance and I aren't broken up. There was a misunderstanding. He was giving me space. He's sleeping at my house right now."

Daisy's eyes got huge. Then they got bright. Then she jumped up from the couch and grabbed onto my forearms with both of her hands and jumped up and down, her enormous head of teased-out platinum blonde hair bouncing with every jump. I didn't look at her cleavage, and luckily she didn't either or there might have been blackened eyes.

"Yee-ha!" she screamed.

I didn't jump with her as I was a head-crackin' mamma jamma, and as such didn't jump around like a girlie-freak. Daisy didn't seem to mind.

Still, I couldn't help but smile.

"This is *so* great!" she shouted then let me go and turned to Clarice. "Isn't this great?"

"Fuck yeah," Clarice said, smiling broadly at me. All the kids knew Vance and I were together and also likely knew Vance and I'd split up. Sniff had been in the building.

"Don't say fuck," I said to Clarice and turned to Daisy. "I need a powwow. Can you get the girls together after work?"

"What's the subject?" Daisy asked.

I kept my eyes trained on Daisy, not wanting Clarice in on the Is-Jules-A-Slut-Or-A-Tease?- If-So,-Discuss Powwow.

"Long story. I'll explain at the powwow. Tell me where and I'll tell May."

"You betcha, sugar," Daisy said. She pulled out her cell phone and started stabbing at the buttons with her long, lethally-pointed fingernail.

Okay, one down, one to go.

I gave Andy his burrito and took mine into the empty yellow room with my cell. I sat down at the table and peeled back the paper and foil on my burrito. Then I scrolled down to Vance's number and hit the green button.

It rang five times (I counted) then he answered, "Yeah?"

"Hey, it's Jules."

He was quiet for a second then he said softly, sounding like it was through a smile, "You know, Princess, I have your number programmed in my phone."

This made me freak out, but again in a good way.

"It's rude just to launch in and talk," I told him, not letting on to my good freak out. "You should always identify yourself."

"I'll keep that in mind."

"Did I wake you?" I asked this even though he sounded awake and alert. Then again he always sounded awake and alert.

"You caught me in the shower."

Oh my *God*.

Major Good Freak Out.

I cleared visions of Vance naked in my shower out of my mind. I was so good at doing this I completely blanked my mind and forgot why I was calling.

"Jules?"

"Um... yeah."

Pull yourself together, Jules.

"I'm meeting the girls after work," I told him.

"When are you gonna be done? I'll make dinner."

This was too much. I could barely process Vance sleeping in my bed, and he'd done it before. I'd even slept in his bed. The shower, dinner, I couldn't hack it.

"Jules?"

"What?"

"Are we done talkin'?"

"No."

"Then maybe you should talk."

God, I was such an idiot.

"You cook?" I asked.

"No," Vance answered.

I blinked at my burrito. "Didn't you just say you were making dinner?"

"There's a tray of what looks like incinerated brownies on your stove. I'm guessin' we'd do better to take our chances with me."

He was probably right. Still, it was slightly embarrassing.

I made a mental note to throw out the brownie tray. "Nick normally cooks. Maybe we should bum a meal off him."

"I like Nick, Princess, but I been away for three days. You just let your guard down and told me you're off with the girls for part of the night. That's about all I'm willin' to share."

Uh-oh.

"Um…" I mumbled.

"That doesn't sound like a good 'um'," Vance noted.

Throughout our conversation he'd sounded mellow, relaxed, in a good mood, amused. Now, he did not.

"I kinda promised to go ride-along with Luke tonight."

Silence.

"Vance?"

"How 'kinda'?" he asked.

"Kind of *definitely* kinda," I answered.

The phone came away from his mouth, but I still heard him swear. Then his voice was back in my ear. "I thought we agreed you'd call him."

"We did."

"You need to call him."

"I did."

Silence for a beat then, "Did you actually *speak* to him?"

"Yes."

"So tell me, how did your tellin' him to back off translate into a ride-along?"

Yes, I was right. Vance had definitely lost his mellow, relaxed, amused, good mood.

"He understands about Yoko Ono," I explained. "It'll be all right."

More silence then, "Maybe you should explain to *me* about Yoko Ono."

The words were a suggestion. The way he said them was not.

"Do you know who Yoko Ono is?" I enquired.

Vance didn't answer.

I figured everyone knew who Yoko Ono was, so I just forged ahead. "Well, see, The Beatles had this thing, no women in the——"

"I know about The Beatles," Vance cut in.

"You do?"

"Yeah."

"You like them? Their music, that is."

I asked because I was curious. Everything with Vance had been so intense, it felt like it had been years and it'd only been a week. I had a lot to learn and I figured no better time than the present.

And anyway, I loved The Beatles. If he didn't like them that would suck. If he was in the house what would I do when I was in a Sgt. Pepper's mood?

"For Christ's sake, Jules, get to the point."

Yikes.

Maybe now was not the time for a "getting to know you" conversation.

"Well, if you know about The Beatles and Yoko Ono then you get it."

"No."

"I don't want to be the woman who breaks up the band."

Again silence.

"Luke gets it. I think he'll be cool," I went on.

He still didn't speak.

"I really want to do a ride-along. I think I could learn a lot."

More silence.

"Vance, you have to trust me," I said quietly.

A beat more of silence then I heard a sigh. "Come back for dinner. When you're done with Luke, I'll be at the cabin."

For a second I didn't breathe. Then my mind shouted, *Yay!*

He trusted me.

And I was getting a ride-along. *And* I was getting to go back to the cabin.

"You have to leave the door open," I told him.

"I always leave the door open. Do you know how to get there?"

Hell yes, I'd memorized it even though I thought we were breaking up.

I wasn't going to tell him that.

"Maybe you should write out directions."

⋍⊨⋍

The Powwow was at Fortnum's at five thirty. I got there late and the crowd had already assembled. It included May, Daisy, Roxie, Jet, Indy, Ally, Tod, Stevie, and for some bizarre reason, Tex.

Tod and Stevie I could understand. Tex seemed like curry powder sprinkled on an ice cream sundae.

Whatever.

I sat down while everyone watched me, all of them grinning but no one saying a word.

"It seems there was a misunderstanding," I started.

Lots of nods.

"I thought we were breaking up," I continued. "Vance thought we were making up. Then he decided to give me some space because things were too intense."

More nods, grins turning into smiles.

"Seems you don't have sex four times while breaking up and saying good-bye," I went on.

Mouths dropped open, except Daisy, who emitted a tinkly bell laugh.

"Vance tells me that's more of a making-up kind of thing to do," I informed them.

Everyone looked at each other and I thought I heard Ally give a snort of amusement.

"This morning, my Rottweiler took a hike," I kept going.

The smiles disappeared and faces turned confused.

I took in a deep breath and told them about my emotional Rottweiler and his disappearance, and even told them about my cute, new, cuddly, squirmy pug puppy.

The smiles came back.

"Last night, I made out with Luke," I continued.

The smiles vanished again.

"And, kind of, the night before."

Eyes bugged out.

"Holy crap," Indy finally spoke.

"What's he like?" Roxie asked.

I just looked at her. She took one look at my face, which obviously said a thousand (good) words, and when her hand went up to her throat it was shaking.

I carried on, "Vance wired my house, put cameras in to keep an eye on me and protect me. He was working the surveillance room last night. He saw the whole thing."

"Jesus, sweet Lord in heaven," May whispered.

"I'd just taken down a furry pimp, some guy who skipped bond and two of his girls, Taser and hand-to-hand. Luke and Ike didn't need to lift a finger.

287

After it was over, I was kind of... jazzed and I'm guessing so was Luke," I explained. "And anyway, I thought Vance and I were over."

More nods.

"The time before, well... it just happened," I shared. "Still, I thought Vance and I were over or no way."

"I hear you, sister," Ally said.

"Luke wouldn't move in if he thought you were Vance's woman," Roxie threw in. "He doesn't do that."

"How do you know?" Tod asked.

"He told me," Roxie answered.

"That seems an odd thing to share," Jet entered the discussion. "Especially for Luke."

"It's a long story," Roxie said.

Everyone stared at her. With everyone's gaze on her, she told us about how Luke told her he was interested if it didn't work out with Hank and something about "Denver men being men".

When she was done, everyone kept staring at her.

"That Luke sure gets around," Stevie muttered.

"Boy needs to find his own woman," May declared.

"You got that right, sister," Jet said.

"Mm," Ally murmured. Her eyes had gone glazed.

"People, fuckin' focus. I'm thinkin' The Law ain't here to talk girlie bullshit. What's this about a furry pimp?" Tex barked.

"That's over. Ike took him in. It took like thirty seconds for me to drop all three of them," I told him.

"Righteous," Ally remarked.

"So what d'you need from us?" Tex asked. "Need a partner when you go out? Want to double up on maneuvers. You get seen harassin' one dealer while someone else douses another's car with vegetable oil? Get them all freaked out that The Law can be two places at once? That kind of thing?"

That wasn't a bad idea.

I looked around the room and was surprised to see everyone's face was eager except Stevie, who was staring at the ceiling looking like he was praying.

"Well, actually, I *did* come here to talk girlie bullshit. See, I'm worried I'm a tease," I admitted.

I saw a couple of blinks but mostly blank stares.

"Excuse me?" Jet asked.

"Misunderstanding the whole make-up, break-up scenario with Vance. Kissing Luke," I explained. "I don't want them to think I'm jacking them around. I don't want to be a tease."

Everyone looked at me.

"Jay-sus," Tex boomed then he got up, stalked behind the coffee counter and started banging on the espresso machine.

"How did you leave it with Vance?" Indy asked, ignoring Tex.

"He's making me dinner after the powwow, and after the ride-along with Luke I'm going to meet him at his cabin."

"Ride-along with Luke?" Stevie asked.

"Yeah," I replied.

"Vance know about the ride-along with Luke?" Stevie went on.

"Yeah, I explained Yoko Ono to him, and to Luke, they understood."

Indy, Ally, Jet and Roxie all nodded sagely, totally getting it. Daisy giggled again. Tod, Stevie and May gave me blank stares.

"It's a long story," I told them.

"Girl," I heard from behind me.

I turned around, my eyes hit a faded black t-shirt and the edges of a black leather vest. I looked up and saw Duke standing behind me.

Uh-oh.

I didn't know that Duke was even there, much less that he was listening in.

"Hi," I said.

He didn't return my greeting.

Instead he asked, "You were a virgin right?"

Shit!

Why did everyone know I was a virgin?

I didn't answer, I just stared.

"Those boys aren't stupid. They know who you are, what you are and a lot more of how a woman's mind works than you'd like them to know," Duke told me.

This gave me pause for reflection because I had more than a small suspicion that Vance had my number.

My reflecting didn't last long.

Duke kept talking, "They don't fuck around because they see a lot of shit in their line of business. They know the risks they take and they know the danger. They don't have time to pussyfoot around and process emotions. They see what they want, they get it. The end."

Oh my God.

I kept silent and kept staring. I couldn't help myself.

Duke carried on, "He knows you were a virgin. It's impossible to be a clueless virgin one day and a tease the next. Or, at least what I seen of you, it's impossible for you."

I hadn't agreed that I was a *clueless* virgin.

I didn't have time to squabble, Duke was on a roll. "Vance knows that. If he's havin' dinner with you and he wants you in his bed, you got nothin' to worry about. And if Luke knows you're with Vance and he wants you ride-along, you got nothin' to worry about with him, either. Yoko Ono my ass."

Well, there you go.

Duke's eyes turned to May. "When Luke's ready, mark my words, he'll get his own fuckin' woman, and God save us all."

Then he stomped away. Everyone watched him go.

Finally Stevie said, "Guess the powwow is over."

"Yeah, well, Duke has a way," Roxie mumbled.

"I'll say," May put in.

"Anyone want coffee?" Tex boomed. "If not, I'm shuttin' her down for the night."

"I have to get home. Lee's taking me to Barolo Grill tonight," Indy said, standing.

"Oh, sorry. I forgot to tell you, Eddie called. Lee and him have something on tonight. I told him to tell Lee I'd tell you," Jet explained.

"You're shitting me." For some reason, Indy looked ready to blow. I suspected she really (really) liked Barolo Grill.

Ally laughed.

"You and Lee and Barolo Grill... not... gonna... happen," Ally told Indy.

"Hank and I were supposed to go to a movie. He's sucked into whatever this is, too," Roxie said.

Indy sighed. "Such is the life of the Woman of a Badass."

"You got that right, sister," Jet said.

Everyone laughed.

I didn't. I was reflecting, and kept reflecting while they all decided to go to Brother's for burgers.

I headed home.
To Vance.

We were lying in my bed.

Vance was wearing jeans and a heathered, dark gray henley with a cool, heavy-buckled black belt. His feet were bare and I had to admit, they were still sexy.

I was wearing low-rider, midnight blue cords, a cool, heavy-buckled black belt of my own, and dark, gray-blue, fitted long-sleeved tee (I didn't figure Luke would have issues with blue cords). My feet were bare, too, and my toenails were painted a dark, electric blue. It had seemed a good idea at the time. I was feeling in a funky-girl mood. I decided I needed a pedicure.

Vance had made quesadillas and they were good. He'd even put jalapeños and bits of sautéed chicken breast in them. When we were done eating I did the dishes while he made some calls (it was only fair, he cooked). He was off that night, back at work tomorrow. He was going to the cabin after Luke picked me up.

When he was done with the phone and I was done with the dishes, he guided me to the steps to the bed and we climbed up.

Luke was due at my house in just over an hour. I figured Vance would go straight for the hanky panky. We had time.

He didn't.

He lay down on his back and tucked me in his side, my cheek on his shoulder. Then his hand went up the back of my shirt, but only to draw mindless patterns on the skin of my lower back. Other than that, he was silent and he didn't touch me or try to kiss me.

Hmm.

His fingers were having an effect. As I'd attacked him that morning, I thought it was his turn. But I didn't know how to communicate this without making it my turn.

"Vance?"

"Yeah."

"What're we doing?"

"Lyin' in bed."

Kristen Ashley

"I know, but... why?"

"Why not?"

I didn't have an answer for that.

Wait, I did. "I'm not good at lying around."

"Princess, you need to learn to be still."

I thought about that, thinking maybe he was right. I was rarely still. I was usually on the go, always had been my whole life. Hard to save the world lying in bed and doing nothing.

"Is this a Native American thing?" I asked.

"What?" There seemed a hint of laughter in his voice, and I got up on my elbow and looked at him.

I was right, definitely laughter. In fact, a full blown grin.

"What's funny?" I asked.

"You."

"How am I funny? I don't know anyone who sits around, doing nothing and being still."

"Lot of people do it. Most the time they fuck it up with their eyes glued to a television set, filling their mind with garbage."

I had to admit this was true. "Is that why you think I'm funny? Because I can't be still?"

"I think you're funny because you asked me if it was a Native American thing."

"Why's that funny?"

"The only thing I know about my culture is what I've read in books. I was off the rez by the time I was twelve. The two years before that, I was bounced around amongst people with good hearts who took me in but not enough patience to deal with my shit. Before that, all I knew was my Dad gettin' shitfaced drunk every fuckin' night of his life, most of those beatin' my Mom bloody while my brother and I watched."

Every muscle, bone and piece of tissue in my body froze including my lungs and heart. Then I snapped out of it, leaned over him, reached high and turned out the light.

"Jules?"

I settled in beside him, put my arm around his waist and pulled him to his side, facing me.

"Jules," he repeated.

I looked up at him. My arm stayed around his waist and I pressed my front to his.

Then I whispered, "I can't do it, Vance. You have to give me time. I need the moonlight." I took a deep breath, then said, "But before you get upset, you have to know that I know it counts, this counts more than any of it."

A change came about him. I could barely see it but I could definitely feel it.

"Jesus, Jules," he muttered, but he wasn't disappointed in me. It was something else. Something bigger, something that made his voice sound kind of husky.

It was something good.

I pushed deeper into him.

"If I had a superpower," I whispered, "I'd go back in time. I'd talk your Dad to an AA meeting. I'd get you back your family."

"Quiet Jules."

"I'd fix your Mom so she was only beautiful and not broken——"

"Quiet."

"And you'd know all about your culture because you should."

He rolled into me, then on top of me. "If you aren't quiet, I'll make you quiet."

"You should at least find your brother, Vance."

His hands came to either side of my face.

"I'll help you," I offered.

He kissed me and he didn't stop there. He did a lot of things that made me stay quiet.

Not exactly quiet, as such, but the sounds I was making didn't have anything to do with a recognized language.

So I guess I figured out how to get Vance to make a move and take his turn.

After we were done, he pulled a soft knit, chenille blanket out of the cubbyhole over the hall ceiling and arranged it on top of us.

He held me front-to-front, my face in his throat.

After a few minutes I said, "I want you to tell me more."

He was silent.

"Please. I know it's hard but——" I went on.

"Later."

"Promise?"

"Yeah."

"Okay."

His arms, already around me, tightened when I gave in.

I lay there, still, and thinking it was not that hard.

Chapter 21
Sometime Next Week

The knock came, and although it didn't take two people to open a door, Vance walked me to it. His arm was curled around my neck in a way that even I, with my significant lack of experience, knew was somewhat excessively proprietary. I had no choice but to wrap my arm around his waist or I would look awkward and be uncomfortable. Surprisingly, the minute I did this I was comfortable, very comfortable.

This was not a bad thing. Just that I thought it was kind of in-your-face for Luke, considering.

Vance opened the door and stepped us both back, keeping me at his side while Luke came into the house. Luke looked at me then at Vance, his face blank. I held my breath.

"We good?" Vance asked.

Luke's lips twitched. "Yeah," he replied.

I blinked. Was that it?

Vance's arm around my neck tightened and he curled me into his body so we were full frontal. When I looked up at him, he was grinning.

Well, I guessed that *was* it.

Guys were so weird.

Vance started talking, "Jules, be smart. Watch Luke and do what he says. I don't wanna have to come back down the mountain to sit in an ER waiting room."

"Okay," I said.

"No drug dealers tonight. Just business. Got me?" Vance went on.

Hmm.

Macho-speak.

I decided against answering and instead I just frowned.

"Got me?" he repeated.

Okay, so I had to answer and I did so snottily. "Are you aiming for our make-up to be the shortest in history or what?"

Vance grinned again. It was his turn not to answer and he did it better than me.

"I kid you not, Crowe, I'm working the King Sooper's stores tomorrow. I'm gonna find me a checkout boy. Safe job, good insurance and he probably won't tell me what to do."

At my threat Vance kissed my forehead. Then he let me go.

I took this to mean he didn't feel the King Sooper's checkout boys were much competition. He was probably right.

"Bye, Boo," I called.

"Meow," Boo called back from somewhere in the house, likely somewhere where he was getting into trouble.

"Be good," I called in warning just in case he was getting into trouble.

"*Meow!*" Boo called back again, sounding harassed.

I turned to Luke. "I'm ready now."

Luke had a full-on smile going. They were rare and they were effective. Some woman was going to be super lucky one day. I just hoped that Luke was just as lucky.

We started to move. Vance grabbed my hand, gave it a tug and I turned back to him. His head bent and he touched his lips to mine.

"Be careful," he murmured, his face close, his eyes soft and warm.

My breath caught.

I nodded and whispered, "I will."

We left and I swung into the passenger side of the Explorer.

"King Sooper's checkout boys?" Luke asked after I'd buckled in.

"My dream men," I replied.

"Babe." He started up the SUV and we headed out. "At least you aren't wearing purple pants tonight," he noted.

"I didn't want to embarrass the team."

"I'm thinkin' that'd be impossible."

Wow.

That was huge.

Even with that hugeness uttered, I decided to take a page out of Luke's book and be quiet.

It wasn't a silent night for Luke.

He talked.

He told me Nightingale Investigations had a varied clientele.

The bulk of which was corporate investigations, background checks on employees, looking into fraud, that kind of thing. This was done in-office, usually by their computer hacker, a guy named Brody, as well as through surveillance.

They also did some domestic investigations: cheating husbands, cheating wives, pilfering money from joint bank accounts.

Luke told me they used to do security, but now only watched Fortnum's and recently my place.

Further, they took on some government contracts, federal, state and local. They also took on specialized cases.

These Luke didn't share much about, but explained they were worked almost exclusively by what I was realizing were the "Top Four": Lee, Luke, Mace and Vance.

Last, the team also did a lot of skip tracing, and this they did nationally if the skip seriously skipped. Mostly it was done in a six or seven state area, which Luke considered "local".

Vance, Luke confirmed, was their top tracker. He also did all their wire work. Further, he was the guy they chose to do most reconnaissance because he was ultra-quiet, something he'd learned during his past as a felon.

Lee was ex-special operations force, Army Night Stalkers. Monty was an ex-Navy SEAL. Lee's specialty was everything. Monty's specialty was planning operations, these operations Luke also didn't go into detail about.

Matt and Bobby, two more of Lee's team, were local boys who should have been cops, but preferred an extra challenge. They spent a lot of time pulling in skips, taking photos during dangerous liaisons, doing stakeouts, providing security (as in bodyguards) when a client needed it, and they acted as added manpower. "Foot soldiers" was how Luke described them.

"Good ones," he said.

Ike had been a cop until something ugly went down. That something ugly wasn't shared by Luke, either. He was tracker number two on the team and was often out-of-town, the same as Vance.

Jack, another guy I hadn't met, was muscle.

"That's it?" I asked.

"Except for taking most night shifts in the surveillance room, yeah," Luke answered.

Mace sounded interesting, mainly from what Luke *didn't* say. Apparently he used to be a world-class surfer. He was half-Native Hawaiian and he came to Colorado to take up snowboarding, something at which he also excelled. Mace, like Lee and Vance, was good at everything he did. He had no specialty. They were all his specialties (except wirework, which Luke explained only Lee, Monty and Vance knew how to do). This was due to a life as an athlete, some of that professional. He knew how to use his body and his instincts and reflexes were sharp.

"How did he go from a professional surfer/snowboarder to a private investigator/bounty hunter? That seems a strange career move," I noted.

I thought of surfers and boarders as Zen masters, riding the waves and the snow, one with nature, not out cracking heads and looking pissed-off all the time.

"Personal reasons," Luke answered.

"What personal reasons?" I asked.

Luke didn't answer.

I gave up mainly because I knew I'd get nowhere as well as the fact that it was none of my business.

"And you?" I went on.

"Me?"

"Why are you in the game?"

He turned to look at me with a half-smile on his lips. "Shits and grins."

His eyes went back to the road.

He was holding back. How I knew this I didn't know. I just knew it.

"Bullshit," I muttered.

The air in the SUV changed rather dramatically, and my body automatically tensed at the feel of it.

Then Luke spoke, and it wasn't with his usual somewhat-teasing, bordering-on-affectionate tone. "Babe, there comes a time when you're sharin' my bed and you feel free to turn your attitude on me with your body pressed against mine, then you'll be in the position to know."

Well then, there you go.

I suspected Luke was "good" with the situation just as long as I didn't push it.

Good to know.

I decided to change the subject. "What's on tonight?"

"Search. Got a client who wants dirt on his wife before he asks for a divorce."

"Is she cheating on him?"

"He's the one who found a replacement. Lookin' for a way to make the divorce payout more comfortable."

Um.

No.

"This guy sounds like a jerk," I said.

"He *is* a jerk," Luke replied.

Luke pulled over and parked in a well-lit street in a neighborhood filled with comfortable houses of the nearly very rich. He made to exit the vehicle.

"Wait," I called.

He turned to me and raised his brows.

"We can't do this," I told him.

"Why not?" he asked.

"It's not right."

Luke twisted his body fully to face me. "We don't make judgments. We send invoices."

I could see right away where there might be a problem with my being on the team. I didn't make judgments, but I sure as hell had a moral code.

I decided not to debate this point with Luke, mainly because I didn't figure I'd change his mind in the few minutes I had.

I tried a different tactic. "I don't see how this is going to help me be more of a nuisance to drug dealers."

"This isn't training, babe, this is a ride-along. You go where I go. You don't like it, I'll take you home and you can have a bubble bath."

In truth, a bubble bath sounded good. However, I figured if I fucked up this chance there wouldn't be another one. I was too curious about what this team of badasses did for a living, considering I was "with" one of them.

I didn't know how to describe my relationship with Vance except that calling him my "boyfriend" sounded pretty stupid. We were exclusive, Vance made that clear, but how to translate that into a descriptive modifier was *unclear*.

Kristen Ashley

Also, I had the impression that the team liked me, respected me. I had this impression because somewhat easily they'd accepted me. If I went home and had a bubble bath I knew that would disintegrate faster than the bubbles.

"Let's do this," I muttered, getting out my side.

As he did last night, Luke walked straight up to the house like he owned the place. He opened the door with a key.

"You have a key?" I whispered, not about to make the same mistake as I'd made last night by being loud and calling attention to us.

He looked at me. "Client gave it to us."

Oh. Right. That made sense.

Luke entered and didn't turn on any lights. He went directly to a massive kitchen like he'd taken that route on numerous occasions. I followed.

He went straight to a small office off the kitchen that even in the dark I could see was decorated by a woman. Luke pulled on a pair of plastic gloves then took a small flashlight out of his belt and started to rifle through the desk.

"What are you looking for?" I asked.

"Anything," Luke answered.

I stood there, watching.

The flashlight often slid along the walls, and I saw one of those bulletin boards with the criss-cross ribbons on it. Business cards, receipts, notes, letters and photos were shoved into the ribbons. The photos were different shots of the same four people, a woman, a man and two young boys.

"They have children," I hissed at Luke.

Luke didn't answer, he kept searching.

I got more uncomfortable. I wanted to pretend it didn't matter, but it went against the grain. So deeply against the grain that the grain was feeling raw.

"Luke."

He straightened and turned to me. "Not our problem."

"But—"

"Babe." His voice was a warning. I was trying his patience.

I snapped my mouth shut and crossed my arms on my chest.

I decided a bubble bath was sounding good. In fact, after we were done here, I was going to ask Luke to take me home. Then I was going to put my bath oil in my bag for the cabin and take my bath there, where, after I was done, I could cozy up to Vance.

300

Fuck this shit.

So I would lose my unofficial place on the team.

Whatever.

Luke lost interest in the office and went upstairs. He was nearly as silent as Vance.

I followed, trying hard not to stomp and throw a tantrum, although I thought the situation warranted it.

We went to the bedroom and Luke rifled some more—drawers, medicine cabinet in the bathroom, nightstand. Then he got on his side on the floor and swung the light underneath the bed. He dropped to his back and shoved in his shoulder.

"Fuck," he muttered.

"What?" I asked, arms still crossed on my chest, hip hitched, one leg out. My stance said "attitude", but I had to admit I was curious.

Luke came out with a box. He'd opened it under the bed. He got to his feet, put the little flashlight between his teeth and with the box open in one hand, he rifled through it with the other.

I walked forward and looked then stared with my mouth open.

It was a little pharmaceutical cabinet. Not just pills (lots of pills), but vials filled with white powder; three of them, two very full, one half-empty, a mirror, a razor blade and a rolled up bill.

"Bitch is a cokehead," Luke remarked after he'd taken the flashlight from his teeth.

"It could be his," I suggested.

"He's payin' us to search his house. You think he'd leave his shit lyin' around?"

Damn.

That made sense.

"Maybe he planted it," I tried again.

"Doubtful. It isn't hers, he'll have a problem proving it if she fights it. Considering what's at stake, she will. Easy enough to find out if she's smart enough to ask for it to be printed."

Damn again!

I glared at him.

Luke ignored my glare, dropped down and replaced the box.

"Don't you need to photograph that or something?" I asked when he was back on his feet and back to searching.

"Call goes out to the husband tonight. They're at a show. He comes home, knows right where to find it, big scene. He asks for the divorce. He's got the dirt to nail her. She has no idea he has a woman on the side. She caves because she's fucked."

His scenario left a bad taste in my mouth. This wasn't about two people, it was about four.

Fuck.

After finding something, Luke's search intensified. In the end he found two more hidden vials of coke, both nearly empty, and another kit with mirror, blade and bill. He also found so many pill bottles hidden just about everywhere that it wasn't funny. Finally he found an envelope taped to the back of the dining room hutch. In it was a stack of receipts from pawn shops. Pill-Poppin' Mama Cokehead was pawning jewelry, silver, Waterford crystal and a goodly number of other household items to finance her habit.

Luke yanked off his gloves and I knew we were done. We left how we came in, got in the car and Luke called it in. I sat there not knowing what to feel.

Those two boys had a cheating father who wanted to screw over his wife and a drug addict mother who, from the looks of it, was either high as a kite or significantly sedated on a regular basis.

After Luke was done describing where the bulk of the evidence could be found, he said, "Out," then he started the Explorer and pulled away from the curb.

"This feels shit," I told him, staring angrily out the window.

Luke didn't respond.

"People suck," I went on.

Luke stayed silent.

I crossed my arms on my chest.

"We gonna go somewhere and crack some heads now?" I asked.

Luke chuckled. "You're gettin' it," he said.

Whatever.

We didn't crack heads. Or I should say, *I* didn't crack heads.

We did something else that rocked my world. It wasn't worse than being left with musings of the terrible life ahead for two little boys I didn't know and would never meet, but it was something that shook my world and what I thought was my place in it.

We went to a bar off Evans, a dive I'd never been to and likely would never see again.

In the parking lot Luke turned to me. "The guy we're gonna meet isn't gonna be happy to see me."

"Why?" I asked.

"He'll be expecting Bobby or Matt. At most, Ike."

"What does that mean?"

"That means he thinks he's flyin' under radar and we aren't takin' him seriously. I walk in there, he's gonna know we're serious. You got your gun?"

I'd put it under my seat. I bent to retrieve it, but he stopped me with a hand on my arm.

"You don't go in there carryin'. With this you're not the one posin' the threat. I am."

This all seemed quite complicated. I wanted to ask questions, but instead I nodded.

Luke entered the bar in his usual manner, body language communicating confidently that he knew who he was, he knew what he was doing and he knew where he was going. I followed, probably not looking as cool and confident as Luke because I didn't know any of those things.

Still, people turned to look when we walked in, and when they saw us their looks became stares.

Luke walked to a booth. A man was sitting in it and he reminded me of Sal Cordova. Ladies man, or at least he thought he was. Caucasian, dirty blond hair, dressed to the nines.

His face showed surprise, and perhaps a hint of fear, when his eyes hit Luke, then he covered it. His gaze hit on me and he stared, but again only for a moment, then his eyes went back to Luke.

"Stark," he said when Luke arrived at the table. "Didn't expect you to be running errands for Marcus. What? You get demoted?"

My body went rock-solid and I looked at Luke. Then I realized what I was giving away and I forced myself to relax.

Running an errand for Marcus?

Marcus Sloan?

Gun runner with drug dealer and pimp on the side?

Luke looked at me and I felt he was telling me something. It took a few beats for me to cotton on, then I slid in the booth opposite Ladies Man and Luke slid in beside me.

"Who's this? The Law?" Ladies Man was joking.

"Yeah," Luke answered.

Ladies Man's eyes cut to me and the forced joviality faded from his face. I could tell he didn't know what to make of me.

I kept quiet.

"She on the payroll now or what?" Ladies Man asked, going on to note, "I heard she took down Warren last night."

"We're not here to talk about Law," Luke said.

Ladies Man's attention returned to Luke. "Hey man, I don't know what this is all about. When I got the message, I was fuckin' stunned. Seems a lot of trouble over nothin'."

For some reason Luke said, "Stop," and I didn't think he was telling him to stop talking.

Ladies Man kept on smiling his good ole boy smile. "What?"

"Stop," Luke repeated.

"I know you're a man of few words, but what? Is this the message? Give me a clue." He turned to me. "Law? Do you know? How many syllables? Sounds like?"

Over the past few days Luke and I had shared a lot, or at least what I guessed in the World of Luke was a lot. So I felt pretty safe in thinking that Luke would not take to this guy being a smartass very well.

I wasn't wrong.

Luke lifted up in a squat, leaned across the table, and I kid you not, grabbed onto Ladies Man's collar and pulled him clean out of his seat. He put his other hand on him then twisted.

I reared back and was just barely missed when Ladies Man's body went flying by me and into the booth behind us.

Oh... my... *God.*

I got the keen sensation that Luke had been holding back in our training sessions.

Like.

A lot.

Luke slid out of our booth and stalked to the other one.

I followed.

By the time I made it to him Luke had Ladies Man by the collar. He'd pulled him out of that thankfully empty booth and whirled, slamming him against a wall.

There was music playing in the bar, but the hum of conversation died as everyone watched Luke.

Luke yanked Ladies Man forward and then slammed him against the wall again. I could hear the crack of his skull against the wall.

Yikes.

Luke held him pressed there, his legs dangling beneath him a foot off the floor, his hands wrapped around Luke's wrist and forearm. Just like in the movies, Luke held him aloft one-handed. I didn't even know people could do that in real life.

It was a sight to see. It gave me a belly flutter and a heart flutter, and I was jealous as all hell.

Luke wasn't just kickass. He was *kickass*.

"Stop," Luke repeated the same word.

Ladies Man wasn't feeling like being a smartass anymore. He looked scared shitless.

"Got me?" Luke asked.

"Yeah, yeah. Got you. Tell Marcus, nothin' to worry about. I'm out," Ladies Man rasped because Luke's hand was wrapped around his throat.

Luke dropped him.

Ladies Man's legs buckled a bit when he landed, but he pulled himself together and his hands went to his neck.

Luke turned his head to me. I got the message loud and clear and we both walked out.

We were buckled in and on and the road before I found my voice. "That wasn't fair. You hogged all the head-crackin'."

Luke was silent, but I could tell he was amused.

"Next time I get to throw the guy across the booth," I announced.

"Not tonight. We're done."

"Done?"

"Done."

"That's it?"

"Yep."

"But we've only been out..." I looked at the dashboard clock, "an hour and a half."

"Nothin' more on tonight's agenda, babe."

Well, that was disappointing.

"You should come on a ride-along on one of my nights out. It lasts longer and is a lot more fun." I told him.

"I'll take you up on that."

Whoops.

I'd said it to be snotty. I didn't expect he'd agree. This meant another conversation with Vance.

Shit.

Luke again walked me to my door, took my keys, pushed in ahead of me and turned off my alarm. This time he didn't head to the kitchen. I thought it best not to offer him a beer.

Then I asked what had been praying on my mind for the last twenty minutes. "Do you guys work for Marcus Sloan?"

"We're on retainer," Luke answered.

I closed my eyes. This was *not* good.

"Babe."

I opened my eyes again.

"He's a drug dealer. He runs guns. He sells flesh," I whispered.

"He's also Daisy's husband," Luke responded.

I felt like he'd punched me in the gut.

Daisy's husband? Daisy was married to a drug dealer? A flesh peddler? A gun runner?

"What?" My voice was so low even I wondered if I'd made any noise.

Super Dude Luke's superpowers included super hearing. "He isn't a good guy, but he's a good ally."

I didn't speak, *couldn't* speak. I was trying to process. I was also trying to breathe. Both I was finding difficult.

"Daisy's clean," Luke told me.

"Does she know what he does?"

"I'm guessin', yeah."

"Then she can't be clean."

"She's clean."

"I think you and I may have different definitions of the word 'clean'."

All of a sudden he advanced. Even knowing I was a head-crackin' mamma jamma, I retreated. I was vulnerable. I liked Daisy. I liked her a lot. I wanted to be her friend, but more, I wanted her to be mine. I'd suffered a blow from which I didn't know if I could recover.

Somehow Luke got me up against a wall and he came in close. This wasn't predatory, I'm-going-to-kiss-you close, this was pay attention to me close.

"People do what people do, to get by or get ahead, or leave shit lives behind. But there are lots of things that define them. How they act, the way they treat people they care about. Daisy lives well off dirty money. The minute she entered Indy's life, Lee investigated her and she's had more bumps than most, enough for her to deserve to live well. She's a good person and she isn't involved in Marcus's business. He's got legitimate shit running alongside his other concerns. Both sides are lucrative. He used to work for whatever he got out of it. Now he works for her. There's beauty in that and it isn't for you to judge."

"But——"

"Jules, it isn't for you to judge."

"I disagree."

"You pull out of that gang, you strike a blow to a good woman who's taken to carin' about you because you think you're too good for her. What does that say about you?"

What he said gave me pause. Pizza, football and facials gave me pause. Daisy taking Clarice shopping and hanging out with her at King's gave me pause.

"Shit," I whispered, and my eyes slid to the side, away from Luke.

His hand came to my neck, thumb at my jaw and my eyes slid back.

He wasn't looking at me like he was swinging toward disappointed. Now his eyes were warm with approval and something else.

"Now that you worked that out, somethin' else you should know," he said.

Uh-oh.

"Luke——"

"Vance is a friend, has been for a while. I like him. I respect him. He's good at what he does and I know he has my back. He knows I have his."

This, I thought, was good.

"I get the barest, fuckin' inkling he's fuckin' you around, I'm there."

This, I thought, was not good.

"I'm in love with him," I blurted.

Now why did I say that? I hadn't even told Vance that. I wasn't even *going* to tell Vance that. Not until he told me. I wasn't going to be out on the limb like Jet was with Eddie for months or for forever, worried about painting bathrooms purple or... whatever.

No way.

"I know you are," Luke said.

My eyes nearly bugged out of my head.

What?

Oh my God.

"How do you know?" I whispered.

"A woman like you, a woman who *looks* like you, doesn't save herself for twenty-six fuckin' years then gives it to a guy she's known a couple of days because she feels in the mood for an adventure."

This was true.

Shit.

This meant Duke was right. Men *did* know a lot more about the way a woman's mind works than we wanted them to know.

I decided this was not a good thing, especially if Vance had figured out the same thing.

I was fucked.

I decided not to think about it at all, ever, or at least not until tomorrow.

"Nearly twenty-seven," I said in an attempt to be amusing and steer us away from a tense subject.

One side of his mouth went up in a grin. I thought that I'd succeeded. I was wrong.

"With Vance or without, you always got me," Luke declared.

I felt that weight hit my chest, tears heavy there, and I sucked in breath to control them.

"Thank you," I whispered because I didn't know what else to say. "You too. You, um, always got me too."

He shook his head, touched his finger to my nose, then he was gone.

I stared at the door that he'd closed behind him.

Wow.

Hazel, Boo and I went right to Vance's cabin without one glance at Vance's directions.

Boo was not used to car rides and told me he didn't like them overly much. Indeed, he described his displeasure at length. Then he asked if this was an unheard of nocturnal visit to his most hated person in the world, the vet. When I assured him we were going to see Vance, not the vet, he sat on my thigh and dug his claws into my flesh to hold on and started purring.

Crazy fucking cat.

We parked close to the cabin door next to Vance's Harley. With my bag and purse over my shoulder, Boo's litter box in my hand and Boo tucked under my other arm, we made our awkward way to the cabin. The curtains were open, the windows were lit and the light coming into the surrounding darkness seemed warm and welcoming.

I opened the door and dropped Boo, who immediately began to explore. I put his litter box in the corner.

Vance wasn't in the room, but the buffalo-shaded floor lamp was lit and the cabin was warm, far warmer than the last time I was there.

It was nearly midnight and I figured Vance was asleep.

I was wrong.

He walked down the hall, feet bare, still wearing his clothes. He stopped at the entry into the living room and leaned a shoulder against it. His hair was not pulled back. He looked relaxed, at ease, at home and *hot*.

"Hey," I said.

"Hey," he said.

"Meow," Boo said.

"I brought Boo," I explained unnecessarily. "I hope that's all right. He doesn't like the way Nick serves his breakfast."

Vance grinned but didn't say anything. I decided to take this as an all-clear for the uninvited feline houseguest.

"Learn anything?" Vance asked.

"I learned that Luke hogs all the action," I replied.

Vance's grin turned to a smile.

I was standing by the dining room table and it seemed that Vance was far away.

I felt weird. I'd never had a sleepover at my boyfriend's (or whatever) house. I mean, I did have a sleepover, but that was a break-up/make-up session that included a rousing fight, unbelievable sex and a heartbreaking misunder-standing. I hoped this wasn't going to be the same (though the unbelievable sex wouldn't be unwelcome).

I needed him to make a move, but he seemed happy where he was.

Hmm.

"I'm going to take a bubble bath," I announced.

The vibe changed, his tractor beam flipped on and I felt my body lean towards him.

Finally he walked to me, grabbed my bag off my shoulder and then walked away. I followed him to the bedroom. He dumped my bag on the bed and then he lay down, picked up his book and started reading.

Okay then, tractor beam malfunction.

I got my stuff, took a long bubble bath, lotioned up with cucumber melon and put on my new nightie; soft, pale lemon silk with an edge of peach lace that hit the tops of my thighs. I yanked on my new lacy white hipsters. I'd bundled my hair in a loose knot with a ponytail holder at the top of my head. I left my bathroom stuff where it was, gathered up my clothes and went to the bedroom.

The house was dark, but the light was on in the bedroom. My bag was now on the floor. Vance was under the covers, Boo lying on his stomach, making himself at home. Vance's chest was bare and he was up on pillows, reading, his fingers rubbing Boo's neck.

When I entered, Vance's eyes cut to me. I rushed to my side of the bed, trying not to look like I was rushing. I dumped my clothes, climbed in and con-fiscated Boo for a cuddle. Boo had been comfy and protested.

"Hush, Boo. Mommy wants a cuddle," I told him.

"Meow."

"Hush."

I felt like an idiot talking to my cat, taking a bubble bath, having a boy-friend.

I was kind of flipping out.

This was normal stuff that normal girls do.

I'd never been normal. I'd always been kind of a freak.

And anyway, Vance was hot. I often forgot how hot he was, what with us arguing most of the time. He was just as beautiful lying in bed reading as he was kicking bad guy ass. Being reminded of that fact without him moving inside me or in a heated discussion with me made me feel... unsure.

We'd not had many quiet, normal, mellow times. Hardly any.

I found I couldn't handle it.

"I can't handle this," I told Vance, letting Boo go. Boo hustled to the end of the bed, plopped down on his side and gave me a glare.

"What?" Vance asked.

"This," I threw my arm out. Boo had given up the glare and started cleaning his face with his paw, likely washing away cucumber melon lotion residue.

"You're gonna have to explain, Princess."

"I can't explain." And I couldn't, at least not without sounding like a fool.

See, I'd never thought I'd have this in my life. I always thought I'd be alone. I was happy with that. I liked being alone, as long as Nick was next door and Boo felt talkative, which was all the time.

What if this worked for us? I got used to taking bubble baths in Vance's cabin. Boo lying on the end of his bed like he'd lived there his whole kitty life. Vance crashing at my place and using my shower and making us dinner.

What if I eventually had clothes here? What if I doubled up on the toiletries, litter box and kitty bowls so I didn't have to cart them back and forth?

What if Vance's jeans hung in my closet and I had to shift my nightgowns so he could have space for his t-shirts?

What if I got used to that? What if I liked it then it was all swept away?

My cute pug was chewing on my fingers, baby-dog teething.

Did pugs go bad?

I started to breathe heavily and I realized I was close to hyperventilating. Shit!

"For fuck's sake," Vance muttered. He'd been staring at me the whole time I was processing and obviously lost patience.

He put down his book, hauled me across the bed and into his arms, right on top of him.

Even though this was a loving gesture and the words he next spoke were in a tone that was both sweet and tender, a tone I'd never heard him use before and I liked it a lot, the actual words were not loving, sweet or tender.

"Girl, it's a good thing you're so fuckin' beautiful or you'd be a serious pain in the ass."

I rested my forearms on his chest and my head snapped up to look at him. "What's that supposed to mean?"

"I'm thinkin' you didn't get it. When you still your body, you also got to still your mind."

"What if you can't?" I asked.

"You can," Vance answered.

"What if you can't?"

"You can."

I made a "huh" noise in the back of my throat.

Vance burst out laughing.

Well then.

Whatever.

I slid off him, but he kept an arm around my waist, holding me to his side. I held my body tense, deciding to hold a grudge even as I rested my cheek on his shoulder.

He picked up his book and continued reading.

I decided tomorrow I was going to break up with him and I started to enumerate the reasons for doing so in my mind. He was too good-looking. I'd have to keep my head-crackin' mamma jamma skills honed to beat off all the bitches who wanted a piece of him. He was too arrogant, lying there, not paying any attention to my negative body language grudge (regardless of my cheek on his shoulder *and* my arm, which had snaked around his waist) and reading like he didn't have a care in the world. He told me what to do all the time, in macho-speak no less, and in front of other people.

While I was mentally enumerating, his fingers pulled up my nightie, his hand slid inside my panties, over the cheek of my ass, to come to rest flat against my hip.

That felt nice.

As in *way* nice.

So nice, my body relaxed, giving up the grudge.

Okay, then I'd break up with him the day after tomorrow.

Or maybe sometime next week.

When I made that decision, I fell asleep.

Chapter 22

Home

"*Meeeeooow!*"

My eyes opened and I saw smooth brown skin.

My head turned and I realized I was partially on my side, partially on Vance. I was pressed up against Vance's side and back, he was on his stomach. My cheek had been resting on his shoulder, my arms cocked, one hand against his side, the other flat on his back. My hips and legs were in full contact, my top leg thrown over his thigh.

Major cuddle action.

Um.

Serious yikes.

Boo was standing on my shoulder staring down at me, each of his kitty paws pressing into me like they weighed a ton, even though Boo himself weighed less than twelve pounds.

He was confused at his unprecedented new location and thinking he was four hours ahead, perhaps in Boston (even though it was doubtful he knew Boston existed), rather than outside Golden and in the same time zone as always. Therefore he'd decided he wanted an early breakfast.

"*Meeeeeeeoooooooooow!*"

Jeez.

I moved away from Vance, trying to do it gently so as not to wake him, if Boo hadn't already.

"Hush, Boo," I whispered, my voice sounding hoarse with sleep. I was a heavy sleeper. I knew it was early and I was *not* happy to have my sleep and my warm cuddle interrupted.

Vance moved, coming up on his forearms and looking toward me.

"I got him," Vance's voice was sleepy, too. Husky-sleepy, *sexy*-husky-sleepy.

"That's okay," I said.

Then I stopped talking, stopped breathing and my belly fluttered in deep Grade Eight, followed by a rollercoaster plummet when I looked at him.

His voice wasn't the only thing that was sexy-husky-sleepy. His eyes were soft, warm and unguarded, and he was looking at me with that "mine" possessive look, but also that other look, too. The one I could never figure out, but I knew I remembered. This time, early in the morning, dawn not even a promise, the room dim and Vance unguarded, the look was magnified.

And I finally remembered where I'd seen that look before.

No one had ever looked at me that way.

No, I'd seen someone else looking at someone else that way.

Nick used to look at Auntie Reba that way.

Like she was breath.

Like she was necessity.

Like she was life.

That was the way Vance was looking at me.

Right then, in the dim room, his eyes half sleepy and half full... of me.

Oh... my... God.

"I got him," Vance repeated not realizing I'd frozen. He leaned toward me, touched his lips to mine and got out of bed. He pulled on his jeans, did up all the buttons but two, rifled through my bag until he found Boo's food and walked out of the bedroom, Boo prancing in his wake, tail straight up.

I collapsed on the pillows and turned my back to the door.

"Oh crap, oh crap, oh crap," I whispered to myself again and again, holding the pillow to me. Then I stopped when I thought maybe Vance could hear.

Something was stealing over me, over my skin, through my insides. In both places it felt like velvet. Then it was all around me like a cocoon, warm and sweet and safe.

Then Auntie Reba's voice came to me, the first time in years.

After she died I'd hear it a lot, sometimes memories, sometimes like she was talking to me. I used to think I was a little insane so I kept it to myself. I didn't even tell Nick. It was my secret and I didn't want anyone to talk me out of having her voice with me. The months passed and it went away, but now it was back. I heard her voice, soft and wise, just like it had been the day she said the words.

Nick was in danger of getting transferred to Springfield, Illinois. I didn't want to go to Springfield. Nick didn't want to go to Springfield. Auntie Reba didn't want to go to Springfield. We were in the kitchen and I was pitching a teenaged fit. Denver was all I knew. It was *home*.

Auntie Reba, on the other hand, seemed totally at peace.

"How can you be so calm?" I'd shouted.

She turned to me, a small smile on her lips. *"Jules, sweetheart, home isn't a place. Home is anywhere, just as long as the people you love are there."*

Nick never got transferred and a few months later Auntie Reba died.

And home was torn away from us. We'd been homeless ever since.

Or we thought we were.

The tears hit my chest with a weight so hard it shoved itself up my throat and I could do nothing about it. It hurt too much to hold them back, they sprang from my eyes.

I was finally, *finally* back home.

But having Nick all these years I realized I'd never left.

"I'm so stupid," I told the pillow.

"Jules?"

I turned in the bed, flat on my back, and looked at Vance standing in the doorway, tears streaming from my eyes.

"I... I'm so f... fucking stupid," I sobbed.

"Jesus," he whispered, took two long strides and then I was in his arms.

"She left and sh... she was... ho... ho... home," I said against his neck, somehow I was in his lap and holding on tight. "And N... N... Nick and now this. I'm so stupid."

I was making no sense. I knew it, but I couldn't help it.

Vance had an arm tight around my waist, the other hand stroking my back.

"She died twelve years ago. *When is it going to stop hurting!*" I screamed over his shoulder.

"I don't know, Princess," Vance murmured into my neck.

I sat in his lap holding onto him and then all of a sudden I shouted, "I'm a *freak!*"

I was bouncing from subject to subject, my mind unable to hold a thought.

He pulled away and looked at me. "Sorry?"

"I'm twenty-seven years old and I've never had a boyfriend. I'm a total, fucking *freak*. I don't know what to do with you. Even though I've semi-gotten over the whole Vance Crowe, badass, super-cool, macho-man, danger-seeker gig, that still, like, flips me out, by the way, now I don't know how to be normal. I don't know what *to do*. Auntie Reba would tell me."

Vance was staring at me like he didn't know what to do either, but was leaning towards a call to the doctor.

"I need to call Nick," I announced, "I have to tell him I love him."

"It's barely six o'clock in the morning."

"He's an early riser."

"Jules, I think he knows you love him."

I stared at him and narrowed my eyes. "Are you sure?"

He grinned at me. "Pretty much."

I nodded my head decisively once. "Okay then."

Vance kept watching me closely.

Finally he asked, "Are you all right?"

"No, I'm not all right. I'm stupid. I'm totally clueless. I'm a mess. I'm a freak. I thought we'd already established that."

His grin faded and the atmosphere in the room went electric. I'd been relaxed even though I was crying, my body using his for strength and warmth. I tensed when the room changed because he'd tensed. In fact he went solid as a rock.

His arms went from around me and he pulled the ponytail holder out of the mess of hair at the top of my head and then twisted, tossing it on the nightstand.

Then he came back to me.

When he did, even in the dim light I saw his eyes were intense, more intense than usual, burning into me. His hands slid through my hair at the sides of my head, his fingers combing through it all the way down my back. His hands came up to either side of my head, holding it in position to look at him, his thumbs coming forward and wiping away my tears. I got the impression he did all this as an effort at control. What he was trying to control, I did not know, but I was about to find out.

"You're a woman who lost her family, *all* of her family, and did what she had to do to keep going. There's not one fuckin' thing stupid or clueless about that."

"Crowe—"

He interrupted me, "I hear you call yourself that again, it's gonna piss me off."

Um.

Yikes.

He already sounded pissed-off.

"Are you angry with me?" I whispered.

He ignored my question and carried on, "If you'd given yourself to someone else, you wouldn't be mine. And that would *seriously* piss me off."

Okay, now he sounded *seriously* pissed-off.

"Crowe——" I tried again.

"Far as I can see, with the time she had, your aunt did a fuckin' great job with you and left you in the hands of a man who handled you with care. I can understand you miss her, but if she was alive, she'd be proud of who you've become."

Oh my God.

That velvet feeling was back and it wasn't only enshrouding me, it had Vance wrapped up in it, too.

"Crowe, stop talking," I whispered.

"You want to know more about me?" he offered and at that moment I didn't. I couldn't take anymore.

I didn't have the choice.

"My life has been shit. I'd never been touched with gentleness, never understood it until I saw you handle Roam in Fortnum's. Then that night watchin' football with Nick, you showed it to me by runnin' your fingers along my jaw after I told you the worst in me. I was once Roam, Jules. You might not think it, but it isn't the kids who have two parents and a stable home who are the luckiest ones. It's the kids who know the taste of shit because they've been eatin' it all their lives, and then someone finds them and offers them a taste of somethin' sweeter and they learn that life can be good. They learn to trust. They learn that if you care about someone you put your ass on the line to keep them safe. They learn that love doesn't come with conditions. Roam and Sniff are the luckiest kids alive. I never had that. No one gave a shit enough to see it through. No one ever offered me that, until you."

It was my turn to hold his face. I put both hands up and kept them there.

"Vance——" I started, but he interrupted me again.

"I've been playin' this cool so I wouldn't scare the shit out of you because you're jumpy as a fuckin' jackrabbit, but I'm done with that now. I won't listen to you call yourself a freak and I'll let you know something else, and I don't give a fuck if it flips you out. If you ever think of takin' off, if you ever get scared enough at what I do for a living that you decide you can't hack it, then you best think again, because unless what we have turns shit like everything else in my life, I'm not ever letting you go."

"Listen to me—"

"Do you understand what I just said to you?"

"Vance, please listen—"

"Do you understand?"

"Yes," I said softly.

He stared at me or, more to the point, *glared* at me.

I decided it was time to come clean, too. "Well then, maybe you should also be aware of the fact that I know you have a reputation as a player and I know a lot of other people know that. If any woman tries to cut into my action, I'm taking her down."

I thought I sounded relatively badass and super-cool, for a girl.

Vance just kept staring at me a beat, still tense, then his body relaxed and his lips turned up at the ends in an amused mini-smile.

Um.

No.

"This isn't funny. I'm serious," I informed him. "I'm a head-crackin' mamma jamma. You're too handsome for your own good. I'll have to deck most of the single female population of Denver."

Even though I was, indeed, being perfectly serious, his body started moving and it felt a lot like laughter. He twisted and we went down, me on my back, him on top of me. By the time he came over me, I knew it was laughter, mainly because it had become audible.

I was offended. "Excuse me! This is *not* funny. How come you can make intense, macho man statements and I can't?"

His lips touched mine. He was still laughing.

"Shut up, Jules," he said there.

"Do *not* tell me to shut up," I snapped.

So he didn't. Using hands, mouth, tongue and other parts of his anatomy, he shut me up a different way.

⊰⊱

Vance made love to me. He did it slow, took his time and it was beyond beautiful.

We took a quick shower, got dressed and went back into town.

In a morning of significant moments, two more were still to come.

First, he told me to leave my stuff in the bathroom.

"I can't, I need it," I told him.

"Buy more," he replied, then walked into the kitchen to make toast. Or, remake toast. I'd had a go, and I'd burned it. Twice.

I added a trip to the mall on my mental agenda for the day and I had no problem with it whatsoever. In fact, my pug had never been to the mall and he was all excited to go (something else about my pug; his fur and face and little wet nose felt like velvet, too).

Second, Vance followed me on his Harley all the way into Denver. I saw him in my rearview mirror and I didn't lose sight of him until I turned my car into the garage behind the duplex. I knew this took him out of his way. His offices were in LoDo (lower downtown). He'd gone ten, fifteen minutes out of his way.

I could not explain why this was significant, but it was. I'd been on my own a long time and knowing someone had my back as, it were, was just plain nice.

I dropped off Boo, his litter and my bag, and went to King's.

May descended the minute I came through the door.

I took one look at her stormy face and asked, "What?"

"You still together with Crowe?"

What now?

"Why?" I asked.

"Tell me," she snapped.

"Yes. Why?" I snapped back.

Her face melted and she was all smiles.

"Just checkin'," she said, storm cloud gone, all bouncy and happy. "You want a pudding cup?"

"May, it's eight thirty in the morning."

"There's no time limit on pudding cups."

Jeez.

She was grinning at me, pleased as punch that I was getting it regular.

I looked at her.

Home. The word came into my head in Auntie Reba's voice and a warm shiver ran along my skin.

"Love you, May," I said softly.

May blinked at me. "What'd you say, hon?"

I walked the step of distance between us, put my hands on either side of her neck, bent at the waist and laid my forehead against hers.

"Love you," I whispered.

I watched close up as tears filled her eyes.

She tried to pull away. It wouldn't be cool for the kids to see us like this, but I didn't care and I held on tight. Maybe they *should* see.

"I think Vance loves me," I whispered as I lifted my forehead from hers, but kept looking in her teary eyes. "He looked at me this morning in a way, May, you wouldn't believe. And he told me he'd never let me go."

May was still staring at me. She'd never heard me share information about myself freely, certainly not something important, not without her having to drag it out of me.

I let her go, but put an arm around her shoulders and walked her toward the office. The whole time my head was bent to hers and I told her about my morning.

"Praise be to Jesus!" she shouted right before we disappeared into the hall.

All the kids (luckily, there weren't that many of them that early in the morning) stared.

⋈

The morning was its usual madness.

I called my doctor to make an appointment to discuss birth control because I was done with the condom business. There might be ways to make it fun, but Vance and I were kind of active (okay, *really* active) and spontaneous, and enough was enough.

My cell rang mid-morning. The display said, "Crowe calling".

I flipped it open. "Hey," I said.

"Got time for lunch?"

I didn't and that sucked. "Not really," I told him.

"I'll bring something to the Shelter."

I smiled into the phone. "That'd work."

"See you around noon."

My pug gave me a sleepy puppy cuddle.

"Okay," I said.

I went in search of Martin and Curtis and hustled them into the yellow room. It was time to get to the bottom of why they'd run away so I could start fixing it, but even though I knew I had their respect, they gave me nothing.

We walked out of the yellow room and one of the tutors, Stuart, was coming at me. The boys took off. Most of the kids avoided the tutors like the plague.

"Hey Stu," I said.

"Got a problem," he told me. "Roam and Sniff had an appointment with me yesterday and today. They missed them both."

Hmm.

Not good.

Roam seemed all fired up to get an education so he could become a badass mother. Clearly he'd lost interest when he thought Vance was out of my life.

"I'll take care of it," I said to Stu and I went in search of the boys.

Not stupid, they knew I'd come after them and I caught them making their getaway. I cornered them outside, in front of the building.

"You missed two tutor appointments," I told them.

"What of it?" Roam asked, all lip and attitude.

"You need to get caught up so we can enroll you in high school, get a foster home sorted, get your life sorted."

"Life's good," Sniff put in in an attempt to assure me they knew what they were doing.

My eyes sliced to him, and the look in them made him clamp his mouth shut for once.

I looked back to Roam. "I thought you wanted to get your diploma."

"Don't matter now," Roam said to me.

"I don't think you understand, what happened with me and Crowe——" I started.

"I understand, Law, you know I fuckin' do. Can't trust no-fuckin'-body. You think they're cool, got it goin' on, and you find out they're just assholes. Everyone's a fuckin' asshole."

Hmm.

Really not good.

I got closer.

"Roam—" I started again, but to my shock (and it must be said, supreme annoyance), he put both hands to my shoulders and shoved me hard. I went back on a foot and then steadied.

"Fuck off, Law," he clipped.

"Hang on a goddamned minute," I snapped, but I'd lost his attention. His already tense body froze and he was looking over my shoulder.

I looked, too.

Vance was not a foot behind me. How he'd materialized, I did not know. I hadn't heard him or sensed him, but I couldn't worry about that at the moment. Vance's face was hard and set, his eyes were scary and his mouth was tight. I'd never seen him look that angry. In fact, the word angry didn't begin to do it justice.

"What the fuck?" Vance's eyes flashed on Roam.

"What are you doin' here?" Sniff asked.

Vance didn't take his gaze off Roam.

"I said," Vance went on, his deep voice quiet, pure silk, but not in a good way. "What the fuck?"

Roam brought himself up to full height, which was an inch taller than Crowe, but he still looked like a boy. Crowe didn't move from behind me and I could feel the white-hot vibes crackling between them.

Roam didn't answer.

"Never," Vance continued in his scary voice, "do you put your hands on a woman in anger."

All of a sudden I was finding it difficult to breathe, realizing belatedly why Vance looked ready to commit murder. Roam swallowed. His eyes darted to me then back to Vance, but he kept his position, his guard up and his mouth shut.

"Okay boys—" I decided it was time to cut in.

Vance didn't agree.

"I see you do that again, I hear you did it, I'll find you and knock some goddamned sense into you," Vance warned, and I knew it wasn't a threat, and I suspected so did Roam. "Now's the time when you nod your head," Vance prompted.

Roam decided to play with fire. "Don't see why it's your fuckin' business. You dumped her."

Uh-oh.

"Roam, there's been a——" I started *again*, and got interrupted *again*.

Roam continued talking, "Thought you were the shit. Thought you knew a good thing. Thought you knew *everything*. You don't know nothin'. You threw away a piece like that?" Roam's head jerked in my direction. "You're an asshole."

Yikes.

"Roam," Sniff said in a cautionary tone. Even Sniff knew Roam was carrying it too far.

"Okay, listen to me right now——" I put in, only to be thwarted again.

"I have another rule," Vance talked over me. His voice was still scary, however now it was *scary*-scary, and I knew he was just hanging onto his control. "You call Jules a piece again and you'll be sucking your meals through a straw. I don't care if you're a kid."

Roam looked from me to Vance and back again and opened his mouth to say something, but luckily Vance got there before he dug his hole any deeper.

"Only reason I don't put my hands on you right now is because you're pissed on Jules's behalf. We had a misunderstanding. I didn't dump her. We're together. Nothing's changed except the fact that I was gonna find you and offer you some time. You want that time, see what I do, understand why you have to be smart, you learn some goddamned control."

Roam's face changed, confusion warring with hope.

My face probably changed too, mainly because Vance just offered to take Roam under his wing. I was finding it hard not to turn to him and kiss every inch of his beautiful face.

"You're still together?" Roam asked.

"Yeah," Vance answered.

"Hey! Cool!" Sniff exclaimed.

"You didn't dump her?" Roam continued.

Vance didn't bother responding.

Roam looked at me. "Why didn't you fuckin' say anything?" he asked, or more like *accused* and I knew he felt like a fool.

"Sorry, Roam. I didn't know I needed to inform you of the intricacies of my love life. I'll add your name to my girlfriend list and invite you to the next powwow," I said it full of attitude, hopefully loving attitude, and went on. "And for fuck's sake, stop saying *fuck!*"

The confusion faded from Roam's eyes, leaving only the hope.

He turned them to Vance. "I'll learn control," he promised.

Kristen Ashley

"I fuckin' hope so," Vance responded.

"It won't happen again."

Vance nodded.

The crackling, white-hot vibes disintegrated.

Crisis averted.

Thank God.

"Go make an appointment with the tutor," I ordered.

"This mean I'll get to be a pall bearer?" Sniff put in.

I looked to the heavens.

Jeez.

"*Ring* bearer, stupid. How many times do I hafta—" Roam started.

"Tutor! Now!" I snapped in my word-is-law voice.

Sniff grinned at me.

Roam didn't, but his eyes were shining.

"Later?" he asked Vance.

Vance nodded again.

They took off.

I turned to Vance.

He didn't look ready to commit murder anymore. He was staring at the front door of King's where Roam and Sniff had disappeared, and he looked like he was thinking about something.

"You okay?" I asked.

His eyes came to me. "That boy'd lay his life down for you."

I blinked.

Then I realized he was right. Not a lot of people would throw attitude at Vance like that, especially when he was promising physical retribution.

I felt that velvet shroud coming around me again and I mentally snuggled into it.

I looked at his empty hands. "I thought you were bringing lunch?"

"I left it in the Explorer. Saw you with Roam and Sniff and didn't have a good feeling about the body language."

He'd come to my rescue.

"I want to kiss you right now," I blurted.

Oh jeez.

Why did I say that?

324

Before I could take it back or affect a head-crackin' mamma jamma pose, Vance's face went soft and sexy and his arms came around me, drawing me into his body.

"Don't," I protested. "We're standing right out front, everyone can see. I already had a public display of affection with May this morning. I can't take another direct hit to my street cred."

His head was descending, completely ignoring me.

"Your street cred?" he asked, his voice silk again this time in a good way. His eyes were amused.

"Yeah."

"Fuck your street cred," Vance murmured against my mouth, and he kissed me. Not a touch of the lips but, full-on, open mouths, lots of tongue. I had no choice but to wrap my arms around his neck, and when I did he leaned in. I bent back and we went at it like teenagers.

It took a while for the catcalls and wolf whistles to penetrate our invisible fortress. It was around the time a kid yelled, "You go, dawg!" that I pulled away.

Vance and I looked to the entrance of the Shelter and at least a dozen (maybe more) kids were standing outside the door. May was there beaming from ear to ear. More kids, along with Stu and Andy, were looking out the windows.

We received an ovation, more whistles, catcalls, shouts of raunchy encouragement and full-on clapping applause.

"Goddammit," I whispered to Vance's neck, trying to pull out of his arms, but they just went tighter.

"I think that should do it," he said to me, and I looked into his eyes.

"What?"

"Don't expect anyone will think you're dumped anymore."

Oh.

Well.

I suspected he was right.

I relaxed in his arms and smiled at him, street cred be damned.

Vance smiled back.

Chapter 23
Toiletries and Tiaras

This was my afternoon and evening:

About ten minutes after Vance left from lunch came call number one. Indy.

"Hey, what're you doin' tonight?"

"I have to go to the mall," I told her. "Vance made me leave my lotion and stuff at his house so I need to double up on toiletries."

"That is *so* cool!" she shouted so loud I had to take the phone away from my ear.

"Um... you want to come to the mall?" I asked.

"Wish I could celebrate doubled toiletries, but I'm meeting a couple of friends of mine, Andrea and Marianne, at The Hornet. Want to pop around there after the mall, have a drink? They'd love to meet you, and we can toast the toiletries. Or are you out with Vance?"

"Vance has an uncertain schedule tonight," I explained. "He's gonna come to my place whenever he's done. I'm thinking about going out and crackin' heads later anyway. Probably shouldn't have impaired judgment."

Or more impaired than normal.

Indy laughed. "Probably not."

"Um..." I hesitated again, "did you ever double up on toiletries with Lee?"

"Negative, sister," she replied, "I moved in with him the first night we were together, kind of."

"Wow," I whispered.

"I know," she said. Then she giggled, and for some strange reason I giggled, too.

About an hour before leaving work came call number two. Jet.

"Hey, what're you doing for Thanksgiving?"

Something felt funny in my belly. Not exactly the flutter. Something else, a flutter mixed with a whoosh of happiness. This was because I was hoping I'd be spending Thanksgiving with Nick and Vance and that would be cool.

Kristen Ashley

"I don't know," I told her.

"Well, Eddie and I are going to Eddie's Mom, Blanca's house, and since Mom and Tex are together, he and Mom are coming, and since Tex is Roxie's uncle, she and Hank are coming, and since Ally is Hank's sister, Ally and Hank's parents are coming. Blanca asked me to ask you if you, Vance and Nick want to come."

"I'll have to ask Vance and Nick."

"Okay, let me know. Eddie and I are going over there for dinner tonight so just give me a ring."

"Cool," I said then, "um... Jet?"

"Yeah?"

"Vance asked me to leave my lotion and stuff at his place this morning."

"That is *so* cool!" she shouted.

I grinned at the phone.

"Did you ever double up on toiletries with Eddie?" I asked. "One set for his place, one set for yours?"

"No. Didn't have to do that. I moved in with Eddie after a few days and never moved out."

Yikes.

What was it with these guys?

I was heading to the mall when call number three came.

Daisy.

"Hey sugar. What's shakin'?"

"I'm on my way to the mall," I told her. "Vance said to leave my lotion and stuff at his house so I'm doubling up on toiletries."

"That is *so* cool!" she shouted.

I started laughing.

I flipped the phone shut after listening to Daisy telling me about how her masseuse was coming that night. It was only after I hung up that I realized I'd just talked to a drug-dealing gun-running pimp's wife and I had no problem with that.

None at all.

How weird was that?

Call number four came about five minutes after Daisy. It was Tod.

"Girlie! You're doubling up on toiletries?"

Someone was obviously talking, and that someone was either a redhead, a platinum blonde or a honey blonde. I was guessing platinum or Daisy.

"That calls for champagne!" Tod screeched. "I'm getting on a flight as we speak and Stevie's in Baltimore. We're both back in a couple of days and then we're having a Toiletries and Tiaras party."

By the way, when Tod wasn't a drag queen, both Stevie and Tod were flight attendants.

"Toiletries and Tiaras?" I asked.

"Everything goes with tiaras, girlie."

There you go.

Call number five came when I was in Bath and Body Works at Cherry Creek Mall. It was Roxie.

"Daisy says you're at the mall." Her tone sounded accusatory.

"Um, yeah. Vance told me to leave my lotion—" I started to say.

"I know, I know. Why didn't you call and tell me you were going to the mall?" she asked then didn't give me time answer. "I'll meet you outside the MAC store in fifteen minutes. We'll shop then get pizza at California Pizza Kitchen and we'll gab." Again, she didn't let me answer, she disconnected.

Roxie and I were browsing in the underwear section of Nordstrom's when call number six came.

Ally.

"Hey chickie. What's this I hear about leaving your lotion at Vance's?"

I gave her the lowdown.

"That is *so* cool!" she yelled then, "Listen, I'm working a shift at Brother's." Ally, I'd found out the other night, was a bartender at My Brother's Bar when she wasn't working at Fortnum's. "Come over, I'll buy you a drink to celebrate."

"Can't. Roxie and I are at the mall. We're looking at undies then we're getting a pizza. Anyway, Tod is going to have a Toiletries and Tiaras party in a couple of days," I said.

"Works for me," All replied, clearly always up for any kind of party.

I was buying three new silky, lacy and satiny underwear sets when call number seven came.

Vance.

"Where are you?" he asked. Not taking my instruction in common civility that you should identify yourself, he launched right in with macho-speak.

"Buying underwear at Nordstrom's with Roxie."

Silence.

"Vance?"

"Give me a minute, Princess."

"Why?"

"I'm enjoying a mental picture."

I grinned at the phone. "Still your mind, Crowe, and tell me why you called."

"Lee tells me you're goin' out tonight."

"How did he...?" I started.

This time, I figured it was the redhead who had the big mouth. Indy.

Jeez.

"Yeah, I'm thinking about it," I said.

"I'm caught up in something. I can't take your back."

"That's okay."

More silence for a beat and then, "It's *not* okay. I don't want you on the streets without someone doin' backup."

"Crowe, I've been doing this alone for months."

"You're not doin' it alone anymore."

Again the macho-speak.

"Crowe—"

"I'll ask around, get one of the guys to ride with you."

"Crowe—" I started again but I heard the disconnect.

"Goddammit!" I shouted at my dead phone.

"What?" Roxie asked.

"Vance is arranging for someone to ride with me tonight, even though I'm perfectly fine going it alone. I mean, I did flip a drug dealer onto his back and nearly shot another one in the foot not a week ago, and two nights ago, on my own, I dropped a pimp and two of his whores!" I snapped.

The customer service representative who was ringing up my sexy, silky, lacy, satiny, delicate, pretty, girlie underwear gasped.

Roxie's gaze swung to her then back to me, and she giggled.

Then she said, "Ask Uncle Tex. He's *dying* for some action."

This was true, he was. But Tex was a little scary. Tex had an old gym bag full of teargas at the ready. Tex, I thought, was not a good idea.

"I don't think—" I started, but she was already hitting the green button on her phone.

"Uncle Tex? It's Roxie, listen Jules needs someone to ride with her tonight..."

I sighed and looked at the customer service representative. She looked pale.

"What can you do?" I asked her.

She shook her head and rushed through my purchase.

Call number eight came while we were walking towards California Pizza Kitchen. I pulled out my phone wondering if it could overheat. I'd never been this popular.

It was Zip, and he didn't have the courtesy to identify himself either.

"What? You got the big boys teachin' you the fancy moves, you don't need me, Heavy and Frank no more?"

Uh-oh.

"Zip—" I started.

"You're comin' in to target practice. Tonight."

"Zip, I just doubled up on toiletries because Vance told me to leave mine at his place. Now I'm getting pizza with Roxie. Then I'm going out to crack some heads. I don't have time to shoot."

"You left your stuff at Crowe's?" Zip asked, "I thought you two had broken up."

"There was a misunderstanding. Apparently we hadn't."

"Yeah. I bet. Heard you've been on the street with Stark. One moves out, the other moves in, the first one decides he doesn't feel so much like movin' out no more."

"It wasn't like that," I told him.

"Don't got time to process your love life. Girl, you are loco. Fuckin' *loco*. You don't leave your stuff at a man's house after knowin' him for a week!"

"Of course not," I snapped. "I've known him for a week and two days."

"Shee-it. Those fuckin' guys," Zip said then gave up. "You're in here tomorrow night. No excuses."

Disconnect.

When our pizzas were served, I asked Roxie, "So, did you ever double up on toiletries with Hank?"

She shook her head. "I lived in Chicago. When I was in Denver, most of the time I stayed with Hank. I went back to Chicago for a few weeks to pack up and when I got to Denver, I moved right in with Hank. I was supposed to get an apartment for six months, but Hank didn't like that idea. As in *really* didn't like it."

I blinked at her. "These guys move fast," I whispered.

She smiled and I realized that she'd been living with Hank for as long as I'd known Vance. She'd moved to Denver the day I met him. Their relationship was still relatively new.

"How's it going?" I asked softly.

Her smile got bright, but her eyes got soft and she didn't answer because she didn't have to.

"I'm so glad, Roxie." Then, before I could stop myself, I reached out, grabbed her hand and gave it a squeeze.

She squeezed back, then she started giggling and again, I did, too.

Call number nine came after Roxie and I said good-bye and I was walking back to my car. It was Luke.

"What the fuck?" He also hadn't taken phone etiquette classes.

"What the fuck what?" I asked.

"I thought you were givin' me a week? Shortest fuckin' week in history, you goin' out tonight with Tex."

"How did you know I was going out with Tex?"

"Clue in, Law. People talk."

I was beginning to realize that.

"I thought our deal went south when Vance and I got back together," I explained.

"A deal's a deal."

I thought about this. I thought about what Vance would think about this. I figured Vance wouldn't like it much. Furthermore, I decided I didn't like ride-alongs, partly because they reminded me that people sucked and partly because Luke hogged all the action.

"You hog all the action," I told him.

"Babe," he replied.

"No, seriously."

"Wasn't me who took down a pimp and two whores single-handed."

Hmm.

He was right.

Time for a different tactic.

"If we keep our deal, I have to explain it to Vance. I'm not sure Vance can take another Yoko Ono conversation," I told Luke.

Silence.

"Luke?"

"Jesus," came the muttered reply.

"What?"

He didn't answer on our primary topic, instead he said, "Tonight, you be sure you take lead. Tex is a nut and Tex is an ex-con. Do not let him do anything crazy. You go down, you got no priors. He goes down, he's fucked. The cops want you off the streets and they'll be aimin' for you. Take Tex's Camino, your Camaro's too visible. And for fuck's sake, keep sharp."

Disconnect.

Call number ten came when I was in my kitchen, punching in my alarm code and Boo was shouting at me for treats, *very* unhappy with my trip to the mall and my gab with Roxie at California Pizza Kitchen, and not afraid to tell me.

I dumped my shopping bags and purse on the kitchen table and snatched out the phone.

Vance.

"What's this about Tex?"

Jeez.

"Crowe—"

"I don't have a good feeling about this."

Time for evasive maneuvering.

"Jet wants to know if you want to have Thanksgiving at Eddie's Mom's house with her and Eddie, Tex and Nancy, Roxie and Hank, Ally and her parents. Or do you just want to have it with Nick and me? Or, erm... did you, um, have to work or something?"

Oh my *God.*

I was *such* a dork.

When Vance answered, his voice was pure silk. Evasive maneuvering was effective and it was clear Vance didn't think I was a dork.

"What do you want, Princess?"

I felt the warm whoosh in my belly.

"Just you and Nick," I replied.

"That's what we'll do then."

I smiled at the phone. Again.

"I'll make pumpkin pie," I said.

"We'll get one at King Soopers."

Disconnect.

I stared at the phone.

"I am *so* sure," I said to the phone.

"Meow!" Boo said to me.

Tex drove a bronze El Camino and Tex played his rock 'n' roll loud.

Therefore, when we went barreling into the parking lot toward the drug deal, the Doobie Brother's "Listen to the Music" was blasting.

Tex screeched to a halt, swinging the wheel at the last minute so we did a 180 degree turn.

We were such a sight to see (and hear) that instead of running, the buyers and seller stared at us in frozen shock, and I didn't blame them.

Then during the Doobie Brothers singing the chorus, Tex got out his side, I got out my side and we lobbed the smoke bombs. Three for him, three for me. The buyers and seller started choking, spluttering, cursing and scurrying.

Tex and I jumped into the car and Tex peeled away.

"That's what I'm talkin' about, turkey!" Tex shouted at the windshield and banged his fist on the steering wheel. He did this every time we'd seen action, except once, instead of "turkey", he said, "sucka".

It had been an active night. We were out of smoke bombs.

Make no mistake, The Law and her sidekick, Tex, the Crackpot Coffee Guy, were on the job.

"We're out of smoke bombs," I told Tex.

"Could swing by your place, pick up the teargas," Tex suggested.

Um.

No.

"I don't think smoke bombs are illegal. I'm not sure about teargas."

Tex was silent for a moment as if contemplating this.

Finally he said, "See your point."

"Maybe we should call it a night?"

"We goin' out again tomorrow?"

Hmm.

He said "we".

I was a loner, or had been until recently. I hadn't seen a lot of alone time in a while, and that had been at night when I thought Vance and I had broken up.

That time wasn't fun.

Furthermore, Tex was huge, burly and relaxed. He caused mayhem like it was second nature. He made me feel safe.

It was a new experience, being out making life a pain for drug dealers with Tex.

I liked it.

"Sure," I said.

"Fuckin' A, woman!" Tex boomed.

I smiled.

We went to his house. He stood on the sidewalk and didn't make a move toward his door until I was in my car and headed down the street.

I was negotiating the alley toward Nick and my garage when a car reversed out of a back drive right into the alley, right in front of me. To avoid it I slammed on the brakes and came to a bone-jarring halt.

I stared out the windshield. The car was dark, no lights.

Fuck, fuck, *fuck!*

I threw the Camaro in reverse and looked over my shoulder, but all I could see was a motorcycle parked perpendicular to my car.

I'd wasted precious time shifting to reverse. I should have locked my doors. I didn't even get a chance to move when my door was thrown open.

Before I could grab my gun or stun gun on the seat beside me, someone reached in, undid my belt and yanked me out of the car.

He slammed the door and then slammed me against the car and got up close, his hard body to my soft one, his heat slamming into me like a physical thing.

When I got a look at him in the hazy alley streetlight, I went still.

He looked like a somewhat younger, tougher, rougher, but just as red-hot handsome version of Eddie Chavez.

This had to be Hector Chavez, Eddie's brother.

Oh my *God*.

Before I could say a word or do a thing, he started speaking.

"Get off the street Law. Shard, Jermaine and Clarence are lookin' for retribution, no matter what protection Crowe is offering. They aren't gonna take you down. They're gonna take you somewhere and play with you awhile, games you won't think are fun."

I'd stilled at the sight of him, but his words sent a chill through my blood.

"When they're done, you'll beg them to kill you," he went on.

Um.

Yikes.

"Do I make myself clear?" he asked.

Without delay, I nodded. He made himself clear all right.

He stared at me. I could tell his eyes were dark, liquid black like his brother's, and I found myself wishing for more light just so I could read them.

He got closer. This wouldn't seem possible, but just like Vance had, Hector did—right deep, face-to-face in my space.

"You tell anyone you saw me, you'll blow my cover, and I won't be happy, mainly because I won't be breathin'."

I swallowed.

"Nod if you understand," he demanded.

I nodded again. I understood.

He was a cop... or something. Likely deep cover if even Eddie and Lee didn't know what he was up to.

"Does that mean you don't want me to say anything to...?" I started.

He looked to his left, nodded once, then back at me. "The boys'll know to keep their mouths shut."

Then, as fast as he'd come, he was gone, disappearing into the night. The car in front of Hazel took off. The motorcycle behind her did the same. I never even saw the drivers.

Wow.

With full body shakes I drove Hazel to the garage, super cautious, eyes checking mirrors, willing my ears to have powers beyond normal. I parked, secured the garage and then ran into the house, even though I wanted to stop and kiss Vance's Harley which was sitting outside my backdoor.

I flew into the kitchen and dumped my weapons and bag on the table. Then I locked the door and armed the alarm.

Boo sauntered in and looked at me.

"Meow," he said.

Obviously Vance had given him treats or pets because Boo was a fuck of a lot more calm than me.

I stared at my cat for a beat.

Then I screeched, "*Crowe!*"

I was standing and hyperventilating in my kitchen when Vance walked in. He took one look at me and came to a dead halt.

"I, you... we... oh my *God*," I said.

"Jesus, Jules. Are you all right?"

I shook my head, then I nodded it, then I shook it again.

He started toward me. I took a step back and he stopped again, this time his brows came together.

"You're not gonna try and break up with me again, are you?" he asked.

This time I just shook my head.

His eyes narrowed under knitted brows. "Is Tex okay?"

I nodded.

"Are you okay?"

I shook my head.

He came forward again and I didn't retreat. "Are you hurt?"

"I just met Hector Chavez," I announced.

Vance stopped again, in my space. I saw his eyes flash.

"What the fuck?" he murmured.

"Just now, he and a couple of his buddies fenced me and Hazel in, in the alley. He yanked me out of the car, warned me off the street. Told me Shard, Jermaine and Clarence were going to hurt me no matter what protection you're offering."

This didn't make Vance look happy. "He say anything else?"

"Nothing I care repeating. Not on that subject anyway. He did say if I told anyone about our chat, I'd blow his cover, which means he wouldn't be breathing anymore... or something like that."

Vance stared at me then he muttered, "Christ."

I wasn't sure exactly what I was feeling, but I thought it might be fear.

A lot of fear.

I wasn't going to admit to that out loud so I just took a deep breath to try and control it. That didn't work so I leaned forward, head down, and collided with Crowe, forehead to his shoulder.

He took my weight without a word, his arms coming around me.

"You gotta get off the street," he said softly.

"If I do, they win," I said just as softly, even though I agreed with him.

Vance didn't respond.

I didn't want to play the games Shard, Clarence and Jermaine had planned for me. I knew I'd be disappointing Tex, but if something happened to me, who'd take care of Roam and Sniff? Who'd have dinner with Nick and drive him crazy occasionally? Who'd give it to Vance regularly?

I didn't want to think of anyone (or multiple anyones) giving it to Vance regularly.

This meant I had to get off the street.

Goddammit.

I looked up at Vance.

"Shit," I said.

His arms got tighter and he kissed my forehead, but he still didn't say anything.

There was something nice about that. He didn't rub it in or make a big deal about it. He just let my decision... be.

Even though I was freaking out, I felt another pleasant whoosh in my belly.

"This sucks," I told him. "Tex and I had fun tonight. He's a great sidekick. We used up all our smoke bombs. He's gonna be pissed we aren't going out tomorrow night."

"He'll get over it," Vance replied.

"I have seventeen rolls of plastic wrap. What am I going to do with seventeen rolls of plastic wrap? I never have leftovers. I don't cook."

Vance grinned at me. "Maybe Nick can use them," he suggested.

"What am I going to do at night?" I went on. "I'm used to nighttime action. I'm going to get bored. I can't go from making an art of havoc to lying around reading a book. I'll go nuts."

His eyes got soft and sexy. "We'll find some way to keep you busy."

My belly fluttered.

Hmm.

"What if you're working or out of town?" I enquired.

"For the time being, I'll work something out with Lee."

"I don't want you getting into trouble at work," I told him.

His grin turned into a smile. "Maybe you don't get it, Princess. Lee wants you fucked up by Shard, Clarence and Jermaine only slightly less than I do. You got nothin' to worry about."

That caused a belly whoosh, too. Not as big as the other one, but it was still nice.

"Crowe."

"You got nothin' to worry about," he repeated.

"I don't think—"

"Shut up, Jules."

It was my turn for my brows to knit over narrowed eyes. "Seriously, for the last time, don't tell me to shut up."

Crowe ignored my attitude, stepped away from me and looked around the room.

"Why are we standin' in the kitchen?" he asked.

I blinked at him, not keeping up. I thought we had begun to bicker. I kind of liked bickering with him. His question threw me.

"What?" I asked.

"Lots of better places for us to be," was his answer.

Before I could reply, he leaned down, put a shoulder in my belly, a hand at my wrist and an arm around my thighs and lifted, wrapping me around his neck. He turned and started walking toward the hall.

I shouted, "Crowe!" as if I minded him carrying me to bed.

Um.

Hardly.

I didn't mind at all.

Chapter 24

Chopped Liver

I woke up to heavy kitty footfalls on my body.

I felt Vance's warmth against my back, his body spooning mine, his forearm resting just below my waist.

I decided this was my Number One Most Favorite Sleeping Position with Vance and I was looking forward to ranking alternates.

Boo walked back and forth across Vance and me. I could tell he was doing this because his kitty feet would leave me and then come back to me a lot further down or up my body.

I opened my eyes. It was still dark, nigh on winter so the days were short, but I knew it was too early for Boo Breakfast.

When Boo was four footed on my body, I did a jerk. He lost his position and slid clumsily down my belly with an angry, "Meow!"

I wrapped an arm around him and tucked him into my body. He started purring loudly.

"Would you break up with me if I killed your cat?" Vance's sleepy-rough voice sounded against the back of my neck.

"Probably."

Vance's arm moved, his hand sliding up my belly, midriff, then came to rest cupping my breast.

I was wrong. There was only a subtle change, but *this* was my Number One Most Favorite Sleeping Position with Vance.

I woke up again and it was later. I didn't know how much later, but I instinctively knew there wasn't much time before the alarm went.

I rolled to my belly, dislodging Boo and Vance's arm. Vance moved automatically, falling to his back. I turned into him, ready to say something, but when I lifted up on my elbows I realized he was still asleep.

I wished I could turn on a light. I'd never seen him asleep. He was always up before or with me.

I studied him. There was something about him asleep from what I could see in the near-dark. He seemed almost... boyish.

God, I wanted to kiss him, as in *really* wanted to kiss him.

This gave me pause for reflection. Not as to why I'd want to kiss him, because that was obvious, but as to why I didn't. He *was* my boyfriend (or whatever). We *were* exclusive. He *was* sleeping in my bed. We'd had incredible sex not seven hours earlier.

Why not? Why couldn't I kiss him?

So I kissed him.

Not a full-on, full tongue, let's-have-sex-*right-now* kiss, but I touched my lips to his.

When I pulled back, his eyes were open.

"Good morning," I said and smiled.

He stared at me and he didn't look boyish anymore.

Um.

Maybe I shouldn't have kissed him.

As he kept staring at me, my smile began to fade.

"Sorry, I didn't mean to wake——" I started.

Then he moved, arms going around me, body rolling into me, thigh pressing between my legs, mouth on mine.

His kiss *was* a full-on, full tongue, we're-*going*-to-have-sex-right-now kiss, and I responded. I had no choice. However, if I was given one, I'd have said yes.

He was all over me and it became clear very quickly he wasn't in the mood for me to be all over him. I figured this out because he eventually pinned my hands to the bed, his at my wrists and he did magnificent things to my mouth, neck and breasts with his mouth and tongue, and shockingly, but very effectively, with his teeth.

When I was making noises I couldn't control and struggling at his hands in order to touch him, he went lower, letting my wrists go so he could spread my legs. Then his mouth was *there*.

Yay! My brain screamed.

My hands slid into his hair. His hands tilted my hips and very shortly after I was panting, rocketing to Grade Ten with my entire body on fire and enjoying the ride.

"Vance," I whispered, coming close.

He kept going and my rocket ride kept ascending.

"Vance," I breathed before I hit the stratosphere, dazzled by the stars, and Vance came up over me. I was still flying high when he rolled us, him on his back, me on top. He pulled up my knees so I was astride him. He came up with me and reached to the shelf, nabbing a condom.

"I'll do it," I whispered, still breathing heavily.

"Quiet."

Obviously he didn't feel like playing around. One second he was tearing the packet open with his white teeth, the next second he was inside me.

My head fell back.

He rolled again, him on top of me, but not for very long. He kept my legs bent and lifted up his torso. Coming to his knees, he pulled up my hips and drove into me. The whole time he moved inside me, he was watching me and I was watching him.

Even though he was far away, the intimacy of our connection, the beauty of him, the way he was watching me with that fierce "mine" look on his face overwhelmed me. And although I'd descended to a Grade Six or Seven after my orgasm, it started coming over me again.

It was helped when his hand took mine, moving it between us so I could feel him sliding inside me. Then his fingers pressed mine deep, just at the right spot, and manipulated them. It didn't take long before I let go, saying his name again.

⚜

While Vance went to the bathroom, I laid in bed thinking that I'd spend my newly-free evenings trying to learn how to knit so I could make Vance sweaters.

I was mentally designing a sexy turtleneck when the alarm sounded. I rolled over and slapped the off button, rolled back and cuddled into the pillows.

Boo said, "Meow," which meant "Breakfast."

"Not now, Boo, Mommy just had two orgasms. She's recovering."

Boo was not impressed with this new and unusual excuse and gave me a kitty pouty face.

Kristen Ashley

Vance came back and curled me into his arms, full frontal, thigh pressing between my legs so I was forced to wrap one around his hip.

"What was that?" I asked him.

"What?"

"What you just did."

He grinned his shit-eating grin. "It was good morning."

"Good" didn't quite cover it.

He sure did "good morning" a lot better than me.

"Next time I get to pin your hands down to the bed and have my wicked way with you," I told him.

I wanted to try the teeth thing on him. That was nice.

He didn't answer, but he looked amused.

"No, seriously. It's only fair," I said.

"You could try."

Hmm.

He said, "try".

Whatever.

I was feeling too mellow to bicker.

"What's on for your day?" he asked.

"First up, doctor's appointment," I started, but Vance interrupted, the remnants of his amused look faded and his body got tense.

"Why?"

"Why what?"

"Why are you goin' to the doctor?"

"Um…"

"Are you okay?"

I felt that whoosh of warmth through my belly at his concern and I couldn't help but smile at him.

"Yeah, we just need to discuss, erm…" Why was this embarrassing? He'd just had his mouth between my legs. I told myself to get over it and forged on, "Contraception."

His body relaxed and he kissed my forehead.

"That'd be good," he said softly. "Then what?"

"Work. I need to get to Fortnum's, break it to Tex that his nights as a sidekick will be short-lived. Then I'm going to the hobby shop and picking up a How-To-Knit Kit."

344

I didn't know if there was such a thing as a How-To-Knit-Kit, but I didn't have time to wonder for long because Vance's body started to shake with laughter.

"How to knit?" he asked, voice still amused.

"Yeah, I'll need to do something in the evenings that doesn't involve getting me kidnapped and other things that freak me out. I tried baking. That, as you could see, didn't work. Now I'm going to try knitting."

Knitting didn't burn when Daisy came over to give you an impromptu facial and you forgot it so I thought it was a safe bet.

Vance rolled into me so he was partly on top of me, partly at my side. He was shaking his head and he had that look on his face, the look that said I was too adorable for words. His hand went to the side of my head and his fingers ran through my hair.

"What's on for your day?" I asked and I found that I liked this. I liked cuddling and talking after spending the night together and morning sex. It didn't cause a belly whoosh or flutter or plummet, it just made me feel warm, relaxed, mellow... happy.

I hadn't felt really happy in twelve years, and it was nice. As in *super* nice.

"I'm gonna take Roam and Sniff out later. Can you bring them to Fortnum's when you talk to Tex?"

Okay, I was back to the belly whoosh.

I nodded, smiling at him again, and this time I suspected it was giddily. This was confirmed when Vance's eyes got warm and soft. Or warmer and softer.

"Doesn't take much with you, does it?" he murmured.

"This may not seem much for you, Crowe, but it's gonna rock Roam and Sniff's worlds."

He didn't respond.

"What does it take for you?" I whispered, and wished I hadn't.

That was a moonlight question. Even feeling mellow and happy, I wasn't quite sure I was ready for a moonlight conversation in the morning. We'd had one yesterday and I was thinking once a week was my quota.

Surprisingly, he didn't hesitate in giving his response, clearly not sharing my moonlight restrictions on deep, meaningful, soul-shattering conversations.

"Making you come, watching you come, hearin' you say my name when you do."

Well, one thing you could say for that: it had a theme.

He wasn't finished. "Not knowin' what ridiculous shit is gonna come out of your mouth and make me smile, Yoko Ono, learnin' to knit, namin' your car Hazel."

Okay, I was back to needing the moonlight. That was too much. Especially since his face had changed and so had the air. He still had that warm and soft look, but somehow it was mingled with intensity and I didn't know what was going to come next. What I did know was that I wasn't going to be prepared for it whatever it was.

"Crowe—"

I was right, he'd saved the real whammy for last and I wasn't prepared for it.

When he spoke again, his voice had that fierce undercurrent and it slid across my skin, shrouding me in velvet. "Knowin' I got something to live for now that you're mine. Keepin' it that way, workin' at keepin' this good like it is right now."

I stopped breathing and he kept talking.

"I can go back now, to the rez, to my family with you on the back of my bike."

My lungs started burning with lack of oxygen, but that was okay considering my heart had also stopped beating. I figured I was going to die at any moment and I was totally fine with that.

Vance continued, "They can see that, despite them, I made it to the other side, past their shit. While they lived their dysfunction, I worked my way to something better, ridin' up with you wrapped around me."

I butted in. It took a great deal of effort, mainly because I was overwhelmed by what he was saying. "Vance, you're defined by more than just me giving my virginity to you."

After I said that he kissed me softly, then he did it again, then again.

Then, his face an inch away from mine, he said, "You're right, Princess. That's not what I'm sayin'. It isn't about that, though that was a bonus. Even if I hadn't been your first, I still would claim you as mine. But any man is defined by the woman who shares her bed with him."

"That isn't true."

"It is, and it works the other way, too."

Oh my *God*.

346

Did he really think that?

"Crowe—"

"Which means, if someone like you, someone as unbelievably beautiful as you, as crazy and sweet as you, filled with attitude and courage with her heart in the right place, in a lot of right places even though her head normally isn't... if someone like you shares her bed with me, then that says something about me."

Oh... my... God.

I was going to let the comment about my head not being in the right place slide because the rest of it was so fucking nice.

"Vance—"

"Shut up, Jules."

I decided to give up telling him not to tell me to shut up and desperately looked for a different topic that was safe for morning discussions. I needed to move on, process this later. Perhaps in the nighttime hours with the moonlight coming in the window and Vance asleep while we were test-driving another Most Favorite Sleeping Position.

Finally I blurted, "You never answered me. Do you like The Beatles?"

He stared at me a beat then asked, "What?"

"The Beatles. Do you like them?"

He totally had my number. I knew it when the intensity slid away, a slow grin spread on his face and he kissed me softly again. Thankfully, he let the moonlight conversation go and I knew this was because he knew I needed him to let it go... for now.

"Yeah," he answered.

"Stevie Wonder?"

"Yeah," he repeated.

I let out an exaggerated sigh. "Well, that's a load off my mind."

He shook his head again, eyes amused, then he switched the subject. "Today, I want you checkin' in with me regularly, and if you can't get through to me then call the surveillance room. Yeah?"

I nodded. I could do that. That didn't sound hard.

Vance carried on, "I'll get a panic button from the office. I'll give it to you at Fortnum's."

Um.

No.

Kristen Ashley

I scrunched my nose. A head-crackin' mamma jamma with a panic button? I didn't think so.

Vance's relaxed grin faded. "I'm not arguing about this, Jules. You either take the panic button or you got a bodyguard, whether you want one or not. Your choice. You're protected one way or the other until we pick up Shard, Jermaine and Clarence and convince them to change their minds."

Hmm.

Macho-speak.

My eyes narrowed.

"Choose, Jules."

"Is there a door number three?" I asked.

"Yeah. They can pick you up, gang rape you repeatedly while alternately beatin' the shit out of you until you wished you were dead. Then I'd have to hunt them down and kill them, and after that, I'd spend the rest of my life in prison. That's door number three."

Um.

Yikes.

"I choose the panic button," I said immediately.

His body relaxed.

He kissed my forehead again and said, "Wise choice."

⌖

We were sitting in the Arby's drive-through in May's Grandma van, May at the wheel and me in the passenger seat. Clarice was in the backseat with Roam and Sniff. She was on the phone taking orders from Daisy, who was at Fortnum's, where we were heading after Arby's.

I had three months of birth control pills in my purse and I was supposed to start taking them after my next period, which I hoped and prayed would come right on schedule in two days. Things were going well with Vance and I; super well, beyond-quantum-powered well, in the way that only these badass boys seemed to be able to pull off. Still, I didn't want to be carrying around a mini-Vance just yet.

I'd told Roam and Sniff that Vance was picking them up after lunch. Roam was playing it cool. Sniff was jumping around the seat, radiating excitement, unable to contain it.

I'd called and checked in three times, once when I got to the doctor's, once when I got to work from the doctor's, and then when I left the Shelter with May and the kids for lunch. Vance had answered his phone each time.

The last time I called, I said, "I'm kind of... um, *over* this checking in shit."

He laughed. "Princess, it's only been half a day."

"You think you could round up Jermaine, Clarence and Shard quick-like? This is cutting into my whole head-crackin' mamma jamma vibe."

"I thought you were going to learn how to knit."

"Yeah, *for now*. Once you take care of the bad guys then Tex and I are back on the street."

Silence.

Then, "Christ."

"Vance."

"Later, Princess."

Disconnect.

Obviously, Vance didn't feel like bickering (or arguing) today either.

After picking up enough utterly delicious processed roast beef covered in orange cheese (and even more orange special sauce) to feed an army, we headed to Fortnum's.

I knew something wasn't right the minute we walked in. I knew this because both Zip and Heavy were there, and neither of them were the kind of guys who hung out at a bookstore.

Indy was behind the espresso counter. Jet was walking up to me and Daisy was sitting on a couch. The skinny, tall lady was behind the book counter and there were about five customers sitting around on the seating area enjoying coffee.

I looked to Heavy and Zip and gave them a smile.

"Hey. What are you guys——?" I started to say but Heavy stormed right up to me.

My Arby's bags were confiscated by Heavy, who shoved them in a surprised Jet's hands. Then Zip, Duke and Tex descended and I was hustled, bouncing off one man into another then another then another until I was down the aisle of the book section and shoved right into one of the rows.

"What's going on?" I asked when they'd stopped me, my back to the books. They had surrounded me, all wearing identical father-about-to-speak-to-recalcitrant-daughter expressions, except Tex, who looked like he wanted to rip someone's head off, and I just hoped it wasn't mine.

"You're off-duty," Zip declared.

"No more night patrol. Done." Tex shocked me by booming.

"Everywhere you go, one of us goes with," Heavy announced.

"If you ain't in Fortnum's, at the Shelter or home, you got an escort," Duke stated.

I looked around the pack of them.

"I take it you heard about Shard, Jermaine and Clarence," I guessed.

"Sure thing, sugar." Daisy had arrived. She burrowed into the beefcake to stand in front of Tex. "My husband gave me the scoop last night and I told your boys. Rumor on the street is you're a marked woman. Whatever they have planned, we're gonna make sure it ain't gonna happen, comprende?"

Shit, now even Marcus Sloan was looking after me.

I didn't know what to do with that and didn't have a chance to process it.

"No discussion," Zip broke into my thoughts. "No, 'Zip' is gonna talk you out of this one," Zip imitated my word-is-law voice when he said his own name and it was hard not to laugh.

The good thing about this was Tex wasn't going to be pissed that we weren't going out that night. The bad news was I didn't much like people telling me what to do. I'd already decided to lay low until the coast was clear. I didn't need the Grumpy Middle-Aged Men Posse and Daisy telling me what to do.

"Listen, folks——" I began to say in my word-is-law voice.

May forced her way into the group.

Not good.

"What's goin' on?" she asked, eyes narrowed. She planted her hands on her ample hips, elbowing Zip and Duke as she did so.

"Nothing, May. Everything's fine," I answered, even though it was an obvious lie. I didn't need May to know what was happening. She'd freak.

May's narrowed eyes focused on me. "You thinkin' of breakin' up with Crowe again?"

"No!" I snapped, exasperated. So I broke up with him once and it almost took effect. I'd learned my lesson. Was I going to pay for it for the rest of my life?

Jeez.

"Vance and I are solid, we're real solid," I went on, assuring May. "We're... good."

I started smiling to myself. I couldn't help it. Vance and I *were* good. Even I, Miss No Relationship or Sex Experience, knew enough to know we were seriously good.

At the sight of my smile, Daisy gave a tinkly bell laugh.

The men weren't laughing.

"Better wipe that goofy-assed smile of your face, Law, and get your fuckin' head in the game," Heavy barged right into my happy thoughts so I scowled at him.

"I have my head in the game," I told him.

"Your mind's somewhere else. Probably knitting baby booties," Zip said, and even though I knew he was trying to goad my head-crackin' mamma jamma to the surface, I still took the bait.

"No! Not booties. Knitting sweaters for Vance. Babies are out of the question, for now."

Daisy gave another tinkly laugh.

"Hon, you thinkin' about babies?" May asked, her face now the picture of motherly worry. "Don't you think it's a bit too soon? As in, *seriously* too soon? I mean, it's only been a week."

"A week and three days," I replied.

"Oh for fuck's sake," Zip said to the ceiling.

"Let me get this straight. A second ago we were talkin' about three angry drug dealers markin' you for rape and torture and now we're talkin' about you knittin' sweaters for Crowe?" Duke asked. "Jesus fuckin' Christ. You fuckin' girls."

At Duke's words, May lost her motherly worry face and it went back to the narrow-eyed, pissed-off face.

Then I watched, fascinated, as her face started to get red.

Zip and Duke moved a bit away from her.

Then she exploded.

"*What?*" she screeched.

"What's goin' on?"

Everyone turned, and Vance was standing at the end of the row.

He had his hands to his hips. He was wearing a black t-shirt, his black leather jacket and black cowboy boots. His hands had pushed the jacket back and you could see a gun clipped to the wide belt on his jeans.

He looked good.

He also looked unhappy.

Before I could say anything, May advanced on him, arm up, finger pointed. She got right into his space and poked him in the chest.

Uh-oh.

That was spitting in the eye of the tiger if I ever saw it.

"What you doin' about this, boy?" she snapped.

Um.

Yikes.

May called Vance "boy". I wasn't sure that was good.

Vance didn't respond. He just looked down his nose at her.

I wasn't sure that was good, either.

"My girl's been marked for rape and torture and you swing by to pick up your Arby's roast beef and cheese?" May continued.

"It's covered," Vance replied.

May's back was to me, but I saw her body go rigid.

"*Covered?*" she shrieked.

Time to intervene.

"May," I said as I pushed through Duke and Heavy and headed toward Vance and May. "It's okay," I told her when I arrived. "I told Vance last night I was off the streets. He's giving me a panic button and I'm checking in regularly."

"Panic... checking..." May spluttered. "I do not *believe* what I'm hearing. What kind of lame-ass bullshit is this?"

I noticed with dismay that Roam, Sniff, Clarice, Indy and Jet had all joined our party.

"Jules has tracking devices on her car and in her bag. Her house is wired and under surveillance. I'm giving her a panic button and I know her schedule for the day. She checks in whenever she arrives somewhere," Vance explained, and I thought it was rather nice of him. He didn't have to. Then his eyes cut to me. "Which you *didn't* do when you arrived at Fortnum's."

Whoops.

That explained his unhappy face.

"That's what I'm sayin'. Lame-ass bullshit," May kept at it, luckily taking me off the hot seat for not calling in.

"May, I can take care of myself," I put in.

"Yeah, maybe you can. Maybe you can't. You're dating one of the baddest badasses in Denver and he's workin' with the rest of the baddest badasses. Indy, Jet and Roxie got bodyguards. What are you? Chopped Liver?" After delivering this tirade, May turned back to Vance. "She look like chopped liver to you, boy?"

Oh no, there was the "boy" comment again.

"May, I think it best you don't call Vance 'boy' anymore," I whispered to her.

"He *is* a boy to me!" May shouted back at me.

I stepped away a bit.

"Jules didn't want a bodyguard," Vance informed May.

"Yeah, well, she didn't want a boyfriend either, and you took care of that," May shot back.

Hmm.

She had a point.

"She's got bodyguards," Heavy joined the conversation from behind us.

"Yeah. Us," Zip added.

May turned slowly and looked the Middle-Aged Man Posse up and down. You could tell she found them somewhat lacking, and I understood why when she turned back to Vance.

"Roxie told me when she was being stalked, Luke Stark was her bodyguard."

I had a feeling, even though he was older, Duke knew what he was doing. After my experience with Heavy, Zip and Tex, I knew for a fact they knew what they were doing.

Still, I had to admit they didn't compare to Luke.

I bugged my eyes out at Vance in a non-verbal "Do something!" but he just crossed his arms on his chest.

I guessed it was up to me.

"May, simmer down. It's going to be fine," I said.

She made an angry and unimpressed noise that sounded like "humph".

"No, really. I have a lot of people looking out for me," I went on.

"Something happens to you, what are those boys gonna do?" she pointed to Roam and Sniff.

"Nothing's going to happen to me," I assured her.

"Something happens to you, what's your uncle gonna do?" she carried on, a dog with a bone, as usual.

"May, nothing's gonna happen to me," I repeated.

She walked to me, got in my space and looked up at me.

Quietly, she said, "Something happens to you, what am *I* gonna do?"

It was then I saw the tears she was trying not to shed shimmering in her eyes.

She was scared. Scared for me. Scared that something would happen to me that decades of using her Mama's-Gonna-Make-It-Better Voice would never heal.

I put my arms around her and held her close. She did the same to me.

I'd never hugged May, and in the back of my head it registered that she gave good hugs.

I looked around and saw Indy, Jet, Roam, Sniff and Clarice at one end of the row, all staring at me. Even Roam, Sniff and Clarice, hardened street kids, couldn't hide their worried expressions.

Duke, Tex, Zip and Heavy were in the middle of the row, still looking like my favorite uncles, all pissed-off and wanting a role in my protection.

Daisy was standing with them. She was hard to read, but I suspected she was patiently waiting for me to make the right decision, and that was huge.

May and Vance were at my end of the row.

Home, Auntie Reba whispered in my ear.

My eyes locked on Vance's.

Then I closed them slowly, and when I opened them again he was still looking at me, but he had that look in his eyes again. And now that I knew what that look meant, a happy shiver slid up my spine.

Shit.

I'd just made a decision.

Even when this was all over, I wasn't going back on the street. Too many people cared about what happened to me and they would get hurt if I got hurt.

With one look at me Daisy knew I'd come to my decision. She smiled and gave me an approving wink. Then she came forward and pulled May away from me.

"Let's get you your roast beef sandwich," she said, guiding May away. Everyone followed.

"I'm first up," Duke said, pointing at me before he left.

I rolled my eyes (just for show) and when I was done with my eye roll, Vance was there.

His arm went around my neck and he pulled me to him.

"Thinkin' something big just happened there," he said, looking down at me.

"Yeah," I whispered.

"Wanna share?"

I shook my head but I said it anyway. "I'm giving up the street."

Vance's body went tense.

"For good?" he asked.

"For good," I answered.

It was his turn to close his eyes, but as with everything Vance, he did it better than me.

In closer proximity, he dropped his forehead to mine, opened his eyes again to look into mine and breathed out on a quiet sigh, "Good."

"You think Lee would let me go out with the boys every now and again, keep my skills sharp?" I tried.

He lifted his forehead from mine and shook his head. "I'm thinkin' Lee might think you're a distraction."

I was afraid of that.

Then I asked the all important question.

I stared deep into his eyes and whispered, "Do you think Park would understand?"

His arm went from around me and his hands came to either side of my face. "Yeah."

I nodded.

Then I let my body relax into his. His arms went around my waist and I tucked the side of my face into his throat.

"What's this about knittin' sweaters for me?" Vance asked.

Shit.

My bed moved when Vance got in it.

Normally, I figured I would have slept through this and I had no idea why I didn't. It could have been the covers moving as Vance slid between them, Vance's heat hitting me, or him pulling my back into his front and his body making contact with mine from shoulders to heels.

He settled into me silently. I settled into him the same way.

After a while, he asked quietly against the back of my neck, "How'd it go?"

I knew he meant my evening.

"Weird," I whispered back.

Duke had been in the parking lot leaning against his bike when I finished at the Shelter that afternoon. He followed me to the hobby shop and was by my side as I made my knitting selections, and even when I wandered into the sticker and card-making sections, just in case knitting didn't take.

I thought this was something which would annoy him, but he seemed to have all the patience in the world for hobby shop shopping.

"You're good at this," I told Duke in the checkout line.

"What?" he asked.

"Shopping."

"Dolores paints," Duke replied then went on, "and does macramé and a bit of cake decorating and dried flower arranging."

Sounded like Duke was no stranger to hobby shops.

I handed over my credit card and turned fully to him. "Why are you doing this?"

"What?" he asked again.

"Protecting me. You barely know me."

He regarded me for a second.

Then he said, "Got a feeling you're gonna be a fixture in Indy's life. Whoever is a fixture in Indy's life is a fixture in mine. Don't got no family outside Dolores and her folks. What family I got walks through the doors of that store on a regular basis. I'm guessin' by the way Vance looks at you, and Indy and her gang have taken to you, you're gonna be walkin' through those doors on a regular basis. I'm gonna do my bit to make sure you continue walkin' through those doors. Where I come from, you take care of your family."

At his words, I'd had to put my hand to the counter to hold myself steady.

For some bizarre reason, maybe because he'd shared so I felt I should do the same, I told him, "I don't have much family."

"You do now," he replied.

I had the strange but strong desire to hug him. I didn't, instead I turned to the clerk and took my credit card back.

Duke followed me home and did a walkthrough of my house, even though I told him there were cameras everywhere. He stayed for a beer and long enough for me to knit and purl my way through a line of wool, all the while Duke reading the directions to me.

Finally he said, "Gotta go or Dolores'll be pissed I let the dinner go cold."

I walked him to the door.

"You go anywhere, you call me or one of the boys. Hear me?" he ordered.

I wanted to be a head-crackin' mamma jamma, but I couldn't, not after what he said at the hobby shop, and not after what happened at Fortnum's that afternoon.

I just nodded.

He gave me a look as if to assess my honesty. I must have passed the honesty test because he nodded and left.

While I was eating a dinner of microwave popcorn (I might not be any good with an oven, but I was hell on wheels with a microwave), Sniff had called.

He was full of stories. He told me of their official tour through the Nightingale Investigations offices, their "cool-as-shit" (Sniff's words) hour-long shift in the surveillance room and working with Brody, Lee's hacker, on the computers.

He told me of dinner at Lincoln's Road House, and I made a mental note to have a word with Vance about taking my (underage) boys to a biker bar for dinner.

He also told me of their ride-along with Vance after they ate.

I was only slightly alarmed to learn that Vance had gone gung-ho. Not starting slowly, he had taken them along on a break-and-enter search that included disabling an alarm, picking a lock and rifling through the possessions and computer files of a possible corporate embezzler. Vance did this so well, the "possible" became "definite", and the boys were high with excitement. They were also left understanding that you had to be more than just physically fit to do the job. It wasn't just about cracking heads. You had to know computers. You had to understand electronics. And you had to be smart, thinking three steps ahead so you didn't get caught.

If Roam and Sniff thought Vance was the shit before, they were even more convinced of it now.

"He didn't make, like, *a sound*. It was like he was a ghost. It was fuckin' cool!" Sniff told me.

I smiled into the phone but said, "Sniff, for the last time, don't say fuck."

After my conversation with Sniff, I knitted and purled a line about the length of my house and took a bubble bath. I was about to head to bed with a book when a knock went at my door.

I looked out the window and saw Tex standing outside.

I opened the door and looked up at him.

"What're you doing here?" I asked.

"You got any plastic wrap?" he asked in return.

I stared at him.

Then I smiled. "Yeah."

He smiled back. His smile was kinda scary, but it worked.

I loaded Tex up with my plastic wrap stash and waved him on his merry way.

My phone rang about ten minutes after Tex left. It was Zip.

"You still breathin'?" he asked after I answered.

"Yes," I replied unnecessarily.

"Good."

Disconnect.

This was rude, but it was also sweet and I felt the warm whoosh in my belly again.

After Zip's call I went to bed.

I told Vance about my adventures in boring, everyone else having fun and me knitting the world's longest micro-scarf and taking a bubble bath.

"How was your night?" I asked.

"I picked up Clarence and Jermaine."

My body went still.

Wow.

That didn't take long.

God, he was *good*.

"And?"

"Mace is workin' with them."

Yikes.

I didn't figure that was good for Clarence and Jermaine. Mace had a reputation for fucking people up and good.

"What's that mean?" I asked.

"I'm thinkin' you don't want to know."

"I'm thinking I do."

Vance pulled me deeper into his body and I felt his lips touch the nape of my neck.

Then he said, "Mace doesn't have a lot of patience with men who fuck with women. He doesn't give a shit if they do it or threaten it. Livin' in fear of gettin' hurt is almost as bad as gettin' hurt. Mace'll do what he has to do to get them to back off."

"What about their boss? Won't he be pissed, you guys fucking with his boys?"

"You already know we've declared protection. Lee drew a line in the sand. Everyone on the street knows you're marked, which means they've stepped over that line. What *that* means is if the bosses back their boys, we're at war. That kind of war has no rules."

Oh my God.

I had no idea this was so huge.

I rolled so I was facing Vance and looked at him in the moonlight. "Does that mean you guys are up against the drug lords?"

He shook his head. "The bosses have cut their boys loose. Shard's got no beef with you. I took him down. He's just an ass. Clarence and Jermaine have gone against direct orders. You're an annoyance, but you're also a social worker. There are lots of ways to put you out of commission that don't include what those boys had planned for you. I made a deal with their boss. They reneged on that deal. Looks bad for the boss. This morning we spread word you're off the street. They should have backed down. They didn't. They're on their own. Not a lot of people would invite war against Lee, at least not about this."

"So now it's just Shard."

"It's just Shard."

"You going to find Shard?"

He shook his head again. "Luke and Ike are tracking Shard."

I figured Shard would shortly be joining Mace's party.

"What about Hector?" I asked. "Did you tell Lee I saw him?"

"Yeah. Lee told Eddie, they intensified Brody's hack. Hector's DEA. Deep cover, been workin' at gettin' close to a local big man for over a year and has had success. Anyone finds out he approached you, he's dead."

Fuck!

I closed my eyes and pressed into him, nuzzling my face in his neck.

I was such an idiot.

What was I thinking, going out and annoying drug dealers? How lucky was I, that in the end I found Vance?

If I hadn't and I was alone facing this shit, I'd be fucked, and not in a good way.

"I'm an idiot," I whispered.

His arms got tight around me.

"You're not an idiot," he whispered back.

"I just wanted to—"

Vance interrupted me, "You got passion. You got courage. Nothing's wrong with either of those. You just got to learn to point them in the right direction."

He was right. I *hated* it when he was right.

"If anyone gets hurt because of me—" I started.

"No one's gonna get hurt."

He said that with such certainty that I believed him.

I willed myself to relax, willed my mind and body to go still.

It didn't work.

"Vance?"

"Yeah, Princess?"

I looked up at his face in the moonlight.

It was time.

I took a deep breath then said, "Do you want me to tell you what I think it says about *me* that you share my bed?"

He was looking down at me.

"No," he answered bluntly.

I blinked. "What?" I asked.

"I don't want you to tell me."

Well, that took the wind right out of my sails, and for some reason it hurt, just a little bit (okay, so it hurt a lot). I thought he'd want to know. I *wanted* him to want to know and furthermore, I was ready to tell him.

Before I could hide my face and my disappointment, his mouth came to mine.

"I want you to show me," he said there.

I looked into his dark eyes close up, and even in the moonlight I knew they were burning into mine.

"Okay," I whispered.

Then I did as he asked.

Chapter 25
Quick Could Be Good

The phone was ringing and my eyes opened.

I knew it was the dead of night and in the nanosecond before he moved, I knew I had a big time contender for Number One Most Favorite Sleeping Position with Vance. On my belly, one leg crooked, Vance pressed into my back, leg bent into mine, arm around me.

Seriously nice.

He disengaged gently and rolled away to pick up the phone.

"Yeah?" I heard, pause, "right."

When I heard the phone hit the cradle, I turned. "What was that?"

Vance's arms came around me and he settled on his back, me in his side (just for your information, I liked this as a cuddle position, but it was in the lower half of the top five as a sleeping position).

"They got Shard."

Hallelujah, I thought.

"No more panic button?" I asked.

"You keep the panic button."

My head came up. "Why?"

"Humor me."

"Why?"

"Because I want you to."

"Why?"

"Because you've made enemies and captured attention. Until we hear no talk on the street, I want to know you're safe."

I supposed I could do that.

I settled in, ready to go back to sleep. So ready in fact, that I didn't realize Vance's body had gone tight.

"You gonna do this for me?" he asked.

"Sure," I replied as if that was a given.

After a few minutes ticked by, his body relaxed and he said, "Jesus, you're a pain in the ass."

"Am not," I mumbled sleepily into his shoulder.

His hand came up and started to play with my hair.

I fell asleep.

⇒⇐

I woke up with the alarm and Vance wasn't in bed, but I heard the shower going.

There was no Boo either.

I hit the off button on the alarm and searched for my nightgown and underwear that Vance had divested me of the night before. I struggled to put them on in a lying position, which was not easy. After I succeeded, I slid off the bed platform.

I walked to the kitchen.

Boo's breakfast bowl was down and had already been licked clean.

I looked at the coffeemaker. There was a pot at the ready.

I walked into the living room. Boo was lying on my chaise lounge, cleaning his face. He didn't even spare me a glance, much less a good morning kitty meow. He was sated and preparing for his morning nap.

I walked back into the kitchen and poured myself a cup of coffee.

Then I stood with my hips against the counter, coffee cup aloft, staring into space, wondering how my world had turned on its head in a week and four days.

I had a boyfriend who fed my cat, made coffee, had a kickass job, took care of me, was great in bed and was *hot*. I had a family of friends looking out for me, calling me and wanting to spend time with me. They even got mad at me when I tried to go to the mall alone.

This freaked me out, but in a good way.

My pug nestled up to me and decided he wanted to play just as Vance walked out of the bathroom. Chest bare, black hair wet and slicked back and one of my mint-green, Egyptian cotton towels wrapped around his hips.

My mouth went dry.

He walked toward me, got in my space, dodging the coffee cup I didn't move, put his hands on either side of my neck and touched his lips to mine.

"Mornin' Princess," he said, not moving out of my space.

"Thanks for feeding Boo."

He grinned and dropped his hands to my waist.

"Thanks for making coffee," I went on.

He kept grinning.

"You done in the bathroom?" I asked.

He nodded.

I put the unsipped coffee on the counter, skirted around him and went to bathroom. I brushed and flossed then washed my face.

I left the bathroom and went in search of Vance.

He wasn't hard to find, considering I only had three rooms in the house (three and a half, if you counted the bed platform). He was sitting on my couch, clothed in the outfit he had on yesterday, pulling on his boots.

"What're you doing?" I asked, staring at him.

"Puttin' on my boots," he replied, looking up at me.

I blinked. "You wore that yesterday," I said.

"Yeah," he pulled on the second boot and stood.

"If you're going to stay here you should keep some clothes here."

Now, why did I just say that?

I was going to freak him out. He was going to think I loved him or something.

I, of course, *did* love him, but he didn't know that. Or at least I didn't think he knew that. Now he'd think I was a clingy, stalker, psycho bitch from hell and moving too fast and I was going to scare him off.

Shit.

"All right," he said.

I blinked again.

"Did you say 'all right'?" I asked.

"Yeah," he replied.

Guess I didn't freak him out.

He came up to me, wrapped a hand around the back of my head and kissed my forehead. "Later Princess."

My body went still.

"What?" I asked, looking up at him as he dropped his hand.

"Later. I gotta get to the office."

I stared.

"What?" I repeated.

He watched me a beat. "Are you okay?"

Kristen Ashley

I thought about it.

Then I said, "No, I'm not okay."

"What's the matter?"

"You fed my cat," I told him.

He watched me again, this time perhaps wondering if my body had been taken over by nonsense-speaking aliens.

"And?" he prompted.

"And now you're leaving."

"I have to get to the office. They're holding three assholes who wanted to hurt you. I wanna find out what's happening."

This sounded plausible. I still didn't like it.

"But we haven't had sex yet," I blurted.

For a second I realized I threw him and he looked surprised. He had absolutely no idea that was going to come out of my mouth. Then again, neither did I.

Still, I'd said it so I was going to have to go with it.

"We always have morning sex. We always have nighttime sex. We can't *not* have morning sex. What does that mean? Next we're not going to have nighttime sex?" I asked.

His lips started twitching as I continued.

"You fed my cat. I always have to feed my cat. How am I going to get used to not being the one who *has* to feed my cat? It's always been just me. And Nick, of course, but that's not the same thing. He doesn't break up Boo's food like you and I do."

I was babbling. I knew it and I didn't care.

I wanted to have sex.

"Jules—"

"You can't just get up, make me coffee, feed my cat and then leave. What's up with *that?*" I went on.

"Jules—"

"We have a ritual," I interrupted him. "I like our ritual. I'm not good with change."

Now I was lying. I had no problem with change.

Bottom line, I wanted sex.

His hands came to the sides of my face and he said again, "Jules."

"What?" I snapped.

"Take off your underwear."

My belly did a rollercoaster plummet and I blinked, *again*.

"What?"

"Do it," he demanded.

Okay, now I was freaking out and deciding maybe I didn't want to have sex, even though I wanted sex now more than ever.

All the while looking at him, I pushed down my underwear and it fell to the floor. No sooner did it hit my feet then he lifted me up, hands at my ass and my arms and legs automatically circled him.

He went down to the floor on his knee then he put me on my back and covered me with his body.

"What are we doing?" I asked, staring into his eyes.

I felt his hand between us, working at his belt.

"We're gonna have to be quick."

"How quick?"

"Real quick."

"I'm not sure I want quick."

His face went into my neck. "You don't have much choice," he said in my ear, which made me shiver. Then I felt his tongue touch me and slide down my neck to my collarbone, which made me shiver more.

"Is quick good?" I asked.

"It can be," he said at the base of my throat. Then he touched me between my legs and I sucked in breath.

His mouth came to mine and I could feel he was smiling, pleased about something.

He looked in my eyes and said, "Christ, you're always wet."

"Is that good?"

"Fuck yeah."

"I think it happened when you told me to take off my underwear," I informed him helpfully.

His finger slid inside me. "I'll remember that."

My hands pushed into his jeans and I ran them over his ass. I was done talking and so was Vance.

And, for your information, quick could be good.

It was near to the end of the day when my cell rang.

It was sitting on my desk and the display said, "Crowe calling."

Looking at it, I smiled.

Vance had called me in the morning to give me the lowdown on Shard, Clarence and Jermaine.

Apparently, Mace had done his job well. This was because Luke and Ike felt like getting in on the act. So they'd all done their job well. They'd done it job so well, Shard, Clarence and Jermaine not only decided not to fuck with me, they also decided that maybe Denver wasn't for them. Luke, Mace and Ike had convinced them to try their luck at ruining people's lives somewhere outside the Mile High City. They weren't only leaving town, they'd already left. Vance knew this because Mace, Ike and Luke had escorted them to the city limits.

This made me feel weird. It was weird because I felt safe and protected, but I also felt badly that they likely had to commit acts of violence in order to make me feel safe and protected.

I spent the morning struggling with that.

Since I figured Shard, Clarence and Jermaine had destroyed a number of lives, by the time the clock struck twelve, I got over it.

Then I called Luke.

"Babe," he answered.

"I don't know what to say."

Silence then, "I'm guessin' you're talkin' about the boys."

"I'm talking about what you and Mace and Ike did for me. I feel like I should do something to repay you."

"Not necessary."

"Maybe I should make you some cookies," I suggested.

"*Really* not necessary."

At first I was shocked at the emphasis to his "really". Then I remembered that Luke had smelled the results of my last attempt at being a baking goddess.

"Okay, maybe I should buy you some cookies."

"That'd work."

Disconnect.

Well then, there it was.

Store cookies seemed kind of a lame "thank you" for driving three drug dealers hell-bent on gang raping and torturing you out of town, but burnt cookies were no thank you at all.

I made a mental note to hit the bakery at Safeway and got back to work.

⌦⏁⌫

Now Vance was calling again and I tried to be cool, but I had to admit (just to myself) I liked to see "Crowe calling" on my display.

I liked it a lot.

I picked up my phone and flipped it open. "Hey," I said to Crowe.

"Hey. Got some things to do tonight. Thought I'd take you to Lincoln's for dinner before I did 'em."

"That sounds good."

"Meet you at your place at six."

"Okay."

"Later, Princess."

Disconnect.

I sat there with the phone to my ear and stayed that way. I liked how I felt even after a quick, meaningless phone call from Vance telling me he was taking me out to dinner. I wondered if I'd always feel like that and I hoped I would.

Slowly I flipped the phone shut and set it on my desk, realizing this would be only the second time we'd been out to dinner. We'd had only one date and we were practically living together. He was moving clothes to my house, I had toiletries at his.

Realizing this, I started to laugh, my body shaking with it.

Vance had done it. Just like everyone said he would, just like Lee, Eddie and Hank before him. He hadn't wasted any time (I, however, had) and he'd moved so fast I didn't even realize it was happening. Hell, it was *my* idea for him to leave clothes at my house.

I was laughing so hard I snorted, and Andy, who was on the phone, looked up at me with knitted enquiring brows.

I shook my head at him and mouthed, "I'll tell you later."

Andy blinked in surprise.

I'd been working with Andy for a while. He'd come to the Shelter about six months after they hired me. I'd never, not once, told him anything personal about me. He was a good guy and he could make me laugh. He had a wife and a little girl. He shared stories all the time about what they'd done, funny things his kid said.

Me, nothing. I never shared.

I'd gone through life alone (my choice), in order not to feel, so I wouldn't get hurt.

Now I knew what I was missing.

What kind a fucking idiot was I?

I struggled with that long after Andy got off the phone. Long after I shared with Andy that Vance was practically moving in with me.

Andy had said, hesitantly and with concern, "Um… Jules, don't you think this is a bit fast?"

Then I'd told him about Indy, Jet and Roxie, his eyes got big, but he didn't look any less concerned.

I kept struggling long after I hit two different Safeways and cleaned them out of their M&M cookies (the absolute best) and picked up some other provisions, doing this randomly, because although Vance was going to be hanging clothes in my closet, I had no idea what kind of food he liked in the house.

This last thought had me cracking up hysterically in the meat and cheese section and people gave me a wide berth. This was a good thing as it meant I had the meat and cheese section all to myself without anyone breathing down my neck to make a selection.

I got over my latest emotional struggle when I put the cookies on the kitchen counter, put the food away and gave Boo his kitty treats, letting him have a few more because I was in a good mood. Then Boo and I went over to Nick's. Realizing it was nearly six, I stopped outside Nick's backdoor and Boo and I went back to my side. I dropped Boo long enough to write Vance a note saying I was on Nick's side. I didn't want him to think he was stood up again. Vance didn't like that.

When I was done, I stared at the note on the counter and went back to emotionally struggling with having to write a note to someone to explain my whereabouts, something I'd never done in my life. This didn't take long because, as I stared at the note, that velvet shroud wrapped around me, and I stopped staring at the note and started smiling at it.

Then I snatched up Boo and we went back to Nick's.

I knocked on the door and stuck my head in. "Nick?"

"Hey Jules, be right there."

I walked in and dropped Boo who immediately went in search of Nick.

I went in search of beer.

I'd just pulled out a Fat Tire when Nick came in.

"Hey," I said.

"Hey," Nick replied, staring at me intensely.

"What?" I asked about the stare.

"I don't know," Nick answered.

"Why are you looking at me like that?"

He leaned a hip against the counter. "I'm waiting to see what you have to say. I don't know if you're gonna tell me someone's been shot, you broke up with Vance again or you've decided to single-handedly plan a march on Washington due to the lack of AIDS medications available to developing countries. I gotta be prepared for anything."

I grinned at him and popped open the beer. Then I handed it to him and leaned a hip against the counter myself.

"I'm going to tell you that I'm off the streets."

His body moved, only slightly, but it still moved. It got tense, then it relaxed in such a way that his relief could be read in every line.

"Good," he said quietly.

I had to admit, I felt guilt at this. Nick's reaction wasn't an overwhelming reaction, but it said it all.

I decided to move onto a different subject before I could figure out an anatomically possible way to kick myself in the backside.

"I'm also going to tell you that Vance is moving some clothes to my house."

Without hesitation he said, "Good."

It was my turn to stare. I thought for certain I'd get a lecture that we were going too fast.

"Don't you think we're going too fast?" I asked.

"Vance the reason you're off the streets?"

"Part of it."

"What's the other part?"

"You."

His body moved again in the same way, then he closed his eyes. When he opened them, what I saw made that velvet shroud wrap closer. My pug snuggled in and licked my face.

371

Kristen Ashley

Before I could struggle with this, too, Nick started talking.

"I like Vance. I like that, since he came into your life, you got girlfriends throwin' you parties and folks showin' up at your house to watch football. I like lookin' out the front window seein' guys I don't know, but I know I can trust, knockin' on your door. I like knowin' you aren't alone over there with just Boo and Stevie Wonder for company. No, I don't think you're movin' too fast. What happened to your family hadn't happened, I'd have married Reba within months of knowin' her. When you know it's right, you just *know*. I got a feelin' Vance knows it's right. I'm glad that you figured it out. I'd be honored to walk you down the aisle, if we were walkin' towards Vance, even if you told me it was happening tomorrow."

I couldn't help it. One night off the job and I was already losing hold on my head-crackin' mamma jamma. Therefore at his words I burst into tears.

Nick's arms came around me, I shoved my face in his neck and I heard Auntie Reba's voice in my ear.

Home.

My tears turned to sobs and now I was emotionally struggling with the fact that I was a big sissy.

A knock came at the door.

"Yeah?" Nick called.

I heard it open and I lifted my, what I was sure was red, wet and scary face away from Nick, and saw Vance standing there watching us.

Shit.

"I'll come back," Vance murmured.

"Think you best take over here," Nick answered, gently moving me towards Vance.

"I'm okay," I wiped my tears with my fingers, but made one of those silly, girlie, sobby hiccoughs.

Vance came forward and his arms went around me. At the feel of them, I started crying again, harder, so I shoved my face in *his* neck.

"What happened?" Vance asked Nick.

"I don't know. Do you ever know? She's a girl," Nick answered.

My body went solid and I pulled my head out of Vance's neck.

"I'm not a girl!" I shouted at Nick. "I'm a head-crackin' mamma jamma!"

"Sure you are," Nick soothed, but I could swear he sounded a little bit like he was laughing.

372

I narrowed teary eyes at him. "I am!"

Vance totally ignored me, but kept his arms around me.

"We're goin' to Lincoln's for dinner. You're welcome," Vance told Nick.

"Nah, game on tonight," Nick answered.

"Another time," Vance said.

"Sure, sounds good. Haven't been there in a while."

"Not much has changed."

"Best part about it."

"Hello!" I shouted, pulling out of Vance's arms and pointing to myself with both hands. "Having total emotional breakdown! Anyone? Anyone?"

Nick started out and out laughing. Vance just grinned at me.

"You done?" Vance asked me.

I rolled my eyes.

Whatever.

I'd finish my total emotional breakdown later when I was alone, possibly while listening to Stevie Wonder singing "All In Love Is Fair", which was the best time to have them.

"I'm hungry," I grumbled, wiping my face with my hands. Then I called, "Boo!"

Boo trotted in, tail straight in the air, equally oblivious to my emotional turmoil.

I scooped him up, glared at Nick, swung my glare to Vance, walked out of Nick's and went to my side.

I was in the bathroom cleaning up my face and repairing makeup damage when I heard Vance return. Then I heard a rustling bag.

When I walked into the kitchen, Vance was eating an M&M cookie.

"Don't eat that! Those are for Luke, Ike and Mace," I snapped.

Vance stared at me for a beat then looked into the bag.

Then he looked at me. "There's at least thirty cookies in there."

"Thirty-three," I told him. Then I scowled at his cookie. "Now, thirty-two. How am I going to divide thirty-two cookies three ways?"

He didn't answer me. Instead he said, "Why are you giving Luke, Ike and Mace thirty-two cookies?"

"They beat people up for me," I replied. "That requires payback. Since I can't bake, I can't *make* them cookies. Knitting is boring, as in *super* boring, so I can't knit them sweaters. I don't think they'd like a homemade card or anything

373

I could do with the stickers I bought. There will likely not be a time where I could beat up someone for them. Therefore," I pointed to the bag, "cookies."

He took another bite of his cookie while walking up to me. His hand went to my neck and he brought me closer to his body by putting pressure there.

I put my hands on his waist and looked up at him.

"Princess?"

"What?"

"You have to be the fucking craziest woman I've ever met."

I was back to glaring at him. "I'll take that as a compliment."

He grinned. "I meant it as one."

Well.

There you go.

I couldn't help it. I smiled.

⊰❊⊱

We were sitting at Lincoln's Road House. It was after we ate, the dirty dishes still in front of us, and we managed the whole thing, from duplex to bike, bike to Road House, door to table, menu to ordering, ordering to eating, all without fighting (or even bickering) once.

It had to be a record.

I was enjoying my second beer, relaxed, mellow, maybe even at peace with the world.

"You wanna tell me why you were cryin'?" Vance asked and my eyes moved to him.

I instantly decided I was not at peace with the world.

"Um... no," I answered.

There was no way I was ready to tell Vance that Nick was cool with walking me down the aisle toward Vance even if it happened tomorrow.

No way in hell.

Vance shook his head and looked away, his eyes moving to the television hanging by the bar, and I had the feeling I'd disappointed him.

"What are you doing tonight?" I asked to change the subject and his eyes slid back to me.

"Got a job. It'll take a few hours."

"Are you coming back to my place when you're done?"

I found I was worried about his answer.

"Yeah."

I found I was relieved at his answer.

"Okay," I smiled at him.

His gaze dropped to my mouth, taking in my smile. Then he looked in my eyes again and his were serious.

"Princess, we're gonna have to do something about your inability to share."

"I'm working on it," I promised.

He watched me a bit and then said, "Somethin' else."

Uh-oh.

He still had the serious look in his eye.

"Yeah?" I asked, but I didn't want to know.

"I'm wonderin' why you bought Mace, Ike and Luke cookies when I'm the one who brought in Clarence and Jermaine yesterday."

I didn't know what to make of this question. The answer seemed obvious to me, but I gave it to him anyway.

"You get naked gratitude," I told him.

He stared at me a beat, and again I knew I threw him.

Then he gave me one of his shit-eating grins.

"A *lot* of it," I went on.

The grin turned into a smile.

"Vance!" a female voice called from behind me.

Vance's eyes cut to the voice, his smile vanished and I looked over my shoulder.

Coming toward us was a fantastic-looking, curvy, leggy, long, wavy haired brunette. She had on a short skirt, high-heeled boots and a tight sweater that was giving some serious cleavage.

She was also smiling at Vance in a way that I *did not* like.

"Hey," she breathed when she got to our table, and I realized instantly that this had been one of the many girls who had come before me.

Poof! There it was. My head-crackin' mamma jamma came out.

"Jackie," Vance replied. He was across the table from me, but I could see his face and it was blank.

I hated his blank look when he directed it at me. I liked his blank look when he was giving it to leggy brunettes in short skirts that he'd fucked somewhere down the line.

Jackie's eyes moved to me, looked me up and down where I sat on my stool, then she dismissed me and her eyes went back to Vance. She turned so her back was slightly to me.

Um.

No.

"What're you up to these days? Haven't seen you in ages," Jackie asked Vance in a way that communicated she thought his answer might just be the key to the meaning of life.

"Jackie, this is Jules," Vance said, I thought making a point and I could have kissed him.

She swung her head (as well as her hair) around and glanced at me again.

"Jules," she muttered, then she swung her head (and hair) back. "So, how're things?" Jackie went on, missing the point.

Vance opened his mouth to speak, but I'd kind of had enough.

"Things are good," I put in and Jackie's head (and hair) swung back to me. Her eyes had narrowed.

"Excuse me?" she asked.

"Things are good," I repeated, giving her a huge, happy smile. Then my eyes moved to Vance. "Aren't they, honey?"

Now that, I hoped, was a point Jackie wouldn't miss.

The corners of Vance's lips turned up.

Jackie didn't wait for Vance to answer.

To me she said, "I'm so pleased for you."

She did not mean this.

Translation: Shut the fuck up, I'm not talking to you. I'm flirting with your boyfriend.

She swung back to Vance and leaned in a bit (the better to show her cleavage), smiled, and said in a voice I was meant to hear but she was pretending I wasn't, "We'll talk some other time. Give me a call."

Vance again opened his mouth to speak, but again I got there first.

"What did you just say?" I asked.

Vance's eyes moved to me.

"Jules." His tone held a warning, but he looked like he was about ready to laugh.

I wasn't paying a lot of attention to Vance. My eyes were on Jackie.

Jackie leaned back and put up her hands.

"Nothing to get excited about," she said.

I came off my stool.

"Are you saying that you coming onto my fucking boyfriend right in front of me is nothing to get excited about?" I demanded. My voice was a wee bit loud. So much of a wee bit people started to stare.

Jackie looked from me to Vance then back to me. "If he's your man, then, girlfriend, you got nothing to worry about from me."

She did not mean this either.

Translation: If he's your man, you better keep him happy. You don't, I'll pounce.

It was at that moment, I really wished I had my gun.

Then she went on, not, I noted, very good at reading body language, as in my body language said I was about to kick her ass.

"We're just friends. Good friends. Hey, Vance?"

I looked at Vance. He was still sitting on his stool and it was evident that he had decided not to intervene. I also noted that his lips were twitching.

"She must have been one of those easy things you were talking about," I said to Vance.

He pressed his lips together and shook his head slowly. This was not a negative headshake that said Jackie wasn't one of his easy things. It was a negative headshake that said he thought I was the fucking craziest woman he'd ever met.

"Excuse me?" Jackie asked again.

Jackie now turned full body to me and I stepped clear of the table preparing to throw down.

"I said you must be one of the easy things Vance told me about. You know, easy pieces of ass. Before he met me," I informed her, my voice dripping with acid sweetness.

"You did *not* just say that," she said to me.

"I sure did," I shot back.

"Jackie, I wouldn't rile Jules," Vance decided to wade in.

"You calling me easy?" Jackie decided to ignore Vance.

"Have you slept with Vance?" I asked, even though I knew.

She leaned forward with a catty smile. "It was the best night of my god-damned life."

"It's good you'll have that memory," I stated calmly as if I was truly happy for her.

"You bitch!" she screamed. Then she came at me, hand out, probably to grab my hair.

I was getting that opening a lot these days. I planted my feet, caught her wrist and flipped her on her back on the floor without barely moving.

Vance did move. He had his wallet out and threw some money on the table. Everyone was staring now. Most of them had turned to us, enjoying the show.

I took a step toward her so I was looking down at her.

"Stay away from Vance," I warned.

She was struggling to get up. "Fuck you!"

"That's Vance's job," I retorted.

Vance had me around the waist and was pulling me toward the door as Jackie made it to her feet.

"I won't forget this!" she yelled after us.

"I hope not!" I yelled back at her, fighting against Vance's arm. "That way, next time you'll keep your fucking mouth shut or you won't find it so easy to get up!"

Then Vance had me out the door. He let me go, grabbed my hand and dragged me to his Harley.

"I cannot believe that just happened," I ranted at his back. "What a bitch! I wish I had my stun gun. I wish I had my mace. What a bitch!" I repeated.

He stopped at his bike and pulled me so my back was to it. I was facing him and he settled his hands at my hips.

I looked up at him. "You could have done something," I snapped.

"And missed the show?"

I hadn't noticed it, but right then I did.

He was grinning, huge.

"You think that was amusing?" I asked.

He stepped into me, arms going around me and he touched his lips to mine.

I stood stiff as a board.

"Princess?"

"What?" I clipped.

"Take your time learnin' to share."

I blinked. It was my turn to feel thrown.

"What?"

One of his hands went to my jaw and his thumb came out to run along my lower lip.

"All the time you want," he said softly, not answering my question.

The velvet shroud came around us again and I leaned into him.

"Am I going to be beating up all your ex-lovers?" I asked.

"No. Just Jackie, she's a bitch."

I didn't want to ask. I knew I shouldn't ask. But I asked.

"What were you thinking, being with her?"

"She's not a bitch to me," he replied.

True enough. It was pretty clear she really liked Vance.

Then for some reason, do not ask me why, I threw myself in the deep end. "Was she good?"

"No," he replied immediately.

This time I sagged into him, glad I hadn't sunk to the bottom of the pool like a rock.

"You're not just saying that?" I asked.

He shook his head.

My hands came up and I started to play with the edges of his leather jacket. "When do you have to get to your job?"

"Gonna see to my other job first," he told me.

"What other job?"

His white teeth flashed. "The job of fuckin' you."

He was teasing me.

I stopped playing with his jacket.

"This isn't really funny," I clipped.

"It's hilarious. That, particularly, was my favorite part."

"I'm *so* glad you enjoyed it," I said, sounding snotty.

He touched his lips to mine. "Let's get you home."

Whatever.

He let me go and got on the bike. I got on behind him.

He leaned back, grabbed my wrists and wrapped my arms tight around him.

I put my chin to his shoulder and we took off.

⌐▷◁¬

Sometime in the dead of night, I didn't feel the bed move when Vance got in it, but I did wake when his warmth hit me from shoulders to heels.

"Hey," I mumbled.

"Hey," he replied softly. "Go back to sleep."

I felt Boo walking up the bed and then heard him slip off the side to the platform with an "I meant to do that" meow.

"It was Nick," I told Vance, still half asleep.

"Sorry?"

"Nick made me cry. He approves of you, like, a lot."

Vance's arm tightened around me and drew me deeper into his body.

"Go back to sleep, Jules," Vance whispered into my hair.

"Okay."

I snuggled in and then fell asleep.

Chapter 26
Shrink-Wrapped

The next morning I woke up before Vance and I tried my new skill of waking him with a kiss. This time I decided to put my lips on other parts of his anatomy.

I was left in little doubt that he appreciated my creativity.

We were showered, dressed and in the kitchen eating bowls of Cream of Wheat that I prepared (because you could cook Cream of Wheat in the microwave). Vance was sitting on the kitchen counter. I was standing with a hip leaned partially into the counter, partially into Vance's knee. Boo was sitting in front of us, tail sweeping the floor in a wide arc, staring at our bowls with greedy eyes.

"What's on for your day?" Vance asked.

I looked up at him and gulped down a bite of Cream of Wheat. "Shelter. Then I should go talk to Heavy, Frank and Zip, tell them the party's over."

"Good idea."

I had one more thing on my agenda, and that was waiting for my period to come. Vance and I were moving fast, but not fast enough for me to share *that*.

Instead I said, somewhat wistfully, "I'm gonna miss the street."

"You left it in good hands." Vance's lips weren't smiling, but his eyes were.

"How's that?" I asked.

"Jack told me a dealer's entire car was shrink-wrapped the other night."

I felt my eyes widen. "What?"

"Tex shrink-wrapped a dealer's BMW. Wrapped the whole thing in plastic wrap and then used a portable blow dryer on it to tighten the plastic. Word has it, it was several layers deep."

I was thankful I didn't have a mouthful of Cream of Wheat or it would have come out my nose, I laughed so hard.

"Tex is a nut," I said when I was done laughing.

"Tex is a nut," Vance agreed.

"What's on for your day?" I asked.

"Never know where the day'll take me," he replied.

Kristen Ashley

I sighed and leaned into his knee. "That'd be nice." I took another bite of Cream of Wheat.

"Jules?"

"What?" I asked with my mouth full (Auntie Reba would have had a conniption). Then I swallowed.

"Wherever it takes me, good to know in the end it'll lead back to you."

Luckily I had swallowed because my mouth dropped open.

Vance watched me a beat and said, "If you fuckin' freak out, I'm cuffin' you to the bed."

My mouth snapped shut.

"Indy says that doesn't work," I informed him snottily.

He watched me another beat, again openly surprised by what I shared. Then he laughed.

"That's more than I needed to know about Lee's relationship with Indy," Vance said through his laughter.

Then a thought hit me.

"Don't tell anyone I told you that," I demanded.

He grinned at me. "Why not?"

"Because it's nobody's business."

"Indy told you."

"Yes but she probably didn't expect me to blab it to you."

"Women talk."

I turned away from him and put my bowl in the sink.

"Women talk! Ha!" I said. "You boys are the biggest gossips I've ever met."

Vance jumped off the counter and leaned into me to put his bowl next to mine. "You ever do a shift in the surveillance room, you'll understand. Gotta have something to break the monotony."

I turned to him. "Well, break it with something else. I don't want to make an enemy of Lee."

His arms slid around me. "That's not gonna happen." His face came close to mine. "The cherry poppin' conversation in your living room was the topic of conversation for days. Mace taped it and played it for the whole team." I was back to staring at him with my mouth open and I thought my heart stopped beating. "Look at this as your way of getting even," he finished.

"That's it!" I declared. "No cookies for Mace. I don't care if he did beat someone up for me."

382

I felt Vance's body move against mine with laughter. Still laughing, he touched my lips with his own and said, "Gotta go."

"Fine," I grumbled.

He grinned, ignoring my grumble. "I get done in time, I'll make dinner."

"Fine," I was still not over the fact that the cherry popping conversation was taped and used for the Nightingale Investigation Team's amusement. Then another thought struck me. "If Dawn ever sees that tape——"

The laughter went out of his eyes. "Dawn is *never* gonna see that tape."

At that, I smiled.

Vance smiled back, grabbed the cookies and then he was gone.

Then I remembered something and, probably too late, I yelled, "Don't forget! No cookies for Mace!"

I heard the backdoor slam.

That afternoon, still with no sign of my monthly visitor who always came on time and was *never* late, I called Vance (though, not to give him a progress report on my monthly visitor).

"Yeah?" he answered.

"Hey," I said.

"I was just gonna call you," he told me.

"You making dinner?" I asked.

"Don't think so, I'm in New Mexico." My body went still and Vance kept talking. "I'm after a skip."

I didn't know what to say. It wasn't often that you were standing in your kitchen in Denver with someone, calmly eating Cream of Wheat in the morning and in the afternoon, without warning, they were in New Mexico.

"Jules?"

"I... okay," I said.

"You all right with this?"

"Um, sure," I lied. I was freaking out. Do not ask me why. I just was.

"Trail's hot. It won't take long."

I didn't want to sound like a clingy, stalker, psycho bitch from hell, but I didn't know what to say at that moment that wouldn't sound like a clingy, stalker, psycho bitch from hell.

So I stayed silent.

Vance kept talking, "I'm off tomorrow. Do you want to spend the night at the cabin? I'll meet you there."

"No," I replied. "I think I'll call the girls, see if they want to go out after I talk with Heavy, Zip and Frank."

"I'll come to your place when I'm done with this."

That, at least, made me feel better.

"Okay."

It was Vance's turn to be silent.

"Vance?"

"You're not okay with this," he said.

"It's what you do," I told him as if he didn't know.

"Yeah."

"I'll get used to it."

Silence.

"You just surprised me," I explained.

More silence.

"New Mexico is only one state away. It isn't like you're all of a sudden in New Zealand."

More silence.

"Though, I've always wanted to go to New Zealand. I've heard it's beautiful there and the people are nice."

More silence.

"I should probably take Roam to a beach during my next vacation so he can learn how to surf."

"Jules?" Vance finally spoke.

"Yeah?"

"Shut up."

I smiled.

⌐⌐

I'd spent some time in the rec room with the kids and was walking down the hall on my way back to the office when I turned my head and looked in the window to the blue room. With the tutor, Stu, sat Roam, Sniff and Clarice.

I kept walking a few paces and then stopped dead. Then I walked backwards and looked into the room.

My eyes were not deceiving me. Sitting in the room with Roam, Sniff and the tutor was Clarice.

Before they could see me, I kept walking.

Clarice had never gone to a tutoring session. Andy was working with her, but she was a no-go. Tough as nails and out on the street nearly as long as Roam had been, I thought she only came to the Shelter to watch television, get a decent meal and brag about her shoplifting escapades.

Now she was working with Stu.

That was a mini-miracle. And the mini-miracle worker was Daisy.

When I got to my desk, I flipped open my phone and called Daisy.

"Hey sugar, what's up?" Daisy answered.

"Vance is after a skip," I told her. "He's in New Mexico. Thought maybe, if you're not busy, you might want to go out and get some drinks, maybe dinner."

"I'll have to check with my husband."

"If you have to do something with Marcus, that's cool, I'll call—"

"What did you say?" Daisy cut in, but she did it on a whisper. It was weird hearing Daisy whisper. I'd never heard it before. She was not a whispering kind of person.

"I said if you have to do something with Marcus, that's cool. I'll just call—"

"You know?" Daisy broke in again.

"Know what?"

"Know... do you know who Marcus is?"

Finally I got it.

"Yeah," I said quietly.

"I've been trying to find a way to tell you. How long have you known?"

"Awhile," I said. "Luke told me."

She was silent a few beats then she asked, "Do you *really* know who Marcus is?"

"Yeah," I repeated, again quietly.

"You don't mind?"

Oh, I minded.

One thing I'd learned in life was that women could bitch about their men until they were blue in the face and you could listen and nod and offer support.

But you never—as in *never*—said something bad about a woman's man, no matter how much she bitched or how much he may deserve it. It always came back to haunt you.

"Just call me after you talk to Marcus," I said instead of answering.

"All right, sugar," Daisy replied. Now her tone was quiet. Not a whisper, but barely there.

"Daisy?" I called.

"Yeah?"

"Clarice is in with the tutors," I told her.

Daisy was silent.

"Thanks," I said.

Then I flipped my phone shut.

⌖

"Oh shit, I know who this is," Zip shouted across his Gun Emporium as Daisy and I sauntered in. "No, no, no. Should I say it again? I think I fuckin' will. Fuck... *no!*"

"Zip," I said in a soothing voice as Daisy and I approached him. Heavy was standing in front of the counter opposite him. Both of them were scowling at me.

"No. You aren't gonna get Marcus Sloan's wife filled full of holes. That kind of shit hits the fan, everyone gets splattered. I do not want to be splattered with shit. Jesus, girl, you are loco." He shook his head then narrowed his eyes and said, "I heard you were off the streets."

"I am," I replied, stopping in front of the counter.

"What're you doin' here?" Heavy asked.

"Thought I'd come by, tell you in person. Then I thought maybe you guys might want to meet us for drinks later."

They stared at me. Then they stared at each other.

"Shee-it. Crowe's dumped her again," Zip muttered.

Daisy giggled.

"Crowe has *not* dumped me," I snapped. "And he didn't dump me the first time. It was a misunderstanding!"

"Why aren't you havin' drinks with him?" Heavy asked.

"He's in New Mexico, after a skip."

The light dawned and both of them looked a lot less cantankerous.

"Where you goin' for the drink?" Zip asked.

"Smithie's," Daisy replied.

"I'm in," Heavy answered immediately.

"Me too," Zip put in.

Smithie's was a strip club. Daisy used to work there (as a stripper, pre-Marcus). Jet did, too (as a cocktail waitress, pre- and start-of-Eddie, but most definitely not now as Eddie wasn't fond of the outfit the waitresses had to wear or the clientele). Jet's sister Lottie (better known as Lottie Mac, Queen of the Corvette calendar) now worked there as a stripper, apparently the best one this side of the Mississippi, and that included Vegas. She was such a good stripper, Lottie was a local celebrity. Even I had heard of her.

"We're going to get something to eat. We'll see you at Smithie's after you close down the shop," I told them.

"Later," Heavy said.

As we walked away, we overheard Zip saying, "Loco, fuckin' loco, what kind of women go drinking at a strip club?"

Daisy turned her head and smiled at me.

I smiled back.

⌖

"Oh my God," I breathed after Lottie was done with her two song dance. "I want to be a stripper."

Roxie giggled beside me. "That's what everyone says."

Lottie was gone, disappeared behind the stage. The crowd was wired, screaming for an encore. I was right with them on my feet shouting for her to come back.

She didn't strip. I didn't know what she did, but it wasn't stripping, though she did dance around in fancy underwear and rip her bra off at the end.

The only way to describe it was a work of art.

We were sitting in the VIP section right up next to the stage.

When Daisy and I drove up in Daisy's Mercedes, I thought we'd never get in. There was a velvet rope and a line clear around the building.

Daisy just walked up to the front of the line, said, "Hey Lenny," to the huge black guy that was the bouncer, and then swanned in like the place was named "Daisy's" and not "Smithie's".

She went directly to a cordoned off area where Jet, Roxie, Indy, Ally, Tod and Stevie were all sitting.

Our asses no sooner hit the chairs when an older, heavyset black guy came trotting up to us.

"Smithie!" Daisy squealed with delight.

Smithie ignored her and pointed at me.

"You!" he shouted, even though he'd stopped not two feet away from me.

I went still and stared at him, mentally inventorying my purse for weapons. I'd so lost hold on my head-crackin' mamma jamma that the only things I could think of to use were my nail file, or I could throw my panic button at him. Neither of these were likely to instill terror in his heart.

"Can I help you?" I asked, slowly standing again.

"You Law?" he shot back.

Oh shit.

I decided on silence.

"I want no trouble tonight. We've had our quota of bar brawls this year," Smithie said to me.

"Smithie," Jet put in placatingly.

Smithie's angry gaze swung to Jet.

"You were the cause of two of them," he snapped.

"Was not!" Jet huffed. "Just one, the other one was a shooting."

Smithie looked to the ceiling.

Jet looked at me. "No one got shot," Jet assured me. "All the strippers jumped the shooter. It's kinda funny if you—"

"It *ain't* funny!" Smithie roared, and everyone around us turned to stare.

"Smithie, sugar, Law's given up the street," Daisy cut in.

"Yeah, right. Trouble follows you bitches around like the plague and more often than not, it traipses its tight ass and long legs in here. Not tonight. Got me?" Smithie declared.

"We're just having a few drinks," Ally said.

"See that you do." He snapped his fingers and a waitress in a red micro-mini and a black skintight camisole with "Smithie's" in red script across the front came tottering to our table on high heels.

Smithie's eyes moved to me and he stared. I stared back.

Then he looked me up and down and asked, "You dance?"

"No!" Indy, Jet, Roxie, Tod, Ally and Stevie all said in unison.

"All right, all right. Shit," Smithie put his hands up and then looked at me again. "Hear you're Crowe's woman."

I nodded that, yes, I was Crowe's woman.

At the thought, I grinned.

Smithie did not. "Shit. Those boys need to get their heads examined."

Then he was gone.

"What can I get you to drink?" the waitress asked.

"I'll take an appletini." This was said from behind me, and I turned to see Shirleen powering through to our table.

"Well, the night is complete!" Daisy hooted. "Shirleen, girl, good to see you."

Shirleen, I was surprised to see, got hugs and cheek kisses from everyone while I ordered a cosmopolitan. Then again, she was Darius's aunt and Darius was Lee's best friend, so I guessed she was part of the tribe.

"Hey Law," Shirleen said, eyes on me and sitting across from me.

"How're things?" I asked.

"Goin' well," she replied, nodding then her eyes got intense. "Real well," she repeated with meaning.

I smiled at her. She smiled back.

"You two know each other?" Daisy asked, looking between the two of us.

Everyone was staring.

"Law helped with a family problem," Shirleen explained.

Everyone seemed okay with that answer so I looked at Daisy and changed the subject quickly. "What did Smithie mean when he asked if I danced?"

Daisy nodded to the stage. "He meant stripped."

My eyes went to the stage. The three women there were gorgeous, their perfect bodies oiled up and glistening, their nipples covered with sparkling pasties. They knew how to move and they had tons of money sticking out of their g-strings to prove it.

Still.

"Um…" I said.

"The word is," Tod began, "yikes."

"Nothin' wrong with strippin'," Daisy said to Tod.

Kristen Ashley

"Not for you, but she's a social worker," Tod retorted. "Social workers don't strip."

Daisy turned fully to Tod and I felt her attitude hit our table like a bolt of lightning. "Why not?"

"Uh-oh, another white people fight and I don't have my appletini yet," Shirleen muttered.

I felt the tension in the air (hell, everyone felt the tension in the air), and to dispel it, I blurted, "I haven't got my period yet."

Everyone turned to me. My tactic worked, maybe too well.

Shirleen craned her head around, looking for our waitress. "Holy shit. This is heavy, I need my appletini."

"How late are you?" Indy asked.

"I should have started today," I told her.

"Not to worry," Daisy said, cooling off her attitude when confronted with a girlfriend problem. "Rule is you don't need to worry until at least a week."

I shook my head. "I always start like clockwork late morning on the special day. I haven't started yet."

"I think I need to stretch my legs," Stevie murmured, clearly uncomfortable with the conversational turn.

"What?" Ally said. "We're talking about menstrual cycles. It's the most natural thing in the world."

Stevie glared at her. "I'm gay but I'm still a man. We don't do periods. I could barely cope with the in-depth cherry popping trip down memory lane."

"Okay, no more about periods," Roxie threw in and looked at me. "Let's just talk about cause and possible effect. How many times did you do it unprotected?"

"Too many," I admitted.

They all stared at me.

"Girlie, I know you were a virgin but you got to take care of yourself," Tod advised, not unkind but slightly impatient.

"What's in Vance's head?" Jet murmured. "At least he should know better."

"I know what's in Vance's head," Indy replied.

Jet and Indy looked at each other and their faces broke out in smiles.

Shit.

"You were a virgin?" Shirleen asked, wide-eyed.

Shit again.

I decided not to answer Shirleen and totally ignore Indy and Jet.

I'd had more than enough conversations about my ex-virginal status and cherry popping. One of them was even on tape.

"Word is you're with Crowe," Shirleen went on.

This time I answered with a nod.

"He pop your cherry?" she asked.

Daisy gave a tinkly bell laugh while I closed my eyes in despair.

"Shee-it. Every girl wished the likes of Vance Crowe popped their cherry. You're livin' the dream," Shirleen continued when I opened my eyes.

She wasn't wrong. I was living the dream.

"Was he gentle?" Shirleen pushed, nosy as all hell.

"Um... no," I answered, and her brows flew together.

"He hurt you?" she snapped.

"Um... no." I was beginning to get uncomfortable.

The waitress put our drinks on the table and I smiled at her in hopes that the current discussion would end now that Shirleen had her appletini.

My hopes were soon dashed.

"You come?" Shirleen kept at it.

"Oh for goodness sake," Stevie muttered the words that I was thinking.

"Well, did you?" Shirleen pressed when I didn't answer.

"I don't think—" I started.

Shirleen leaned forward, not to be denied. "Did you?"

"Three times," I gave in.

Shirleen's brows flew apart and her eyes nearly popped out of her head.

"Three times in one go?" she breathed as if she, personally, was going to find Vance and give him an award for Best Cherry Popping in the History of the World.

"Two, um... goes," I answered.

"Still..." She sat back and gave me a huge smile. "Hold on to that one," she commanded.

I nodded again. That I would try my damnedest to do.

"We're with them," we heard from behind us and everyone turned to look as a bouncer was trying to keep Heavy and Zip away from our table.

"Hey guys!" I called, thankful the menstrual cycle-slash-sex talk was done before Heavy and Zip got there.

"See!" Zip snapped at the bouncer, and he and Heavy pushed through.

I got out of my chair and made introductions. Neither Heavy nor Zip looked too happy to be sharing libations with the ex (hopefully) drug dealer Shirleen, but they kept their mouths shut. They sat down, ordered drinks and trained their eyes to the stage, making it clear they weren't there for small talk at a strip club with a gaggle of women and two gay guys.

"Ain't this fun?" Daisy said, wiggling in her chair, happy as a lark.

I couldn't help myself. Even after the cherry popping third degree, I smiled at her.

"Yeah," I said low.

Daisy's eyes came to me, they got soft and she winked.

My pug liked Daisy's wink. He got all squirmy happy and gave me tons of sloppy puppy kisses.

We drank. We chatted. We drank more. We watched the strippers. We drank more, getting tipsy. We laughed and giggled because we were getting tipsy. We drank more. Lottie came on and we all went as nuts for her as the rest of the audience.

We were settling in our seats with fresh drinks, the other strippers had started to do their thing post-Lottie when I heard, "*You!*"

This was a high-pitched, female screech and I turned to look.

"Oh shit," I muttered when I saw Jackie, Vance's ex... whatever, pushing through the crowd toward us.

What on earth was *she* doing there?

Considering the fact she was a woman and she was gorgeous, the bouncer didn't even try to hold her back.

I came out of my chair.

Jackie got right into my space and right into my face and my body went still.

"You bitch!" she screamed.

"Uh-oh," Ally muttered.

"What the fuck?" Heavy asked. I could feel him moving behind me, coming in close.

"Move away," I warned. I didn't want Smithie to get mad at me and I didn't want our fun night to end by being ejected from a strip club because I had to kick one of Vance's ex-bimbo's asses (again).

Four other girls pushed in around Jackie and Jackie swung her head (and hair) around to them.

"This is the bitch I told you about," Jackie informed her friends, and all five of them turned to glare at me, mouths in girlie bitch pouts, hands on hips.

I feared I wasn't going to get my earlier wish.

"Who you callin' a bitch?" Daisy was up, and even though she was at least five inches shorter than any of the women confronting us, she was all bitch pout, hand on hip, attitude right back at them, and it must be said, a lot scarier than any of them.

"Stay out of it," one of Jackie's friends snapped at Daisy.

Um.

I didn't think that was good.

"Don't tell her what to do," Ally entered the fray. She was up and moving around the table.

Fuck.

That *definitely* wasn't good.

"You stay out of it, too," another of Jackie's friends disengaged from the pack, getting ready to confront Ally.

Indy was up and tense. So were Jet and Roxie.

I didn't figure Lee, Eddie and Hank would pat me on the back for getting their women into a catfight at a strip club even if it was against a bitch bimbo skank from hell.

"Ladies——" Stevie tried to play peacemaker and I had the fleeting hope that Stevie's quiet magic would work.

"Shut up, homo," Jackie sneered at Stevie and she barely got out the "mo" part of "homo" when I lost all thoughts of peacemaking and worrying about my friends.

It was then that my head-crackin' mamma jamma snapped into place and I moved.

I took Jackie by the wrist, swung it in a wide arc, spinning her around. I ducked, positioning myself and her. I bounced her off my back and she went flying into the tables. She crashed, as did the tables and all of our drinks (and a number of empties), to the floor.

I watched Jackie struggle amongst the overturned tables, her arms and legs pumping, soaked with appletinis, cosmopolitans and rum and Cokes when I felt my hair being tugged backwards.

I reached back, grabbed both wrists of the hands that were in my ponytail and whipped one of Jackie's friends around to my front. I felt another girl grab at me, but I stayed focused and planted my feet, dropped one of her wrists and flipped her on her back using what had become my signature move. She landed with a thud of flesh on flesh, right on top of Jackie, and both women grunted in very unladylike ways.

Then I dealt with the next one who was pulling at my shirt. I tagged her with a calf in the back of her knees. She teetered, I gave her a nasty shove in chest and she landed on Jackie and the other girl with a high-pitched screech.

I spun around and confronted the last two, lifting my hands and wriggling my fingers at them. I was too focused to notice that everyone had stopped to stare. Everyone, even the strippers.

"You want a piece of this?" I taunted and jumped forward once. They jumped back, bitch pouty looks gone, their eyes wide with fear.

I smiled at them and came back around. Jackie's friends were up and were helping Jackie up, too.

I pushed forward, shoved her friends out of the way and grabbed onto Jackie's sweater, taking a bunch of it in both of my fists. I advanced, forcing her backward until she was at the stage. I leaned in and she had no choice but to arch her back over the stage.

"Stevie come here!" I yelled, my face in Jackie's, her eyes wide and freaked out, my hands not leaving her sweater.

"Girlie, I'm here," Stevie said quietly from my side. "You can let the skank go."

"Apologize," I snapped at Jackie, not listening to Stevie.

"I... I'm sorry," she stammered, not taking her eyes off me.

"Not to me, you stupid bitch, to him. Apologize!"

"Holy crap," I heard Indy say from behind me.

"You got that right, sister," Jet muttered from behind me, too.

Jackie's eyes moved to Stevie and she repeated her apology.

"You ever gonna use that word again?" I asked when her eyes came back to me.

She shook her head (and hair). I moved back, pulled her up with me and then pushed her away from me so she staggered back into the stage.

"Am I ever going to see you again?" I kept at her.

She shook her head (and hair) again.

"Go!" I clipped.

She stood frozen.

I took a step into her. "Move!"

She moved and her friends moved. They moved as fast as their high heels would take them. I watched them go until they disappeared.

I straightened my back and cocked my head to the side quickly as I turned back to the room. The whole place—not just my posse, but everyone—was staring at me.

Smithie was close, standing by Daisy, arms crossed, eyes on me.

Fuck.

We were going to be ejected, I was sure of it.

"Sorry. I'll pay for any damage," I said to him.

"Shit, bitch. I'm thinkin' about askin' you to make that a regular feature at Smithie's." He shocked me by saying. "Hot babe kicks ass. They'll line up to see it."

"Fuck yeah!" Shirleen yelled. "Girl, you are *the shit*."

"Righteous!" Ally shouted.

Jet started clapping. So did Tod. Roxie did, too. Indy joined in, and then so did everyone else, including the audience and the strippers. Daisy gave a whooping shout and Stevie hugged me.

The bouncers righted the tables and Smithie shouted, "Get these bitches some drinks!"

I was about to sit down as the applause died away when I caught Zip and Heavy's eyes.

"You do a man proud," Heavy said to me, and the look on his face echoed his words.

Zip nodded.

I smiled and my pug wiggled in close, proud of me too.

I sat down and ordered another cosmopolitan.

Chapter 27

Home Part Two

I'd barely got Boo and I settled in bed when my phone rang.

After Lottie's third act we all left Smithie's. Daisy was too drunk to drive so she left her Mercedes at Smithie's. One of Marcus's men came to get her and Shirleen grabbed a ride with them. Since I was in the 'hood, I caught a ride with Lee, who came in one of the company's Explorers to get Indy, Tod and Stevie. Roxie was designated driver for Jet and Ally.

We all hugged and told each other we loved each other, waxed on about how great the night was and that we'd be best friends forever for about ten minutes before Lee grabbed Indy and my upper arms and steered us to the Explorer.

They dropped me first, if you could call Lee walking me to the door and making sure I got safely inside "dropping me", and they took off. As I watched out the window, Indy, Tod and Stevie waved at me as Lee drove.

I weaved a bit and giggled to myself, cooing to Boo, "Mommy's *drunk!*" as I walked to the bathroom. I washed my face, slathered it with moisturizer, changed into a nightgown and Boo and I climbed somewhat gracelessly up into the bed.

Then the phone rang so I grabbed it.

"Hello," I sang happily (okay, more like drunkenly).

"Go set your alarm," Vance said in my ear.

"What?"

"Bobby just called me, told me you got home. Lee walked you to the door, but you didn't set your alarm. Go set it."

"Okay," I said, again happily (yes, more appropriately drunkenly) and scooted to the end of the bed.

I took the phone with me and held it to my ear as I jumped down, stumbled a little and muttered, "Shit," before giggling.

Throughout this there was silence in my ear. Then, "Are you drunk?"

Shit.

"Um…" I mumbled.

Vance was an alcoholic. I was a social worker so I knew all about alcoholics. Still, I'd never read a book about how to deal with one when he was your shit-hot boyfriend. Actually, I was pretty sure I had, but I was forgetting in my drunken state what it said.

Therefore I stayed silent after my initial "um".

"How drunk are you?" Vance asked as I made it to the alarm keypad in the living room.

I didn't answer, intent on the task at hand. I punched in some numbers and the keypad started beeping angrily.

"Whoops," I said and narrowed my eyes at the keypad.

"Jules," Vance said in my ear.

"Quiet, I'm concentrating," and I was.

I heard him chuckle.

"Quiet!" I demanded.

His amusement still came at me as I punched the right code in and the alarm stopped beeping.

"Did it!" I announced as if I'd just cracked the code to the security system protecting the Hope Diamond.

I started walking back to the bed as Vance asked again, "All right, Princess. Now tell me. How drunk are you?"

Oh well, honesty, Auntie Reba and Nick always told me, was the best policy.

"Five cosmos drunk," I told him.

"Five?"

I decided to fib by omission and leave out mentioning the shots, when I started up the steps to the bed platform and cracked my head against the hall ceiling.

"Ouch!"

"Jules?" Vance said in my ear.

"Okay. It's okay. I'm okay. Everyone's okay," I declared as I shoved myself in the opening and collapsed on the bed.

Vance was laughing again.

"You aren't mad?" I asked.

"Fuck no. Five cosmos drunk means you'll still be drunk when I get back."

"Is that good?"

"Yeah, Princess, it's good."

"Why?"

He didn't answer, he just said, "The skip was wanted in C Springs. I've just processed him at a station there and I'm passing the Academy now. I'll be home in a little over an hour."

"Okay," I replied happily (this time more happily than drunkenly).

"Take off your underwear."

My breath caught and I went instantly sober.

"What?" I whispered.

"Go to sleep without any underwear."

"Vance," I was still whispering.

"Princess, do it." His voice was silk and it slid through the phone and across my skin like it was alive.

"Okay." Yes, still whispering.

"See you soon," he said.

"Okay."

Disconnect.

I laid there a second, wondering if I could sleep without my underwear. Considering the fact that I was seriously turned on, I figured I wouldn't sleep anyway so I took off my underwear, turned off the light and settled in, cuddling Boo and waiting for Vance.

In about two minutes, I was asleep.

⌁

I was yanked off the edge of the bed with hands at my ankles.

I let out a surprised gasp. Boo went flying, I landed hard on the floor and an arm came around my waist while a hand went over my mouth.

I stared up, thinking (or, more like hoping) I'd be seeing Vance, but in the darkness I saw Hector Chavez.

I screamed against his hand and started struggling.

He pushed me into the bed platform, his body hard against mine, and again I felt his immense heat.

"Quiet. Roam's in trouble," he hissed at me. I stopped struggling immediately at his words and he dropped his hand and stepped away from me. "Get dressed. Get your gun. Now."

Kristen Ashley

Without asking a single question and flying through the house, I grabbed my clothes and shoes then ran into the bathroom and dressed.

I thanked my lucky stars I had worn a longish nightgown to bed because I was still panty-less when Hector pulled me out. I also thanked my luckier stars that fear for one of my boys made me sober as a nun. Vance wouldn't be happy I was sober, but maybe I'd do a shot or two of tequila when I got done with this gig.

After I dressed, I exited the bathroom, knelt in the hall and put my black Pumas on. "What's happening?"

"Cordova got him," Hector answered.

"Goddammit," I snapped.

I went to the sliding doors under my bed, opened a drawer and rooted through my underwear until I had my gun. I knew Cordova had been released from the hospital (it *was* only a flesh wound), but I thought he'd been released to jail.

As I looked for my gun, I asked, "Why?"

"Fuck knows. He's pissed at you. Maybe he thinks he can use Roam to make you pay."

"I thought Cordova was in jail," I said while I tucked my gun into the back waistband of my cords.

"Bonded out."

"Fuck," I muttered.

"Let's go," he said.

We went.

It's important to note at this point there were a lot of things I should have done.

I should have taken my purse. I had my panic button and phone in my purse. Not to mention a tracking device.

I should have called Vance, told him where I was going so he wouldn't worry.

Not doing that, I should have left a note.

I should also have called the surveillance room at Nightingale Investigations. Even the Nightingale Men didn't go into a situation without backup.

400

But I had Hector. Hector was deep cover DEA, which meant he was his own brand of badass mother, perhaps scarier than them all, and this was Sal Cordova we were talking about. Sal was an idiot.

So I didn't do any of these things.

I should have.

Bobby

Bobby Zanzinski hated nighttime surveillance. All of the Nightingale Men hated nighttime surveillance except Jack, though Jack was kind of a weird guy.

Nighttime surveillance was boring as hell. It meant Fortnum's was closed and Vance was normally at Jules's (or Jules was asleep) so you couldn't watch her wandering around saying stupid shit to her cat.

Bobby could watch Jules for hours. Any of them could. That woman was *smokin'*.

He sat in the surveillance room and came instantly alert when Hector Chavez approached the house. Bobby watched Hector break into Law's duplex then disable her alarm.

"Fuck," he muttered.

He knew who Hector was, but Bobby was still alarmed. Those deep cover DEA guys were nuts, pure and simple. Fuck knew why Hector was breaking in, so Bobby leaned forward, turned up the volume to her speakers and got ready to call Vance.

As he reached for the phone, on another monitor Bobby saw Vance drive into the underground parking area. Vance would come up and drop the keys.

Bobby decided to wait and tell him when he got there.

Lord knows The Law can take care of herself, Bobby thought on a smile.

Shirleen

Shirleen heard her phone ringing.

She rolled, reached out, grabbed it and put it to her ear.

"This better be good," she mumbled.

"Aunt Shirleen," Darius said in her ear.

Shirleen came instantly awake *and* sober. "What's up, son?"

"Got word. Shard's back."

Shirleen felt a chill snake down her spine. Anyone with an ear to the ground knew what was on Shard's mind, namely making Jules pay.

"I thought Lee's boys——" Shirleen started.

"Shard's back and he's pissed. He's goin' after Law's kids. Gonna draw her out."

Shirleen threw back her purple, satin covers.

"Call Lee," she ordered.

"I'll take care of it. I've got some boys out lookin' for him."

"No, boy. You call Lee. Let the professionals handle this."

"Aunt Shirleen."

"Boy——"

"I'll handle it."

Disconnect.

Shirleen stared at the phone in the darkness for two seconds. Then she turned on the light and ran to her desk to find Daisy's home number.

⌖

Sniff

Sniff was running. He was running, crying, snot coming out of his nose, breathing heavy.

He had to get to Law. He had to get to her. He had to get to her *now*.

When Cordova took Roam, Sniff had seen it. He'd followed them, knowing that Cordova was an idiot and an asshole. Roam could handle Cordova. Hell, their geeky tutor Stu could handle Cordova. Sniff could even handle Cordova.

Sniff had caught a ride with some Mexican gang-bangers he knew who put up with Sniff because they thought he was funny. They took him to Cordova's place then they'd peeled out, leaving him there.

Sniff had approached the house thinking to get a giggle while Roam kicked Cordova's ass and when he saw what he saw through the window, he'd taken off.

He was so freaked out, he'd dropped his fucking, *fucking* (and he vowed to himself he'd never say "fucking" again if Law got Roam out of this) phone somewhere along the way, and as usual he had no money to make a pay call.

A car came down the street. Sniff stopped and put out his arm to flag it down, desperate, shouting.

The car passed him.

Without hesitation, he kept running and trying to keep the vision of Roam, bloody and what Sniff hoped was only unconscious, out of his brain.

Worse still, the vision of a dead Cordova.

It wasn't working.

Sniff turned onto Colfax, running down the busier street, hoping he could flag down a ride.

He was miles away from Law. He'd never make it.

He saw a black Porsche pass him. The brake lights lit and then the Porsche pulled over. Sniff ran toward it, opening his mouth to yell when the door opened and Luke Stark knifed out the driver's side.

Sniff could have jumped for joy.

Instead he stopped and, as Stark approached him, he doubled over, a stitch in his side, and sucked in breath.

"Sniff," Luke put a hand to the back of his neck.

Sniff looked up at him, not caring even a little bit that this super cool guy was going to see his tears and snot and he said, "We gotta find Law."

Stark took one look at Sniff's face and his own went hard in such a way that Sniff felt a thrill of fear mingled with hope.

"Get in the car," Stark ordered.

Sniff ran to the car.

⌖

Roam

Roam was awake but pretending to be out.

Cordova was dead. Shard had shot him, like, seven times. Right in front of Roam. Roam had never seen so much blood in his life, and Roam had seen a lot of shit in his life, including blood, including his own, but not *that* much.

Roam had not put up much of a fuss when Cordova took him at gunpoint to his house, mumbling stupid shit about making Law pay, getting her attention. Roam figured he'd find some way out of it. Anyway, he knew Sniff had seen them and Sniff would call Law. His idiot, big-mouth friend had done it before, he'd do it again. Everyone knew Law could handle Cordova. She could handle just about anyone.

They'd got to his house, Cordova still ranting, telling Roam to sit, continuing to talk about Law and how she was just playing with him and she really wanted him and Roam thought it was kind of funny. It'd be a good story, it'd make Law laugh. He liked to make her laugh. She had a good laugh. She was one fucking hot white bitch normally, but when she laughed her face was amazing.

Park made her laugh all the time. Park had worked hard at it. He loved to make Law laugh.

Hell, everyone did.

Then Shard had walked right in the front door, as calm as you please.

Cordova turned to him, saying, "What the—?" and that was it.

Bang, bang, bang, bang, bang, bang, bang.

Dead.

Roam had been frozen in shock.

He should have run.

If he'd been like Crowe he might have had his head together enough to do something, if not to save Cordova, then to save himself.

Roam wasn't like Crowe.

But when Shard turned to Roam, he didn't shoot him. He beat the shit out of him. Roam put up a fight, but even all beaten up himself (his face was a swollen, bruised mess) Shard was still stronger, older and smarter than Roam.

So finally, nose bloodied, face cut, ribs burning and after he'd spit up blood the second time, Roam feigned being knocked out and went down.

And he waited.

Shard stood over Roam. Roam felt him there instead of opening his eyes. He listened as Shard called someone and said, "Got Roam. Tell the bitch I'm at Cordova's. She comes alone or I put a bullet in his brain."

Then he flipped his phone shut and waited.

Roam hoped Law wasn't stupid enough to come alone. He'd never seen her in action personally, but Martin and Curtis said she was the shit.

Still, Roam hoped she'd send Crowe.

Jules

Hector stopped his car and turned to me.

"Let's roll," he said.

I went out my side, he went out his.

He disappeared into the night.

I ran to the house Hector told me was Cordova's, one block and three houses down.

Hector, still trying to protect his cover, couldn't be seen. He was running backup for me only if I needed it, and while he was positioning himself at the back of the house I was going to the front.

I hadn't brought my phone and Hector didn't know who had his tapped. We figured I could call the police or Vance once I sorted out Cordova. It wouldn't take long.

It was a stupid plan.

⌘

Bobby

Bobby watched Vance shoot out of the underground parking area on his Harley.

He had his earpiece in his ear, phone on in his jacket pocket.

Bobby eyes were on the GPS screen and he was going to give Vance directions to Cordova's house via speakerphone.

By the time Vance made it up to the offices, Bobby had heard Hector telling Jules why he'd broken in. Bobby had already had the GPS directions to Cordova's house on screen when Vance opened the door and stuck his torso in.

"Keys," Vance had said, obviously not intent on hanging around. He tossed the keys to Bobby without fully entering the room.

"We got a situation," Bobby told him after he'd nabbed the keys, "Law."

Vance's face got tight and without hesitation he entered the room. Bobby briefed him in thirty seconds.

Vance had his earphone in his ear before the door to the surveillance room closed behind him.

"Turn left," Bobby told Vance.

Jesus, Cordova's a fuckin' idiot, Bobby thought, *Crowe's gonna feed him his balls for dinner.*

"Next street, turn right," Bobby said out loud.

⌘

Lee

The phone rang beside the bed. Lee gently rolled away from the soft, warm body of a dead-to-the-world Indy and snatched his cell off the night table, flipped it open and put it to his ear.

"Yeah?" he answered.

"Lee," it was Darius.

Lee got tense.

Darius went on, "Shard's in town. He's got one of Law's kids. Roam."

"Fuck," Lee clipped.

Lee was out of bed, dressed and out of the house in two minutes.

Indy didn't wake.

Shirleen

Shirleen was pacing her living room.

The phone rang and she pounced on it.

"What?" she snapped.

"He's got the brother. Kid's name is Roam," Darius told her.

Shirleen closed her eyes. "Call Lee."

"Already did. We need to find Law's other kid. I need Daisy's number."

"I called her. She's got Marcus on it."

"I'll call Marcus."

Disconnect.

Shirleen sat down on her white couch. She put her elbows to her knees and her head in her hands, and for the first time in a long time, she prayed.

Luke

Luke listened to the phone ringing in his ear, it rang twice before connect.

"Yeah?"

"Lee. I got Sniff. He says Shard's back in town. He's got Roam. I'm headed to Cordova's."

"Why're you headed to Cordova's?"

"Sniff says Shard's there. He looked through the window. He says Cordova is dead, Roam isn't in good shape. I found Sniff runnin' down Colfax headed to Law."

"Darius called, told me about Shard and Roam, though he didn't know where he was." There was a pause then, "*Fuck!*" Lee exploded and Luke's mouth tightened as he heard Lee uncharacteristically lose control. "Luke, I don't have a good feeling about this."

Luke didn't either. He had a fucking shitty feeling about this.

"Sniff's leading me to the house, he doesn't know the address. I'll get it to you when I get there," Luke said.

"I'll call the office for directions," Lee returned. "Out."

Disconnect.

Luke drove, Sniff gave directions. The kid had gotten control, stopped crying, wiped his face on his sweatshirt and was pointing the way with more certainty than Luke would have expected him to in his state.

Luke's phone rang again.

Luke flipped it open and put it to his ear. "Yeah?"

"Pick up the speed, Luke," Lee said. "I called the office. Hector got word about Roam. For some fuckin' reason he went for Law to get him. She's probably already there. Out."

Disconnect.

"*Fuck!*" Luke snarled.

He flipped the phone shut, threw it on the dash, put his foot down and the Porsche shot forward.

⥤⥢

Jules

Never, not in a million years, would I have thought Sal Cordova would have hurt Roam.

He wanted me, then he was going to get me.

But he wouldn't hurt Roam.

Maybe bore him to death with idiot stories about being a supposed ladies man, but that wouldn't be physically painful, just mentally painful.

That was why, just like Luke, I went up to the front door, cocky as all hell, knocked three times and shouted, "It's Jules!"

Then without hesitation, I pulled out my gun, put my hand to the door handle, turned it and went in.

I saw in a quick heart-stopping scan of the room that considering Sal was dead—not just dead, *very* dead—that I was right, he couldn't hurt Roam.

I also saw that somehow Roam *was* hurt, unconscious and bloody and lying on the floor.

Without a thought (I really should have thought), I ran into the room toward Roam, but to my surprise he surged up shouting, "Law!" his eyes behind me.

I whirled and saw Shard, gun up, pointed at me, his bruised and swollen face grinning, eyes hard.

"Fuckin' bitch," Shard said.

Then he fired.

Unfortunately Roam had enough chance to get himself in front of me. His body jerked when the bullet slammed into it and he went down at my feet.

Rage shot through me. I screamed bloody murder, lifted my gun, pointed and fired.

Shard fired too.

My first bullet hit him in the shoulder. I didn't aim to hurt him overly much.

His first bullet hit me in the gut. He aimed to kill me.

The burning sensation in my belly was nearly overpowering.

The will to live, thankfully, put the "nearly" in my previous statement.

With a gut wound, knowing his intention, Roam at my feet not moving and Shard's gun still aimed at me, I had no choice but to fire again, this time, with a different aim.

His second shot hit me in the chest.

My second shot went straight into his frontal lobe.

⚒

Luke

Luke saw the Harley in front of him, Vance astride it. Luke flashed his lights, Vance lifted his hand. Luke parked the Porsche behind the Harley two doors down from Cordova's house.

"Stay here, kid," Luke ordered Sniff.

Sniff nodded but Luke didn't see him. He was already out of the car.

"I take front, you take back," Vance said when Luke made it to him, already approaching the house at a jog.

Luke nodded, jogging beside Vance, then Luke separated, beginning to move across the lawn of the house next to Cordova's, heading toward the back.

Then they heard the shot then the scream and the second they did, they both sprinted forward at a dead run to Cordova's front door.

By the time they made it and Vance kicked in the door, four more shots had been fired.

⇁⊢⇀

Jules

I fell down on my ass, reached out toward a prone Roam. I couldn't find the strength or my breath to make it to him so I fell to my back.

I closed my eyes, fighting the pain and thinking about getting to a phone. When I opened my eyes again, Vance's face was the only thing I saw.

"Hey," I said because I figured I'd passed out (I didn't think I died; the pain of multiple gunshot wounds hurt like a mother and I didn't figure they had pain in heaven) and this was a dream so I smiled at him.

"Hey, Princess," he replied, eyes on me, hands working somewhere else. Then I felt my shirt ripped open from hem to collar.

"Get a goddamned medic here." I heard Luke bark from somewhere in the room.

I turned my head to see where Luke was, but instead saw Hector kneeling over Roam.

I looked back to Vance.

"Is Roam okay?" I asked.

"Let's worry about you right now," Vance said. He moved away from sight and I saw his hands catch something. When Vance wasn't filling my vision I was pretty certain I was seeing things because I could swear I caught a glimpse of Darius, and then Vance came back to me.

I was losing it, fading, and I knew it. My body was going into shock. I could feel the warm blood sliding out of me even as Vance put pressure on the wounds to stop the bleeding. I didn't know, if I went unconscious, if I'd wake up again.

I blinked.

"Crowe," I called.

His eyes had moved from mine to my torso but they came back to me. "Yeah?"

I had a lot of things to tell him, a lot of things I needed him to understand, and I knew I didn't have a lot of time.

I lifted my hand but couldn't keep it up. Before it fell Vance caught it.

I looked into his eyes as his strong fingers closed around mine, and I said the only thing I could think to communicate everything he needed to know.

"Home."

Then everything went black.

Chapter 28
Waiting

Jet

It was the middle of the night and Eddie's phone was ringing.

This happened a lot seeing as Eddie was a cop, so we were kind of practiced at him answering it without disturbing me (too much).

I was curled into his side. His arm went to the nightstand. He nabbed the phone, flipped it open one-handed and said quietly, "Yeah?"

He listened for five seconds then I felt his body go completely solid.

My head shot up.

Eddie rolled away and turned on the light. When he rolled back, his black eyes were on me. I didn't like what I saw and I pushed up, one hand at his abs, one hand in the bed.

"Where're they takin' her?" Eddie asked.

Oh no.

No, no, no.

My first thought was Mom. My Mom had a stroke nearly a year ago, and it had been bad but she had made it. My greatest fear was that it would happen again and worse. Without asking, I whirled around, threw back the covers and jumped out of the bed.

"Right. Later," Eddie said, his voice urgent.

I was hopping around, pulling on my jeans when Eddie caught me by the waist.

"Jet," he said softly.

I turned to him and pushed off, going back to pulling on my jeans, but looking up at him. "Is it Mom? Where is she?"

"It isn't your Mom," I stopped and stared at him. He didn't make me wait. "It's Jules. She's been shot."

"Oh my God," I breathed.

"It's not good," Eddie said.

I couldn't move. I just stayed still, a foot away from Eddie, staring at him.

"How not good?" I finally asked.

"Chest and gut."

I felt somehow as if an imaginary bullet tore through me in each place.

"*Twice?*" I cried, my voice shrill.

"*Cariño.*" He came forward, but I jumped away, pulling up my jeans at the same time.

"Let's go," I said.

"There's nothin' we can do."

I yanked off his t-shirt that I'd drunkenly pulled on before I'd fallen into bed what seemed like only minutes ago and I turned to the chest of drawers. I pulled out a bra and put it on while I glared at him.

"Let's go."

He stared at me a beat then bent to grab his jeans from the floor.

Within five minutes we were out the backdoor and in the garage. I was yanking open the passenger side door to Eddie's red Dodge Ram when Eddie shoved it closed. I turned to him, mouth open to ask him what he was doing when he put a hand to my belly and pushed me up against the truck, following me there and pinning me with his body.

His forehead came to mine, his one hand between us at my belly. His other hand came to my neck and we just stood there, looking into each other's eyes and breathing.

"Fuck," Eddie murmured.

"I love you," I told him.

His mouth touched mine and with his lips still there, he said, "Me too."

I nodded, my forehead rolling against his. He took in a deep breath and moved away. We got in the truck and he drove us to Denver Health.

Indy

"Hey, gorgeous," Lee said in my ear.

I opened my eyes and in the dark I could see his hips clad in jeans on the bed beside me.

I was tangled up in the sheets. This meant I'd been sleeping alone for a while. I was an active sleeper. If Lee was with me, he controlled it by pinning me deliciously to the bed with his hard body. Sometime between me drunkenly falling into bed, wearing nothing but my underwear, and now, Lee had been somewhere.

I came up on my elbow and Lee reached out and turned on the light.

I stared as he did it.

Lee's work had no office hours, but he went to pains to make certain this didn't affect me. Never in five months of living together had he turned on the light when he got home in the dead of night, which happened a lot. Every time he came home he woke me up, as he'd promised, to let me know he was okay, but he'd never turned on the light.

My eyes moved to him and my heart started beating hard in my chest.

Lee was sitting there, for that I could be thankful. But a lot of people I loved had dangerous jobs. Hank for one, Eddie for another. My Dad, who was a cop, Lee's Dad, who was a cop, too, and then there was Lee's whole workforce.

"What is it?" I asked.

"Jules has been shot."

I sucked in breath, not expecting to hear that, and came up to a sitting position.

Lee's eyes moved with me, never leaving mine. "Chest and gut. It isn't good. She's at Denver Health. Vance wanted to go get her uncle but I told him we'd do it."

"Of course," I mumbled, pulling the sheets away from my body.

Lee's hands took mine and my eyes went back to his. "Vance didn't agree. Said he needed to do it. I want you to be there for him and Nick. They're gonna need you. Vance agreed to that."

"Okay," I whispered.

"Hurry, Vance is waiting downstairs."

I flew from the bed, got dressed faster than I ever had in my life and ran downstairs.

Vance was standing, staring out the front window. I noticed he was wearing one of Lee's sweaters and I didn't want to know what that meant.

Lee was on the phone.

Lee said, "Gotta go," into the phone when he saw me and flipped it shut.

Vance's eyes moved to mine and I felt my stomach pitch by what I saw in his.

Or more to the point, what I *didn't*.

I bit my top lip and swallowed, then released it.

"Hey Vance," I said.

He lifted his chin.

"Let's go." Lee was already moving to the backdoor.

Lee had the Explorer blocking the back alley. I wanted to sit in the back, but Vance opened the front door for me and motioned me in.

"You..." I started.

He shook his head.

I didn't delay any further.

Lee drove the two blocks to Jules's house while I was turned in my seat to Vance. "What do you want me to do?"

Vance was looking out the window, but when I asked my question his eyes moved to mine again and he said, "Just be you."

I nodded, not really knowing what that meant, but thinking I could at least do that.

Lee stopped and idled and Vance was out the door. I looked at Lee. He jerked his chin toward my door. I nodded again and trailed Vance to Nick's door.

Vance knocked and I stood next to him. I felt stupid just standing next to him so I reached out and touched his hand with my knuckles. Immediately his hand twisted and his fingers closed over mine hard. I bit my upper lip again as his hand crushed mine, but I didn't make a peep.

The outside light came on, the door opened and Nick stood there. He looked through the screen at Vance then at me then back to Vance.

Vance and I watched as he closed his eyes tight, and before Vance or I could say a word he opened his eyes again and I had to suck in both of my lips at the pain written on his face.

Then he pushed open the screen door and he said, "Come in and sit while I get dressed."

⚞⚟

Roxie

Hank's phone rang.

I was warm and cozy, stuck between the heat of Hank and our chocolate lab, Shamus. I felt the cold air as Hank rolled away.

"Yeah?" I heard him say. I was already falling back to sleep, cuddling into Shamus's warm, soft fur, when I heard Hank say in a quiet, tortured voice I'd never heard him use before, "No."

I turned and looked at him in the dark and as I did that he sat up, twisted and switched on the light. Then his whisky-colored eyes moved to mine and what I saw there made me stare.

"We'll be there. Yeah. Shit. Yeah." He flipped his phone shut.

"Whisky?" I called.

He put his hands under my armpits, pulled me toward him, across his lap and buried his face in my neck as his arms went tight around me.

"Whisky," I whispered, beginning to tremble. Something was wrong, really wrong.

His head came up and his eyes found mine. "Sunshine, Jules has been shot. Twice. It's bad. We gotta go."

My breath caught painfully at this news, but Hank either didn't notice or he wasn't going to be delayed. He got up, arms around me taking me with him. When he was standing, he set me on my feet.

We dressed silently. Hank finished first (as usual) and let Shamus out the back for a quick break before we left.

We made it to the hospital and I saw Eddie and Jet first. They were already in the waiting room. Jet was sitting with Sniff, arm around him, and he was staring at the floor. Eddie was pacing. My eyes scanned the room and I saw Indy with Jules's Uncle Nick, both sitting, Indy holding his hand.

I kept scanning and Vance was there, too, standing and staring out a window. Lee was with him, not close, but also not far.

Hank started to go to Lee, but stopped when the door opened behind us and Bobby walked in. Lee's eyes had come to us when we arrived, but when he saw Bobby he came our way.

"What?" Lee asked Bobby when he arrived at us.

I peeked at Vance. His eyes hadn't moved from the window.

I found this alarming. Vance was a Nightingale Man, an action man, Mr. Alert, and he hadn't even moved, not a muscle. Not when Hank and I arrived, not even when Bobby arrived.

My gaze swung to Jet, who caught my look and shook her head, then to Indy, who did the same. I felt suddenly cold and was about to move to Vance when Hank's hand squeezed mine and Eddie hit our huddle.

"We had to lock Luke down," Bobby told Lee, and I drew in my breath at this latest bit of shocking news. "Mace did it. Luke lost it. Totally pissed at Hector for taking Jules to Cordova. Doesn't give a shit that Hector didn't know about Shard." Bobby's eyes moved to Vance. "I thought you might need me… Vance."

I didn't know what he was talking about, but whatever it was, it certainly wasn't good.

"Vance is hangin' in there," Lee said.

Bobby nodded and his eyes moved from Vance to Lee.

Then Bobby drew in a deep breath.

"I waited," Bobby said on an exhale and he blinked slowly then kept talking, "until Vance got up to the offices. I saw him on the monitors parking the Explorer. I figured I could wait to tell him about Hector breaking into Law's place until Vance got upstairs. Five minutes could have—"

"Get it out of your head," Lee ordered.

"I shouldn't have waited," Bobby replied.

Lee leaned in, face tight and serious. "Bobby, right now, get it out of your fucking head."

Bobby nodded once then his gaze sliced to Vance. He shook his head sharply, then he turned and was gone.

We all watched the doors close behind Bobby and my heart went out to him because obviously he was blaming himself for something, but I turned as Lee spoke.

"Fuck," Lee whispered, "he shouldn't have fucking waited."

I leaned into Hank and Hank's lips went to my ear.

"Go to Vance now," he told me.

I nodded. Hank dropped my hand. I walked across the room and slid my arm around Vance's waist.

He turned to me, and when his eyes hit mine I blinked.

His eyes were dead. They weren't blank, they were dead.

I felt my nostrils burning as I stared at him and I knew I was going to cry. I turned into him, pressed my forehead against his shoulder, breathing deep to control the tears, and his arms went around me.

We stayed that way for a long time and I managed to hold back the tears. He let me go and I took his hand.

We stood together, Vance looking out the window, me standing beside him. Daisy arrived with Marcus. Shirleen arrived with Darius. Ally arrived with Carl. Tex arrived with Nancy. Duke arrived with Dolores. Heavy and Zip came separately. May charged in like a madwoman, tears streaming down her face. Finally Tod and Stevie walked in, carrying enough donuts from some all night Winchell's to feed an army.

Coffees were bought. Eddie or Hank, badges on display on their belts, walked to the nurse's station and asked (okay, more like demanded) updates, even though there were none to be had.

Then the kids started coming. First Clarice, Daisy's friend, came in alone and sat down next to Daisy. Daisy put her head on Clarice's shoulder, and I didn't know that it was a small miracle that Clarice didn't move away.

Then another couple kids came in, two young boys who took a look around. Their eyes hit Sniff, then Vance, then they walked to a wall, slouched against it and stayed silent.

Then another kid came in. A couple more, a gaggle of girls, a posse of boys. After a while the room was filled with the Rock Chick Tribe and Jules's kids.

All of us silent or talking quietly, sipping coffee and eating donuts.

All of us waiting.

All the while Vance looked out the window while I held his hand.

Indy

Dawn was breaking when the doctor walked in wearing clean scrubs and Crocs. He looked around the room, filled to capacity with people, and Nick stood. I stood with him.

"Juliet Lawler?" the doctor asked the room at large.

Lee came up beside me, but I moved close to Nick.

"Me. Here. Me. I'm her uncle," Nick said and he hadn't spoken since we arrived so his voice was hoarse, croaky. He cleared his throat and I got closer.

The doctor walked to Nick. I saw a movement behind him as Vance materialized and stood at his side. Roxie was not far away, Hank at her back. Eddie and Jet moved in beside Lee.

The doctor stopped at Nick, his eyes scanning the crowd again. They settled on Nick and he said, "She's pulled through. Your niece is a fighter. She's in ICU, critical. We'll watch her, but it looks good."

I took Nick's hand as his shoulders drooped and I squeezed. He squeezed back.

My eyes moved to Vance as Nick asked, "Can I see her?"

Vance's body was tense, but I was relieved to see his eyes were alert. They were alive. He was back from whatever hideous place he'd been for the last several hours. I wanted to smile. Hell, I wanted to scream, but I kept my mouth shut.

"A quick visit," the doctor told Nick and started to move away.

"Roam!" We heard shouted, and everyone's eyes swung to Sniff.

The doctor turned back. "I'm sorry?" he said to Sniff.

"My friend, Roam. The black kid. He was shot too. Is he okay too?"

Everyone's gaze swung to look at the doctor.

"Does he have family here?" the doctor asked.

Everyone looked at each other.

"Information can't be released to anyone but family," the doctor said.

Eddie and Hank both moved forward. Information could be released to cops.

"Sho 'nuff, he has family. I'm his grandma," Shirleen lied through her teeth and bustled up to the doctor. "Tell me, how's my baby?"

The doctor stared at her a second then said, "I'll find out."

"You do that doctor," Shirleen said and the doctor turned to Nick as Shirleen's eyes slid to Sniff, then she winked.

Nick let go of my hand and followed the doctor, but he stopped. He looked at the floor behind him as if expecting to see something there, then he lifted his eyes.

"Vance?" he called.

Everyone's eyes swung to Vance, but he was already moving towards Nick.

Then they were out the door.

⚹

Jules

I opened my eyes and it seemed like I was lying in a bed, but I felt absolutely nothing, like I had no body. I figured, since a little while ago I'd been in pretty significant pain and bleeding a lot and now I felt nothing, that I was dead. And I decided kind of woozily that I was obviously an angel.

I saw movement so I looked sideways, and there was Vance staring down at me.

His handsome face was tight, worried and maybe a little pissed-off looking, and my angel-self smiled at him because clearly I'd been given the chance to have a chat with Vance before I flew on my fancy, new, fluffy-white angel wings to Heaven.

"Hey," I said. My voice sounded really weak, raspy and quiet rather than sounding super sweet and melodic like an angel's.

"Hey," he replied.

"Do you see my angel wings?" I asked, my voice still sounding raspy. "Are they pretty?"

He stared at me a second then I was pretty certain his lips twitched.

"Yeah, Princess. They're gorgeous."

"Yay," I whispered.

"You're gonna be okay," he told me.

"I know. I don't feel my body." I didn't realize I wasn't making any sense and wouldn't have cared anyway. Angels probably didn't have to make sense. They could fly around for eternity talking nonsense, who was to care?

I was thinking about my angel outfit, wondering what angels wore, and tried to look down at myself, but I found I didn't have a lot of energy so I stopped trying and my eyes slid sideways to look back at Vance.

"This angel stuff is exhausting," I informed him.

"I bet." His lips weren't twitching anymore. He was grinning flat out.

I really loved his grin.

That was when I remembered.

"Did you get it?" I asked, realizing suddenly that I needed to take an angel nap and soon.

"Get what?"

"Home," I said.

"Sorry, Princess, I can't hear..."

My eyes closed and I didn't have the energy to open them so I didn't bother. I figured angels could fly blind. They had to have angel-like sonar or something like that. Anyway, I would only bump into clouds even if I couldn't fly blind, and I didn't figure clouds would hurt.

But before I took off to Heaven, I had to know, or more importantly, Vance had to know.

So I asked Vance, my eyes still closed, "I said earlier 'home', did you get it?"

I felt him get close, and I thought that was strange since I didn't have a body anymore, not really anyway, so I shouldn't be feeling anything. But I was certain I felt his cheek pressed against mine, his stubble rough against my skin.

"No, Jules," he said into my ear. "I didn't get it."

I sighed huge and felt the angel nap tugging at me.

"Jules?" Vance called and he sounded far away, but it felt like his lips were at my ear.

"Home..." I whispered and then slid closer to somewhere else, maybe Heaven. I didn't know. There sure as hell weren't any bright lights. Oh shit, they probably didn't say "hell" in Heaven. Oh *shit*, they probably didn't say "shit" in heaven, either. I was already getting angel demerits and I hadn't even been to angel orientation yet.

I had to finish my thought. It might be my last chance.

So I whispered in Vance's ear because it seemed like it was really close to my mouth (although I knew it couldn't be because I didn't really have a mouth anymore as I didn't have a body).

"You're home. See, Auntie Reba said home isn't a place, home is anywhere just as long as the people you love are there."

Then I slid into heaven, except weirdly, right before I drifted away, I felt some pain in my fingers, like someone was holding my hand too tight.

Chapter 29
No Matter What

I was an angel in heaven for two days. Or at least I thought I was.

Really, I was whacked out on drugs and in ICU.

During these two days, I saw Vance once and Nick three times. I had no idea they came by often to spend time with me while I was taking angel naps. When I saw them I regaled them with stories of what it was like being an angel since, for two days, I thought I *was* an angel. I figured they could write a book about it and become millionaires. I even shared this idea with Vance.

The nurses told me it was the only time they'd ever heard that much laughter in ICU.

After two days, when it became clear I was going to survive, they moved me to a normal room. I stayed in the hospital a long time, but it wasn't uneventful, mainly because nothing in the World of Rock Chick was uneventful.

꧁꧂

Vance decided he didn't feel much like adhering to visitor's hours. The staff kept telling him he couldn't spend the night, sleeping in a chair next to my bed, but he did it anyway, and Vance seriously was not the kind of guy they wanted to argue with so they let him be.

I also told him, considering his job meant he always needed to be rested and alert, that he should stay at my place. He didn't pay one bit of attention to me and still came to the hospital anyway.

We bickered about it (because I didn't worry about arguing with Vance).

I lost.

Really, it wasn't fair for him to bicker with me when I was in that condition.

I informed him of this, but he just grinned at me.

꧁꧂

Kristen Ashley

A couple of days after I was moved from ICU, in the middle of the night, I heard weird noises.

Considering hospitals weren't the most restful places in the world, I suspected some doctor or nurse was there to check up on me. Instead, I saw Vance and Hector in a death-lock at the door, torsos together, legs planted. Clearly Hector was trying to get in, and just as clearly Vance didn't feel like allowing that.

"Vance," I whispered, and both men froze in death-lock position and looked at me. "Let him in."

"Princess," Vance said low.

"Let him in."

Vance hesitated a moment then stepped out of the death-lock, but he didn't pretend to be happy about it.

Hector approached the bed.

"I didn't know about Shard," Hector told me the minute he hit my bedside, and I noticed he also hadn't gone to etiquette school to learn you should start a conversation with words like, "hi", "hello" or "glad to see you aren't dead".

"I know," I told him.

"I thought Roam wouldn't want one of Lee's boys saving him from Cordova. Cordova was a moron, Roam would lose face. I thought he'd prefer you to take care of it."

"I know," I repeated.

"If I'd have known——"

"I was cocky," I broke in and my eyes slid to Vance, who'd moved to the other side of my bed. I didn't exactly want him to know this part since it might piss him off. However, I also didn't want Hector to go on blaming himself for something that was my fault.

I went on, "Earlier that night, I'd had too much to drink, and I didn't tell you that. I walked right in. I didn't think. I saw Roam and just went in. It wasn't your fault. It was mine. I didn't think."

"I shouldn't have——" Hector began.

"You did the right thing, I didn't. Please don't worry about it. It was my fault."

He stared at me a beat and I stared back, noticing, even though he still was in undercover-disheveled-mode (and seriously needed a haircut, but who

422

was I to say all that thick, dark hair needed to be cut; mainly because longish and messy, it looked hot), he was a seriously good-looking guy. He had Eddie's edge, the one that made you wonder about him, made you think he could turn to the dark side in a nanosecond.

Eddie had it under control. Hector did not.

After we stared at each other awhile, he nodded and left without even a glance at Vance.

When the door closed behind him, Vance called, "Jules."

My gaze slid to him. I took one look at his face and then I closed my eyes.

"I need an angel nap," I said, and I wasn't lying. I did need an angel nap. I also needed an excuse to avoid a Vance Lecture, and that was where angel naps came in handy.

Before I slid into my angel nap, I heard, "Jesus, you're a pain in the ass."

⇥⇤

Roam was released before I was, for some reason to Shirleen, who the hospital thought was his grandmother. A fact that Andy came from the Shelter to confirm, lying like a pig in mud.

The bullet had hit Roam in his right side, luckily missing any vital organs. He was motionless on the floor because on his way down he smashed his head against Cordova's coffee table and it knocked him out. So not only was he beaten bloody and shot, he also had a serious concussion.

During a visit to me, Sniff explained that Roam didn't feel much like letting Shirleen mother him during his convalescence at her house. This was mainly because Shirleen wasn't a motherly-type person who cooed and spoiled and ran herself ragged making certain that Roam had every comfort. Instead, she told Roam what to do, like, a lot. Things like rest and study with Stu (who came over to work with Roam and Sniff) and not to fill his head with too much junk by watching television, but instead she gave him books to read. I knew it freaked out Sniff, but Roam put up with Shirleen. Then again, he was probably scared not to.

Where Roam went, Sniff went, so Sniff was staying with Shirleen, too.

When Roam was fit enough to take to the streets again, Shirleen told both him and Sniff they were welcome to stay as long as they liked.

Kristen Ashley

They told me since Shirleen lived in "one phat crib" they decided to stay awhile, even if staying with her had rules.

It was a long time later that I realized that during all of Roam and Sniff's visits they never cursed.

Not once.

※

By the way, Roam and I never talked about it, him trying to save my life and me taking two bullets to save his.

However, once, while I was still in the hospital, I caught him looking at me funny. I grabbed his hand and mine went tight.

So did his.

For a second.

Then he pulled away.

With a fifteen year old runaway that was all that needed to be said. It was the best he would allow me to give him and it was the best I was going to get.

I was happy with that.

※

Needless to say I wasn't pregnant. I'd asked a nurse in a quiet moment and she told me there was bleeding, but what kind of bleeding she couldn't say.

After I got out of the hospital, my periods resumed as normal and I went right on the pill.

My body, the nurse told me, had been through too much trauma not to miscarry.

Whether I had been or hadn't been, I'd never know.

※

About four days out of ICU, the girl gang showed up one afternoon with a juicy piece of gossip.

Indy, Ally, Jet, Roxie and Daisy all waltzed in grinning like fools. They hung around my bed as Indy told me that Lee had fired Dawn.

424

I didn't gasp because that was a luxury I didn't have at the time (it hurt like a bitch; so did laughing, moving and breathing). So I just widened my eyes and my mouth dropped open.

"Apparently," Indy began, loving every minute of this, "Mace and Monty were in the surveillance room and for shits and giggles they flipped on the sound and visual to the reception area. Dawn was on some call to a girlfriend and she was talking about you. I don't know what she said, but Mace and Monty went ballistic. They called Lee and Lee was with Luke."

Daisy let out a tinkly laugh and rubbed her hands together and I knew that we were getting to a good part.

"Lee and Luke went directly to the offices," Indy continued. "Lee walked right in and told her to pack up her desk. She was fired."

"Luke escorted her out of the building," Roxie threw in, her eyes alight.

"They taped the whole thing," Jet added.

"Brody even cut it into a music video with some old footage of her scowling and glaring and making catty phone calls. He gave it a soundtrack 'The Bitch is Back'. It's fuckin' righteous! I can't wait for you to see it," Ally said, grinning like a loon.

"Yeah, we all went down there and watched it a billion times. Dawn was totally pissed when Lee fired her. It was great!" Indy finished.

Considering the fact that I'd had a near death experience, I knew I should be a better person, live my life doing good deeds and not be bitchy, even when it was being bitchy about someone who was a bitch. Nevertheless, I couldn't help being pleased that Dawn had been fired. Especially since everyone seemed so happy about it.

And of course, the stupid bitch was talking about me.

Luke came to visit me.

I was getting a lot of visitors. The girl gang, Tex and Nancy, Tod and Stevie, Duke and Dolores, Shirleen, Heavy and Zip. May came by all the time, full of stories from the Shelter and carrying with her purloined pudding cups. Frank slunk in, talked to me for five minutes and slunk out, clearly uncomfortable with sunlight shining on him, even through a window. A bunch of my kids came and the Nightingale Men came, too; Mace, Ike, Bobby and Monty. Then, of course, there were Nick and Vance, who spent the evenings with me, mostly kicked back and boring me to death by watching endless football games, talking about who would win the Heisman Trophy and shit like that. Luckily I was drugged out most of the time and slept a lot.

It was a while before Luke came.

I was sleeping, and when I woke up I saw him sitting in a chair pulled up to the bed, his fingers linked and resting on the side of the bed. He was bent forward, his forehead resting on his hands.

I was a little stunned at his posture. It was seriously un-Super-Dude-like.

"Hey," I said.

His head snapped up and he looked at me.

This stunned me, too, because Luke was not the kind of guy you could take by surprise, and he was so lost in thought, I'd done that.

"Hey," he said, face serious, mouth tight. He sat back and put his forearms to his knees.

"You okay?" I asked.

He stared at me and said, "I'll be okay when I can close my eyes at night and not see you lyin' on the floor among a mess of dead bodies and blood."

Yikes.

Not, I feared, a visual that led to sweet dreams.

"I'm sorry," I whispered, and wished there was something better to say.

There wasn't.

He kept staring at me but didn't say anything.

Then, with a voice low and quiet, he said, "You killed a man."

I nodded.

Shard was dead. I shot him in the head. The police waited until I was out of ICU, and with Vance standing next to me holding my hand, I'd made my statement. Roam and Sniff had made theirs, too. The police were not going to press charges, as obviously I'd done it in self-defense. Shard had killed Cordova, shot me and Roam. They were more than happy to close the case on him.

For my part, I was trying not to think about it.

"You gonna be able to live with that?" Luke asked.

I nodded again. "I don't have much choice."

Luke kept staring at me so I kept talking.

"It's the difference between him being here and Roam and me being here. I picked Roam and me. I think that was the right decision."

"It was. It's still gonna fuck with your head," Luke told me.

I had no doubt he was right.

"It starts fuckin' with your head, you talk to Vance," Luke went on. "You can't get to Vance then me, Lee, Monty, Mace, Ike. Any of us'll listen, and we'll know where your head will be at."

It was my turn to stare at him. If I was reading his underlying message, he was telling me they all had killed someone.

"Now I'm really one of the boys," I said softly, testing out my theory.

"Welcome to the club," he affirmed my guess.

He said this in jest, but he wasn't amused and neither of us laughed.

"I was stupid. I shouldn't have——" I started, but he got up suddenly and leaned into me.

Then he stunned me again by kissing me. Not a Luke, teasing, sexy kiss, but he put his hand to the side of my head and touched his lips to mine. He pulled back a couple of inches and stared me in the eyes.

"You can go over it again and again, relive it a million different ways. It isn't going to change anything. You saved your boy and you both are breathing. The end," he said.

He stayed where he was for so long I felt the need to respond.

"Okay," I said, but it was kind of shaky.

"You start relivin' it, you talk to Vance or me or any of the boys. Don't hold it inside. Again, we'll listen."

I nodded and was finding it hard to breathe, and not because I'd been shot in the chest, but because Luke was a great guy. Looking at Luke, hanging with Luke, you'd never know Luke could be like this. His face was hard, but he was close and I saw the soft concern in his eyes and it made a normally fucking handsome guy look downright knock your socks off beautiful.

He trailed his thumb slowly across my cheekbone, his eyes never leaving mine.

Then he took his hand away, touched my nose, gave me a sexy half-grin and he was gone.

⚜

I didn't get Thanksgiving with just Vance, Nick and me. The Rock Chicks had a huge Thanksgiving bash in my hospital room.

They brought the whole meal and all the fixin's and stood or sat around, carting in chairs from other places, eating and chatting. All the women played a massive marathon game of Trivial Pursuit while the men watched football.

Of course, I had to suck my meal through a straw and eventually the nurses had to come around and tell them they had to go, but still, it was fun.

⌖

Martin and Curtis had come to visit me.

The whole time they were there they didn't cuss, either.

Instead they told me why they were on the street. I'd been working with them for months and I had to get shot for them to open up to me.

I didn't complain.

Instead, once they left, I called Shirleen and we had a chat.

Then I called Andy and told him Martin and Curtis were ready for a reunion with their Mom. She had a new boyfriend they didn't like. They had reason not to like him, a really fucking good reason, and Andy knew what to do.

Martin and Curtis's Mom either dumped a boyfriend that was abusive to her boys or her boys were moving in with Shirleen.

Their Mom dumped her boyfriend.

Then she pressed charges.

With what he did, her ex wouldn't have much fun in prison.

⌖

They released me after a few weeks and I went to Vance's cabin.

Vance and I bickered about this. Nick and I bickered about it, too. They didn't want me sleeping on my couch nor climbing up to the bed platform.

They ganged up on me. It was clear they had made the decision without my input before I was released and I had no choice. This I found alarming, as it might not bode well for my future.

My head-crackin' mamma jamma was still with me. However my strength had leaked out onto the floor of Sal Cordova's living room, and it was going to take a little while longer for me to get fighting fit.

So I gave in.

428

Vance took me to his place, driving a new black GMC Sierra (that Ally told me that Indy told her that Lee told *her* that Vance bought because he didn't want me riding around in his rickety old truck and I was certainly in no shape to ride on the Harley).

Daisy and Roxie had packed up a bunch of my clothes. Nick had packed up Boo, his litter, food, treats and toys and he took my cat and stuff Vance's cabin.

Unfortunately for Vance and Nick (it was fortunately for me, I thought it was hilarious), the cabin wasn't nearly as restful as they thought it would be, namely because everyone came with great regularity, and stayed for great lengths of time. Tod and Stevie set up an ongoing Yahtzee tournament that lasted for weeks (Jet won). Heavy even brought a punching bag there, set it up in Vance's second bedroom, and when I was up and around, he sat eating Ding Dongs and Oreos and other chocolate-flavored snacks with dubious cream-like filling and drilled me relentlessly.

⚡

Vance worked through my recovery, though Lee never assigned him to anything that would take him out of town. He also was never given night shifts in the surveillance room. This meant Vance was home by eight o'clock, usually earlier, every night.

⚡

In late December, close to Christmas when I was still recovering but getting stronger all the time, I stood in Vance's bathroom, wearing nothing but lacy, pink hipsters and staring into the mirror at my red, ugly, puckering, very, *very* slowly fading scars.

They would fade, but they'd never go away, and they were not at all attractive.

I put on a t-shirt of Vance's. I'd not worn a sexy nightie since getting shot. The bodice of all of the ones I had showed the scar. I knew this because I tried them all on and checked.

I walked to the bedroom.

429

Vance was lying in bed, chest bare, sheet to his waist, naked under the sheet. I knew this because Vance slept naked, not that I'd acquired x-ray vision during my recent trauma.

He was reading.

Boo was on his belly, eyes closed, but his was head up.

I rounded the bed, flicked back the covers and lay down, pulling the covers up to my neck.

It was safe to say that multiple gunshot wounds put a serious crimp in your sex life. A crimp I wasn't all fired up to iron out.

In fact, I didn't think I ever wanted Vance to see me naked again.

"I think we should break up," I blurted to the ceiling, and then closed my eyes tight when I felt his mood change and fill the room with dangerous white-hot electricity.

"Sorry?" he asked.

I opened my eyes and looked at him. I shouldn't have. He was looking at me. His brows were knit and his eyes were narrowed and I'd learned that was not a good combo with Vance.

"I think we should break up," I told him.

"Jesus, you're a pain in the ass," he muttered and went back to his book.

"Seriously, Vance."

"Shut up, Jules," he said without taking his eyes from his book.

I rolled to my side, reached out and pushed his book down. His eyes cut to me, and with one look in them I rethought my actions, but it was too late.

"Crowe—" I started, but Vance turned. Boo flew off his belly and Vance put his book to the nightstand. Then he came back to me and rolled toward me. Arm going around my waist, he pulled me to him. He did this gently, how he'd been touching me for weeks, but this time it had meaning.

"What's in that fucking head of yours?" he asked when we were lying side-by-side, face-to-face, our bodies touching.

"I... you... well..." I stopped then started again, "It's pretty clear you're the kind of guy who has to have sex, um... a lot of it and, um... we can't have sex anymore."

"Why can't we have sex anymore?"

"Well," I started and halted. Did I really have to explain it?

I looked at him. He was glaring at me.

I guessed I did.

"I'm kind of gross," I finished.

"Gross?"

"Yes, gross."

"How are you gross?"

Now I was getting pissed.

"I can't believe you're gonna make me spell it out for you," I snapped.

His hand moved, it went down over my hip then up under my shirt before both his arms wrapped around me.

"He could have blown off half your face, you survived, you'd still be lyin' beside me."

I blinked.

He didn't pause for me to wrap my head around that mind blowing statement. He went on.

"One of those bullets could have torn through your spinal cord, you'd be lyin' beside me."

Oh my God.

His arms got tighter, pressing my body against his, and his face came super close.

"This is it. You and me. No matter what," he declared.

"Crowe——" I whispered, so stunned, so moved, I thought my heart had to have stopped beating.

"No matter what," he said, his voice fierce and strong and rumbling through me. "You told me I was home to you and I get it. You're home to me. I've never had a home. I like the one I found and I'm not losin' it. No matter what."

I couldn't help it. I didn't want to, but I started crying. It wasn't the wracking loud sobs kind of crying, it was the tears filling your eyes and spilling over silently kind of crying.

He watched me cry and didn't say a word, he just held me close.

"You... you said..." I stammered, "if I ever changed my body——"

"Show me," he murmured, his voice and eyes had grown soft.

I stopped crying immediately and asked, "What?"

"Show me, Princess."

I stared at him for what seemed like ages, knowing exactly what he meant.

His mouth came to mine and he said again, "Show me."

Kristen Ashley

I sucked in a breath in an attempt to buy time to decide if I had the courage to show him. Then, deciding I did—in fact I had to—I pulled away and he let me go. He pushed down the covers. I pulled up the t-shirt and I closed my eyes.

I opened them again when I felt his mouth on me.

It moved, touching my scars gently, his hands roaming my sides, my hips, and then he pushed me on my back.

He came up, kissing the scar at my chest, then he moved his mouth to my breasts, spending a lot more time there, first at one then the other. It felt great and I totally forgot how gross I was.

Then his mouth went lower. Lower. He rolled between my legs and his mouth was there.

That was when I *really* totally forgot how gross I was.

After a while he pulled off my panties and made me come with his mouth.

It was fucking fantastic.

He rolled to his back. I got on top of him and wrapped my hand around him.

"Jules, you don't—" he started, but I leaned down and kissed him quiet.

Then I guided him inside me and moved on top of him. I took my time, mainly because I'd just had an orgasm so I had all the time in the world, not to mention it felt really good.

Vance wasn't really into slow though. I figured he'd taken care of himself somewhere along the way, but maybe I was wrong. He got impatient and sat up, his hands at my hips coaxing me to go faster. They slid up my sides and his eyes locked on mine.

"I wanna take off your shirt," he said, his voice hoarse.

I shook my head.

He kissed me deep and hard.

Then he repeated, "I wanna take off your shirt."

I was a bit muddled from the kiss so I said, "Okay."

Gently, he pulled the t-shirt over my head.

His mouth was at my chest, my scar, my breasts; his hands pressing in to make me arch my back and expose myself to him. I moved faster, faster and he tipped his head back. His fingers slid into my hair, tilting my face down to his, and he kissed me right before he came.

I guess he wasn't grossed out by my body.

We had Christmas at Nick's, just Vance, Nick and me.

I gave Nick tickets to an upcoming Springsteen concert. I gave Vance this kickass choker with a thick, braided leather band and two small, silver medallions at the front, one of an eagle and one of a buffalo. He tied it on, and usually I didn't like jewelry on guys, but that leather and silver on him looked hot.

Nick stole my bracelet while I was recovering and had three more links put in.

One with an emerald, for Nick, which, days later, I found out signifies goodness, fidelity and love.

One with a blue topaz, for me, which signifies sincerity, courage and wisdom. When I read this out to Vance and Nick, Nick said, "Don't know about that last one." This comment Vance thought was so funny, he threw back his head and laughed, which meant I had to try and tackle him. But he just caught me, swung me up in his arms and kept right on laughing, his face buried in my neck).

And last, one with a pearl, for Vance, which signifies nobility, beauty and peace.

How was that for perfect?

Of course I burst into sloppy tears when I opened it, which pissed me off because I seemed to be crying all the time those days, but Vance pulled me into his lap and held me until I was done crying. Which, head-crackin' mamma jamma that I was, I still had to admit was super nice.

Zip dropped a gift by Nick's. It was gun holster with a note attached that said, "Just in case".

I laughed my ass off.

Vance and Nick didn't think this was funny (at all).

We had Christmas dinner at my place because I had a better dining room table.

I cooked dinner while Nick looked worried and Vance looked amused, mainly because I banged around and cursed a lot through this process.

I'd been practicing cooking at Vance's cabin while I was recovering and wasn't doing too badly. However the Christmas pork tenderloin somehow ended up kind of raw. I swore to both of them it was *not* my fault, it had to be my stupid oven. Then Nick asked me what temperature I cooked it on and I said, "One fifty, like it says in the cookbook."

Nick got the cookbook and showed me it said *three* fifty, which I guess proved it wasn't the oven.

Vance, for your information, stayed silent through this exchange. However he wore his shit-eating grin the entire time.

Luckily, Nick cooked a backup pork tenderloin (just in case) so all was saved.

Vance gave me my present later in bed when nothing but the moonlight was shining down on us. It was an ultra-wide hammered silver ring that went all the way up to my knuckle. It was *gorgeous*.

I put it on my right ring finger and Vance took it off and put it on my left, but not before kissing my finger and looking at me with that "mine" expression on his face.

I could see it, even in the moonlight.

What was more, I could feel it.

Since then, I've never taken that ring off.

The week between Christmas and New Year's was busy because I was going back to work after New Year's and Vance and I had a lot to do, considering we were splitting houses.

He brought a bunch of his stuff to my house and I moved some of my stuff back, but left a lot of it at the cabin.

We doubled up on kitty paraphernalia so Boo could go back and forth with us (Boo liked riding in the Sierra, by the way, crazy cat) without us carting around litter boxes and kitty bowls.

I bought Vance some bookshelves for his cabin. He bought me a stereo so I could listen to music there. He also put in decent locks so no one would steal the stereo, which I thought was a smart move.

He gave me a key.

Lee *was* recruiting new Nightingale Investigations Men, not to mention a new receptionist, and he hit the jackpot that week before New Year's.

Darius, finally disentangled from the drug trade, went to work for Lee. Word on the street, Vance told me, this was not a popular move. Though I didn't think anyone at Nightingale Investigations ever cared if something was popular.

Hector, who miraculously didn't blow his cover, ended his long investigation by getting his man. After that, for reasons only known to Hector (and I knew this for certain because Indy tried naked gratitude on Lee, like, seven times, and got nothing), he quit the DEA and went to work for Lee.

The kicker was Shirleen, also now drug-trade-free, was looking for a way to spend her days. She and Darius also owned a bar and ran a poker game. She shut down the game, hired a good manager for the bar and became Lee's receptionist.

No one really knew why Lee hired a crazy, ex-drug dealing woman with a huge afro and no experience whatsoever to be his receptionist (and we talked about it a lot, mostly over brunch at Dozens), but then again he'd also hired Dawn, so go figure.

⁂

The only downer about the New Year's Party Indy and Lee threw at their duplex was when the fireworks started going off and I freaked out.

I didn't mean to, but I couldn't control it, the noise... I just panicked.

Once he ascertained I wasn't going to go off half-cocked and run screaming into the night, Vance left me with the girls (and Tod and Stevie) all crowded around me. Then he, Luke, Mace, Lee, Hank and Eddie (not to mention Tex and Duke) took off, each one wearing a scary-angry look on their face. In about ten minutes there was no more noise and they all came back with a shitload of confiscated fireworks.

So in some ways it was good being a badass's girlfriend.

Though the kids who were enjoying their firework celebrations probably wouldn't agree.

⁂

Kristen Ashley

In March, we packed Sniff and Roam into the GMC. Nick waved us off, promising to break up Boo's wet food, and the four of us headed to Ignacio, Vance's hometown.

A week before we left, Vance had called his Mom and told her we were coming to visit.

She obviously hadn't been expecting a call from her long lost son and she flipped out then burst into uncontrollable sobs. That was when Vance handed the phone to me and I gave him a dirty look, which he ignored. I calmed his Mom down and found out that we were more than welcome, we could come anytime.

Anytime.

She said this, like, fifteen times.

About an hour out of Ignacio, I was fidgeting in my seat, more than even Sniff normally fidgeted, totally flipped out.

I looked at Vance, who was sitting back, driving with only his left wrist on the steering wheel, eyes on the road, thoughts hidden, cool as a cucumber.

He sensed my agitation, his eyes slid to me and he said, "Still."

"Still, my ass," I murmured.

Vance chuckled. So did Roam.

We drove up to the house and Vance barely got his new, shiny, black truck stopped when the door flew open and a beautiful Native American woman, a hint of gray in her thick, black hair and cheekbones I'd sell my soul for, came flying out of the house.

She ran half the way to the truck then halted. Her body went solid and she stared at her grown son, seeing him for the first time in twenty years.

Vance dropped down from the truck (still, I might add, cool as a cucumber, acting as if he came to visit every weekend) and he waited for me to round the hood to get to him. He took my hand and we walked up to his Mom, Roam and Sniff hanging back.

She was a tiny, little thing and she watched us coming, her eyes leaving Vance only once to slide to our linked hands and then to gaze momentarily at me. When we got close, she looked up at Vance like pretty much everyone did—like he was a god fallen to earth (sometimes, normally post-orgasm, I suspected that he was, but I never told him that; though I did share my suspicions with Ally, Indy, Jet, Roxie and Daisy, and they'd all laughed themselves stupid).

"My son," she whispered as if she couldn't quite believe it.

436

"Yeah, Ma," Vance said.

At his words, she burst into tears.

Unfortunately, so did I. What could I say? Even a head-crackin' mamma jamma and a social worker who'd witnessed dozens of reunions was going to lose it in the face of *that* kind of reunion.

Vance held his Mom. Roam slid his arm around my shoulders and I stuffed my face in his neck.

Finally, after a good long bawl, she looked at me.

"My name is Roslyn," she said, wiping her face and trying to get control.

"I'm Jules," I told her, doing the same as she was.

Then, for some ungodly reason, we burst out crying again, moving into each other's arms.

The guys just left us to it and unpacked the truck, though I heard Roam mutter, "Shit, silly bitches."

"Don't say bitches!" I shouted at his back just as the screen door slammed.

Roslyn laughed.

I watched her, and it hit me that her son looked a lot like her.

⌇

We stayed with Roslyn for a couple of days. His Dad was mysteriously "on a fishing trip" which Vance took in stride, but it pissed me right the hell off. Though, with effort, I kept my mouth shut.

We found out his brother, Owen, was living in Santa Fe. Owen and his family came up on our last day when Vance's Mom had a barbeque for us at noontime before we were going to take off.

The reunion with Owen didn't go so well. Owen sized up Vance immediately and didn't like what he saw (pure jealousy, if you asked me).

Owen was married with two young boys, was shorter than Vance and clearly took after his Dad in the looks department. Vance looked like his Mom, as in gorgeous. Owen wasn't much, but then again I could be prejudiced. Owen was kind of a jerk, I thought that right off.

Around about the dessert stage of the festivities, Owen teetered over the rim of happy-drunk and got shitfaced drunk, loud and obnoxious in a way you knew he did it a lot, especially when both Roslyn and Owen's wife got very tense and started to shrink into themselves.

Kristen Ashley

The whole time we were there Vance had been... well, Vance. Cool and laidback. It put Roslyn and all of us at ease and our time with his Mom had been good. She was funny and sweet and obviously happy to have us with her. Sometimes, though, I'd catch her looking at Vance in a way that was lost and infinitely sad. Thank God Sniff was there. His motor mouth usually served to snap her out of it.

But his brother's drunken behavior got a reaction from Vance, who looked at his two nephews, his mother and sister-in-law then he took his brother around the front of the house for a chat.

The chat degenerated when Owen became not only drunk, loud and obnoxious, but also seriously pissed-off. We heard the shouts all the way to the back and I got up and ran around to the front, the whole party following me. I tried to intercede as Owen yelled in Vance's face and Vance stared him down.

Owen turned an enraged face to me and screamed, "Shut up, bitch. Who the fuck're—?"

Quick as a flash (as was the way of Lightnin' Crowe), Owen was up against the house, Vance's forearm to his throat and Vance in his face.

There went the reunion barbeque.

Owen looked stunned that one second he was five feet away and shouting mad and the next second he was pinned and powerless against the house.

"Not smart," Vance said in a scary, quiet voice. H shoved off and looked at Roam. "Pack it up."

Roam, not looking all that happy himself, didn't hesitate. He grabbed Sniff and they ran into the house.

"But we haven't got to the pie yet!" Roslyn cried.

Vance was not in the mood to change his mind. We were packed up and ready to go in fifteen minutes. Owen had disappeared. His wife and kids stood by Roslyn as we said our good-byes.

"You'll come back?" Roslyn asked Vance, standing a foot away, not touching him and the sound of her voice made tears crawl up my throat.

"I'll be back," Vance told her.

I was standing at Vance's side and her eyes moved to me.

"You'll bring him back?" she asked, even though Vance had already answered the question.

I smiled at her. "I'll bring him back."

I gave her a hug and told her to come visit us in Denver.

438

Vance touched his young nephews' heads, nodded to his sister-in-law and turned to kiss his mother's forehead.

Then we were gone.

⌖

After the emotional start to our vacation, we spent the rest of the week camping.

Two street-smart, urban runaways roughing it in the mountains outside Ouray was pretty hilarious. They didn't have a clue.

Vance was a patient teacher.

I, on the other hand, never stopped giving them stick.

⌖

It was late March, and May and I were hanging in the surveillance room with Vance, Monty and Mace.

May and I had brought a lunch of calzones from Pasquini's for the boys and Shirleen. We were consuming them and giggling ourselves silly while watching Tex and Duke argue about what happened at Kent State (though I didn't understand what the argument was about, considering it sounded like they both agreed) when Vance got tense and he leaned forward.

He turned down the volume to the Fortnum's monitor and moved to the monitor that showed a visual of the reception area.

Shirleen was sitting behind the reception desk, consuming her own calzone while alternately painting her fingernails, a mean feat. A woman had walked in.

I looked at her and liked her immediately.

Tall, curvy, super pretty and definitely cool in a female James Dean throwaway cool type of way. She was wearing a pair of *very* faded Levi's. So faded, they were worn nearly through in some advantageous areas, a pair of black flip-flops, a black Green Day t-shirt over a white thermal, silver rings on nearly every finger, several silver necklaces around her neck, a mess of silver bracelets on both her wrists and wide silver hoops at her ears. Her long, streaked-blonde hair was up in a twisty, untidy knot with chunks falling around her face in a way that looked artless and kickass.

Her look was sah-weet. She had Rock Chick written all over her.

Vance turned up the volume to the reception monitor in time for us to hear Shirleen say, "... help you?"

The woman was looking at Shirleen and she didn't look happy. Why I couldn't fathom, but she looked like she wanted to be anywhere but there and was about ready to turn on her flip-flop and leave.

She hesitated for a moment then said, "I'm looking for Lucas Stark."

Uh-oh.

I drew in breath.

"You got an appointment with Luke?" Shirleen asked, looking through the total mess on her desk as if she actually kept appointments for Luke. Luke didn't even take appointments. Luke was wherever Luke was, and if you caught him you could count yourself lucky.

"No, I'm an..." the woman hesitated, licked her lips and finished, "old friend."

"Holy fuck," Monty muttered under his breath, staring at the monitors with a pained expression and shaking his head. "Here we go again."

May and I looked at each other and grinned.

"He ain't here, girl. You want, I can call him," Shirleen told her.

"No," the woman said quickly and she sounded downright relieved. "I'll just..." she hesitated again and looked around. She still looked tense and I was pretty certain she was about to bolt. "Forget it. Could you please just tell him Ava Barlow was here? I'll try to catch him later."

Yep, I was right, she was about to bolt. Vance picked up the phone and hit a button.

Shirleen was smiling huge. "No problem to give him a bell. I got his number on speed dial."

"No!" Ava cried suddenly them continued. "Really, thanks, but I'll just go. I've got to be somewhere anyway." She was edging away, definitely losing it now. She was beginning to look jittery.

I heard Mace laughing softly behind me.

Vance spoke into the phone. "Luke," pause, "you got a visitor." I could hear the smile in Vance's voice even though his face was turned away. "Says her name's Ava Barlow."

"Just hang on one tick," Shirleen said, getting up, waving her hands to dry her nails. "I'll just talk to the boys in the back. Maybe they know where he is."

In the surveillance room, Vance said into the phone. "Looks scared as a fuckin' jackrabbit. She's about to take off." Immediately, his eyes sliced to Mace and he did a flick of his hand, index finger pointed to the door, saying, "Luke'll be here in five."

Mace disappeared and seconds later we saw him hit the reception area and move to block the exit.

"Luke just called in," Mace lied to the staring Ava (it was hard not to stare at Mace, especially upon first sight of him). "He'll be here in five."

I could swear I saw Ava's face grow pale.

"I'm thinkin' Ava Barlow don't have a prayer," May whispered to me, but she was looking at the monitor and her whole body was shaking with laughter.

I found myself hoping Ava Barlow was good enough for Luke Stark, and thinking that was a tall order.

She liked Green Day though, so I figured that was a start.

Vance put down the phone and sat back, picking up his calzone. His gaze moved to me and mine moved to him.

His eyes were amused but soft and sweet, and he had that "mine" look on his face. These days it was less intense, less raw, more settled, more content and I liked that.

I liked it a lot.

Home, I heard Auntie Reba say in my head.

I know, I said back.

My pug puppy curled up in my mental lap and sighed a happy puppy sigh. My eyes still on Vance, I smiled.

The Rock Chick ride continues
with **Rock Chick Revenge**
the story of Luke and Ava

CPSIA information can be obtained at www.ICGtesting.com
Printed in the USA
BVOW02s1932241115

428249BV00002B/218/P